GRAY WIDOW'S WEB

GRAY WIDOW'S WEB

BOOK TWO OF THE GRAY WIDOW SERIES

DAN JOLLEY

Charlotte, NC

FALSTAFF
BOOKS
WWW.FALSTAFFBOOKS.COM

For Tracy — Always

1

Dennis Belmont ran, his breath ragged white bursts in the moonlight as the shadow creature glided after him. He wiped blood out of his eyes with the sleeve of his coat. The laceration on his forehead throbbed in the frigid wind.

A late-winter cold front had drenched Atlanta in freezing rain for the last four days, and Dennis almost crashed to the ground when his foot hit the edge of a frozen puddle. The lights of a passing car threw his own shadow long in front of him, and he rasped out, "No, no no, please no," praying the creature wouldn't emerge from it. Ahead of him on his right, a rail overpass crossed Arizona Avenue, and sodium-vapor lights flooded the space beneath it with a harsh yellow glare. Dennis ran faster, lungs aching, legs on fire. If he could just make it to the light…

He skidded to a stop in the middle of the underpass and half-collapsed against the mural-covered wall, heaving, panting. Hands on his knees. The yellow light surrounded him, welcome as the sun's rays—

—until he noticed one image, nestled among the mural's stylized shapes. No bigger than the palm of his hand, but staring at him. Accusing him. He knew what it was called: The Eyes of the Widow.

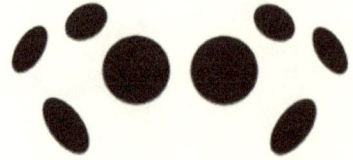

The truth of the situation clicked in his head. Dennis said, "Oh shit," just as the shadow creature stepped into the light at the far end of the underpass.

She was tall, towering, her long, lean frame hugged tight by gray segmented body armor. The black spots on her helmet mirrored the symbol on the wall, the rest of her armor dabbed with paint like a pattern from a spider's abdomen, and involuntarily Dennis breathed out her name. "*Gray Widow.*"

Steel knuckles glinted gold from her clenched fists. One of them still dripped with Dennis's blood, where it had sliced open his forehead. The Widow's words crunched out into the near-freezing air. "You're only making this worse."

Dennis screamed and ran again. Out from the underpass, off the road, into a stand of trees, a prayer on his lips that he could lose her. It wasn't his fault. He said it to himself again and again, chanted it, it wasn't his fault. There was no way he could've known how old that girl was. No way. She came onto him! He couldn't control how drunk she was! Dennis crashed through the trees, zigging and zagging around trunks and bulling through undergrowth, and between the branches whipping at him he saw a parking lot ahead. Maybe he could get to a car, hotwire it, get the hell away from there. Away from her.

Something caught Dennis's foot. He crashed chin-first into the frozen ground, scrambling and flailing to get away, sure that the Widow's armored hand had clamped around his ankle. But when he turned, ready to kick and fight, the dim light filtering into the trees from the parking lot's streetlights showed him what had entangled him. Dennis froze. Staring. Staring as steam rose into the night air from the mangled horror still caging his foot.

2

Dennis screamed, and kept screaming, hysterical tears running down his cheeks, until the Gray Widow stepped out of the shadows behind him and delivered a pile-driver blow to his jaw with a steel-knuckled fist.

D ammit, J. There's proper ways to do this. And you're not doing it the proper way."

Janey Sinclair ducked her head, since she knew Feygen couldn't see her facial expression behind the helmet's faceplate. "Sorry. I thought you'd want to see this before anyone else did. Before the press did."

Not quite half an hour had passed since Janey had knocked Dennis Belmont unconscious. Belmont now sat in the back of Detective Zach Feygen's car in the nearby parking lot, handcuffed and eager to tell anyone who would listen that yes, he had assaulted an underage girl earlier that night, that no, he'd had nothing to do with the corpse in the woods and, if asked, that at no time had he seen or interacted with the vigilante known as the Gray Widow. He'd stumbled, literally, across the corpse and, having one of Detective Feygen's cards in his wallet, placed a call. Janey had ensured Belmont's cooperation with a few brief, pointed words after he'd awakened but before Feygen had arrived. She'd put particular stress on the ways she'd break his legs if he said anything he wasn't supposed to.

Now Janey and Feygen stood beside the corpse that had tripped Belmont up, Feygen illuminating it with a powerful flashlight. Feygen said, "Yeah, well, uniforms'll be here soon, and I know you don't want to stick around for that. So...exactly what the *fuck* am I looking at here?"

Janey wished she knew what to tell him. Her gorge rose, and she had to swallow hard and take a couple of deep breaths to keep her voice steady. Stretched out on the ground just inside the woods lay the body of a woman Janey guessed to be in her early- to mid-thirties. The woman's name, according to the Waffle House employee name tag on the ground beside her, was Carol, and from the neck down, Carol had been...what? Janey wasn't sure what to call it. She said, "I don't think this was an animal attack."

Feygen grunted and shined his light on Carol's face. A few thin wisps of steam still rose from the ruined body. "I think you're right. See where the wounds stop? Right at the neck—nice clean line." He looked up at Janey. "This isn't like what Simon Grove did, is it?"

Janey shook her head. "No. He drained people. Sucked their blood out through their skin. This is..." She didn't have words for it. The corpse's skin had been split open and peeled back, down the torso and along the lengths of all four limbs, and the muscle tissue beneath it was just...gone. The organs inside the ribcage and the intestines remained, untouched as far as Janey could tell, but—the thought appeared in her head, grisly and unwanted—all the *meat* had been taken. Janey crouched and peered at the exposed knee structure. "Look at the marks on the bones here. And the ligaments—severed. What made those marks? What kind of cutting instrument did the killer use?"

"Beats me. That's a question for the M.E."

Janey stood and moved around to the corpse's head. Carol, when she lived, had been a woman who took care of her hair. She had a lot of it, dark blonde, thick and carefully maintained. Janey started to reach for it, thought better, and snapped open an aluminum police baton. With the tip of the baton, she moved a section of Carol's hair, and sucked in a sharp, queasy breath.

Feygen joined her. "What? What is it?" He trained his light on the corpse's scalp. "Oh...*fuck.*"

A smooth-edged, round hole the size of a ripe lemon had been bored into the top of Carol's skull, and Feygen's light illuminated nothing inside the cranium but darkness. Feygen took a couple of steps backward. Janey said, "Someone or something stripped all the meat off this woman's bones and sucked her brain out of her skull."

Feygen rubbed his face. "Succinctly put."

Past the parking lot, blue and red lights appeared, approaching rapidly. Janey said, "First thing either of us hears about who or what might've done this, let's let the other know, okay?"

"You got it." The lights got closer and brighter. "Go on. That'll be the lieutenant. We'll take it from here."

Janey collapsed the baton and slid it into the holster on her thigh, stepped back into the thickest of the darkness among the trees, and with a brief, smoky flicker she disappeared. Steam hissed from the leaves of nearby trees in her passing.

2

Seven days after the discovery of the body amid the trees, Janey Sinclair stepped off the elevator on the eleventh floor of the LaCroix Building and moved aside, allowing plenty of room for Tim Kapoor. Tim maneuvered deliberately out into the hallway, and Janey fell in next to him, conscientious about staying on the side opposite the cane. As they walked, slowly and carefully, toward Sha'dae Wilkerson's apartment, Janey entwined her fingers in his. Tim smiled a little when she did that, but didn't look at her. He couldn't. He wasn't able to turn his head. Janey reminded herself that the neck brace had only been off for a few days.

Janey's leg, which had snapped halfway between the knee and ankle on the same night Simon Grove did so much damage to Tim, didn't hurt at all. She had tested it plenty, but it had healed. She felt pretty sure the only evidence the break had ever happened would be an x-ray.

Tim wasn't as lucky. The beating he had taken at Simon Grove's hands had left him with multiple broken bones, nerve damage that the doctors said might be permanent, and a reliance on painkillers that, Tim had confided in her, he was terrified would become an addiction.

Janey didn't know what to say to him as they traversed the hall-way's threadbare carpet. With a lump in her stomach, she acknowl-edged to herself that "not knowing what to say" had become her default position.

"We don't have to go to this thing, y'know," Tim said. "Or—what I mean is, *I* don't have to go."

Janey squeezed his hand. "I thought you wanted to?"

She began to hear conversation emanating from Sha'dae's place. She couldn't tell how many voices. At least half a dozen. Her pace slowed.

"Sha'dae's more your friend than mine. And I like her, don't get me wrong. I just…don't want to be a drag."

Janey stopped, and faced him, and brushed her lips against his. "You're not a drag. Nothing about you is a drag." She stopped short of, *Why would you even say that?*

She knew exactly why he would say that. Tim's parents had hired the best physical and occupational therapists they could find, the best in Atlanta, but his recovery hadn't been anywhere near fast enough to suit him. It hadn't helped anything, either, that Janey's cast had come off after only three weeks.

He gave her the tiny smile again. "Okay."

They closed the distance to Sha'dae's front door, but neither of them made a move to hold hands again. Janey patted her messenger bag-style purse to make sure Sha'dae's gift was in it before she knocked.

The door opened seconds later, and Sha'dae Wilkerson's perfect white teeth practically lit up the hallway. "Janey! Tim! Come in, come in! The pizza just got here, it's still all steamy, help yourselves!"

Sha'dae moved aside as they entered, and shut the door behind them. She was twenty-four, three years younger than Janey. *No. Four years.* Janey had just had a birthday, and didn't yet think of herself as twenty-eight. Janey often thought Sha'dae could have been a model, if —and it was a huge, prohibitive if—her personality and culture hadn't so decisively ruled against it. She wore a light blue hijab over a mostly shapeless long-sleeved tunic and a pair of baggy white pants that didn't quite drag the floor as she walked. The blue of the hijab contrasted perfectly with the rich, dark brown of her smooth, unblemished skin, and set off her eyes, which were every bit as deep and dark and warm as Tim's.

Janey gave her a hug. "Congratulations. I never doubted you'd do it."

"Thanks!" Sha'dae turned to Tim and hugged him too, but very carefully. Janey watched Tim's face over Sha'dae's shoulder, as appreciation for the hug mingled with chagrin over the need for its delicate nature. "But don't congratulate me yet. I still have to find a job."

Tim leaned on his cane. "I feel your pain, there. But your Master's of Engineering'll be about a thousand times more helpful in the job market than my Bachelor's of English."

Sha'dae smiled. "Well, then, maybe save the congrats till I pay off my student loans?"

Janey slipped her arm lightly around Tim's waist. To her relief, he didn't pull away. "See, this is why I didn't go to college at all."

Sha'dae said, "Smartass," but didn't lose her smile.

Janey dug in her purse, and Sha'dae's face lit up when Janey pulled out an oblong box. "Happy successful thesis day."

"Is this what I think it is?" Sha'dae tore the wrapping paper off and pried open the lid, and squealed loudly enough that everyone in the apartment looked at her. She yanked the object free and waved it above her head. "You got me a Hermione wand!"

Janey let the corners of her mouth curl up. "Straight from Universal."

Sha'dae flourished the wand at a red Solo cup. "*Wingardium leviosa!*" The cup didn't move, but Sha'dae giggled. "Clearly I have to practice! Thank you so much!" She threw her arms around Janey and hugged her tightly. "You are absolutely the best!"

Janey's phone buzzed in her pocket. She disengaged from Sha'dae —"Hang on, sorry"—and shot an apologetic look at Tim. His forehead wrinkled, but he shrugged. Janey stepped out into the hall and tapped "Accept."

"Hello."

Over the phone, Garrison Vessler's voice came out even more gravelly than in person. "I've got a line on Simon Grove's mother."

"Not his father?"

"His father's dead. But get this—his mother is Anna Grove."

"The *actress*? But…how…a famous actress's son goes on a killing spree, and no one knows about it? How is that even possible?"

"It's got Derek Stamford's greasy fingerprints all over it. Media control. No easy feat these days."

Janey paced back and forth outside Sha'dae's door, tuning out the murmur of voices from within. She had never met Derek Stamford, Vessler's former business partner, in person. Just glimpsed him once, right after Simon Grove died, and then only for a few seconds. The way Vessler talked about him, he sounded like the kind of government boogeyman a conspiracy theorist would invent.

"So where is she?"

"I'm working on that. She had a big place in Louisiana, but she sold it four months ago. I'll let you know when I find out."

"Okay. How's Scott?"

"He's good. I have to go."

The line went dead as the conversational murmur grew louder. Janey slipped the phone back in her pocket and turned to face the door, where Tim leaned against the doorframe, watching her. His expression wasn't quite accusatory, but didn't miss it by much. He silently mouthed the name: *Vessler?*

She nodded.

"What did he have to say?"

Janey hesitated. Even as the words formed in her head, she realized how much of a cliché they sounded: *The less you know, the better.* And *You need plausible deniability.* And *I don't want to put you in any more danger.* That last one was beginning to sound like a broken record, even to her. "Nothing, really. Just checking in."

"Nothing?"

"Nothing important." She went to him, and took his hand and squeezed it, and managed not to sigh with relief when he returned the gentle pressure. She kissed him on the cheek, and on the lips. "Let's just go back in, okay?"

He nodded. "Okay." She kept his hand in hers as they entered Sha'-dae's apartment.

Ten people—Janey quickly counted—sat around the living room or stood in the adjoining galley kitchen, eating pizza and sipping soft drinks and picking from the hors d'oeuvre-covered table. Almost all of them looked like college students, male and female, and if Janey had been forced to guess, she would have put all of them squarely in the Engineering department. Sha'dae had a playlist of what sounded like early-90s boy bands going on the stereo, a selection for which Janey decided to forgive her, but most of the sound came from the TV. Sha'dae had hauled out her old Wii, and a guy and girl, neither of whom Janey knew, were in the middle of a boxing match.

Janey and Tim drifted over to the table. Janey dipped a baby carrot in some ranch dressing and nibbled on it. Tim lightly bumped her shoulder with his, and under his breath, said, "Now who's uncomfortable?"

Janey let her eyelids slide closed as she chewed. "Is it that obvious?"

He shrugged, and gathered up a slice of pizza. "I think maybe engaging in some socializing might be just as good for you as for me."

Janey swallowed the bite of carrot, and was about to say something else, or at least try to think of something else to say, when the guy in front of the TV let out a whoop and turned to face the crowd. He threw wiry arms in the air and cried out, "Teenage reflexes for the win!"

It was Nathan Pittman.

As casually as she could, Janey turned away from him, hoping Nathan hadn't noticed her, and maneuvered so that she could get a better look at him reflected in a wall mirror. Tim picked up on her sudden anxiety, and lowered his voice. "What're you doing?"

"That's Nathan Pittman. At the TV."

Tim glanced over her shoulder at the teenager. "The kid who got shot?" Janey nodded. "Okay...but he doesn't know who you are. Right? Why turn your back on him?"

Janey had no clear answer for that. Worry? Guilt?

Nathan didn't appear quite as pale and hollow as he had in the hospital, when Janey had flickered into his room to get a look at him in person, but he didn't look exactly well, either. Judging by the photos she'd seen in the local paper, Nathan hadn't had any extra body fat to lose, and after he was shot he'd gone from "thin" to "emaciated." Some flesh had found its way back onto his bones now.

Sha'dae came to stand beside Janey, and to Janey's horror, beckoned to Nathan. "Hey! Nate! Come here, I want you to meet some more friends of mine."

Nathan held up a finger in a *just a second* gesture, and Janey leaned close to Sha'dae. "How, uh, how do you know him? He's not in college, is he?"

Sha'dae's dazzling grin flashed. "I picked him up on my straydar."

"Sorry, your what?"

"I've got a habit of attracting strays. I call it my 'straydar.' People who don't really fit in, exactly? They wind up in my orbit a lot of the time."

Janey's mouth quirked. "Is that what I am, then? One of your strays?"

Sha'dae's eyes twinkled. "You're my *best* stray."

Nathan ambled over, snagging a bottle of Diet Coke along the way. Gaunt or not, he seemed in great spirits as he stuck his hand out. "Hi! Nathan Pittman."

Janey kept her face very carefully neutral as she shook his hand. "Janey Sinclair." She gestured at Tim. "This is, uh—" *This is my boyfriend. This is the man I'm in love with. This is the man I almost got killed.* "This is Tim Kapoor."

Tim switched his hold on the cane and shook Nathan's hand as well. "You look familiar. Weren't you on the news?"

Nathan grinned and ducked his head. "Yeah, 'fraid so. I tried to stop a robbery, and got perforated for my troubles." His fingers nimbly undid the top buttons of his shirt, and he pulled it open to display what could have passed for a subway map of scars. "That's what you get for trying to imitate a vigilante, right? I got better, though." The buttons closed again as fast as he'd opened them. "And, like I told the cops, the Gray Widow can keep that job. You've only gotta shoot this white boy three times for him to learn his lesson."

Janey saw Tim shoot her a discreet look, like *How do you want to play this?*

Before she could think of a response, Nathan asked, "So how'd you guys meet Sha'dae? Known each other long?"

Janey smiled at Sha'dae and shook her head. "About, what, five months?"

Sha'dae smiled back. "About that, yeah."

Janey said, "It was right after Tim got home from the hospital. Sha'dae had just moved in, and she spotted me helping Tim onto the elevator with some groceries and came over to lend a hand carrying bags and such. And pretty much ever since then—"

Sha'dae's eyes twinkled. "—we've been finishing each other's sentences."

Tim watched them both with a mild expression. To Nathan, he said, "They only *think* they're joking about being sisters in a past life."

Pleased with how steady she was keeping her voice, Janey asked, "So, how do *you* know Sha'dae?"

Nathan grinned again and shoved his hands in his pockets. "We only just met, actually. I'm the new maintenance guy, here in the building. Well, I say maintenance, but it's really more like take the garbage out, clean up any messes, y'know. Accept people's rent checks. Whatever needs doing."

Tim said, "Wait, hang on—my father hired you?"

Nathan's eyes widened. "Oh! You're Mr. Kapoor's son? Jeez, I didn't even make the connection, *duh!*" He shot a look at Tim's cane. "Your dad said you were in charge of the place, but you got sort of laid up for a while, so yeah, I'm just, like. Helping out." He wiggled a finger at the cane. "What happened? Car wreck?"

"I got mugged," Tim said tightly. "It's been a pleasure to meet you, Nathan. If you'll all excuse me, I'll be right back." Without a glance in Janey's direction, Tim crossed the living room and slipped out the front door.

Janey stood there with Sha'dae and Nathan Pittman, drowning in sudden, awkward silence. She breathed a silent sigh of relief when the girl Nathan had been boxing with called out, waving a Wii controller. "Hey! Nate! I can feel my arms again. Want a rematch?"

"Sure!" Nathan flashed an aww-shucks grin at Sha'dae and Janey, said, "Great to meet you!" and headed back to the game.

Quietly, Sha'dae said, "Is Tim all right?"

Janey took a deep breath and let it out slowly. "He's been awfully down on himself since he got hurt. And now, if he's feeling like his dad's replaced him?" She eyeballed the front door. "I better go after him."

She slipped out the door as Sha'dae waved her new wand at Nathan and shouted, *"Expelliarmus!"*

Outside, by herself and with no phone call to take, the hallway seemed so quiet Janey's ears almost rang. She hadn't realized how much ambient noise had been bouncing around inside Sha'dae's apartment. It took her a few moments of concentration before she heard Tim's voice, faint with distance.

Tim's, and someone else's. She padded down the hall, the voices getting louder, until she reached the stairwell, where she heard someone she didn't recognize say, "You're wrong, man. You're *wrong.*" The words slurred together. Janey pushed the door open to find Tim seated on the landing, his cane across his knees, facing a tall, thickly muscled man in a gray tank top and a pair of badly frayed jeans. Janey figured the man to be somewhere between thirty and thirty-five. What hair he had left was a rusty sort of red, draped across his skull in an unconvincing comb-over.

The man held a can of beer in his left hand, and sloshed a bit of the amber liquid out as he gestured at Tim. "You're not...not *listening* to me." He breathed hard. His eyes narrowed. "I'm tellin' you, you're *wrong."*

Janey let the stairwell door swing shut behind her. It latched with an echoing click. "Tim? Who's your friend?"

Tim angled his torso enough so that he could glimpse her out of the corner of his eye. In an oddly calm tone, he said, "This is Burt. He stepped into the stairwell to have a smoke, and found me here, and we've been conversing for the last couple of minutes."

Burt raised his narrowed eyes and peered at Janey. He swayed a little.

Janey moved over to Tim and held out a hand. "Well, I really think we should be getting back to the party. Nice meeting you, Burt."

Burt belched. "That party. Down there, that's that rag-head girl, right?"

Janey felt her throat constrict. "Pardon me?"

Burt jabbed a finger in Tim's direction. "What we was just talkin' about. Got these rag-heads livin' in the building. You a rag-head too, *Tim*? Got you a, what's, got you a turban? Where you from, anyway?"

Janey took a breath to speak, but Tim beat her to it. "Burt, I'm every bit as much an American as you are. Now if you'll excuse us."

"Bull *shit*." Burt's lips peeled back. He was missing both his front teeth. "I know who you are. I been payin' your daddy rent for six months now. And what about you, sugar-lips?" He winked at Janey. "You got some white in you. I can tell by the eyes. But you ain't white. Not by a long shot."

Janey said, "Come on, let's go," and Tim took her hand and tensed his legs to stand up, and Burt reached out with his free hand and put it on Tim's shoulder and shoved him back down into a sitting position.

"You ain't goin' nowhere till we finish our talk," Burt said, and Tim grunted in pain, and Janey moved.

Before Burt could react, she stepped past him to a lower stair and punched him in the back of the right knee. His leg buckled, and Tim said, "Janey, Janey *don't*," just as Burt yelped when his kneecap hit the corner of one of the steps. Janey grabbed the back of Burt's collar and hauled him toward her, so that he fell against her, and his sheer bulk would have knocked anyone else off-balance and sent both of them tumbling down the stairs.

Janey wasn't anyone else, though, and her muscles rippled as her arms clamped around Burt's throat. He thrashed against her for two seconds—three seconds—and sagged. She held him for another two before laying him down on the stairwell. He had crushed the beer can in his fist, spraying beer all over himself, and the odor mixed with another distinctive scent as he lost control of his bladder.

Janey sprang back up the stairs to Tim's side. He had already pushed himself up to his feet, and wasn't looking at her, and when she reached for his arm to steady him he shook her hand off. "Are you okay? Did he hurt you? I know your back's been giving you trouble—"

"I'm fine." Tim opened the stairwell door. He still didn't look at her as he stepped out into the hallway.

Janey followed. "He'll be okay, if that's what you're worried about, he'll wake up in a few minutes, and if anyone finds him, they'll just think he passed out…"

Tim stopped. "He was just a drunk, Janey."

"I—I know, but, he might've…I mean, I couldn't let him—"

Tim's shoulders quivered. He smacked his cane against the wall. "No, you couldn't, could you?" He cranked himself around enough to look her in the eye. "I need to lie down. I'll see you later."

Janey mentally kicked herself as Tim stumped off toward the elevator. What guy wanted his girlfriend protecting him? Fighting his battles for him? She might as well have popped his balls off and thrown them in the garbage. But at the same time, her heart thumped out the words she'd been hearing for the last six months: *I can't let him get hurt again. I can't. I won't.*

Janey stood there for a solid minute after Tim had disappeared inside the elevator, before she headed back to Sha'dae's place.

She did not see Nathan Pittman step out of a shallow alcove, two doors past the stairwell. She did not see him go to the stairwell door, glance inside, and gasp. She did not see the grin filled with trembling excitement that stretched his lips as the stairwell door clicked shut again.

J aney made her excuses and said her goodbyes fifteen minutes later. She knew Sha'dae would understand. Since moving in to the La Croix building, Sha'dae had proven herself to be the most sympathetic, understanding person Janey had ever met. Janey often thought of what seemed like the audible *click* when they met.

She caught Sha'dae's eye and motioned toward the door with her chin. Sha'dae disengaged herself from the conversation she was having with a portly fellow sporting a waxed, curled mustache and came over.

"I'm taking off."

Sha'dae nodded. "So...going after Tim? Not as successful as you were hoping?"

Janey's face creased with pain. She turned her head away so that no one else would see it. While she thought of what to say, Nathan Pittman whooped again in front of the TV, throwing Wii punches. Janey said, "Maybe I could come by later? Talk it out a little?"

Sha'dae put her hand on Janey's forearm. "Of course. Of *course*. Anytime."

Janey hugged her and left. Trudged down the hall, alone. Rode the elevator down to the ninth floor, alone.

The door to Janey's apartment squealed when she opened it. *Wonder if Nathan Pittman's going to show up with a can of WD-40 now?* She didn't bother turning on any lights. The shadows in her living room were plenty thick, so Janey strode to the middle of the floor, concentrated, and vanished with a burst of heat.

She emerged into the Basement. That was how she thought of it, anyway. The huge, low space was actually part of an underground parking structure below an abandoned, half-demolished theater—a place where her father, under the stage name "The Astounding Alexander," had performed years ago. Now half the concrete walls were lined with cloth-draped paintings, oil on canvas, while the other half boasted an array of human-outline targets fastened to hay bales, and a peg-board festooned with an arsenal of blunt and edged weaponry.

Next to the long work-bench below the weapon-covered peg-board, the Vylar suit rested, laid out across a loveseat someone had abandoned on a curb. Janey had made a few minor improvements to it in the last six months. Now, instead of a tight-clinging mask, a slim gray full-face helmet sat beside the armored, steel-knuckle-bearing gauntlets. She had made sure to copy the spider-eye pattern from the mask onto the new headgear, and had touched up the paint on the rest of the suit, reinforcing the arachnid theme of it.

Two other additions lay on the loveseat's worn cushions: a black pouch about the size of a knapsack, and a katana.

Janey had realized the need for a kind of "portable darkness" during her final fight with Simon Grove. If he hadn't been wearing that long coat…if she hadn't been able to reach into the pool of shadow inside it…Janey shuddered. Now, thanks to a series of straps, the pouch would fold flat and ride against her back, barely even altering her silhouette until she decided to use it.

The only reason she had survived that encounter was that she had reached through the shadows and grabbed her father's katana, which had then taken Simon's head off, putting him down once and for all. But her father's sword was much more for show than for function. Which was why she sought out and found a newer one. A better one.

No lights burned in the Basement. Janey stood there in what any other human would have considered perfect darkness. But when she willed her night vision on, picked up the new sword, and slid it carefully out of its scabbard, her eyes took in the rainbow sheen as if standing under a noonday sun. The blade glistened like an oil spill on top of a pool of water.

"Beryllium-bronze core," she recited. "Clad in titanium-alloy semi-ceramic." If what she had read about the sword was to be believed, there were very few substances on the planet it couldn't cut, given sufficient force behind the blow. She had already sliced through bricks with it, and found the blade hadn't dulled at all.

Janey hadn't paid a dime for the Vylar suit, or its new accompanying helmet, or what she couldn't help but think of as the "rainbow sword." Her ability—her Augmentation, as Garrison Vessler had called it—the power to disappear into one patch of darkness and reappear from a different one, lent itself superbly to theft. Janey swung the sword. She didn't feel a bit guilty about taking these items. The Vylar suit had been developed for the U.S. military, but proved to be so expensive even the Pentagon wouldn't approve the funding, so the prototype had sat in a lab, gathering dust.

Likewise, the sword had been little more than a conversation piece, a demonstration of an industrial engineer's metallurgy prowess. Technically, the company he worked for now owned the sword and the patent for it, but hadn't had the vision to put the engineer's process to use. So, like the Vylar suit, it had sat in a case in the engineer's office. Until Janey utilized it.

Janey stretched. Did a few jumping jacks. Tensed her legs and performed a backflip that would have made an Olympic gymnast proud. She walked over to the workbench, picked up a burner phone, and dialed the one number in the phone's memory.

Atlanta Police Detective Zach Feygen answered on the second ring, his low, rumbling voice a hiss of static as the signal fought its way down to the Basement's depths. "Damn, woman, you reading minds now?"

"What?"

"I was just about to call you."

She sighed. *Thank God.* "Where are you?"

It took Janey ten seconds to buckle herself into the Vylar suit. She grabbed up a pair of telescoping police batons, slid them into the sheathes along her thighs, and with a flicker and a burst of heat, vanished from the Basement.

In the seven or so months that she had been active as the vigilante the media had insisted on dubbing "the Gray Widow," excluding the weeks it had taken her to heal from the broken leg, Janey had developed a pattern for moving through the streets and parks and backyards of Atlanta. Her flickering, as she called it, worked only in line of sight—unless she wanted to risk a fatal disaster by teleporting blind—but she had yet to reach the limits of how many times she could teleport. Consequently, a minor wave of unexpected heat crossed the city as Janey flickered from one pool of darkness to the next, until she reached the house where Zach Feygen waited for her. A back window with no curtains over it allowed her access, and between one heartbeat and the next, she stood behind Feygen as he stared out the front window with a pair of binoculars.

Janey cleared her throat, and took a perverse pleasure in watching Feygen jump.

"Jesus Christ, J. You 'bout gave me an infarction."

"Is this about the body? The skeletonized one?"

"No. No movement on that."

She tilted her head. "What about forensics? Didn't they come up with anything?"

"Look, that's not my case. Not my precinct. I'm keeping track of it best I can, but I'm not lead on it, so there's limits. Right now, far as I know, they got nothing. But that's not why I called." He peered at the patches of black mesh covering her eyes and frowned. "That's new. Right? The helmet? Used to just be a, like a gray stocking pulled over your head, didn't it? I thought it looked different, in the woods."

She rapped the side of her head with her knuckles. "Got a little padding now. Plus some rigidity. Might just hurt really bad if I take a round to the skull, instead of cracking it open."

"Makes sense. Anyway. Reason I called is across the street."

He turned and peered through the binoculars again, and Janey marveled at how *comfortable* they had gotten with each other. She remembered vividly finding Feygen's card in the ruined theater, directly above the Basement, with his handwritten words scrawled on the back: *I know who you are. Call me.* Zach Feygen hadn't outed her to the press or the cops, and she figured if he hadn't done it by now, he wasn't going to.

He said, "Couple days ago we had a body turn up missing a head. Looked like it'd been taken off with some sort of razor-sharp blade, except the surface of the stump—the wound itself—was curved. Like, concave. Like his head'd been sliced off with a giant, sharp-edged melon-baller."

Janey grunted. "Okay. Weird."

"It gets weirder. Next day, we find another guy, and he's got a hole where the middle of his chest should've been. The missing part was globe-shaped. Like a sphere just disappeared out of him."

Janey joined him at the window. "Why are you here by yourself?"

"Budget. Manpower limitations. Discretion, too. Our skeletonized corpse had the brass on edge already, and now this? You try keeping a lid on something like that and covering all your bases at the same time."

"But you don't see a connection between the corpse in the woods and these guys with the, uh, the missing pieces?"

"Don't think so. M.O.'s completely different. I mean, yeah, they're both freaky as shit, and if it's not something to do with, y'know, people like you—no offense."

"None taken."

"If it's not, I'm gonna be awfully surprised."

She nodded. "Okay. And the connection between the two missing-pieces victims is what?"

"One guy, near as we can tell. Julian Roth." Feygen pulled out his phone, thumbed through photos, and showed her one of a chubby, bashful-looking African-American boy. "He's twenty years old, decent kid from what I can tell, but his parents say he went through hell and back in high school. There was a crew, three guys, that singled him out. Tortured him, basically, every chance they got."

"Ah. Your victims."

"Yup. Two of the crew. And the third one lives in this house across the street. We've got eyes on the back entrance, and we swept the place earlier tonight. Our survivor, Antonio Griggs—he was the ring-leader of his little crew of tough guys—he came home right before dark." Feygen flipped a couple of photos over on his phone. Antonio Griggs looked at least partly Hispanic, but his defining feature was a severely pock-marked face. "He never turned any lights on, never turned on the TV. He's sent no texts, made no calls."

Janey folded her arms. Drummed her fingers against her biceps. "Maybe he went to sleep?"

"Maybe he did. And if he did, fine. We'd just like to know."

Janey smiled under the mask. "So you want me to pop in and take a look."

"Discreetly, of course. But yeah."

She scanned the street, and the tiny yard in front of the house. "I can get in there. Just observe and report?"

"*Strictly* observe and report. Otherwise I'm up to my neck in inadmissible evidence." He turned and favored her with raised eyebrow. "You *can* do that, yeah? It doesn't all have to be broken arms and smashed noses."

Janey turned and leaned against the windowsill. "How much has crime dropped since the Eyes of the Widow started showing up around the city?"

Feygen made a noise halfway between a grunt and a sigh. "I don't want to talk about your little googly-eye symbol."

Janey chuckled, glanced across the street again, flickered and vanished.

She emerged in the shadow of a City of Atlanta trash can tucked close to the house, just behind the front porch. A small window let her peer into a half-bath. Another flicker—the distance short enough so that the heat of her passing didn't warp the window's glass—and she put her ear to the bathroom door, concentrating, listening.

Janey heard something. She couldn't tell what it was. From inside the tiny bathroom, it sounded like...bees? A buzzing of some kind, faint, just loud enough to hear. Janey cracked the door, reached through the shadows back to the Basement, and picked up a dentist's mirror from her workbench. The burst of heat made the door handle hot enough that she was glad for her Vylar gloves as she cracked the door open.

Janey slid the mirror through the tiny crack between the door and the frame, and almost dropped it. If she hadn't been using her night vision, she wouldn't've seen it; to the cops outside, the house must have appeared perfectly dark and still. But it wasn't. With one more wave of heat, Janey dropped the mirror back in its place on the workbench, snapped open her police baton, and pushed through the bathroom door.

Something crouched over the body of a man in the middle of the living room floor. Janey tried to focus on the crouching thing, and couldn't, and when she tried again, she felt a low, dull pain blossom somewhere deep inside her head. It looked like...like smoke. Like smoke in the shape of a man, but the smoke flickered, shimmered, danced back and forth, sometimes only the size of a human body, sometimes wider—much wider—like an image on an old television with bad reception.

The figure hadn't noticed her yet, or she didn't think it had, and she took a silent step closer. Whatever it was, it was breathing, and with each exhale, vibrations hummed and thrummed through the air. Waves of power emanated from it, creating the bee-like buzzing, but it wasn't just air molecules being touched. A set of keys on a nearby table rattled. A shot glass on a coffee table tipped over and rolled onto the floor. Janey felt the vibrations in the floor, coming up through the soles of her boots.

Flicker. Shimmer. The crouching thing blurred. Coalesced. Blurred again.

And looked up at Janey.

She froze in her tracks, her knuckles inside the gauntlet white as they gripped the baton. The blurred, shimmering thing was Julian Roth.

Except that the plump, self-conscious boy in Feygen's photo was gone. The young man who stared at her now was at least fifty pounds lighter, maybe more, his eyes peering from deep within sunken sockets, his cheekbones thrusting out against the skin of his face. Julian Roth stood, and between shimmers and blurs, Janey saw that he was dressed all in black. He reached up and pulled a black ski mask down over his face, shimmered, and vanished, and the vibrations stopped the instant he disappeared.

Janey thought her heart might crack in half. Julian Roth was an Augment. And he had some version of the same ability she did.

Moving more on autopilot than truly controlling her actions, Janey moved gingerly over to the dead body. His pock-marked face left no doubt in her mind: Antonio Griggs lay dead on the floor. But unlike Griggs's two deceased cohorts, Julian Roth had taken his time here. Griggs' torso looked like…like Swiss cheese. Like a target at a gun range.

She realized with a dull thud in the pit of her stomach that Julian Roth had killed his high-school tormentors by teleporting sections of their bodies away.

3

Splinters.

The world had fractured.

Like a jagged mosaic, grating and grinding across itself as the pieces shifted, shattered, joined, shattered again. One piece sliding against the next, shards that made up a razor-edged whole, alternating perception, one reality juxtaposed with the other.

"I see the world...the world sees me..."

Aphrodite Lupo nodded to herself and crouched down tighter next to the trunk of the tree, trying to make herself as small as possible and perfectly motionless, so no one passing on the sidewalk below would have reason to look up and see her perched on the branch.

The half-frozen, rain-slick street broke apart in her eyes, re-joined, broke apart, shifted, re-joined again. Two realities dancing, fighting, clawing at each other. Aphrodite sighed. It was so much easier to give up and let the world fracture. She wondered how and why she had ever tried to resist the splintering, lacerating dance.

Her name echoed and reverberated inside her skull, as it often did, and she turned it over and over, sliding her tongue across it, pressing her nose against it, tasting, smelling, touching. The perfect name.

Aphrodite Lupo. Aphrodite, the goddess of love, because wasn't she beautiful? Wouldn't men and women and children see her and love her, adore her, do her bidding? And Lupo. The wolf. The hunter. The teeth behind the beauty, the ferocity behind the love. Consequence. Dishonor her? Disobey her? Defy her? Any such attempt would bring forth the wolf.

Wolves feed. Teeth like splinters.

Aphrodite's eyes wavered and pulsed, wavered and pulsed, and the deep-blue-on-white gave way to the red and yellow display, the ruby sparks against the topaz field. She never tired of staring into a mirror when her eyes were like this. When the doctors came and took her mirror away, took it out of her room, that was when she knew it was time to leave. First the light in the sky, then the splintering, then the mirror.

Soak in the light, soak in the night, reach out, take them, claw and tear and bite.

Aphrodite's night eyes fixed on the mailbox across the street. With the tiniest bit of effort, she pulled the image closer to her, the numbers growing larger, clearer, until she could read them as easily as if they'd been printed huge on a billboard.

1547.

Aphrodite watched as the numbers exploded, re-formed, broken and twitching.

1 for A, 5 for E, 4 for D, 7 for G. What does it mean? What can it mean?

Aphrodite pursed her lips. Her brow furrowed. The blood-red sparks swirled in her eyes as if caught in a windstorm. A E D G. D A E G. E G D A. "Every girl."

Good. Good. Keep going.

"Every girl deserves absolution."

Someone who lived at that address was good, and right, and proper—fit for her. Prime. Ripe.

From some distance away, Aphrodite heard a door open and close. She recognized the sound: the back door at number 1547. She had watched the house long enough to have memorized its distinctions. A light came on, probably in the kitchen, dim through the front windows being that far back inside the place. Another light flared to life in an upstairs window. "Karen's home," Aphrodite breathed, and slithered down the trunk of the tree as sinuously as if she'd been a snake herself. The waitress's shirt snagged on a bit of bark and tore. Aphrodite didn't care. She'd have a new wardrobe soon.

Aphrodite stayed in the shadows, darting between parked cars, and dashed across the road so fast and so low to the ground, she knew anyone watching would think they'd seen an animal rather than a girl. She stayed that low as she circled around to the back of the house, to the doggy door she'd seen earlier. The LeFevre family had lost their Yorkie a week before, but hadn't yet removed the little dog's access point to the backyard. The door was much too small for a grown man to wriggle through, and almost too small for someone Aphrodite's size, but that made no difference. Aphrodite's bones cooperated as she narrowed her body and crawled silently through.

The LeFevres made good money. Not good enough to buy land, she didn't guess, since they lived in a mansion orchard with barely ten feet between their fancy house and the next one, but still more money than Aphrodite had ever seen. Hardwood floors everywhere. Marble countertops. A TV so ridiculous that it took up most of one wall in the living room. Golf clubs in the hallway corner. A pang of jealousy found its way to her heart.

Aphrodite whispered, "Remember, we need this," in her ancient, dust-dry voice, and climbed the stairs.

Karen LeFevre lay on her bed, gazing into the screen of her laptop. Seventeen years old, all skinny legs and elbows and eyes too big for her face. Aphrodite made no noise as she walked into Karen's bedroom, and over the girl's shoulder read the headline of the article she'd pulled up on *Huffington Post*: ATLANTA POLICE STILL KNOW NOTHING ABOUT THE GRAY WIDOW.

Aphrodite froze.

Gray Widow. Gray Widow. G for 7. W for 23. 7 for luck. 23 for the number of human chromosomes.

Karen LeFevre's body splintered, shifting, two worlds, black and white, alive and dead, real and unreal. A flush made its way through

Aphrodite's body. She felt the whispers making their way to the surface.

Gray Widow. Ghost Woman. Great Warrior.

Aphrodite's heart pounded, her breathing quickened, and before she could try to stop them, the whispers burst from her skin, electrifying the air around her, vibrations traveling in every direction. Karen LeFevre gasped, the skin of her bare legs erupting in gooseflesh as the temperature in the room plummeted, and when Karen heard the whispers she looked around and saw Aphrodite standing there, and she drew in a breath for what would surely be an ear-splitting, headache-inducing scream.

Aphrodite couldn't have that, so she struck before the girl made a sound.

Hirsch LaFevre threw open the back door and hit the stairs at a dead run. "Karen! Karen, where are you?"

"In my room, daddy." Karen's voice quavered with sobs.

Hirsch burst into Karen's room. Aphrodite took a moment to savor the image. The ex-Green Beret father, still huge and thick with muscle, broad chest heaving, eyes wide with anxiety after receiving a panicked call from his only child. Aphrodite had waited until Mrs. Hirsch was out of town before moving on her target. The father. Alone. Aphrodite watched, rapt, cataloguing every detail of the cinema that played out in the following seconds. Every movement of the man's face as he took in the sight of the bloody, broken, ruined mess that had been his daughter, only her face left pristine. Aphrodite wanted to make sure Hirsch LeFevre understood it was Karen he saw there, crumpled on the bed. She watched as all the blood drained away, falling out of his bronze, heavy-featured face, leaving him the color of ash. She watched as his body convulsed, convulsed again, his knees collapsing, watched as his flailing, grasping hands knocked everything from his daughter's dresser as he struggled to keep his feet. She listened intently

27

as words melted away from him, leaving only a rasping, keening cry.

It took only a handful of heartbeats to see enough. She stepped out from behind the closet door, wearing Karen LeFevre's shape and hair and face. Taking on her appearance had hurt. It always hurt. But she felt it worthwhile, to see the shock, the confusion, and—yes, yes, *there* —the spark of hope.

Hirsch LeFevre's face splintered, hope and fear, joy and dread, sliding, grinding.

"Karen? But..."

Aphrodite launched herself across the bedroom. LeFevre's eyelids didn't have time to slam shut before her stiffened fingers stabbed into his throat. Silenced, he staggered, and she slipped behind him and wrapped her arms around his skull and broke his neck, and watched as his head flopped, his neck as limp as the finger of a glove.

"There, there," she murmured. "I've got you. There, there."

We will need him. The strength he offers. The power. The knowledge.

Aphrodite didn't bother moving Hirsch LeFevre from the floor of the hallway outside his dead daughter's bedroom. She knelt over him and stripped off his clothing. She didn't bother with buttons or snaps or zippers, she simply took handfuls of the cloth and tore it length-wise, so that in a few seconds he lay naked on the hardwood, the shreds of his shirt and pants and underwear lying beneath him. Aphrodite didn't care about his shoes, but as she sat back on her haunches, surveying her work in progress, she decided it would be aesthetically unappealing to leave them on. So she pushed the leather loafers off his feet and pulled off his socks.

Hirsch LeFevre's corpse looked better than most men did while still alive. Clearly he had kept up his physical fitness, perhaps not to the level of a soldier, but enough to keep himself maintained. Aphrodite trailed delicate fingertips along the lines of his arms, his chest and stomach. She grasped his penis with one hand. It was still warm. She wondered what it might have looked like aroused. Her fingers left his groin and caressed the long, thick muscles of his thighs.

"Now. Now. Now."

Aphrodite closed her shifting, swirling eyes. The temperature around her dropped so quickly that ice formed on Hirsch LeFevre's broad chest, and the whispers echoed throughout the upstairs, maybe through the whole house. Aphrodite's upper and lower jaws changed. Extended. Twisted sideways, the teeth absorbing into the bone that burst free of the disappearing gums, until two wet, red, curving blades protruded downward from her skull. They slid against each other, past each other, with the delicate rasping sound of scissor blades.

A long, red, grasping tongue flicked out and licked the residual blood clean from the curved bone blades. Aphrodite focused on Hirsch LeFevre's left thigh and bent to her work.

Aphrodite had never bothered to learn much about computers, or programming, or anything that could be considered technical. She knew she could pick up whatever knowledge she needed later. Her mission now took precedence.

Still, she had heard a few terms, a few bits of jargon, on shows in the hospital's TV room. What she had done with Karen LeFevre, taking her appearance...that was temporary. A quick fix. Now, as she stood naked in front of a full-length mirror in Karen LeFevre's bathroom, she knew she was about to perform what could be called an "upgrade." A...what was the term? An update of her core system. Something like that. With a tiny shock she realized she still wore her patient wristband. A flick of two fingers tore it away. Flushed down the toilet.

Aphrodite had been eighteen for several weeks, but knew she could still pass for twelve. Her entirely un-lined face. Her frail arms and legs...only the barest hints of hips...the tiny breasts, tipped with petite pink nipples...the delicate, downy hair at her groin.

"I'm not a little girl."

No.

"I'm a leader. A commander."

Then look like one.

Aphrodite Lupo's ice-blonde hair fell in a fine, silky sheet down over her shoulders. She decided that could stay. Her dark blue eyes could stay, too. But the mass she had stripped from Hirsch LeFevre's bones, and from the waitress before him, needed places to go, and Aphrodite sent it to her bones first.

Imitating Karen LeFevre had hurt.

But this…this was the most exquisite torture.

Aphrodite turned from the mirror and clutched the edge of the sink, her head bowed, her teeth grinding as her body forced itself to elongate. She fought back a scream, no, a *shriek*, as her legs and arms stretched, as her back lengthened. In seconds she gained five inches of height.

Her muscles already commanded power unlike any normal female's, but she needed more. More flesh. Needed to look like a *woman*.

Keep going, Aphrodite. Keep going.

Her calves and thighs and buttocks increased in mass, filling out from the pipe-cleaner limbs she'd had moments before, followed by her biceps and triceps and shoulders. Muscles encased her core, hardening, flattening. She channeled fatty tissue to her breasts, willed her nipples to grow and darken, and allowed faint creases to appear around her mouth, between her eyebrows.

The splintering of the world around her made a sound.

"Whisper to me. Tell me. Tell me."

Like hushed voices from far away, the whispers drew closer and closer, every splinter sliding past the next, locking, breaking, pushing, tearing.

The whispers became a roar. Every surface in the bathroom crackled as crystals of ice formed and expanded and coalesced into a thin, hard sheet.

Aphrodite never stopped screaming. If she hadn't been directing new tissue to her vocal chords, lowering her voice from a girl's to a woman's, she might have lost the ability to speak entirely.

Finally, the agony stopped. Breathing hard, her vision dark around the edges, Aphrodite straightened up and looked at herself in the mirror again. Gone was the girl who could've been mistaken for a child. The new Aphrodite Lupo let a slow, satisfied grin stretch her naturally ruby-red lips. She ran her hands over the flawless curves, up from her hips, across her abs, between her heavy breasts, along the perfect jawline. She didn't think Karen LeFevre's clothes would fit her now. "Maybe her mother's..."

Aphrodite left the bedroom and padded down the hall, past Hirsch LeFevre's ravaged corpse, toward the master bedroom.

Fourteen hours later, Aphrodite walked out of a TJ Maxx store carrying two large bags of clothes. She knew better than to use stolen credit cards, but Hirsch LeFevre's wallet had yielded not quite six hundred dollars, and his wife's taste in clothing did not suit a commander.

Neither did anything in TJ Maxx, but Aphrodite needed clothes that fit her new taller, fuller body, and this was the closest place within easy walking distance.

You'll need a car soon. Begin planning for that.

"A car...yes..."

Careful reconnaissance had led to the discovery of a pool house in the backyard of an elderly woman. The pool didn't appear to have had any water in it for years, the yard had grown up into weeds, and Aphrodite doubted the old woman had set foot in the pool house in recent memory. As far as Aphrodite could tell, the woman—Mrs. Florence Gadsworth—lived alone and had no family. The brick wall around the property was easy to climb, and Aphrodite had been squatting in the pool house, unseen and unheard, for the last week. She had carefully chosen clothes that would require no ironing or other upkeep to look normal, as she couldn't risk using any electricity.

Aphrodite was about to cross the parking lot, headed across the street into Mrs. Gadsworth's neighborhood, when she heard a burst of laughter from off to her left. A comics and games shop stood next to the clothing store, and in front of it stood two teenage boys, one of them smoking a cigarette.

The one not smoking turned his head and looked at her, and Aphrodite stopped dead still as the whispers shouted inside her head.

The boy just barely topped six feet, but looked taller because he was so thin. She could tell by the way his T-shirt hung from his not-too-narrow shoulders that he had virtually no body fat. She liked that. His hair had been buzzed off to almost nothing, but he had colored the stubble fire-engine red, and he had four...no. She counted. Five piercings. One in each ear, one in each nostril, and a curved jade spike jutting from his lower lip.

The boy's body splintered. Shifted. Re-formed. Five piercings. Five for "E." Electric. Energy. Everything.

Aphrodite slowly pivoted and began walking toward the boys. The red-haired one saw her coming, and turned his head, a blush creeping into his pale cheeks. Aphrodite walked past them, to the shop window, and looked inside while she listened.

The other boy, a tall, fat young man with a beard that grew exclusively out of his neck, said, "Okay, okay, but seriously, you look at it from a law enforcement perspective? The Gray Widow is *totally* a criminal. I mean, as soon as she touches somebody, that, like...ruins the, uh...the chain of custody or something."

The boy with the piercings said, "Oh my God, dude, you are *so* full of shit. Look, it's like this. Yeah, the Gray Widow is technically a criminal. What she's doing breaks the law, breaks a fuck-ton of laws. But, like, she's outside the legal system! You get me? She's bypassed it! It doesn't matter that she's breaking the law, because she's got her *own* law. And from where I'm standing, it looks like she's doing better enforcing hers than the cops are with their whole, like, legal code."

The neck-bearded one sputtered. "Nathan, c'mon, man, my uncle's a cop. And he fucking *hates* her. He says she's stomping all over the Constitution. That's a sacred document."

Nathan. His name is Nathan. Remember that.

Nathan snorted. "Sacred my ass. The Constitution is this, right here: it's the best a bunch of white guys could come up with at the time."

"But it's the law!"

"Right, and without law, there'd be anarchy, right? People running wild in the streets. Looting, raping, pillaging, all that great Viking stuff. But let me ask you this: how much of that's going on in Atlanta, now that she's here? Now that *that's* here?"

Nathan pointed at something on the wall beside the window, and Aphrodite couldn't help but turn and look. There, scratched deeply into the brick, was a symbol she'd never seen before—six oblong shapes arranged around two circles. It took no more than a second for her to realize that the shape represented a spider's eyes.

Gray Widow. Ghost Woman.

Aphrodite whispered, "Great Warrior," but too softly for Nathan to hear her.

Nathan went on: "I'll tell you. People feel safer. They're not as worried, 'cause they know she's out there. That she's got their backs."

The neck-bearded boy scoffed. "You could do that with a bunch of beat cops, though."

Nathan looked around theatrically. "Yeah? And do you *see* any beat cops? Where are they? Hiding in the bushes? Invisible? Yeah. There aren't any beat cops anymore, man. There's just *her.*"

Inside the window, a display advertised a new edition of a game called "Munchkin," and listed its sale price as $19.95. As soon as Aphrodite's eyes lit on the number, the whispers rang out inside her skull, and she had to struggle to keep them from bursting out of her skin.

Turn. Turn and look. His car.

As casually as she could, Aphrodite turned and faced the parking lot. Only one vehicle was parked near the comic shop, a fast-looking four-door that had at one point been all-black, but now was part white and part red. The license plate read 918 TMM.

See it. See it!

Aphrodite struggled.

9 for I. 1 for A. 8 for H. And T. And M. And M. See it for what it is.

I Am The Messenger.

Heed Me.

Aphrodite pulled her eyes from the car to Nathan, and walked up to him. She only had to tilt her head a tiny bit now to look him in the eye. "Hi. What's your name?"

It seemed to take him a moment to understand that she was talking to him, and another moment to swallow hard before he spoke. "Uh. Hi! I'm, I'm, my name's Nathan. Nate. You can call me either one. Nathan Pittman. Or, or Nate. Nate's fine, too." He gestured at his friend. "This is—"

She cut him off. "My name is Aphrodite. Aphrodite Lupo."

Nathan faltered. "Are you serious?"

Aphrodite let her eyelids lower, and pretended not to notice the tiny bits of body language as Nathan urged his friend to leave. "Why would I lie about something like that?"

"No, no, I don't think you would, I just—that's just the most baller name I've ever heard in my life. Is all."

Aphrodite moved closer to him. Not a full step. Just enough so that he noticed. "Nathan…tell me more about this 'Gray Widow.'"

4

———————

Janey's connection to the Basement was on a completely different level from the other places to which she teleported. She had spent days there, weeks, maybe months by now, and knew the place as intimately as she knew her own bedroom. Because of that, she didn't need the line of sight necessary to flicker to other destinations. Because of that, she could reach into any dark place and access the Basement. She sometimes wondered what that would look like—a hand and arm emerging from out of nowhere, grabbing something off the peg-board or workbench, and disappearing again. Of course, no one would ever witness such a thing, first because she never intended to leave anyone alone in the Basement, and second because it wouldn't work if enough light were present for anyone else to see it.

Since appearing on a local television show and spectacularly announcing her presence to the world, Janey had followed through on her promise to place the "Eyes of the Widow" symbol around the city, and tried to add a new one each week. She cultivated the same kind of connection to each of these places as she had with the Basement, so that she could flicker directly from one to another without the line of sight. It had turned out to be a tricky proposition. She couldn't teleport directly to the symbol itself. She didn't dare. Four times now she had caught police surveillance units focused on different locations bearing the Eyes of the Widow, and while she knew they weren't aware of her limitation to darkness, she couldn't take the chance of flickering in and setting off an array of klieg lights.

Simon Grove had trapped her with just such an arrangement. Her leg ached faintly when she thought of it.

Instead, Janey picked a spot near each symbol where, once the sun set, thick shadows congregated. That way she could teleport in, see if any police lingered nearby, spot any criminal activity, and flicker back out.

That was another reason to place as many symbols as she could. Police manpower stretched only so far. There was no way for them to monitor every location. She wondered if they had plans to install discreet cameras. Maybe motion-activated ones. But even if they did, all the cameras would produce would be evidence of her dealing with muggers, or violent pimps, or gang members, or anyone else she caught.

After reporting to Zach Feygen, Janey flickered from symbol to symbol, her mind whipping through what she'd seen—determined to distract herself from the debacle with Tim. Her conversation with Feygen played on a loop in her head as she traveled.

"So, you're saying Roth is...like you? He's—fuck, I don't even know the word for it."

"Call him an Augment. And I'm not saying he's exactly like me. I'm just saying there are similarities."

Janey flickered onto a fire escape, her night vision rendering the alleyway below her crystal-clear. She could see the Eyes of the Widow etched into a metal delivery door. A drunk man leaned against the wall, and as she watched, he vomited onto his shoes, but there was no one else there, so she flickered out again.

"But he can do what you do? Disappear and shit?"

"At least. Yes. It looked...I don't know. I've never seen anything like it before, but that's not saying much, because I don't even know how I got this

way myself. It looked like he was, maybe—I'm just guessing, here—it's like he was stuck."

Janey emerged from the shadows on the roof of a house in a neighborhood the media would call "economically depressed." She crouched next to a chimney, near the power pole where she had carved the Eyes of the Widow. There had been a rash of burglaries in the area in the last week, and Janey flickered from roof to roof, eyes peering through the darkness, until she caught sight of a slim teenage boy trying to open a dark house's back window with a small pry-bar. Janey teleported directly behind him, spun him around and took the pry-bar away. "You're about to break the law," she growled. She had been working on her growl. "Run away. Don't let me catch you again. Next time will be much, much worse."

Janey dropped the pry-bar on the Basement workbench and, listening to the sound of the boy's running feet as they faded in the distance, flickered away.

"What do you mean, 'stuck'?"

"When I...teleport...there's a process to it. A series of events. It happens very, very quickly, but there's a sequence. And it's like Roth is...I don't know. Like he's hung up in the middle of the sequence."

"Jesus."

"But, Feygen. Listen to me. He's killing people by teleporting chunks of their bodies away. Now that the three guys he hated are dead, maybe he'll stop. But maybe he won't. Maybe now he's got a taste for it. Either way, regular police are not equipped for this. You try to take him and he's likely to kill you all."

Janey stepped out of the shadows next to a dilapidated apartment building, one of a dozen in a complex. Across the oil-stained parking lot, the Eyes of the Widow looked out from the frame of a MARTA bus stop shelter. An enormous young man—Janey figured him for college age, at least six-five, with shoulders that would brush both sides of a doorframe—held a teenage girl against a car, his hand clamped over her mouth. The girl struggled, squirmed, and got her mouth free long enough to shout, *"Get off me!"* before he silenced her again.

"You ain't walkin' out on me, bitch," the young man said, and Janey appeared from the darkness right behind him and kicked him in the back of the knee. Unlike Burt on the stairs, however, as the man dropped, Janey cranked his head around and rode him to the ground, where his nose shattered on the pavement.

Behind her, the girl gasped, "He's got a knife *he's got a knife!*"

Sure enough, the enormous young man had a switchblade in one hand, which poked uselessly into Janey's Vylar-protected calf. Janey knocked it aside, switched her position, and pressed her knee into the back of his neck. He yelped in pain, and a blister formed on his skin as Janey used the darkness next to his oversized skull to reach back to the Basement. She grabbed three thick, black plastic zip-ties, and within seconds she had the young man hog-tied.

"Call the police," Janey growled. "Report a citizen's arrest." She stood, not waiting for the girl to reply, and disappeared into the darkness beside a nearby SUV.

"So what am I supposed to do? Somebody sees him again, we...what?"

"You call me. Same if you find any more bodies like the ones he's already left. Just being honest, Detective, I don't know what I'll do to try to beat him, but I'd rather it be me than you."

"Fuck. Jesus H. FUCK. What is this? People like you and, and that Grove freak, and whatever did that to the Waffle House waitress, you're just going to start popping up all over the place?"

"As soon as I know what's going on, I swear to God, I'll fill you in. Say hi to Heather for me."

Janey smiled to herself at how Feygen had sputtered as she vanished into the shadows. The smile faded as the image of Julian Roth came back to her, a man made of smoke and shimmer and static. Janey finished her patrol, returned to the Basement and stripped off the suit, and flickered back to her apartment to wash it out. That wasn't as nasty a job in early Spring as it was during Atlanta's punishing summers, but she never let herself put it off.

Once the suit was back in the Basement, drying, Janey flopped down on the couch in her living room and stretched out. She wore a pair of boy-shorts underwear, an old, soft, hole-riddled T-shirt, and not even a molecule of makeup. She glanced at the clock, saw that it was 3:32 a.m., and sighed. She plucked at the shirt. "Me at my sexiest."

She had Tim's number set as the first of her favorites. He'd been having bouts of severe insomnia since he got hurt, and she knew the chances he'd be awake at that hour were pretty good. Her thumb hovered over the "Call" button...and hesitated...and with a groan she dropped the phone beside her on the couch. What right did she have to involve Tim in any of this? What right had she ever had to involve him in her life at all? It'd already gotten him nearly killed, and left him with injuries that he might never get over. She buried her face in her hands.

3:32. That meant the nurse at the O'Brien Home wouldn't check in for an hour and a half.

Janey made sure her phone was on silent, pulled on a pair of jeans and a sports bra and a non-holey T-shirt, and flickered away into the darkness.

A tiny night-light burned just above the baseboard beside the door to Adam's *en suite* bathroom. Janey knew where it was, and where its light failed to reach. She stepped out of the shadows beside the tall wooden wardrobe. Her bare feet made no noise on the tile floor, or the thick shag rug beside his bed.

Adam lay there, a thin white sheet covering his pajama-clad body, the weak illumination from the night-light still making his golden hair shine. The nurses had let it get longer than usual, she saw. The glorious waves and curls fell down to his shoulders. His lips were parted, his chin relaxed, but he didn't snore. Adam had rarely snored. She knew, from before as well as from the time he'd spent here...after he got hurt...that Adam slept like a stone. Some of the nurses laughed affectionately about how difficult it was to get him out of bed in the mornings.

Janey didn't laugh when they told her that.

When had she last laughed?

When I was with Tim. Tim makes me laugh.

Standing there, gazing down at Adam, Janey fought back tears.

She crossed the room and carefully, gently, lay down next to him. Only for a few minutes, she promised herself, and double-promised. Adam made a soft sound and rolled onto his side, his back to her. Janey lay there, her eyes closed, for most of a minute. Then she repositioned herself and spooned against him.

So warm. Adam had always radiated more body heat than anyone else she had ever known, so much so that she called him her "personal heater." That was great for cool winter nights, but more than once in the summer he'd proven too much, so that she'd had to scoot away from him. He was just as warm now.

And he smelled the same. Earthy and clean at the same time. Like...like rain.

Adam shifted his head, just a fraction of an inch, but it was enough to shift a long, curling lock of his hair. It fell across Janey's cheek. *That hair.* Back then Janey had sported her own ferocious mane of chestnut curls. How often had they joked about clogging the shower drain?

She knew it wasn't fair, doing this, just being here. Not to herself. Not to Adam, either, if he woke up, though he couldn't understand it the way she did. But with the heat of his skin soaking into her, and the scent of his hair, and the lines and contours of his body that she knew so well, so intimately, pressed against hers...

Janey rolled over onto her back again, filled with shame and a deep, familiar grief. Adam didn't move. She lay there and listened to his deep, even breaths, the scent of him still in her nostrils, and repeating the words *only for a few minutes* to herself, she closed her eyes.

When she opened them, she was perched on a stool in the corner behind the counter at the art supply store where Adam worked, her sketchbook on her lap and a charcoal pencil in her hand, waiting for him to get back. She had a sketch of Adam half-finished. Rain hammered down outside, and the wind blew with such force that every few minutes the big front door swung open a couple of inches and the art books in the spinner rack near the register ruffled and slapped at each other. The rain seemed to have driven away any potential customers, and for the last half hour it had just been Janey and Adam. She liked to keep him company as he straightened the merchandise and stocked the shelves.

The door swung wide, and Adam—who had just ducked into the coffee shop next door to get them a couple of lattes—came in, soaked to the skin and no lattes in sight, with something cradled in his arms. "Hey. Want to meet the friend I just made?"

Janey put aside her sketchbook and pencil and came to the counter, where Adam set down a tiny, bedraggled orange kitten. The kitten trembled, and made a sound sort of like *meep*. Adam said, "There's some towels in the bathroom, would you mind—" but before he could finish the sentence, Janey had sprinted to the back.

She returned to the counter seconds later with a fuzzy brown towel, and Adam used it to pat the kitten dry instead of rubbing it. "I don't want to hurt it," he said, when she gave him a quizzical look. As he dried it off, Adam petted its head and scratched under its chin. His grin was infectious, and Janey gave him one of her own. "Where did you find it?"

"In front of the coffee shop, under a car. It was all alone, just sitting there shivering with its fur stuck to it."

Adam worked diligently until the kitten's fur had dried and returned to what looked like its normal state of fuzziness. The kitten stretched, extending its petite needle claws, and started purring. Adam set the towel down and cradled it, and the purrs got louder, and when he held it against him it climbed up and nuzzled against his neck. He swayed a little, as if rocking an infant, and stroked the kitten's back, and murmured, "There, there...look at you, little one... you're just perfect, aren't you?"

Janey watched the two of them. She knew she needed to be the voice of reason, and knew just as well how pointless it would be. "Adam. First off, you're soaking wet yourself. You need to dry off or you'll catch pneumonia."

Adam set the kitten on the counter and used the same towel to give his hair a once-over. "I'll be fine." He danced his fingers back and forth on the countertop. The kitten chased after them. "You look like a...Pericles. Don't you think? Isn't he just the little elder statesman? We could call him Perry for short."

Janey put her hand out and tried to get the kitten to come to her, but it showed not even a shred of interest in that. The animal might as well have looked Adam square in the eye and said, "All right, I'll be your cat now."

"You know we're not allowed to have pets."

The kitten skittered and scampered across the counter. Adam said, "Ah, I'm sure I can work something out with the landlord."

"And neither one of us knows a damn thing about taking care of cats."

Adam picked Perry up and cradled him again. The kitten immediately nuzzled against his neck and turned the purrs back on. "We can learn! We can *totally* learn. There's websites for that and everything." The kitten climbed up and stood on Adam's shoulder, its pointed little tail stuck in his ear. He laughed and carefully disengaged its claws and cradled it again. "Besides, we can't just put it back where I found it. And I won't take him to the pound." He scratched the kitten's chin again. "No, sir. No I won't."

Janey reached out and stroked the kitten's back. It closed its eyes and stretched again, and began pawing slowly at the air with its front feet. Adam laughed. "My neighbor's cat used to do that! He called it 'making biscuits.' It's supposed to mean the cat's comfortable."

"Okay. But soon it'll be hungry. Do you know what to feed a kitten that small?"

Outside, the rain diminished and stopped, and seconds later a ray of sun lit up the sidewalk. Steam began to rise.

"I'll look it up. Or...*you* could look it up? Could you take Perry back to our place, and as soon as my shift's over, I'll come and we can take him to the vet together, get him checked out?"

Janey sighed. She'd seen this coming, the second she saw the kitten in Adam's arms. She'd also known she wouldn't be able to say no. Not when he was this happy. "Yeah, I can do that. Got a box he can ride in? ...Is he even a 'he?' I'm not sure how to tell."

"Thanks, sweetie! And yeah, I've got a box that'll work for that." He took a step around the corner of the counter, the kitten still cradled in his arms. "In fact, y'know what, I could take three or four of these boxes and make him up a little, like, what do you call them? A kitty condo! It'd fit right in the corner of the living room!"

Movement on the sidewalk caught Janey's eye. A middle-aged man walked by, looking around on the ground, as Adam disappeared into the stock room. Seconds later, a young girl, seven or eight, followed after the man. Tears flowed from her puffy red eyes. Both the man and the little girl were every bit as soaked as Adam had been. Janey went to the front window, and saw the man checking under parked cars along the sidewalk.

Adam came back to the counter holding a small box, the orange kitten riding on his shoulder. Janey turned to him, and when he saw her face, his grin faded and disappeared. Janey said, "I'm sorry, babe. I really am." She pushed open the front door and called out, "Sir? Excuse me? Have you lost something?"

The man looked up, and Janey felt Adam brush her shoulder as he joined her, and the little girl turned toward them and her face lit up like the sun itself. She shouted, "Harry!" and bolted toward Adam, her hands stretching up toward the kitten.

The girl's father followed right behind her. "You found him! Oh thank God! We only stopped for a minute, literally just long enough to run in and run out, but when we came back out he was gone! I had the window cracked—trying to give him air, y'know? I didn't think the little bugger could climb up and get out that way."

Adam carefully took the kitten off his shoulder and handed it to the girl. She started crying again, but they were very different tears now, and she said, "Thank you thank you thank you!" and dashed away to a car in front of a dry cleaners.

The father pulled out his wallet. "Seriously, I can't thank you enough. She loves that kitten more than she loves me, I'm pretty sure." The man took a fifty-dollar bill and held it out. "This is the least I can do."

Adam smiled, and shook his head. "Nah, that's not necessary. I'm just, y'know. Glad he's got a good home."

Doing her best not to sound accusatory, Janey said, "Yeah, just, maybe don't leave him alone in the car, huh?"

The father shrugged. He looked sheepish. "Definitely. Definitely. Well...you're sure you don't want it?" He waggled the bill.

Adam shook his head again. "Nah, it's fine. You guys take care."

The father shook Adam's hand, and Janey's hand, and went after his daughter.

Adam closed the door, watching the man and the girl as they climbed into their car with the kitten. "Guess we don't have a cat after all, huh?"

Janey wrapped her arms around him, feeling his disappointment, and held him as tightly as she could...

...and opened her eyes in Adam's room, still lying on his bed. Adam had awakened at some point, and sat next to her, his legs crossed, his back to the wall. Watching her. The dim glow of the night-light accentuated the deep indentation above his temple where the bullet had blasted away all the true parts of him.

"Hi, Janey," he said, his voice light and simple.

Janey sprang off the bed. "I, I, Adam, I'm, I'm sorry, I didn't mean... didn't mean..." The clock on the wall read 4:47. She had thirteen minutes before the nurse came in.

"I rolled over, and bumped into you, and woke up." A tiny bit of saliva ran down from the corner of his mouth. He swiped at it with his sleeve. "Are we having a sleepover? I've heard about sleepovers."

Janey knelt beside the bed and took his hands in hers. "No, sweetie. This is...this is a dream. You're just dreaming. You should go back to sleep now."

He tugged a hand loose and touched her face. "But..." He pushed his fingers into her hair. "But you feel like real."

"No, no. You're just dreaming." Janey pulled his hand back down and put it on his knee. "Lie back down, sweetie. Okay?"

Adam nodded. "Okay." He stretched out on the bed. His long,

golden hair spread out around his head on the pillow. "It's still dark out. When it's breakfast, it's light."

"That's right, sweetie. That's why you need to go back to sleep."

Adam closed his eyes. It took no more than ten seconds for his breathing to even out again.

Janey moved into the deepest of the shadows and flickered away, half-blind with scalding tears.

J aney woke to the sound of a knock at her front door. She squinted —the sun was well into the sky, and she had to grope around for something to put on—and saw that, according to her bedside clock, it was five past noon. Vaguely ashamed of herself for sleeping so late, she pulled on a short, lightweight robe and went to the door.

She told herself how ridiculous it was to feel bad for sleeping late, when she'd been out half the night taking care of the city. It didn't make the shame go away.

She peered through the peephole, and a twinge of mixed excitement and anxiety shot through her, and she opened the door to reveal Tim standing there, leaning on his cane. He had a paper sack in one hand, and gave her a solid grin as he held it up. "Breakfast?"

"Oh my God. Bagels?"

"Cinnamon. With cream cheese."

She hugged him, and let her lips linger against his neck for a long moment. He made a low, satisfied sound in his throat, and shifted the paper sack to the hand holding the cane, and pressed his free one into the small of her back. Janey leaned away from him just enough to plant a tiny kiss on his mouth before covering her own mouth with one hand. "Sorry. Morning breath. I just got up." She ushered him into the apartment and closed the door.

One fresh pot of coffee later, they sat at Janey's comically small breakfast table, and Tim watched her with what appeared to be continued satisfaction as she wolfed down one bagel and started on another. Janey took a sip of coffee. "There's another one in there. Are you sure you don't want it? I'm just saying, if you don't, I'm going to eat it, and I don't want you to have any food-based regrets."

Tim chuckled. "No, I already ate. More than I should have, really. Mom served up biscuits and smoked sausage this morning, and then I had a steak salad at lunch."

Janey's cheeks darkened. *Normal people have already had lunch, and you're just having breakfast.* "So, um...not that I'm not thrilled to see you and your bagels, but—did we have plans today? Have I forgotten about something?"

Tim tried to shake his head, frowned at the pain in his immobilized neck, and drummed his fingertips on the tabletop. "No. No, it's just, I'm free today. I mean, I don't have any physical therapy scheduled, and I'm feeling pretty good. Better than I have in a while. I just thought we might hang out." His eyes widened, and he threw up protesting hands. "Unless *you* have plans! If you have plans, I totally understand, I didn't mean you should just drop everything because my schedule's clear."

Janey swallowed a bite of bagel, and let her eyes twinkle. "What did you have in mind?"

"Well, maybe not trail hiking." When Janey laughed, he went on: "Maybe an early movie, and a meal? Maybe go to the High? They've got a new Peruvian exhibit I've heard is pretty amazing. I don't know. It's still a little nippy for a picnic in the park, but I'm game if you are."

Janey's father had once told her something that hadn't made any sense to her at the time. She'd been...what, thirteen? Freshman year of high school? Yes—because her first school dance was coming up. She couldn't remember the context, but she could hear her father's voice clear as a bell. "Janey, loving someone is a decision you make every day."

At the time, she'd shrugged those words off. They didn't fit at all with the rom-com version of true love Janey had seen over and over. And she didn't have both parents to provide an example. It was just her and her dad. So she'd let the words fly in one ear and out the other, and hadn't given them a second thought until a year after Adam had been shot.

It had taken her that long even to entertain the thought that she might, someday, somehow, love someone else.

Adam was her first love. Her first true love. But…

Say the words. Admit it. Adam is gone.

Her heart kicked and pounded. She felt as if she'd just set herself a dare.

Janey set down the bagel, pushed the flimsy table out the way and stood. Tim said, "What're you—" but she shushed him, crossed the space between them, and straddled him, settling into his lap. He started to say something else, but she cut him off with a kiss.

"Tim, I know how…well, how spectacularly fucked up things have been between us. But I've been doing a lot of thinking. And I don't want there to be any more obstacles. I want…I want us to move forward." She kissed him again. Longer this time, deeper, and she felt his hands travel up from her waist, across her ribs, and—

Tim grasped both her upper arms and pushed her away. "I'm sorry, but you sitting on me—my back's spasming—"

Janey leapt off of him. "Oh shit, oh shit, I'm sorry, I didn't mean to hurt you, I swear I didn't mean to hurt you!"

Tim nodded, his eyes squeezed shut, and dug in a pocket. "I know. Janey, I know." He pulled out a prescription pill bottle and shook a couple into his palm, and pointed at her coffee. "Mind if I…?"

Janey handed him the coffee quickly enough that she almost slopped it over the side, and he swallowed the pills with it. "What can I do? Do you need to lie down, do I need to get you back to your place, do I need to call your therapist?"

He made a dampening gesture. "I'll be okay. I promise you. It was just, I wasn't expecting you to do that, and I wasn't in the right position, and it sort of pinched a nerve, I guess." He re-settled on the chair. Wincing. It made her hate herself.

Janey turned away from him and braced both hands on the kitchen sink, her head bowed. When her phone went off, Janey felt a stab of relief, and then a wave of guilt for feeling relieved. She ran and grabbed it off her nightstand.

"Yeah?"

"It's me." Janey knew Garrison Vessler didn't smoke, but his voice made him sound like a human chimney. "I'm about to text you Anna Grove's new address. She's got a place outside Knoxville, Tennessee. You still sure you want to talk to her? It might open up a bigger can of worms than you're prepared to deal with."

"Well, do *you* have any answers about how we got this way?"

Janey expected Vessler to say the same thing he always said when she brought up the mysterious source of the superhuman "Augmentations" she and Vessler and a minuscule number of other people had: "No one knows how this happened." Instead, Vessler paused. She could hear him breathing.

"Vessler—what is it? Has something happened?"

The pause continued for several more heartbeats before he said, "Maybe."

"What? What? Tell me!"

"It could be nothing. But...you remember, I told you right after we first met that there had been some speculation about an unidentified object in orbit."

"Yeah...uh, you said something had been detected up there, right? But nobody knew anything past that?"

"Right. Well, I've got a contact at NASA. And for the last few weeks, they've been trying to track something in low orbit."

Janey turned to Tim, and saw him watching her with obvious keen interest. "So is it the same thing?"

"They can't tell. It fades in and out. Sometimes they can see it, sometimes they can't. Most of the time they can't. And they can't predict where it's going to be, because its orbit started out erratic and has been getting more so as it goes."

"So...it might not have anything to do with us at all."

"Correct."

"But it *might*."

"Correct."

"So what do we do about it?"

"We wait. See if NASA can predict where it's going to be, and if they can get eyes on it. In the meantime...Anna Grove doesn't seem to be going anywhere."

"All right. Thanks."

She ended the call, and knew Vessler would destroy the burner phone he'd used to contact her. She had no idea where he and Scott Charles were, since he refused to tell her and she had no way to track him, but she liked to imagine the two of them in a log cabin beside an icy lake somewhere. Maybe with a barrel full of burner phones in the corner.

Without looking at Tim, Janey scooted the breakfast table back into place and sat down across from him again. "How, uh...how's your back?"

"It's fine. The spasm died down, and the pills'll start helping soon."

"Good." Janey didn't know what to say past that, and smeared cream cheese on another bagel.

Tim said, "Listen..."

"Yes?"

"I could hear little bits of what Vessler was saying. You've got an address for Anna Grove, right? Simon Grove's mother?"

Janey's phone blipped as Vessler's text came through. "Yeah. Here it is. Can you believe it's *the* Anna Grove?"

Tim shrugged. "I never saw any of her movies. But what I was going to say...you want to go and see her. Right? And if we try to hang out today, you're going to be distracted, thinking about her, all day."

Janey opened her mouth to answer, but hung her head instead. "Probably."

Tim leaned forward and put his hand over Janey's. "Then let's go see her together."

That brought her head back up. "Excuse me?"

"Not...doing the, the flickering thing. No teleporting. We've both got cars. Let's take one and go see her. Together. Knoxville's not that far away. We can be there by five or six, allowing for traffic."

"Are you sure? If we spend much time talking to her—if she'll talk to us at all—that'd put us back here awfully late."

A mischievous smile crept onto Tim's lips. "Well, if it gets too late, maybe we can carefully, very carefully, find a hotel."

Janey stood and leaned over and kissed him. "Let me get dressed."

5

Nathan Pittman hadn't had a clear thought in the last five days, and as Aphrodite bucked and squirmed beneath his lips and tongue, the last shreds of his coherent thinking disappeared out the window. Her scent, her taste, filled his mouth and his nose and washed across his skin. He drank it in like a man dying of thirst. "Yes, just like that."

Rain pelted down outside the window of the pool house where Nathan lived, away from the apathetic eyes of his parents. Nathan knelt beside his bed, where Aphrodite lay crosswise, her flawless ass at the edge of the mattress, her thighs spread wide and her feet braced on his shoulders. He had two fingers inside her, moving and pressing gently, exactly as she had taught him, and his other hand reached up to massage her breast, carefully rolling and tugging the nipple.

"Harder." Her fingers grazed the back of his hand as it caressed and kneaded her. "A little harder." He pulled more firmly on her nipple— *Oh God I hope that's not too hard*—and she groaned and raised her hips further. She groped at the back of his head, but his hair was too short to grip, so she put her palm against the top of his skull and pressed his face more firmly into herself.

"*There!*" Her hips rose and fell, rose and fell, as his tongue kept up the pace she had asked for. *Don't stop, she said don't stop, don't stop and don't go faster, just keep doing like this unless she tells me.*

Aphrodite's hand left his head, and he snuck a glance upward and saw her clawing at the sheets, and her back arched and as she moaned he felt her clamp down on his fingers, and again, and again.

I'm doing it right! Fuck yes!

Her back hit the bed again, and a long, lingering sigh escaped her. He started to pull away, but her hand flew back to his scalp and kept him in place. "No. Don't move. Don't move." She breathed deeply, raggedly. Pressed his hand against her breast again. "Now..." Her voice trembled. "Now, a tiny bit of suction...right where your tongue is..."

Nathan did as he was asked, and Aphrodite rewarded him with another long, shuddering moan. He swirled his tongue around her. "Yes. *Yes.* Now a little faster." Her legs quivered as he worked. "Oh God. Oh God. Oh *fuck.*" She grabbed Nathan's head with both hands and held him tight against her, soaking his mouth and his chin and the fingers she had guided to the precious place inside her. "Don't stop. Don't stop. *Don't stop...*" His eager tongue moved against her like a soft machine. As the quivering in her legs intensified, Nathan broke Aphrodite's rule—*Don't do anything unless she says to, but this feels right* —and sucked harder, pulling the delicate bit of flesh farther between his lips, covering it with the gift of his tongue, and Aphrodite erupted in a hoarse shout, a shout so loud it startled him, and she sat upright and ground herself against his mouth...

...and with a prolonged groan collapsed against him, her body draped over him. Nathan turned his head to the side so he could breathe. They stayed like that for...he wasn't sure how long. Two minutes? Five? Eventually he reached up, and put his hands on her shoulders, and carefully moved back. Not even the width of his own scarred, narrow body, but enough to look her in the eye as she raised her head, ice-blonde hair damp and clinging to her face.

Aphrodite gave him a lazy, sweaty smile. "You...Nathan Pittman... are a *very* good student." She slid backward and collapsed on the bed, and beckoned him to join her. He climbed up and lay down alongside her, and as he propped himself up on one elbow to gaze down at her, he caught sight of their reflection in the mirror on his closet door.

Nathan knew they didn't go together. They didn't *fit*. For one thing, even though she hadn't told him her age, he knew she had to be too old for him. He wasn't even out of high school, not quite yet, and Aphrodite must have been at least twenty-five. For another... *Talk about punching above my weight class.* Nathan had never considered himself anything special as far as his looks, and now that his torso was more scar than unaffected skin, he had no illusions about his physical appeal. Whereas Aphrodite...

Aphrodite could have walked the runway for Victoria's Secret. Aphrodite could be on the cover of *Sports Illustrated*'s swimsuit edition. Aphrodite could have her pick of rich, handsome, Ferrari-driving assholes. And yet here she was with him.

Nathan took a second to look at himself instead of at the sheer glory of Aphrodite's body, and used the edge of the sheet to wipe off his chin as discreetly as he could manage. Her scent still filled his nostrils. It was everywhere. He drew in a slow, deep, delicious breath.

Aphrodite's eyes had closed as soon as her head hit the bed, and she kept them closed as she said, "No bones. I have no bones now. I'm like a dish rag. Wrung out." She ran a hand along his arm, and down to the tip of his cock. "Oh! But I see someone's ready to go again." She opened her eyes and rolled up on her elbow, mirroring Nathan's pose, and took hold of him. "What would you like me to do with this?"

Nathan had read something in one of his dad's old issues of *Penthouse*. He had never thought he'd actually get to try it, though, and never in a million *years* with someone who looked like Aphrodite. He opened his mouth to speak, but stopped.

"Nathan. Are you blushing? You're *blushing*. My God, that is adorable. Especially after everything we've done this week."

Before meeting Aphrodite, the closest Nathan had ever come to having sex was a fleeting touch of a girl's breast when they rode the log flume together at Six Flags. And that was four years ago. Since meeting Aphrodite...he felt as if he'd won some kind of lottery. Or found out some dead relative had left him a vast treasure. Things he'd thought about, dreamed about, wished for. Aphrodite had made them all come true, one by one.

She poked him in the ribs. "Come on. Tell me."

Nathan tried again, hesitated again, and finally had to cup a hand around her ear and whisper it. He saw Aphrodite's eyes get bigger and bigger as he talked, and when he leaned away, her plump, ruby-red lips curved into a wicked smile. "Nathan! That almost made *me* blush." She shoved his shoulder, pushing him over onto his back, and climbed on top of him. "But I think I can accommodate. Now." She took his wrists and pinned them to the bed on either side of his head. "You'd better hold on."

Aphrodite crouched on the floor of Nathan's bathroom, hugging her knees and doing her best to keep her sobbing silent. Nathan lay asleep on his bed. He was a heavy sleeper. She didn't think her tears would wake him.

"I've done well," she muttered. "I'm doing well. I shouldn't be sad." Except the sadness crept along her skin and slid inside her joints and burrowed through her bones. "Except it wasn't supposed to be like this. Happen like this."

The tiles splintered. The whispers built around her, and she knew the truth.

Intelligence must be gathered. It is vital.

Aphrodite groaned quietly. "I had...had ideas about...about how it would be. My first time. I know, it's often awkward, because you don't know what you're doing, so it's sex, but it's exploring, too. Two people exploring each other. But my first time, with this boy, it was...as if I wasn't even a part of it. The waitress, what we took from her. All her experience. Her confidence. I felt as if the waitress was doing every-thing. And I was trapped in here. Just watching."

The jagged, shattered-glass world around her shifted, the whispers growing harsh.

"Don't you understand? It felt like...felt like I was getting..." She hesitated to use the word. *Rape.* "I felt violated."

These emotions are inconsequential. We have been gathering intelligence. Nothing more.

Nathan stirred in the bedroom. "Aphrodite? You talking to somebody?"

Aphrodite rose to her feet. She used a bit of toilet paper to blot her face. A splash of cool water, and no one could have told she'd been crying.

Aphrodite walked out into the bedroom without a stitch on. She wanted to blush furiously, watching Nathan squirm at the sight of her, but she seized control of her blood and forced it away from her face. Aphrodite crawled onto the bed, slowly, moving so that her heavy breasts swayed just right. She ran her tongue from Nathan's thigh up across the scar tissue. Circled one of his nipples as she straddled him. "I wasn't talking to anybody, baby. You must've been dreaming. So. Before. You were saying you thought you'd figured out who the Gray Widow really is?"

She had had him only twenty minutes earlier, but she felt him rise beneath her. "You really want to talk about this now? Seriously?"

She moved back and forth on top of him. "I do. And then we can get back to having fun."

Nathan draped a forearm across his eyes. "Um. Okay. Well. I mean, I sort of know. Maybe. I mean, I think so. I don't know for sure."

"So? Tell me."

"Mmmm...I...think I'd better not. I mean, not until I do know for sure. Y'know? What if who I think it is really *isn't* who it is?"

She traced one of his scars, down his chest and across his flat, tight abdomen. A tiny smile played across his lips. He said, "You know, you're the only person I've met who doesn't get totally grossed out by..." He gestured at his torso. "All this mess."

"Then you've only met fools." She moved against him again. Slower. More firmly. "Come on. Nathan. *Tell* me. Atlanta has a real, live superhero? Who is she?"

He groaned, and the more she moved, the louder the groan got. "Okay! Okay. I think... I think her name is Janey Sinclair."

Aphrodite had to struggle not to flinch as something like an electric shock played up and down her limbs, just at the sound of the name alone. The bedroom around her fractured and split into a billion shards as realities overlapped.

"How do you know? I mean, what makes you think it might be her?"

Nathan reached up and took her breasts in his hands. "I was flying blind at first. I'm no detective, y'know? But every report I read about her mentioned how tall she was. And I'm thinking to myself, how many women in Atlanta are *that* tall, and *that* badass?"

"Right...?"

"Right, so, I got the idea to research local martial arts schools. Started pulling up photos of the students? And *bam.* There's Janey Sinclair, with a black belt in judo, and she's like a freaking skyscraper, head and shoulders taller than every other woman in the class. So... check this out...you know that part-time job I got? It's at Janey Sinclair's apartment building."

Careful to keep her voice even, Aphrodite said, "And what does this Janey Sinclair look like?"

Nathan grinned and let go of one breast to reach for his phone. "I actually got a shot of her at this party." He paged through photos, landed on the one he wanted, and handed the phone to her. Aphrodite took it, and for a moment her hand trembled.

Everything about Janey Sinclair screamed *strength.* Supple, agile strength, like a jaguar waiting to pounce.

Aphrodite handed the phone back. "All right." She didn't shout. Didn't scream. Didn't tear Nathan Pittman's windpipe out of his throat. She simply smiled. "Now...where were we?"

Aphrodite scaled the brick wall surrounding Nathan's property and made her way down the sidewalk. She hated the hiding, the creeping, the need for such measures.

I am a leader. I am Command. Stealth is beneath me.

The splintered world whispered in her ear.

Janey Sinclair is too powerful to approach on our own. We must demonstrate our leadership. Our dominance. Otherwise she will have no respect for us.

Aphrodite nodded again. "But how will I find what I need? Find *who* I need?"

Your desires are our desires. Your mission is our mission.

Aphrodite smiled.

The whispers led her to a corner where taxis waited. Aphrodite took one to a train station, and rode the train south to College Park. Three blocks west put her on Conley Street. She stood there on the edge of the cracked pavement, her breath escaping from her in long, white, measured plumes. "Is this right?"

The whispers strengthened. Guiding her.

Aphrodite squinted at a street sign. "Conley. Conley..." As she stared at it, the letters detached from the sign. Floated in space and rearranged themselves. Aphrodite tilted her head. "Ceylon? No..." She took a deep breath and surrendered to the splintering. "C O N L E Y. E C O Y N L..." The razor-edged fragments shifted, shifted again, locked in place. Meaning emerged. Aphrodite's eyes widened. "Emergent Conscription of Your New Lieutenant."

The secrets reveal themselves if allowed. Now. Reach out. Sense him. Feel him.

Her breathing grew shallow. Her heartbeat sped up until it whirred like hummingbird's wings.

"I can. I *can.*"

Energy pulsed and thrummed from a house up the road. Aphrodite sprinted to it. The house sat alone, surrounded by an unkempt quarter-acre of weeds and grass grown long. It might have once been a place of pride for someone, but now the craftsman-style cottage seemed on the verge of falling apart, and the front porch had separated from the rest of the house by a good five inches. Aphrodite circled the place and headed for the back door.

Aphrodite steeled herself. She walked up the short flight of concrete steps leading to the back door and entered the house without knocking...and gasped. Frozen. Staring.

A cloud of living darkness danced and shimmered in the cramped living room. As it turned toward her, shimmering and throbbing, expanding and contracting like a heart made of shadow, she saw the face within the cloud. The face told her its name.

"Julian Roth," Aphrodite said. "I've come here for you."

The Texas night sky stretched on and on over James Brittain's ranch, the kind of star-filled black ocean that can only be appreciated from specific places on Earth. One light burned—the light on Brittain's front porch—and its minimal glow did nothing to obscure the stellar infinite that stretched past the horizon in every direction. No one moved on Brittain's ranch. No people, no animals. The ever-present western wind failed to find even a tumbleweed to send skittering across the sandy, barren land.

Above the ranch, a new star winked into existence. It grew brighter and brighter as it plummeted, and tiny jets of white-hot gas sprayed from it, slowing its descent. In seconds, the glow of atmospheric entry faded, revealing a silvery metallic object shaped very much like a spear. The silver metal spear fired its jets again, adjusted its course, and with a brittle, splintering crash, drilled through the roof of James Brittain's empty cattle barn. The spear punched through the hayloft, leaving a red-ember-edged hole in the wooden planks, and burrowed into the earth beneath the structure.

From appearing in the sky to disappearing beneath the ground, the entire incident had taken seventeen seconds.

Stillness descended over the ranch again. The kind of stillness found only in places where no living creatures dwelled.

Over the next hour, a series of sounds emanated from the hole the spear had dug, some of them harsh and metallic, some wet and liquid. At three minutes past the one-hour mark, long, writhing, serpentine ribbons of silver metal began to flow up out of the hole and stream away from it. Pinpoints of light gleamed and scintillated just beneath their metallic surfaces, red and blue and green and purple. One after another they escaped the hole and slithered out, across the barn's packed dirt floor.

Each metal serpent measured not quite eight feet long and as big around as a man's wrist, and after a few seconds' experimentation, they began traveling laterally across the ground, in the fashion of the sidewinder rattlesnake. Still more and more metallic sidewinders emerged from the hole. Each of them took a different path away from it.

The sidewinders crawled and slithered over every inch of the cattle barn, the multi-colored points of light inside them flashing and winking. They emerged from the barn and crossed the empty space to the house. Some of them moved past the house, down the long dusty driveway to the road. One sidewinder coiled up and around the sign-post next to the mailbox and ran a light touch across the sign, across the letters it bore: FOR SALE. CONTACT JACK BUSKINS. BUSKINS REALTY.

Others glided over the ranch house, touching every bit of its surface, before sliding through an open window into its interior. They traveled through the living room—lingering over the television—and through the kitchen, where pinpoint colored lights flashed as they probed through cabinets, around dishes, and into the pantry. They made their way down the short hall, into the dust-covered spare bedroom, and across into the master bedroom, where the day-old corpse of James Brittain lay in the bed.

Behind them, in the cattle barn, a larger metallic object pushed up through the hole the spear had made. Half again as tall as an average man, it looked like nothing more than a broad cylinder, until a vertical seam lit up and the cylinder opened as if on a hinge. More serpents clustered inside it, their lights rippling and undulating.

In the ranch house, sidewinders slid across James Brittain's body, under the threadbare pajamas, along his limbs, in and out of his mouth. Others lingered in the kitchen, swaying over a stack of mail, touching envelopes that bore words such as "URGENT" and "THIRD NOTICE." Still more twined and pulsed around the array of photographs on a built-in shelving unit in the living room. Photos depicting a much younger James Brittain, tall and solid, standing next to a smaller woman. Both of them smiling.

Two hours later, the sidewinders began removing items from the house, clutching them in metallic loops as they undulated back across the dry earth to the cattle barn. Pops and cracks and crashes sounded out from the house as the sidewinders tore through walls and pulled down paneling, seeking out the copper and other metals they needed. Pipes from the kitchen and bathroom, the television broken down into its components, the entire engine from the battered pickup truck under the carport. Parts of the truck's body. All of the carport's steel supports. A flood of metallic scraps wriggled and wove their way into the cattle barn.

The barn's interior flooded with multi-colored points of light as the sidewinders delivered their cargo to the metal cylinder planted beside the hole. The serpents inside the cylinder took the parts, and when enough had been received, the cylinder closed. A thrumming so deep and loud issued forth from the cylinder that dust fell from every rafter of the barn, and the ceramic dishes in the ranch house kitchen rattled and danced against each other. The thrumming continued for another hour, as one by one, the sidewinders disappeared back down the spear hole.

Finally, the thrumming slowed and stopped. The cylinder opened along its vertical seam again, and a human-shaped figure stepped out of it. As the figure walked out of the barn, its gait careful and measured, its immense weight pressed footprints two inches deep into the dry, packed earth.

6

Tim had hoped that the road trip to Knoxville would result in some long, honest, open talks between Janey and him. Not far into the journey he realized how sorely disappointed he was likely to be.

Sorely disappointed! His back was already killing him. *Ha! I'm a riot.*

Tim shifted in the bucket seat of Janey's Honda Civic, trying to find a position that didn't hurt. It was a losing battle. The damage to his lower back had led to persistent sciatica, and the edge of the seat dug into his thigh in *just* the right way to make him feel the pain shooting down his left leg. He could counteract that, he found, by sliding farther down in the seat, but that put pressure directly on both his lower back and his all-but-ruined neck, and he knew if he stayed that way for long he'd be hard pressed to walk at all. And, of course, the lack of mobility in his neck meant he couldn't turn his head to look at Janey, so the only way he could face her was to crank himself around in the seat. That set off flares of pain down his right arm and made his fingers tingle unpleasantly. Finally, Tim reclined the seat as far as it would go and lay there, staring at the ceiling.

"You okay?" Janey rested a hand lightly on his thigh. He took her hand in his, and she gave it an affectionate squeeze—then reached up and adjusted the rearview mirror so that they could look each other in the eye without Tim having to turn his head.

He chuckled and managed a grin. "I should've thought of that. And yeah, I'm okay enough. It's just...a little tougher than I thought, getting comfortable."

"Can I do anything? You want to stop somewhere and get, like, a pillow or something?"

"No, no, this is fine. I mean, if you don't mind me riding along like this."

Janey shook her head. "I don't mind a bit. You want to listen to some music?"

The last thing Tim wanted to do was listen to music. Words had been building inside him for months, words that had built up into an entire lake's worth of bitterness and self-loathing, held back by a dam of desire not to be any more trouble than he already was. Cursing himself for a coward, Tim said, "Sure. What do you have?"

Janey plugged in the auxiliary cable and handed him her phone. "You can be our musical navigator."

Tim thumbed through her library, and let out a long, low whistle.

"What? What's the whistle for?"

"Oh, just realizing how good a road trip is for learning things you don't know about people."

She laughed. "You are *not* disparaging my musical tastes."

"Disparaging, no. Marveling at, maybe. I just never pegged you for a Marilyn Manson fan."

"There's only a couple of songs!"

"Followed immediately by Marty Robbins."

Janey shot him a challenging look. "'Ghost Riders in the Sky' is a classic."

"Never let it be said that you don't have eclectic tastes." He cued up "El Paso." Janey sang along, not quite at the top of her lungs, he didn't think, but close. Tim didn't see her having a future as a professional entertainer, but she carried the tune, and her singing voice had a warm, rich quality he appreciated.

When the song finished, Janey said, "I hope you realize, you're the only person on the planet I would *ever* sing in front of."

He grinned. "I'm honored."

"You should be. Play me something else."

"Hmmm…how about some Chris Isaak?"

"Perfect."

The next couple of hours passed that way, with Tim playing DJ. Sometimes Janey sang along with the songs, sometimes she didn't. Tim kept trying to decide on a good spot to pause, so that he could introduce some of the subjects he'd been agonizing over. He corrected himself: there was only one subject.

"I feel like a cripple, and we still haven't had sex, and I'm afraid you're going to leave me, and I'm scared to bring it up because I don't want to sound pitiful and needy, but I don't want to ignore it either, and I waffle between wanting to tell you how I feel and wanting to crawl into a hole and pull the hole in after me."

Sure. Say it just like that, you silver-tongued devil. Put that insecurity right out there in the spotlight.

They stopped to get what Janey called "road chicken"—chicken nuggets that could be easily eaten in the car while driving—at a fast food place off the Cartersville exit. Tim slowly, painstakingly got out of the car and stretched and hobbled from one end of the parking lot to the other, trying his best not to imagine what he must look like. Or what a prize he must appear to be in Janey's sight.

Once they got back on the freeway, Janey said, "Road trips like this are the only time I ever eat fast food." She dipped a nugget into a little plastic tub of buffalo sauce. "It's kind of a treat, in a gross, self-destructive way."

Tim had put the seat back upright, and wondered how Janey could drive and eat chicken nuggets so gracefully. He kept getting crumbs all over his lap.

Janey chewed and swallowed, and took a long sip from her cup of Diet Sprite. "Listen, I…I want to apologize. About what happened on the stairs."

Tim gazed down at his lap. *Ah yes. I had almost forgotten about my girlfriend protecting me from the big mean man.* He grimaced. *That's not fair. She was only trying to protect me. Because I need protecting.*

He said, "There's no need."

Tim heard Janey take a breath to speak...and pause. Another breath. Another pause. He wondered, in an abstract sort of way, if she felt anywhere near as awkward in this relationship as he did. He wondered if they even *had* a relationship. Was it just guilt? Or pity? Or both?

Janey said, "Why don't you play me some more songs?"

Tim nodded, wiped his greasy fingers on a paper napkin, and picked up the phone.

O nce they reached Knoxville, Garrison Vessler's directions took them west, out of the city again, into the countryside, and finally into a thick patch of woods. Tim was grateful for Vessler's turn-by-turn instructions, as Janey's GPS didn't include the gravel road they were supposed to turn down.

"Hey, slow down, slow down. We're here. I mean, this is the turn."

"You sure?"

Tim stared at Janey's hand-written directions, as dictated to her by Vessler, in the glare of his phone's LED light. "It's got to be. He described the curve of the road and the color of the mailbox. And I'd be pretty damn impressed if a Google Street View car had made it out here. How'd he get these directions? Spy satellite?"

"I didn't ask."

Janey navigated the Honda onto the gravel and around a bend, out of sight of the paved road, through a dense growth of pine and oak and hickory. Shortly, they came to a place wide enough to turn around, right in front of an imposing metal gate set into an even more imposing stone wall. Tim said, "This has *got* to be the place." Janey pulled the car up to a call box, rolled down the window, and hit a big green button labeled "CALL."

After a few seconds, a red light popped on next to a small camera lens, and a female voice said, "Yes?"

Janey cleared her throat. "My name is Janey Sinclair. This is Tim Kapoor. We'd like to talk to Anna Grove, please."

The red light stayed on, but silence stretched out. Tim had been right when he'd said they'd arrive here in late afternoon. The sun had begun to set, and slanted bars of golden light pierced the canopy of the woods around them.

The voice crackled. "I'm sorry, Ms. Grove isn't accepting visitors."

Janey leaned part of the way out the window and, even though they were alone in the middle of the woods, pitched her voice low. "It's about Ms. Grove's son. Simon."

More silence.

From somewhere out in the trees, a rain crow called.

The red light on the call box winked out, and the massive metal gate swung open with a hum of electric motors. Janey rolled up her window and squeezed Tim's hand. "Here we go."

Beyond the gate, the gravel road became a smoothly paved drive-way. It wound through the woods for another quarter of a mile before the trees fell away, revealing a house that didn't quite qualify as a mansion, but only just. Massive white marble pillars adorned the front porch of the two-story gray mountain-stone home, and Tim spotted a four-car detached garage off to one side. The broad lawn looked freshly mowed. Warm lights burned in half the windows.

Tim sighed. "One of those columns costs more money than I will ever make in my entire life."

Janey brought his hand to her lips and kissed a knuckle. She didn't say anything else as they parked and made their way to the front door. A camera mounted above the door clicked on, another red light like the one in the call box, and swiveled to point straight at them. The red light went off again, and the front door opened.

A woman of about forty-five stood there, ash-blonde hair done in a braid that draped over one shoulder, dressed in a plain blue button shirt and jeans and sandals. Tim thought, if you looked up the defini-tion of "wary," her photo might have been there next to it. She scanned them up and down. "My name is Jessica. I work for Ms. Grove."

Janey took a deep breath. "We'd like to talk to her about her son. We have information, and...and questions."

Jessica put a hand against the doorframe. Her eyes flicked past them, out into the dark. "Is he here? Is Simon here?"

Janey shook her head. "No, ma'am. I'm afraid Simon Grove is dead."

Jessica's eyes filled up. "Damn it. *Damn.*" She sniffled, and stepped aside, her head lowered. "You'd better come in."

Tim followed Janey into the house, through a marble-tiled foyer, into a formal sitting room filled with furniture built from cream-colored leather and mahogany. Huge, gorgeously-framed paintings hung on the walls, and Tim recognized several Vermeers. He couldn't tell if they were reproductions or the genuine thing, but if they were the real thing, his mind balked at how much they must have been worth. Though Tim considered himself dirt-poor, his parents had done well for themselves in the property management business—or, rather, he and his parents had always *thought* they'd done well. This was Tim's first in-person exposure to actual wealth. It made his stomach tighten.

A door on the other side of the room opened, and a woman walked through it, and Tim forgot all about furniture.

He'd googled Anna Grove before they made this trip. She might have been considered a "flash in the pan" in Hollywood terms. Appearing in five movies over an eighteen-month period, Anna Grove had prompted people to use terms such as "rising starlet," and "next big thing." And then...nothing. Tim hadn't been able to figure out whether her exit from Hollywood was voluntary or not, but it had been sudden and final. He wondered how much she'd been paid for those five movies, and how well she'd invested once her career had ended.

Anna Grove stood about five-four, and for the life of him Tim couldn't tell how old she was. She didn't have the fresh-faced, unlined look of a teenager, and he knew she must have been at least forty to have had a child Simon's age, but her utterly flawless skin showed no wrinkles, no crow's feet, no hint of any sagging around the neck or jowls. She could have been anywhere from twenty-five to fifty-five. What stopped Tim in his tracks and halted his breathing, though, was her beauty. Anna Grove looked like a goddess. Blue eyes flashed beneath black hair, so black it had blue highlights, and her immaculately sculpted nose and wide, sensuous mouth completed a face like...

Like a work of art. She's a work of art.

Tim didn't realize how blatantly he'd been staring until Janey discreetly elbowed him in the ribs.

When she spoke, Anna Grove's voice rang like a pure, mellow bell. "Who are you? How do you know what happened to my son? And how did you find me here?"

Janey said, "Ms. Grove, could we please sit?"

Anna Grove smoothed her hands down her pale yellow pantsuit. Tim wondered absently if it was made of silk. It looked like silk. "No. I heard you say my son was dead. How? How did he die? When did this happen?"

Janey's hands moved to her mouth. When she didn't say anything, Tim stepped in. "Ms. Grove, we're sorry to have to tell you this. But Simon's the reason I have to walk with a cane. He tried to kill me. Tried to kill both of us."

Anna Grove's face went pale. She moved behind a wing-back chair and gripped the top of it, knuckles turning white. "...And?"

Janey murmured, "I killed him. I had no choice."

Anna trembled. "How? How did you kill him? How did he die?"

Janey stared at the floor. "I...he was...decapitated."

Anna came around the chair, eyes flashing, and Janey took a step backward, but Anna grabbed her by the upper arms and stared up into Janey's face. "And you saw his body? You *know* he's dead?"

Janey nodded.

Anna let go of Janey and hugged herself. "Thank God. May He forgive me. Thank God. Thank God my son is gone."

M inutes later, Janey and Tim sat on a couch across from Anna and Jessica, who each perched in a wing-back chair. Janey said, "All I'm trying to do is figure out how all this happened. The source of it. Is it some kind of natural mutation? A government experiment? What?"

Jessica said, "So...you're like Simon?"

Janey shook her head. "No. Everything he did was...was about changing his body. The shape of it. I can do...other things."

Tim leaned forward. "Ms. Grove, do you know why Simon was the way he was?"

Anna chewed on her lower lip. The pause she took stretched out long enough to make Tim wonder if she were going to answer at all. Then, finally: "It's because of me."

Tim saw Janey's muscles tense. Her fingers dug into her knees. Tim said, "And how is that?"

Anna sat up very straight and closed her eyes. Jessica said, "Anna, no, don't. Don't."

If Anna heard her, she gave no sign of it. A tiny crease appeared between Anna's eyebrows, and as they watched, Anna Grove's hair turned from raven-black to a rich, lustrous auburn. When she opened her eyes again, they had gone from blue—the same blue as Simon's eyes—to a startling emerald green. "Changing the body. He...he got it from me."

Janey's breathing grew ragged.

Tim said, "And...is this something you were born with?"

Anna let out a long, slow exhalation, and her eyes and hair returned to blue and black. "No. It happened when I was a teenager. Fifteen, I think. Before, I was...well... 'plain' would be generous. No one looked at me. No one acknowledged me. But then, one night, I saw a star in the sky, and it burned *so bright...*"

Janey gasped.

Anna went on, "After that, slowly at first, I learned to change things. Little things. Cleared my skin up, made my teeth straighter. Dropped some weight..." She made a general gesture around her chest. "Except where I didn't want to. Bit by bit, I changed myself into…into what I wanted to be."

Jessica hadn't missed Janey's reaction. She said, "What was that? When Anna mentioned the star? That meant something to you, didn't it?"

Janey rubbed her hands on her thighs. "My father. One night in his early twenties. He saw a light in the sky, and after that, um…" She gazed up at the ceiling, and Tim saw tears start in her eyes. He put a hand on her back, and she gave him a quick smile. "He could do what I do, except on a much smaller scale."

Tim said, "Ms. Grove, did you ever find out what the bright star was?"

Anna shook her head.

"Not a clue? No explanation at all?"

Anna dabbed at her eyes with a lacy handkerchief. "Sorry. Sorry. I'm a sympathetic crier. But no. Honestly, I never questioned it that much. I was afraid if I went poking around, it might…it might go away. And I'd have to go back to the way I was before." She sniffled. "Janey, maybe I could talk to your father? Compare notes, so to speak?"

Janey stood. Tim started to get up after her, but she gestured for him to stay put. "Sorry, I need to move." She mashed at her eyes with the heels of her hands. "My father died, Ms. Grove. He was murdered because of what the light in the sky let him do. You might've had the right idea, not to 'poke around.'"

Anna said, "I'm so sorry…What about your mother? Did she—was she affected, too?"

Janey's shoulders hunched as she turned her back to the group. She wiped furiously at her cheeks. "My mother died when I was nine. Thank you for your time. We won't trouble you any further."

Anna and Jessica both made sounds of protest, but Janey was off like a shot. Tim struggled up off the couch and went after her.

A phrodite Lupo held the image of Janey Sinclair in her mind. Let it permeate her. Felt herself grow taller...felt her skin and hair and eyes change.

She had studied all of the photos Nathan had gathered of the woman—not that there were that many, Sinclair seemed terribly camera-shy—but in almost all of those, Janey Sinclair had sported a spectacular, dense mane of tight chestnut curls that swayed and bounced when she walked. Such was no longer the case, as evidenced by the photo Nathan had taken in the Muslim girl's apartment. To confirm, Aphrodite had lurked around Sinclair's apartment building earlier that day, keeping out of sight, waiting to catch a glimpse of her target.

It had paid off. Janey Sinclair and a Middle Eastern-looking man had walked right past her, and even stood and talked for a moment before climbing into Sinclair's eight-year-old Honda and driving off. Now Aphrodite knew exactly how tall Sinclair was, exactly what shade of golden brown her skin was, even exactly how she smelled. She also knew that Sinclair wore her hair shaved down to stubble on the sides and in the back, with only a cursory nod to her former glorious curls on top.

As she climbed the stairs to the ninth floor, which she did thanks to her abject hatred of elevators, Aphrodite muttered, "I don't know why I couldn't have just taken her right then." The grating hiss of the splintering whispers answered her.

Someone as powerful as the Gray Widow needs to be studied. We must discover everything about her. We must know all there is to know, and even what there is not to know. She is the key to our success. The key to our survival in the coming War. Go. Go and learn.

Aphrodite walked down the hallway to the door of Janey Sinclair's apartment. It had only a simple lock. Blocking any view of it with her body, Aphrodite concentrated on the tip of one of her fingers, watched it elongate and become rigid, and slipped it inside the lock. Once inside, the fingertip expanded, feeling the mechanism of the lock, exploring, until it assumed exactly the right shape. Aphrodite swiveled her wrist, and the lock clicked open as easily as if the actual key had done the job.

"Janey?"

Aphrodite stiffened at the sound of the voice from behind her. She slid her finger out of the lock and let it return to its normal shape before glancing over her shoulder to see who had spoken—and let Janey Sinclair's mouth spread into an easy smile.

The young African-American Muslim woman Nathan had told her about stood there in the hallway, dressed in shapeless clothes, a scarf wrapped around her head. Aphrodite had read that such a scarf was commonly called a *hijab*. That was roughly where her knowledge of Islam ended. "Hey," Aphrodite said, grateful that she had heard Sinclair speak. Sinclair's voice flowed easily from her vocal chords. "How are you?"

The Muslim woman held up a couple of envelopes. "I got some of your mail. I was just going to slip it under your door—what happened to your road trip?"

Aphrodite leaned against the door frame. "Excuse me?"

The Muslim woman walked right up to her, and Aphrodite saw that she wore a CVS Pharmacy nametag that read SHA'DAE, and below that, SALES ASSOCIATE. "I thought you and Tim were headed up to Knoxville. For some sort of family thing."

"Oh...right. Yeah, that got postponed." Aphrodite's smile grew brighter as a perverse thought struck her. She pushed the door open. "You want to come in?"

Aphrodite knew that if this Sha'dae woman realized who she was really talking to, she could simply kill her. She also knew of one sure-fire way to dispose of a body that wouldn't leave any trace. She didn't like to eat bones and organs, but could if pressed.

Sha'dae shrugged. "Yeah, okay, but just for a few minutes. My dad's on his way over to check on me. Again. You know how many gaskets he'd blow if he knew I'd had a party? Alcohol or no alcohol." She threw up her hands and fluttered her fingers. "*Anyway.* I don't mean to sound like a broken record."

Aphrodite followed Sha'dae into Janey Sinclair's apartment and stopped for a moment to look around. Sha'dae still had her back turned, so Aphrodite took advantage of the opportunity to scan the place.

Her first thought was, "God, how depressing." Janey Sinclair took the whole concept of Spartan living to an extreme. The place could almost have passed for a nun's quarters, with its white walls and neutral floors and utter absence of decoration. No knickknacks on the kitchen counter, no art of any kind on the walls...no shoes thrown in the corner, no baskets of clean laundry waiting to be folded. It was like the apartment of someone who had almost finished moving out.

Aphrodite flashed another grin as Sha'dae turned. "Want something to drink?" She walked into the kitchen and opened the refrigerator. "I've got...wow. Not much." She pulled out a Brita water pitcher. "Filtered water okay?"

Sha'dae slid onto one of the two barstools on the other side of the kitchen counter. "Sure, that's fine. You sure seem like you're in a good mood today. Something happen I don't know about?"

Aphrodite pulled a drinking glass from the dish drainer resting on a towel beside the sink. As she poured the water, she said, "What makes you think I'm in a good mood?"

Sha'dae accepted the water and took a sip. "Well...this is just the most I've seen you smile in...I don't know. Ever? I mean, I know you've been trying to stay in good spirits to help Tim out."

Aphrodite leaned on the counter, resting the weight of her upper body on her elbows. "Nah, nothing special happened. I did read this article, though, that said there's supposed to be an actual connection between smiling and elevating your mood. Not the other way around —it said, if you smile, that actually triggers something in your brain, and you feel better. So, y'know. I'm just giving it a shot." Was this too much talking? She wasn't sure how to judge.

Aphrodite considered taking this Sha'dae woman whether she grew suspicious or not. There was something about her bone structure, something about the glow of health in the skin of her face... Aphrodite hadn't planned to grow any larger, not yet, but maybe now was the time after all. The hijab hid Sha'dae's neck, but Aphrodite could see the minute movement of the fabric as the blood pulsed beneath it. Movement no human eyes could see.

Sha'dae said, "I guess that sort of makes sense. Like, reverse muscle memory? Kind of Pavlovian..." She took another sip of water and stared off into space, clearly lost in thought. Aphrodite wondered how often Sha'dae zoned out like that. It would make her a truly easy target.

Sha'dae said, "Maybe I could get my dad to try that. He is so uptight, I'm telling you, *all* the time. You know he runs his own construction company, right? I told you that?"

Aphrodite nodded. "Mm-hm."

"He's got this favorite phrase. Well, he's got a bunch of favorite phrases, but one of them is—" Sha'dae raised one finger and held it across her upper lip, simulating a mustache, and spoke in a pronounced Pakistani accent. "If you see a penny on the ground and you do not pick that penny up, you are not worth that penny!"

Aphrodite's hands tightened into fists as she laughed in what she hoped was a convincing way. She forcibly relaxed her hands, even as she anticipated how Sha'dae's flesh would feel in her grip, how the bones would crack, how the muscles would tear. Aphrodite's mouth ached with the desire to shift sideways, to become the scissor-mandibles.

But she was learning about Janey Sinclair. This was a fact-finding exercise. She couldn't forget that. "Speaking of things I read. I saw this personality quiz in..." Aphrodite thought fast. What did normal women read? "...in an old issue of *Cosmo*. It made me wonder, how would you describe my personality? How do people see me? What am I like?"

Sha'dae left her contemplative haze and smiled. "Well. How people see you and what you're like are two different things, aren't they?"

Aphrodite straightened up, and hopped up to sit on the counter. "You think so?"

Sha'dae shrugged. "Well, it's just...you don't really let people in, do you? I mean you, specifically, not the general you. But, also, it's not like you actively turn people away, either. You just don't put yourself out there for anyone to find. You're kind of the most private person I've ever met. It wouldn't take much for you to become a hermit, I don't think. You and your paintings, y'know, all crouched in a cave like Gollum."

Paintings? Gollum? Aphrodite filed those away. "Okay. Go on."

"Seriously? You want more? Okay, well, but, see, you're not *really* walled off. Not to the people closest to you. Which, granted, I think that list stops at Tim and me."

Aphrodite let her head tilt to one side. "So if you had to describe me in a word or two…?"

Sha'dae laughed. It sounded nervous. "A word or two? Well, I guess…I guess I don't think I know anyone more generous, or loyal. Or kind-hearted. Sorry, that's three words. Maybe four."

Generous? Kind-hearted? This is the ruthless vigilante?

Sha'dae looked at her phone. "Oh, shoot, I've got to go. My dad's almost here. Thanks for the water."

Sha'dae slid the glass across the counter and went to the front door. When her hand was on the knob, Aphrodite said, "Anytime, Sha'dae. See you later." Sha'dae paused, and glanced over her shoulder, and Aphrodite saw the pupils of her eyes dilate. "What's wrong? Forget something?"

Sha'dae smiled brightly. "Nope! See you later!" And she was out the door and gone.

Aphrodite whispered, "Well? Have we learned enough?"

Loyal and kind, but only to a couple of people. Withdrawn from society. Emotionally disconnected from the world. We have found the perfect recruit—someone few people would miss. And if those two do miss her—

"Right. Eliminating a couple of obstacles would be easy."

Aphrodite drank the rest of Sha'dae's water and went to explore the rest of the apartment.

7

D erek Stamford lay on his back in a darkened, sound-
proofed room, virtual reality goggles strapped around his
head. An IV tube attached to a port in his left forearm fed
him a steady stream of nutrient-rich fluids. His fingers and toes
twitched erratically. His rigid penis strained against his pants.

Occasionally a wisp of steam rose from his body. If his clothes and
the chair he reclined in hadn't been fashioned from fire-proof material, they would have burst into flame.

Stamford and a team of VR engineers had spent two years and just
north of sixteen million dollars developing a software suite that
catered precisely to Stamford's needs. Now, encased within an envi-
ronment optimized for sensory input, Derek Stamford learned.

He thought of it with a capital L: *Learned.*

Eight separate data streams made their way into Stamford's mind
simultaneously. Multiple internet news sources kept him up to date
on current events; digitized versions of every known encyclopedia
emptied their vaults of knowledge into him; but most important of all,
Stamford absorbed languages.

Every dialect, every colloquialism, every nuance he could find,
Derek Stamford learned and retained, and the act of doing so filled

him with a euphoria unmatched by any other experience he'd ever had. It encompassed sex and sensuality, but far surpassed them. Each new word, each new thought, wove fingers through his hair and slid across his skin and massaged his muscles and bones with a firm, hungry grace.

Stamford knew a time would come when he would discover that he had learned and absorbed every language on the planet. He wondered if, at that point, when his mind had nothing else to conquer, he might die. Tremors ran through his thighs, his testes drew up tight against his body, and his penis throbbed with an ache simultaneously painful and delightful. If that time ever came, Stamford had decided years ago, his death would be worth it.

"End program."

At his words, the VR display dimmed and switched off, the lights in the room came up, and with the hum of an electric motor the chair pivoted upright. A nurse wearing pale gray scrubs came in and, without saying a word or looking Stamford in the eye, disconnected the IV. His body pulsing with energy, Stamford grabbed the silver-headed cane that rested against a small table and grunted as he got to his feet.

Transitions were the hardest on him. Sitting or lying down, not a problem. Standing, walking, not pain-free but certainly manageable. Shifting from sitting to standing, however, sent pain shooting down his right leg, and he squeezed his eyes shut as the nurse left the room.

A moment on his feet and the pain passed.

Stamford idly rubbed his cock through his pants. Pre-ejaculate had soaked through and left a wet patch. He knew he'd be able to take care of that soon enough.

With the practiced, deliberate gait that minimized his discomfort, Stamford crossed the room to the hook by the door and took down his suit jacket. The double-breasted long cut hid the erection that still bulged so insistently. He left the VR room and walked across the hallway to his office.

Derek Stamford had put a lot of thought into the décor of his inner sanctum, and had decided on function over form. The thick

Berber carpet had a low enough knap to make sure he wouldn't lose his footing. The ergonomic desk sported none of the knurled mahogany one might have expected from a Fortune 100 CEO, but he could sit behind it for hours without feeling fatigue. He'd had the chair custom-built, and for the price he'd paid, he knew he could have demanded whatever aesthetic approach he'd felt like, but the plain, stainless-steel-and-black-leather chair suited him. And while it could have passed for a display-floor model at an Office Depot, every inch of it had been crafted and assembled according to the exact dimensions of his body.

The only strictly non-functional element of Stamford's office was the series of two-by-three-foot black-and-white framed photographs running along one wall, but they served just as much a purpose as the carpet and the desk and the chair. Stamford gazed at each one as he walked from the door to his seat.

The photos depicted the aftermath of a head-on collision between a mid-90s sedan and an enormous pickup truck. The EMTs had already come and gone by the time the photos were taken, so the smashed, ruined body of Stamford's wife Helena was nowhere to be seen. Likewise, the driver of the pickup, who had been flung through his own windshield with such force that he had burst through Stamford's windshield and crushed Helena to death with the mass of his own body, had also been carted away. By the time these shots had been taken, Derek Stamford himself lay on an operating table, where surgeons had saved his spinal column and prevented his paralysis, for the price of a lifelong disability and flares of unpreventable pain.

Stamford took in the photos, one by one, as he did every time he entered his office. They reminded him of how fleeting life could be. Of how his time on Earth could end with little more warning than the screeching of tires and a shrill, truncated scream.

Of how power must be seized as if there were no tomorrow.

Stamford settled into his custom chair, hissing at the ice-pick stab of pain in his hip, and picked up the encoded message his assistant had left for him. It took up most of a page, column after column of letters, many of them adorned with diacritical marks, and before he had even gotten to the bottom of the page Stamford knew it was a Polish book cipher.

The rush of euphoria swept through him again.

The paper yellowed where he touched it as heat built up in his fingertips.

Book ciphers worked when the person encoding a message and the person receiving a message both had identical copies of a particular book, with the encrypted material corresponding to specific words on specific pages. Without knowing what exact book was used, book ciphers verged on impossible to crack.

Unless one had access to every book ever published. Which was, of course, impossible.

And unless one could cross-reference the encryption with each and every one of those books. Also patently impossible.

The pupils of Derek Stamford's eyes glowed with a faint yellow light as he stared at the book cipher. One by one, like the tumblers of a lock, the meaning began to click into place. First he located the specific book—a science-fiction novel called *Head-On*, by Rafał W. Orkan—and as the seconds ticked past, each relevant word on each page of the novel revealed itself. Five minutes later he had neatly transcribed the full text of the encrypted message onto a yellow legal pad.

Stamford sat back in the black leather chair and sighed. A portion of the jangling, pent-up energy inside him had dissipated, but not the most important part. His thighs still quivered. His cock still raged.

A knock sounded at his door. "Come in."

A tall, lean, gray-haired man in gray slacks, a white shirt with the sleeves rolled up, and intensely polished shoes opened the door and padded across the carpet to stand in front of Stamford's desk. There were no chairs in the room besides Stamford's. He preferred people to stand when they spoke to him. "What is it, Reg?"

"You asked for updates on the anomalous object. The one in low orbit."

Stamford set aside the legal pad. "That I did. And?"

"We can't get a fix on it, sir. Its path is...erratic."

"You're telling me an object in low Earth orbit is, what?

78

Zigzagging?"

"Not regularly, sir, no. It only becomes visible on screen for point-oh-four seconds at a time, and we can't predict where it'll be based on its trajectory. Also…"

Stamford drummed his fingertips on the desk. With his other hand, discreetly, he rubbed his granite-hard erection. "Also? Also what?"

"It's been throwing off pulses of radiation. We haven't been able to match it to anything in our databases."

Stamford put both elbows on the desktop and steepled his fingers. "So it *is* man-made. What is it? Some kind of drone?"

"Impossible to say. Yet. Sir."

"All right. Keep monitoring it as best you can."

Reg Fasolo's face, ordinarily solemn, creased with traces of indignation and frustration. "Sir…the subject in the Interview Room is not cooperating."

"Oh?"

"I would say it's time for a judgement call, sir."

Stamford nodded once. He grabbed his cane, exhaled sharply through the momentary agony of standing, and followed Fasolo out of the office and down the hall to the elevator. Neither man spoke as they rode down several floors, and the silence stretched out as they traversed the gray concrete corridor to the Interview Room. Stamford knew Fasolo well enough to guess what the man was thinking: *I did everything I could, I used everything we had, this is not my fault.* He also knew Fasolo well enough to know that it *wasn't* his fault. Reg Fasolo had never done anything halfway in his life.

Stamford pushed the heavy steel door open and paused in the doorway. The subject, naked and shackled into a heavy chair in the center of the room, wore a thin, glistening sheen of blood that seeped down from a series of small, precise lacerations in his face and scalp. The blood had hardened at the blackened areas around his nipples and genitals where electric current had been applied. The man trembled and shook as if he were freezing to death, and Stamford reasoned he was on the verge of shock.

Stamford paced across to a metal chair. He set it facing away from the subject, straddled the chair, rested his forearms on the chair back, and propped his chin on his arms. The subject stared at him and continued trembling.

Stamford knew the man's name, but didn't care about that. He knew the man was forty years old, single, and was until last year a successful car salesman. Stamford didn't care about that, either. What he cared about was the telepathic Augmentation the man had manifested. The control wasn't there, not yet, but when the power kicked in, the subject was able to comb through the mind of anyone he touched and pluck information out of it as he saw fit.

"You're being unreasonable," Stamford said.

The subject spat blood at Stamford's feet. "Fuck you."

Stamford looked over his shoulder at Fasolo. The gray-haired man said, "I only resorted to the physical techniques when none of the psychological ones worked. And now, just to be a dick about it, he's resistant to the physicals, too."

Stamford looked back at the subject. Dropped his chin on his arms again. "High threshold of pain, is it?"

The subject sneered at him. "Fuck. You."

Stamford straightened up in the chair and shook his head. "I don't understand. We offered you employment. All you had to do was take the job."

"I won't be part of this!"

Stamford almost recoiled from the sudden ferocity in the subject's voice.

"I saw! I saw what you do! You're murderers! Monsters!" The man's trembles turned to a violent thrashing. "Kill me! Go ahead and kill me! I know you're going to! Get it the fuck over with!"

Stamford decided to give it one more shot. "Look, since you don't want to work for us of your own accord...we do have ways. We will break you. Sooner or later. It's really a lot better if you don't resist."

The subject's eyes narrowed. "I *will* resist. I'll resist until there's nothing left of my brain but a pile of gray mush. Won't be able to use me then, will you? *Will you?*"

Stamford's heart rate skyrocketed. He could feel it pounding in his cock. It was all he could do to keep from letting out a low, joyous moan. He rose and gestured with his chin toward the door. Fasolo stepped out into the hallway, where Stamford joined him seconds later, shutting the door behind him. By then he had regained his equilibrium. "Is he right? Will none of the techniques work?"

Fasolo sighed. "My professional opinion? Yeah, he's right. I've never seen anything like it, sir. He feels the pain. I know he's hurting. He just...won't break."

Stamford shrugged. "Then we need to stop wasting time on him."

"All right. I'll have him taken care of."

"No." Stamford put his hand on the door handle. "I'll do it."

Fasolo stayed in the hallway as Stamford re-entered the room. The subject hadn't stopped trembling, and now tears had formed and spilled from his eyes, washing away the blood in narrow streaks down his face. Stamford walked up and stopped right in front of him. "You know what's going to happen now?"

"I know you. I saw you. In the thoughts of your people...I saw what you've done. What you've ordered done. I know the devil when I see him."

Stamford pursed his lips. Shook his head. "No. No, you've only seen the surface. You deserve the truth." And he laid his palm flat against the subject's brow. He felt the subject's Augmentation kick on, the thrum of power against his skin, and the man's trembles faded and died. When Stamford took his hand away, the subject stared up at him with wide eyes, pupils constricted to pin-pricks. Urine pooled on the floor at the man's feet. "Now. Now you understand?"

The subject's eyelids slowly slid down over his eyes. His head lolled on his neck, exposing all the vessels necessary to do the job. He made a soft, whimpering sound, and more tears slid down his cheeks, and Derek Stamford took the knife from his pocket, snapped open the blade, and cut the subject's throat from ear to ear.

As the subject gurgled and died, Stamford felt the dam break open inside of him, all the energy rushing out in a vast, profound torrent of relief, mirrored by his explosive, shuddering orgasm.

8

Tim didn't try to initiate any conversation until they were eastbound on I-24. When he finally did—when he didn't think any more tears would well up in Janey's eyes—he decided to start small. "Um...you okay?"

Janey sighed and rapped the steering wheel with her knuckles. "More or less. I was hoping for some actual answers." She paused. "I don't guess I can blame Ms. Grove for keeping her own Augmentation to herself."

"Maybe not. But if she hadn't kept quiet about what her son could do..." Tim let the words trail off, but the thought hovered there in front of him, clear as crystal.

He might not have done this to me. I might not be so damn useless.

"You learned a little, though, right? Your dad could teleport small stuff, and you can do your whole body and other people. Simon's mom could change small stuff, and he could, uh, do what he did."

She nodded slowly. "True. True. But we don't know if Simon could do it from birth and it just got more potent as he got older, or what. It seems to be all about seeing this light in the sky—Anna Grove saw it, my dad saw it. I was indoors the first time I flickered, so I don't know if I did or not, but it seems likely. Did Simon, though? I need to know for sure."

"Not to mention we need to find out what the light in the sky *is*."

"Well, yeah. I was considering that a given."

Tim reached over and rested his hand on her thigh. Janey took it in hers and held it, driving one-handed. She said, "I know this a ridiculous thing to say. I know it isn't how life is. But not knowing? Being able to do these things, having other people out there like me, and not knowing *why*? It isn't fair. I mean, if all of this went public, and some reporter put a microphone in my face and said, 'So what caused these so-called Augmentations?' I'd have to shrug. I'd have to say, 'Beats me. Sure would be nice to know, huh?'"

They rode in silence for a few minutes. Watching her in the angle-adjusted rearview mirror, Tim saw Janey glance at the radio a couple of times, and really wanted to head off another long stretch of no conversation at all. He took a deep breath. "You reacted pretty strongly when Ms. Grove mentioned your mother."

Janey's grip tightened on his hand for a second. Not quite hard enough to hurt. The muscles in her jaw rippled. Since she hadn't broken any of his bones, he decided to forge ahead. "You've never talked to me about her. You've always just said that it was you and your dad. I'm assuming…she's no longer with us?"

Janey opened her mouth. Closed it again. Frowned. Let go of his hand and put it back on the steering wheel. She glanced at him, and her right lower eyelid twitched. "You know how sometimes you've heard a song all your life, and you never really thought about it, and then one day you really pay attention to the lyrics and realize there's a whole meaning to it that never registered with you before?"

Tim took a second to answer, trying to decide whether this was a deliberate subject change, and if so, how wise it would be to try to steer things back around. "Hmm. Got an example?"

She drummed her fingers on the wheel. "My dad liked Lynyrd Skynyrd. We'd go places in the car, and he'd sing along—that's some of my earliest memories, my father doing bad karaoke on road trips. And, y'know, a song you hear that early, it's easy not to think about it. It just becomes…sort of…part of the landscape. It just *is*. But then, years later, I think I was twenty or twenty-one, 'What's Your Name' came on the radio while I was driving somewhere, and I hadn't heard it in so long, and for the first time I paid attention to the lyrics. And I realized that the song my dad used to sing with his five-year-old daughter in the car was actually about a touring musician having sex with a groupie."

"Oh. Yeah. Wow. So, kind of disillusioning, I'm guessing?"

"Well…nah, not really. I mean, not like traumatizing or anything. I was just surprised. Like, how could I have missed that? How could I not have gotten that sooner?"

Tim nodded. "Okay. Yeah, I've got one. Like, the first time I saw *The Road Warrior,* I guess I was six or seven. And, y'know, you've got those barbarians on motorcycles, right, the guys Mad Max was fighting? And one of them—I think the character's name is Wez—Wez is this giant, brutal dude with war paint on his face, and he pulls up on his motorbike, and on the seat behind him there's this, this boy. I mean, he was grown, but he was this thin, really pale young guy with long blond hair. And at the time, y'know, as a little kid, I just thought, 'Okay, that guy rides with Wez. They must be friends'"

A whisper of a smile touched Janey's lips. "And then you saw it later?"

"Yeah. I guess I was eighteen or so. And the whole thing smacked me in the face—especially the blond guy's thousand-yard stare. I mean, clearly, I was looking at Wez's sex slave, y'know, the poor guy was a broken shell of a human being. He even had a collar with a chain attached to it. God only knows what Wez had put him through. But when I was a kid, *zoom.*" He waved a hand over the top of his head. "It just flew right past me."

Janey frowned again. Cleared her throat. "My mother died when I was nine."

Tim shifted in his seat. Determined to keep his mouth shut and listen.

"She and Dad, Dad especially, shielded me from most of it. I knew she was sick, and I knew she had to go to the hospital a lot. I was there when they brought in the big hospital bed and set it up in the living room. I wanted to know why Mom was all of a sudden sleeping there, out in front of everybody, and not in her room with Dad anymore, but...there didn't ever seem to be a good time to talk to either of them about it. And I remember, vividly, when Dad took me out into the backyard and sat me on the swing and told me that I had to go and stay with some friends, and that Mom had to go away. That we wouldn't see her anymore. Mom was asleep when I had that talk with Dad. She was asleep when I left. Every now and then she'd make a sound, and I could hear her breathing. But she never woke up."

Tim swallowed. Janey seemed to want to say more, and took a couple of small breaths as if to speak, but didn't.

"What did she have?"

"Cancer. What I was saying about not realizing things till later... When I was twenty-two, I found my father's diary."

"Oh. Oh God." Tim put his hand back on Janey's leg as a new tear sprang up in her eye. She tilted her head forward, and the tear dropped onto the back of his hand. He left it there.

"It was like learning about my own life. Learning all the secrets Mom and Dad thought would be too painful for me to know. 'Dedifferentiated chondrosarcoma.' That's what she had."

"I...I'm sorry. I don't know what that is."

"It was cartilage cancer. Really fucking rare cartilage cancer. Mom was walking down the stairs one day, and her leg broke. High up..." She tapped her left upper thigh. "Here. The mass—the mass they didn't know was there—it had eaten into the bone. Weakened it. She had what you call a 'pathological fracture.' And they didn't know it, no way they could've known it, but when her leg broke? That was it. That was the end. The mass ruptured when the bone broke, and spilled into her bloodstream."

"But they tried to treat it?"

She nodded. Swallowed hard. "First with an emergency hip replacement. But that was before the biopsy results came back. Before they knew what they were really dealing with, when they just wanted to get the leg fixed. So she had to go through that—"

Her words choked off. Tim put what he hoped was reassuring pressure on her thigh. "Janey, if this is too much, I mean, if you don't want to tell me this—"

"No. No, I do." She picked his hand up and pressed it to her lips. Placed it back on her thigh. "They did the hip replacement, and she had just started on the physical therapy when the oncologist called them in. He explained what kind of cancer it was, and…I remember the words in the diary, in Dad's handwriting, I can see them. The doctor said, 'This kind of cancer is very good at taking lives.' He put the survival rate at ten percent."

"Jesus."

"And he explained that their best option was amputation."

"*Jesus.*"

"If they took the leg, she'd have a ten percent chance. If they didn't, she had no chance. But it wasn't just the leg. He had to take what he called a 'wide margin.' So part of her pelvis had to go, too." Janey paused. She sniffled again. "There's, there should be some napkins or something in the glove compartment, could you…?"

Tim popped open the little door and scrounged through stacks of receipts. He found a couple of Hardee's napkins underneath the Honda's owner's manual and handed them to her. She dabbed at her eyes with one, and braced the steering wheel with her knee as she delicately blew her nose with the other.

"That's the part I never even knew about. Dad always made sure I sat on her right side, see? And they…they put a pillow under the sheet on the left, so I couldn't tell that…that she didn't have a leg anymore…" A sob like a hiccup escaped her. "I *never knew.* I was right there, and, and, I mean, what could I have done? I was nine! But they never told me, and I never got to tell her that it didn't matter to me, I never got to let her know that it wouldn't have scared me, that she was my mother, that I loved her no matter what. That they didn't have to hide it."

"But, Janey, that was twenty-two-year-old you thinking that."

"I know. I know. I know that *here.*" She tapped her temple with a fingertip. "Maybe it *would* have scared me then. Maybe they did the right thing. But I'll never know." She blotted her eyes with another napkin. "Taking the leg didn't make any difference. The cancer showed back up. In her neck."

Tim sucked air between his teeth.

"It moved. Into her skull. And one morning she didn't know my name. I remember that. I came into the living room, and she looked at me with her big brown eyes, and she said, 'Are you my daughter?' I thought she was *playing*. Teasing me. She liked to do that, act goofy with me, make me laugh. I said, 'Of course I'm your daughter, Mama!' and Dad picked me up and took me out of the room, and that was the day we had the talk in the backyard. So while Mom was asleep, Dad sent me to stay with his assistant, Tonya, and her girlfriend. I don't remember the girlfriend's name. But I was there for a week, and Dad came to see me every day, and at the end of the week he told me Mama was gone. I never got to say goodbye to her."

Tim groped for words, desperate to say something, but Janey went on before he could find any.

"Everything in that last week, that was what Dad was protecting me from. Page after page in his diary. The cancer ate through her skull and got into her brain, and she didn't know Dad anymore, didn't know the nurses. She retreated into some place inside herself, some place in her past. And there was..." She drew several deep breaths. "There was a lot of screaming." Janey blinked her eyes hard. "I read all that in Dad's diary. He never said a word to me about it. Never even a hint."

"Janey. My God. I don't, uh...I don't know what to say."

Her winter-sky-blue eyes found his in the rearview. "I lost my mother. Horribly. Seven years later I watched my father murdered. Tim, I know. I know I've been hovering. Helicoptering, I think? That's the term? But I can't lose you, too. I can't. I just *can't*. I hope you can understand that."

Before he could begin to formulate a response, the car veered, and a deep *whump-whump-whump* came up through the floorboard. Janey said, "Shit," and guided the Civic over onto the shoulder.

Tim said, "Sit tight," and popped his door open.

Janey put a hand on his arm. "Tim, wait—don't you think I should—"

"Relax. I've changed more tires than I'm even comfortable admitting. If I'd ever been a Boy Scout, I would've gotten a merit badge in tire-changing."

"But, with your back?"

Without thinking about it, he tried to lean over and kiss her cheek, but his neck stopped him short. Relieved that moving like that hadn't sent his back into spasms, he said, "Just let me do this for you, okay?"

Janey nodded.

Tim got out and surveyed the damage, grateful that the flat tire was on his side instead of the one facing the stream of late-night traffic. He grimaced at the stink of gasoline fumes that always seemed to hover over freeways, pushed his hair out of his eyes when a passing eighteen-wheeler blew it into his face, and opened the Civic's hatchback. A couple of minutes later, Tim had the spare tire leaning against the back bumper, the jack positioned in front of the flat, and the handle in full crank mode as he slowly raised the car off the ground.

Once the car's weight was off the flat, he pulled the handle out, reversed it, and fitted the socket over the first of the lug nuts. He took a deep breath, grabbed the handle with both hands, pulled—and gasped as a sharp pain shot through his lower back. He steadied himself against the car. The passenger window buzzed down and, leaning over from the driver's seat, Janey called, "Are you all right?"

Tim nodded and waved a hand. "I'm fine, I'm fine. Just need to use a different technique." As Janey watched, her brow furrowing, Tim repositioned the socket on the nut so that the handle pointed toward the trunk. He changed his grip, putting the whole weight of his torso directly above the end of the handle, straightened his arms and pushed.

His back didn't hurt this time.

But the lug nut didn't budge, either.

He tried again, pushing down as hard as he could, and just when he thought the nut might begin to move, the pain stabbed up from his lumbar region all the way into his neck. Tim let out an involuntary groan and sagged against the car, sliding down till his butt hit the gravel-strewn pavement.

Tim shut his eyes, breathing deeply, and dug the bottle of pills out of his pocket as he heard the driver's door open and close. He popped a pill into his mouth and swallowed it while Janey walked around the car, and when he opened his eyes again she was squatting on her haunches in front of him.

"I know how to change a tire, too. Will you please let me take care of this? There's no need for you to hurt yourself."

"Any further." That's what she means. Hurt myself any more than I already am. He groaned inwardly. *Don't be a dick, Tim. Don't be that guy who's too macho for his own good.*

He found that more easily said than done.

Waving away her offered hand, he got to his feet himself. Janey said, "Tim…" but he waved her words away, too. Silently he got back in the car. He saw Janey in the side-view mirror, standing there, looking after him. He wondered what she was thinking. Maybe trying to decide if she should come and say something? Maybe trying to decide if it was worth it to talk to a sullen, pointless cripple when he was in the middle of a pout? Tim knew he was wallowing in self-pity, and knew how attractive it must have been making him.

She'll want you now more than ever.

Tim watched in the side-view as Janey took hold of the handle and broke the lug nut loose with one hand. She had the flat changed in three minutes.

As soon as they were back on the road, Tim turned on the radio and reclined his seat and closed his eyes.

Janey didn't try to talk to him.

The digital clock in the Civic's dashboard read 11:53 when they pulled into Janey's parking spot at the La Croix. Tim had lain there in the reclined seat with his eyes closed for long enough that he was pretty sure Janey thought he'd fallen asleep, and he hadn't disabused her of that notion, even when she'd stopped to fill the tank and use the restroom at a gas station south of Chattanooga.

He'd been keenly aware when she had reached up and shifted the rearview so that she could see the road behind her again, rather than using it to look him in the eyes.

"Tim?" She touched his knee. "Tim, we're back."

He stretched—carefully—and returned the seat to upright. He couldn't look at her, and not just because it hurt to shift around enough to focus on her with both eyes. *What a stunt you pulled. What a whiny little baby-man. You piece of shit.* He'd played the events in his head on an endless loop ever since Janey had changed the tire, waving her off like that when she was trying to reach out to him.

You're hurt, so you feel sorry for yourself.

You feel sorry for yourself, so you push her away.

You push her away, so you feel sorry for yourself.

You titanic, chrome-plated dick.

"Janey..."

"Yes?"

Tim did crank himself around then, pain be damned. *Say it! Say everything! Even if you babble like a fool, for God's sake, talk to her!* "Janey, listen, I—" He broke off, squinting past her. "Who's that?"

A shadow lounged against the wall next to the building's side entrance. Someone tall and scarecrow-thin. Janey leaned forward, her eyes narrowed, and said, "That's Nathan Pittman."

Tim blinked. "Wonder if Dad's got him working late hours?"

"Don't know. I don't think so."

Tim was about to say something else, but Janey opened the door and got out, so Tim followed, and almost tripped over his cane in the process. When he'd gotten his footing sorted and closed the door, he turned to see Nathan Pittman, clear now in the glow from a nearby streetlamp. Nathan had stepped away from the wall and was approaching Janey.

"Ms. Sinclair. Hi. Uh, do you, uh, remember me?" He stuck his hand out. "From Sha'dae's place? I work here now? Hi, Tim."

"Nathan," Janey said, but made no move to shake his hand. Tim just stared at him. "What can we do for you?"

Even under these odd circumstances, Tim caught that pronoun: *we.*

Maybe there's hope yet.

As Tim made his way to Janey's side, Nathan ran a hand over his buzzed-off hair and tugged at one of the piercings in his ear. His voice trembled. "Look, uh…I need to talk to you. In private? Is that okay?"

Janey put a hand on Tim's shoulder. "I think anything you've got to say, you can say to both of us."

Tim had to fight to keep a big, dumb grin off his face.

The grin vanished when Tim heard Nathan Pittman's next words.

"Um. Okay." Nathan rubbed his head again. "It's just, I might've done something I shouldn't have. I mean, said something I shouldn't have said, and I don't want to cause trouble, but I told someone, and now I'm thinking it was a bad idea."

Janey frowned. "What exactly are you trying to say?"

Nathan said, "It's just, see, I know you're the Gray Widow. And I need to talk to you about it."

9

The Plowman felt no kinship with the inhabitants of this muddy planet. It didn't matter that his consciousness had transferred completely into the body constructed from Terrestrial elements, fully linking his own perceptions to its physical senses in a way indistinguishable from his own nervous system. He was not one of the slimy, gas-filled, bipedal earthworms that had dominated this world, and never would be. Adopting a body shaped like one of theirs was concession enough. He felt no need at all to adopt a proper Terrestrial name. A quick assessment of the dead human in the farmhouse had led to the designation "Plowman." The probes had modeled his shell after the general physical attributes of the farm's sole inhabitant, and "Plowman" conveyed enough respect for the imitation as far as he was concerned.

"The Experiment's bad enough already," the Plowman said, trying out the vocal synthesizers installed in his throat. He made sure none of his recording devices were active before uttering the words. His superiors allowed no dissension among the ranks.

The Plowman walked from the farmhouse to the barn, still adjusting his gait to look as human as possible. While the probes had fashioned his body's exterior to resemble the dead farmer, they had

also taken into account the Plowman's need for protection and dura-
bility, making a few concessions regarding aesthetics and accuracy. So
while the Plowman did look somewhat like James Brittain, the farm's
deceased owner, he also towered to six feet ten inches in height, with
shoulders broad enough to brush both sides of the house's doorways.
His feet left deep impressions in the dusty earth.

In the center of the barn, a six-foot-wide circular ramp
corkscrewed down into darkness, spiraling around the shaft sunk by
his landing craft. The probes had packed the dirt so hard it resembled
concrete, and his feet left no marks in it as he walked down the ramp.
His eyes, designed to be a brown that matched the most common
human pigmentation most of the time, glimmered yellow as the
sensors inside them switched to infrared.

Twenty-seven feet below the barn's floor, the walls of the spiral
shaft opened up and shifted to metal, and the Plowman walked out
into the telemetry station he had been sent to this planet to establish.
The metal of the walls curved, unbroken, onto the ceiling and floor,
and rising from that floor—waving slowly and gracefully in the air,
not unlike images the Plowman had seen of Terrestrial marine plant
life—were score after score of pliant metal columns, their rounded
tops coming up to the center of the Plowman's chest. The tiny, multi-
colored points of light floating within the columns' metal provided
enough illumination for the Plowman to see via his human-style optic
receptors, so the glimmering yellow faded back to brown.

"Status?"

The nearest column's surface glimmered green. The column bent
toward him, and when the Plowman extended his hand, his skin
rippled and changed from James Brittain's weathered tan to a fine,
near-translucent silver. The same vast array of tiny, brilliant pinpoints
swam and flowed inside him as in the sensor columns, the same as in
the serpentine probes that had explored the landing site and built his
armored, human-replica body.

The Plowman's finger touched the sensor column. His own array
of lights flashed a deep, iridescent blue, and the blue surged into the
column. As he watched, every column in the vast chamber flooded

with the same color, and the Plowman closed his eyes and saw the whole world.

The pulse pushed out into the atmosphere by the sensor array could not have been detected by Terrestrial technology. From hydrogen atom to hydrogen atom the pulse leapt, surging outward along the curvature of the planet like a drop of oil colliding with a pool of water. The array filtered as much as it searched. Even as technologically primitive as this world was, the Plowman's mind could not have processed the towering wave of information the pulse returned to him. It didn't have to. He only searched for energy signatures unique to his home. He only searched for the Sender.

There—to the east. A cluster of...

No. Those were Experiment subjects. The pulse crossed the body of water known to English-speakers as the Atlantic Ocean.

There! No...more subjects. Two in the British Isles. Seven scattered from western Europe to the Caucasus. Sixteen between India and China and Russia.

The Plowman filed those identifications away as the pulse circled the globe and surged forward again.

Odd concentration in... His database pulled up the name of the city. *Washington, D.C.* Again, he filed the locations for further exploration. His synthetic jaw clenched.

"Increase power. Find him."

The iridescent blue deepened two shades. A faint hum sounded out from the columns and reverberated around the metal cave.

There!

The Plowman sent out the strongest direct signal the station would allow. Hailing. Questioning. *Joyful.*

He got no response.

"Why isn't he answering me?"

The hum in the metal cave grew louder, and when the next influx of information reached him, the Plowman knew that if his body had been genuinely human, the blood would have drained from his face.

"End pulse."

He disconnected from the column and watched as the blue faded from the array, returning to its multi-colored light swarm. The hum faded to silence. For long moments the Plowman stood there, fully aware of the results he had received, fully aware of the truth of the situation, but unwilling to accept it. Finally, he reached out to the column again, which obligingly bent to meet his fingertip. This time the lights within his skin burned a piercing yellow-orange. As the sensor array followed suit, the metal cave lit up like a forest fire.

"Initiate comm. Tell them..."

A new hum rolled out from the sea of columns. Higher-pitched. Shrill.

"Tell them the Sender's orbit is decaying. He is dying."

The yellow-orange lights flowed and glimmered. The Plowman stood, patient, silent. Connected.

When the reply came, the part of his brain dedicated to blending in with the human species translated it to the dominant language of the region where he had touched down. The message itself impacted him immediately, within nanoseconds, and as the English words formed and played in his mind, each sound, each syllable stretched the pain out endlessly.

"The Sender is beyond our influence. Wait for impact and recover his body."

I n the seventh sub-basement below a building in upstate New York that Redfell had purchased eight years prior, Derek Stamford walked slowly down a stark white hallway, favoring his bad leg a little more than usual. A low-pressure system was moving in. That always made his knee ache.

Stamford glanced through small, ballistic glass windows set in heavily reinforced doors as he passed. Checking in on the children, just like a good father. Except that Derek Stamford was no one's father, and in no way did he think of any of the creatures huddling on the other sides of these doors as children.

"Children having children," his grandfather had often said. "That's what's going to be the death of this country." Stamford allowed himself a tiny grin. *No, Papa Jack, that's what's going to save it.*

Stamford disliked the word "eugenics," at least as it applied to what he was doing here in Sub-Basement 7, not only because of the Nazi connotations, but also because if one were engaging in a eugenics program, he felt that that implied one should be dealing with humans. And these subjects weren't people. Not really. People came from human DNA.

That was why Derek Stamford had gotten a vasectomy shortly after his own Augmentation.

Stamford turned a corner and passed a small attendants' desk. He didn't think of the men and women who worked here as nurses, despite the RN required for their employment. Again—nurses treated people. These were more like zoo workers. Or lab technicians, clipping toes off rats and measuring how much eye liner one of the greasy little rodents could eat before it developed cancer.

Reg Fasolo waited for him at the end of the corridor. Stamford could have hurried up a bit without causing himself undue pain, but he didn't. *Let him wait. It's not as if Anastasia's going anywhere.* Fasolo shifted his weight from foot to foot until Stamford got there.

"How's she doing?"

"I believe we've had a breakthrough, sir."

Stamford peered through the tiny window in Anastasia's door, just as he had with all the other subjects on his way here. "The MRI finally worked?" After Garrison Vessler had fled with Scott Charles, Redfell employees had reclaimed everything in the remote safehouse, including the portable fMRI device that had allowed Scott Charles to project what he was seeing onto a monitor.

"No, sir, it didn't. We're still working on that. But Anastasia's powers of both observation and description appear to exceed Scott Charles's by, I'd say, an order of magnitude. She described what Jenny was doing, in her cell, right down to the positions of the pieces on the chess board."

Stamford turned a baleful eye on Fasolo. "She described what *who* was doing?"

Fasolo studied his shoes. "Sorry. Subject 5499."

Of course Stamford knew Subject 5499's name. Jennifer Benton. He knew all the subjects' names, and in a few instances, had even been the one to name them. But just because Subject 3501's name was Anastasia Coletti didn't mean she should be afforded the dignity of being addressed as such. Not by the help, anyway. Stamford considered a few different approaches to take, once he finally opened the door and spoke to the girl. Idly, he said, "This breakthrough didn't come a moment too soon, did it?"

"No, sir. She was scheduled to be put down by end of day Friday."

Stamford made a *tsk tsk* noise. "Was the cause of her infertility ever determined?"

"No, sir."

Stamford turned the latch on the door. "That'll be all." Fasolo nodded and headed off down the hall as Stamford went in to see Anastasia Coletti—Subject 3501.

Anastasia raised her head as Stamford stepped into the room. She sat on her cot, cross-legged, bent over a book, and the harsh fluorescent lights gleamed off the narrow, pale patches of scalp showing through her light brown hair. Anastasia didn't make a sound, didn't act surprise, but she carefully closed the book and scooted all the way into the corner, watching him. As far from Stamford as she could get. Her huge brown eyes, a brown that matched her diminishing hair, didn't blink. Didn't look away from him.

Aside from the cot, the room contained a small metal desk, a straight-backed metal chair, and a cloth screen to hide the toilet, sink, and shower in one corner. A few books lay scattered across the desk. Stamford spared them a glance, frowning inwardly that a subject as promising as Anastasia would waste her mind on frivolities such as fantasy and science-fiction. He set the chair a few feet away from the cot and sat down.

"I'm told you made everyone very happy today," he said in his best neutral voice.

Anastasia nodded. A strand of hair turned loose and fell from her scalp. She didn't seem to notice. Her bony arms and legs poked out of the white linen tunic and shorts like dry twigs, and with her cheeks sunken in as they were, her eyes appeared twice as big as normal.

"You concentrated on another subject here, and you saw what she was doing, correct?"

Anastasia nodded again.

"Good. Good. That deserves a treat. What kind of treat would you like?"

Her huge brown eyes still didn't blink, but she finally spoke. "Pecan pie."

"Pecan pie! A nice slice of delicious pecan pie. I think we can arrange that. Now, tomorrow, we'll be going even farther away than the end of the hall. All right? Are you ready to try to see something farther away?"

Anastasia's tone didn't change. She simply stated it, matter-of-factly. "I already have."

Stamford hesitated. Cocked his head to one side. Leaned forward, his elbows on his knees. "Excuse me? Say that again?"

No change in volume. "I already have."

Stamford cleared his throat and moved the chair closer. "Now, I want you to listen to me very carefully now. Because this is important. Are you listening?" She nodded again. "When you say you already have, what do you mean? Exactly? Are you saying you've already seen something, the way you saw Subject 5499, but farther away?"

Maybe she saw the light in his eyes, or heard the excitement in his voice. For whatever reason, Anastasia seemed to realize that her words were making Derek Stamford happy. She finally blinked a couple of times, and moved half an inch closer to him. "Yes, sir. About an hour ago. I've been trying ever since to figure out where it was."

Stamford could scarcely breathe. "And did you? Figure out it, I mean?"

"I think so, sir. I think I know where. But...what I saw...I don't know how to tell you what it was."

Stamford pulled out his phone and sent a text to Fasolo: *GET DOWN HERE*. He put the phone away. "Well, we'll work on that. But first, tell me where you saw this puzzling thing."

Anastasia squeezed her eyes shut. Stamford imagined her pulling up the image she had seen. Studying it. She took a few deep breaths, and Stamford began to grow impatient. "Come, now. I already told you how important this was. I don't want to find out that you've been wasting my time. If it turns out you've been wasting my time, Murray will bring out the hose again."

The huge brown eyes opened. "I don't mean to waste your time, sir. It was in Texas."

Stamford fought to keep his eyes from bugging out of his head. "You saw something...in *Texas?*"

A knock on the door, and Fasolo stuck his head in. "Sir? We're set to move on Trent Davis."

Stamford didn't take his eyes off Anastasia. "I'll be right there." To the girl, his voice lowered, he said, "We'll talk about this more when I get back. Have answers for me."

She nodded, head bowed.

Ninety minutes later, Derek Stamford studied Trent Davis through a pair of high-powered binoculars. Davis sat in his recliner in his living room, a can of beer in his hand and fifteen empty ones strewn around him, watching a pre-recorded NASCAR race on a tiny, old, shitty TV worthy of a college student's dorm room. "I cannot for the life of me understand why people don't draw their curtains. It's fine during the day, but at night you might as well put a neon sign up —COME LOOK AT ME."

Stamford sat sideways in the backseat of a company car, parked at the curb across the street from Davis's house, while Fasolo drove. Without looking up from his phone, Fasolo said, "Most people are fucking morons." Fasolo thumbed the phone's screen. "I hate Atlanta. Every time I go outside I'm breathing gnats."

Stamford chuckled. "You've never been to southern Georgia, have you?"

Fasolo snorted. "This is as far south as I want to go, thanks."

"You've got his file pulled up, yes?"

Fasolo nodded.

"Give me the highlights."

"Trent Ronald Davis, fifty-five years of age, widowed, no children. Active member of a KKK chapter around Stone Mountain in his twenties and thirties, tried to found one here in his forties. Didn't work. Half a dozen arrests for...let's see..." Fasolo scrolled down on his tablet. "Disorderly conduct, public drunkenness. Demographics of his neighborhood started to change right around the time his wife died. Davis refused to move—got loud and drunk, to no one's surprise —and multiple witnesses gave an account of an altercation between Davis and his new next-door neighbor, one JaCarlton Clifford, thirty-six."

In his living room, Davis belched and scratched his balls. Stamford said, "That's the one that ended up dead?"

"Four years ago. Back door smashed to kindling, kitchen trashed, and Clifford, I'm quoting the police report here, 'mauled to death.'"

"They tried to blame it on a wild animal?"

"A bear."

"An adult bear. In College Park."

"Best they could come up with."

Stamford sighed. "I don't guess I can blame them. I wouldn't have believed it either. All right, let's see what we can do here." He leveled a pointed look at Fasolo. "You realize this would probably go better if you hadn't let him crawl so far inside a beer can."

Fasolo turned and put an elbow on the back seat. "Well, two things. One, Anastasia spotted him forty-five minutes ago. Two, approaching him tonight was your call. Sir."

A crease appeared between Stamford's eyebrows. After a few seconds he shrugged. "Fair enough. Grab the boys and let's go talk to the man."

Fasolo tapped his phone. "We're going in. Come on."

As Stamford and Fasolo got out of the car, a huge, brick-like Humvee rolled up the street and parked behind them. Stamford had paid to have the Humvee specially reinforced, and considered it money well spent. Its frame creaked and groaned with the shifting weight of its driver and passengers. One by one they got out: Matt Binkovski, a thirty-two-year-old Polish-born man who'd been a video game designer before his Augmentation appeared; Graham Salvatore, forty-five, former owner and operator of a newsstand in northern New Jersey; and Ned Fields, the driver, a mousy, bland, utterly forgettable little man whose last job before Redfell had been as a dog groomer. Before Stamford and Garrison Vessler found him and trained him and assigned him to Scott Charles's protective detail.

The three men shared the same kind of Augmentation, and had become known around Redfell as "the Heavy Boys."

Fields nodded to Stamford as the three of them assembled before him. Stamford nodded back, keeping his face neutral, but every time he looked at Ned Fields his blood pressure rose. Fields still bore a scar on the back of his neck where that bitch in the gray spider-eye mask had shocked him with a modified stun gun—shocked him badly enough to kill any normal human. It was Fields's failure that had cost Redfell Scott Charles and his ability. Now and then, Stamford still considered getting rid of Fields. Their discovery of Anastasia mitigated Scott Charles's loss, though, and lent Stamford a bit of charity.

Fields, the senior among the three operatives, tilted his head toward the house. "How do you want to do this?"

"We're just going to talk to the man," Stamford answered. "No displays of force. No action unless provoked, and then only to contain. This is a potential recruit." All three Heavy Boys nodded, and Stamford led the way across the street and through Davis's weed-grown yard to the front door. There was no doorbell, so Stamford rapped on the screen-and-glass aluminum storm door with his cane.

Trent Davis opened the inner door and peered at Stamford with red-rimmed eyes. Those eyes tracked past Stamford, taking in Fasolo and the Heavy Boys, and a sneer made its way across Davis's mouth. "The fuck're you? What d'you want?"

"Mr. Davis, my name is Derek Stamford. I've come to present you with a financial opportunity. May I come in?"

The reddened eyes narrowed. "You from the gubment? You look like you're from the gubment."

Stamford allowed himself a smile. He tried to make it as charming and non-threatening as possible. "Hardly, sir. I represent a private concern."

Davis swayed in the doorway. "And…what's it you want?"

"Well, sir, the long and the short of it is that you have the opportunity to make a fair amount of money."

"I'm fine where I am. Get the fuck off my property."

"Mr. Davis…I know you've been a shut-in since the unfortunate incident with your neighbor, Mr. Clifford."

Davis bristled. "That was a animal attack. News said so."

"But we both know what really happened, don't we? Mr. Davis— that's why I'm here. I understand what happened to you. What made you able to do what you did. It's a worthwhile thing, sir. Something my company can make use of. Something that can benefit both of us. If you'll just hear me out."

"Fuck you!" Davis bellowed loudly enough that Stamford came close to wincing, and Binkovski took a menacing step forward, his fists clenched. Stamford motioned Binkovski back and put on his best smile. He didn't need neighbors calling cops. "Fuck you!" Davis said again, more quietly this time, but with just as much venom. "Gubment shits! You git! You git outta here! Go on, git!" Davis slammed the door. Stamford heard a deadbolt engage.

When Stamford turned from the door and came back down the two concrete steps, Fasolo said, "Take him?"

Stamford nodded. "Yeah, now that the formality's out of the way. Standard procedure." He gestured at the Heavy Boys. "He's a brick, like you guys, so you don't have to worry much about hurting him. Confine, sedate, get him in the truck."

Binkovski, Salvatore, and Fields headed back to the Humvee to get the necessary equipment.

Trent Davis stared out at the government bastards through the window next to the door. Adrenaline surged through him like a riptide, and when he heard the groaning creak of tortured metal, he realized he'd bent the iron fireplace poker in his trembling, white-knuckled hands into a corkscrew.

"They know what happened." He whispered the words, making real the hideous act of violence he'd committed on the night the star had shined on him. "They know what I done, they gon' take me away."

"No, they won't, Mr. Davis," a feminine voice said from behind him, and before Davis could turn around, all the hairs on his arms stood straight up. His skin tightened, his stomach rolled over, and as he turned to face the people standing on the other side of his living room, he knew for sure that the Devil had sent a couple of demons to drag him down to the Lake of Fire.

One of them—the one that had spoken—looked normal. Beautiful, even. On the tall side, tight jeans, good-fitting sweater that showed off heavy tits. Pale skin and blonde hair and the kind of dark blue eyes he knew would sparkle in sunlight.

But right behind her was a straight-out demon, a monster, a thing shaped like a man, except he was like...like a cloud of darkness. The monster's outline kept shifting back and forth, one second human, the next some kind of squirming, boiling cloud that stretched wall to wall. His black, bony face looked a skull made of coal, and every time he blurred and snapped back, blurred and snapped back, the lights in Davis's house flickered, and Davis felt a buzzing in the air, some kind of vibration, pushing through his skin and his muscles and down to his bones.

The girl turned her dark red lips into a sultry smile. "Mr. Davis, we don't have a lot of time. We know about you. We're like you. And we're *nothing* like the men outside. If you let those men into your house, they will take you and either kill you or brainwash you into becoming their slave. If you come with us...a whole world of possibilities awaits you."

Davis squinted past her. "What is that? That thing behind you? Looks like a nigger."

Davis had no time even to blink before the cloud-demon was on him, surrounding him, and Davis lashed out. Trying to punch, grab, anything, Davis whirled, desperate to connect, to feel something break under his touch. But his world had become nothing other than darkness, swirling darkness, and the coal-skull whispered in his ear.

"Listen. Listen to her. We ain't here to hurt you."

Panting, Davis stopped his flailing. The twitching, impossible cloud parted, and the blonde girl stepped into it. Right up to him. Took his hands in hers and looked him in the eye.

"Trent. It's time to move past all the old hate and fear. I know what you can do. I know what you *are.* We're alike. You and I, and Julian here."

The cloud of inky darkness coalesced into its human shape. The coal-skull nodded to him as the girl kept talking. "My name is Aphrodite Lupo. This is Julian Roth. We are part of something bigger, we three. We have a destiny much greater than petty squabbles and old-fashioned prejudices." The girl's blue eyes drilled into Davis's brown ones—a brown so deep and dark, he knew, he had always known, that he had to have some black blood in him, somewhere far back.

But as Aphrodite spoke, a new sensation stole over Trent Davis. Like the wind that stirred up the choppy waters of his soul was fading, dying, calming down more and more with every word she said.

"The men outside represent the old way, Trent. The dead way. The *human* way. But the star spoke to you. I know it did, I can feel it. I can feel the energy radiating from you. Join us, Trent. Join us, pledge your loyalty to me, fight shoulder-to-shoulder with Julian, and I will give you a new world."

There was something happening to Davis's brain. He knew it, and knew he couldn't do anything about it. It was like...like some wall in his head had trembled and cracked, and opened up, and on the other side of it was...

…was Aphrodite Lupo. Her words came to him direct. No interference. No distance to travel. Her mind connected straight to his.

Davis's jaw went slack as he tried to make sense of what his reality had just become.

He had his house, which he'd finally paid off last year, even though the carpet had gotten moldy in the back bedroom, even though the foundation had cracked, even though it needed a new roof. He knew the place, backward and forward, inside and out. He felt safe inside it. But the longer he stared into Aphrodite's eyes, the wider that crack in the walls of his mind opened up. The more his house seemed false. A shell, something fake, something plastic, nothing but a place to hide. Aphrodite's voice settled inside him, penetrated him, and he thought about the argument he'd had with Clifford next door, complaining about the noise from the barbecue the man had thrown in his backyard, thought about the way he'd smashed through Clifford's door like it'd been made of Kleenex, the way he'd grabbed Clifford and torn him and broken him and ripped him.

No human could do that.

That's why he'd hidden in his house for the last four years. Having all his food delivered to him. Communicating only by mail.

When he finally spoke, Trent Davis had lost all sense of the passage of time—he could have been staring at Aphrodite Lupo for a minute or a day or a year—and his voice sounded more like a little boy's than a grown man's. "Can you…can you tell me what happened to me? Tell me how I got like this?"

"Oh, Trent." Aphrodite brought one of his hands to her lips and kissed it. "I can do so much more than that."

The last sound Trent Davis heard before the swirling darkness engulfed him was the splintering of wood as Derek Stamford's men broke down his front door. Then he was gone.

10

Janey stood rooted to the spot as if flash-frozen, an effigy of herself.

Part of the reason she had decided to wear the full-body Vylar suit—aside from the identity protection and the decreased chance of a to-the-head gunshot proving fatal—was that she had never had anything like a poker face. As she stood there, staring at Nathan Pittman, she could tell by looking at *his* face that the truth was written all over *hers*. His grin wasn't nasty, or malevolent, or even self-satisfied. He just looked as if he felt vindicated.

Tim said, "Janey—"

Nathan Pittman cut him off. "I *knew* it."

And before Janey could put two coherent thoughts together, from behind her, Sha'dae's voice said, "What did he just say?" Sha'dae stepped up on Janey's other side. "Nathan—*what* did you just say?"

Janey put her hands over her face. Her grip on reality had come abruptly unmoored, and she half expected her hands to just pass through her cheeks and eyes, as if her body had become nothing more than an illusion, a shade of a woman. "Sha'dae, what're you doing here?"

Sha'dae gripped Janey's upper arms and turned Janey to face her. "Say that again. Say my name again."

Tim said, "Is something wrong?"

"Say it again! Please! Just humor me!"

Janey let her hands fall to her side. "Sha'dae. What is this?"

Sha'dae gave Janey a quick, fierce hug, and stepped back to address Janey and Tim. Nathan hovered nearby. Janey thought he looked like someone whose thunder had been stolen out from under him. "You and Tim just got back. Didn't you. From Knoxville."

Tim frowned. "Yeah. Just pulled in, and found Buzzcut here waiting for us."

Sha'dae made an impatient gesture. "Did you not get my texts? Or hear the phone ring?"

Janey said, "Oh, shit," and dug into her purse. "I had my phone on silent." She pulled the phone out and tapped the home button, and sure enough, the screen had filled top to bottom with messages from Sha'dae. "Why were you calling me?"

Sha'dae glanced at Nathan. "Sorry, Nate, but I think this conversation needs to be had in private."

He threw his hands up. "Fine! Great! I guess figuring out somebody's a famous vigilante doesn't matter! Sure, go have your conversation, I've got nothing better to do."

Tim groaned.

Sha'dae looked back up at Janey. "So he's serious. He thinks you're the Gray Widow." Janey took a breath to speak, but before she could, Sha'dae's eyes widened. "Oh my God. You are the Gray Widow, aren't you?"

Nathan jumped up and down. "See? *See?* I'm not crazy!"

Janey rubbed the back of her neck with one hand. "Nathan. You were waiting to talk to me. Sha'dae, you just came out of nowhere. Were you waiting, too?"

"Yes! That's what I've been trying to tell you! That's why I left you all those messages! Janey, *there was somebody in your apartment who looked like you!* And it wasn't just some kind special-effects disguise, because she *sounded* exactly like you, too! Except I could tell she wasn't really you because she said my name wrong. She said it like 'shuh-DAY.' Not SHAH-DAY.' And I was scared to stay, so I left, but I was scared of what would happen if you came home and found her there, so I hung around outside to wait for you, and I was scared to call the cops 'cause they'd think I was nuts and have me thrown in the loony bin..." She paused, panting a little, and pointed at Nathan. "I didn't realize he was lurking around, too."

Tim peered up at Janey's window. She followed suit, and saw no lights burning inside. "So is this other person still up there? Do you know?"

Sha'dae shook her head. "She left about an hour after I spoke to her. I saw her. Janey, I swear, she looked exactly like you. *Exactly like you.* How is that possible? *Nobody* looks exactly like you!"

Janey turned to Nathan. "You said you might've told someone you shouldn't have. Who? Who'd you tell?"

Nathan seemed to shrink a bit under the combined weights of Janey's, Tim's, and Sha'dae's stares. "My, uh, m-my girlfriend. I mean, I don't know that I should really call her my girlfriend, and I've only known her for about a week, but that's what made her talk to me in the first place, I think, was me saying something about the Gr—about you. Ms. Sinclair. And, like, it's not like she's just out of my league, she's *so* far out that I'd have to have binoculars to even *see* her league, and she kept on...kept on asking questions about you, and it all just struck me weird—finally—and, uh, that's why I'm here. I wanted to warn you."

Tim pointed at Nathan with his cane. "Does your girlfriend look like Janey?"

Nathan shook his head. "No. No! Not even a little."

Sha'dae said, "Could be someone the girlfriend's working with. Still, it was so weird, I mean, I can't even—whoever it was, it wasn't just an impersonator. It's like it *was Janey.*"

Janey squeezed her eyes shut. "Okay, I need to think. Give me a minute."

Can't go up to my apartment. Not yet, not with people in tow. Who knows what this woman who looks like me left up there.

Headlights washed over the four of them, and they moved to the side of the aisle as another tenant pulled into the lot and parked. No one said anything while Mr. Benjamin, the retired tailor who lived in 4B, unloaded his groceries and went inside. Once he was gone, Janey faced everyone again.

"Look, we need to talk. And we can't talk here." She chewed her lower lip for a second, glanced around at the streetlights ringing the parking lot, and made a decision. "Tim, we're going to the roof. You first."

Tim started with, "Wait, what do you mean, 'me first'—" but when Janey put a hand on his shoulder and guided him a few steps away, he said, "Oh. Really?" His eyes darted to Sha'dae and Nathan. "You sure?"

"Mostly." She touched him, and in the next heartbeat they stepped out onto the roof of the La Croix Building. Being up there brought memories slamming back into Janey's mind of the horrible, crippling fight she and Tim had endured with Simon Grove, and when she saw Tim's face she instantly regretted bringing him here, but he read her expression and shook his head.

"I'm fine. Go get everybody else."

From down in the parking lot, Janey heard Nathan's voice, faint with distance. *"Holy shit! Holy shit fucking shitballs!"* She sighed.

Two more flickers, first Sha'dae and then Nathan, and Janey stood there facing all three of them, twenty stories above the ground. Tim came to stand beside her. To Nathan and Sha'dae, he said, "Look, I know how disorienting that is the first time. Just take a few deep breaths. You're fine. You're just...on a roof now, instead of in a parking lot."

Nathan turned in slow circles. He seemed to be speaking to himself more than to any of the rest of them, and Janey had a hard time making out his words. "Knew it...I knew it...knew there had to be something out there like this..." He whirled to face Janey and jabbed a finger at her. "You've gotta tell me how this happened! What was it? Alien meteorite? Did you follow a meteorite after it crashed and it was all glowy and blue and you touched it? Did an alien give you some kind of extra-dimensional artifact?" He took a step closer and glared at her balefully. "Do you have an alien parasite inside you?"

Out of the corner of her mouth, Janey asked Tim, "How did this happen to my life? Why do I have to answer questions like this?"

Tim took her elbow and turned her away from Nathan, who'd gone back to muttering to himself and turning in circles. Softly, Tim asked, "Why didn't you take us all to your Basement? Why the roof?"

Nathan went pale and shouted, "Or is it *magic?*"

Janey grunted. "I'm pretty sure I can trust Sha'dae, but I barely know Nathan. I don't want to show him any places he doesn't already know about."

Tim didn't look convinced by that, and thinking about it, Janey wasn't sure the reasoning held up. It wasn't as if they'd know where the Basement was if she took them there. But the roof of the LaCroix didn't have any easy lines of sight to the surrounding buildings, as evidenced by the lack of witnesses to their showdown with Simon Grove, and for what amounted to a split-second decision, she figured this would do. Janey glanced over her shoulder at Sha'dae, who up to this point had just been standing quietly, watching her, like a shy kid in a classroom afraid to raise her hand for fear of getting called on. Janey went to her.

"You're not freaking out. Aren't you surprised?"

Sha'dae's ink-black eyes locked with Janey's blue-gray. "Nnnn... not really."

"No?"

Sha'dae touched her temples with her fingertips. "It's the weirdest thing, but...no. I'm not surprised. It's like...kind of like déjà vu? When you think you've been someplace before? Except it's like I've *known* this before. Like I knew it before I even met you."

Tim had followed after Janey, and spoke to Sha'dae. "You're taking it a lot better than I did. I was more like—" He gestured at Nathan, who had gone from turning in circles to walking in a broad circle, his muttering now joined by big arm movements and near-hysterical laughter. "Not quite as bad as that, but close."

Sha'dae tossed a smile in Nathan's direction. "He's kind of cute, actually." Then, to Janey: "So—what happens now? We're up here. The, ah, the cat's pretty much out of the bag, right? So what's next?"

Janey pinched the bridge of her nose. "First things first, we have to figure out exactly who was in my apartment. What she wanted. Whether or not she had anything to do with some other people...like me."

Nathan spun and charged over to Janey. "There *are* other people like you! And you know about them! Holy fucking shit, this is the greatest night of my life!" He waved his hands in circles. "Are there shape-shifters? Are there?" Janey and Tim exchanged uncomfortable glances, the specter of Simon hanging between them, and Nathan continued, "'Cause that might explain who was in your apartment! An honest-to-God doppelganger!" He rubbed his hands together. "This is the greatest night of my fucking *life*, y'all."

Janey tilted her head back, expecting to see the light-dampened, gray-black vault of the Atlanta night sky—and her eyes snapped to one point of light directly overhead. She frowned. "What is that? I don't hear a helicopter."

Tim twisted his torso and craned his neck as much as he was able. "Nah, it's too high to be a helicopter anyway. Probably a satellite."

Sha'dae had looked skyward along with Janey and Tim. "But it's not moving. Satellites are supposed to move, aren't they? Might be a drone. Except, uh...is it just me, or...is it getting brighter?"

The light in the sky.

Barely whispering, Janey said, "Oh no...oh God, no..."

The point of light flared, and Janey Sinclair's body caught fire.

Not literally. She did not burst into flames. But Janey stood there, rigid, locked into place as the light in the sky spoke to her, fired words and thoughts and raw information and horrible, paralyzing torture straight through her eyes into her brain, and Janey's skin and flesh and bones and blood lit with an agony hotter than the surface of the sun.

She tried to scream.

She couldn't.

Somewhere far away, somewhere outside of her, she knew Tim

was there, shaking her, shouting at her, shouting her name. She heard Sha'dae screaming, heard Nathan say something about ambulances, and the pain-fire inside her built to the breaking point and exploded.

Janey never moved, her bones clamped into place by muscles as hard and unmoving as marble, but the pain-fire streaming into her from the light in the sky found its release. Janey felt it rip through her, using her body as a conduit, an antenna, and she knew that the signal blasting down from above sought new targets. New opportunities. New *subjects*. She had no idea how she knew this. The knowledge simply appeared, etched onto her brain in lines and angles and loops of acid burns, and as she stood there, rigid, the pain-fire flowed out of her body and into Tim and Sha'dae and Nathan, and the agony finally overwhelmed her and Janey Sinclair fell out of the world.

Janey stood with Adam in line for the roller-coaster. He didn't really want to ride it—the spinning teacups were more his speed, he was afraid he'd get sick if it had too many super-fast downhill plunges—but she'd given him a Dramamine pill and insisted he'd be fine. "Well, you're definitely tall enough to ride this ride," he said, hugging her to him. When she giggled, he said, "Did I tell you what my grandmother used to say about tall women? Every time she saw one, she'd say, 'Damn, if she fell over, she'd be halfway home.'" Janey giggled harder and

and

Janey lay with Adam in the bed in their hotel room, panting, her lion-coat skin glistening with sweat, the new wedding ring just a hair loose on her finger as she traced patterns across Adam's chest. She considered every penny they'd spent renting the honeymoon suite worth it by far. Adam said, "Do you ever feel like you're supposed to be in a certain place, at a certain time, in your life?" Janey didn't know how to respond, and hadn't caught her breath yet, and worried that speaking might interfere with the aftershocks of pleasure that still sent tremors through her legs, so she snuggled tighter to him instead of answering. Adam skimmed fingertips along her shoulder, her arm, her breast, traced circles around one dark-brown nipple. "I was supposed to be here. Right now. With you. This is one of the things my life was meant for." Janey smiled and kissed his lips and his throat and

and

Janey sat with Adam as he lay on the gurney in the back of the ambulance. She couldn't make herself look away from the mangled, ravaged skin and bone where part of his head used to be. She couldn't make herself look away from his clear green eyes that stared, empty, sightless, at the ceiling. She couldn't make herself look away from the movement of his hands and feet, how they twitched and lay still, twitched, lay still. She knew the EMTs were saying things, important things, things directed at her, but she couldn't do anything at all but sit there and hold his hand and wonder how her life had just come apart, every bit of it, blown apart like Adam's skull, and

and

and

And Janey lay there, on the roof of the La Croix Building, motionless, senseless, helpless, alongside Tim and Sha'dae and Nathan, their bodies in crumpled heaps.

The gray-black Atlanta sky swam back into focus for Nathan Pittman. At first he wasn't sure if his eyes were even open or not, but after a few seconds, during which he tried and succeeded to wiggle his fingers and toes, he decided they were indeed open, and he sat up.

Oh God. Wish I hadn't done that.

Something was wrong with his inner ears. Or at least that's as close as he could come to understanding how he felt. Nothing spun, it wasn't vertigo, but...the world seemed to be dragging down. Sinking.

No—getting heavier.

Get home. Gotta get home.

The sensation of weight mashed itself into his brain. He had some dim recollection of the events leading up to his awakening, but they didn't seem real, couldn't be real, so he decided he must have been dreaming. Or drunk. *Did I get drunk? How did I get drunk?* Nathan got to his feet, his distorted vision locked on a stairwell doorway in front of him, and with his first step he pitched forward and landed squarely on his face.

Oh shit...oh shit, I just broke my nose. I'm gonna have a face full of road rash.

But he scrambled up to his knees, and touched his lips, his cheeks, his nose. Nothing *felt* broken. His fingers didn't come away bloody. He got to his feet again and moved slowly, carefully. Gravity seemed to waver with each beat of his heart. One foot dragged impossibly across the roof, but the next step moved normally, and weird spikes of adrenaline kept stabbing through him. His right arm weighed seven hundred pounds and hung straight down from his shoulder as if his fist were a three-ton wrecking ball—and then swung freely, so he overcompensated and stumbled forward, and he wasn't sure how long it had taken him to arrive at the door, but his flailing fist struck the handle and smashed it completely out of the frame.

Nathan stood there and stared at the ruined, dangling lock, trying to make sense of it, but it was too much, and another wave of heavy gravity crashed through his brain, and he pushed through the wrecked door and half-walked, half-limped down the stairs.

That took a long time, but the repetition of it—*stairs, turn, stairs, landing, stairs, turn, stairs, landing*—let him concentrate on gaining control of his body again. Around the fourteenth floor he tripped and fell, and was pretty sure his head struck something hard, but he felt no pain, and though he didn't understand where the gray-white dust in his hair had come from, he got up and kept going. A glance behind him let him see a semi-circular chunk missing from one of the concrete steps.

Must've been what made me trip.

Nathan pushed open the door marked EXIT and wandered out through the parking lot. He knew he'd forgotten something. Something important, maybe *really* important, but the heavy waves crashing through his brain jarred and distracted him every time he tried to bring it into focus. He only had one coherent thought: *home.* Nathan stopped on the edge of the lot and stared at a street sign, trying to get his bearings. Home was...that way? Maybe?

What's my address? He pulled his phone out, thumbed it on, blinked his eyes to clear his blurry, wavering vision. *Lyft. I'll call a car.* Nathan hit the "Lyft" icon and yelped as his thumb went all the way through the screen and touched his palm. He tried to drop the destroyed phone, but it wouldn't come off his thumb, and as he shook it the phone flew to pieces, scattering bits of glass and plastic and metal on the sidewalk in front of him.

"Nathan?"

He turned toward the voice just as another wave of gravity compressed his brain, and he almost fell, but staggered and righted himself. "Aphrodite?"

Aphrodite stepped out of the shadows behind a tree and came closer. "What're you doing here? What's going on?"

Nathan put both hands on the sides of his head in an effort to steady it. It worked a little, enough for him to notice that someone else was still over there in the shadows. No—*two* someones. *Two peoples. People.* "God, my head feels weird." Nathan staggered again, and when he put a foot down hard to steady himself, the concrete cracked and cratered underneath it.

He heard Aphrodite suck in a sharp breath. "Nathan, why are you here? What's happened?"

Nathan dropped his hands and shook his head. "I was...I was on the roof..." More waves of gravity crashed through his brain. It was so hard to think. So hard. "The...the roof..." He gestured at the La Croix, and when he did, every single bit of what had happened up there came flooding back into his mind in a raging torrent. Nathan clapped a hand over his mouth so that his words came out muffled. "I, I uh, I shouldn't've have said anything, I mean, about that, I don't, I mean I—"

His words died, and he made a tiny choking sound, as Aphrodite's eyes turned a vivid yellow. Sparks of red shifted and swirled within them, and Nathan came very close to losing control of his bowels.

Aphrodite said, "Trent. Julian."

A tall, skinny, gray-haired white guy stepped out from behind another tree, grinning and cracking his knuckles, and right behind him...

A demon from hell followed the white guy. A black skeleton

wrapped in a cloud of darkness. Nathan couldn't do anything but stare as the white man moved behind him and wrapped an arm around Nathan's throat.

Aphrodite shifted her unholy fire-spark eyes to the roof of the La Croix building, and spoke to the soot-black demon. "Take us up there."

11

Janey sat bolt upright, gasping, her vision dim around the edges.

What just happened?

She patted herself down—nothing broken—and from off to one side she heard Tim groan. Janey scrambled over to him. "Tim! Are you okay? Can you move? Wiggle your feet for me!"

Tim propped himself up on his elbows and shifted his right foot, then his left. "I can move. I guess I'm okay. What the hell was that?"

Ten feet away, still lying prone, Sha'dae said, "I can move, too, thanks for asking."

Janey sprang up and went to Sha'dae's side, a hand extended. "I was—"

Sha'dae waved Janey's words away as she got to her feet, her voice mild. "—checking on Tim first because of his back, I know, I know." Sha'dae dusted herself off, and Janey made a small choking sound. "What?"

Janey put a finger under Sha'dae's chin. "Here. Look at me. Look right at me."

Sha'dae did, frowning. "What? What? Is there something on my face?"

Janey stepped back, her own frown mirroring Sha'dae's. For just a second, maybe less than a second, Sha'dae's eyes had glowed violet. Or was Janey seeing things? She didn't know what had just happened to her. Hallucinations might be normal at this point. "You feel okay? You're sure you're not hurt?"

Sha'dae shrugged. "I don't think so." Her eyes remained their normal, placid black.

"Okay. Okay, never mind. C'mon, give me a hand with Tim."

Janey and Sha'dae carefully helped Tim to his feet, and Janey give him a quick but intense hug. "Sorry. Sorry, I know I hover. Just, when you—I mean, when *we*—"

"Yeah." Tim leaned on his cane. "Speaking of which, I'll ask again. *What the hell was that?*"

"An excellent question," said an unfamiliar female voice, and Janey whirled around to see two people she knew and two more she didn't. Nathan Pittman, wobbling and listing as if he were hammered out of his mind, stood beside a tall, pale, jaw-droppingly gorgeous young woman with long, straight, ice-blonde hair and movie-star blue eyes. A lean, gray-haired man with skin like a baked potato loomed behind her, and at the back of the group…

Janey's breathing grew fast and shallow.

Julian Roth lurked there, visible as little more than flashes of teeth and eyes in the static-filled, volatile cloud of darkness.

Janey put her hands out, palms backward. "Get behind me." Tim immediately moved, but Sha'dae stood rooted to the spot.

"Who are…" Sha'dae's words choked off. She started again. "What am I even looking at?"

The gray-haired man's lips peeled back from tobacco-stained teeth. "Fuckin' raghead." He spoke to the blonde woman. "You didn't tell me I'd get to kill a fuckin' raghead."

"You're not doing a goddamn thing until I say," the blonde snapped back, and the gray-haired man fell silent. The blonde's own lips thinned, and Janey wondered if she were trying for a friendly smile. If so, it was a disastrous failure. "Allow me to make introductions. My name is Aphrodite Lupo. This is Trent Davis. That's Julian Roth behind us, whom you met briefly, and I believe you already know Nate Pittman."

Nathan took a step toward Aphrodite, but Trent Davis threw out an arm and blocked him. Nathan's face twisted up as he stared at the blonde. "Aphrodite, what're you doing?" She ignored him and kept her eyes on Janey.

Janey took Sha'dae by the wrist and pulled her back to stand beside Tim. To Aphrodite Lupo, Janey said, "What do you want?"

Janey watched as Nathan's eyes flicked from Aphrodite to her and back. His balance left him, and he fell to one knee, and Janey sucked in another breath at the crater in the roof left by the impact. Nathan said, "Aphrodite—how'd you...what's..." He wrenched himself back up to his feet, and waved a wild hand at Trent Davis and Julian Roth. "Who are these guys? *What* are these guys?"

Aphrodite finally turned her head and spared him a smile, half-patronizing, half-impatient. She snapped her fingers at Julian Roth. "Put him somewhere out of the way, would you? And come right back."

Nathan shoved Trent Davis out of the way—shock spreading across the older man's face at Nathan's strength—and grabbed Aphrodite by the upper arm. "Why? Why're you doing this?"

Aphrodite gave him a smile that might have had traces of actual tenderness in it, and Janey understood that Nathan and Aphrodite had been sleeping together. Aphrodite patted his cheek. "Oh, Nate. You were good practice. But you already had suspicions about me, didn't you? That's why you came here. Yes?" Her eyes darted at Roth. "Julian?"

The cloud of darkness flowed forward, twitching, roiling, and Nathan and Julian Roth winked out of existence. Half a second later, Roth reappeared. Alone.

Janey spun to face Tim and Sha'dae. *Got to get them out of here, both of them, take them to the Basement, nobody can find us there*—she reached out, fingers grasping, aiming for Tim's shoulder, but before her fingertips could touch him, Roth's cloud of darkness settled around her, shutting out all light and cutting off her night vision as if a hood had slipped over her head.

Janey flailed, grasping, touching nothing. As swiftly as it had manifested, the darkness receded—just enough time for Aphrodite and Trent Davis to close the distance—and Tim made a soft gurgling sound as Davis clamped an arm around his neck. Twenty feet away, the cloud appeared, swirled and parted, and revealed Julian Roth holding a knife to Sha'dae's throat.

At Janey's shoulder, Aphrodite Lupo whispered in her ear, "You're going nowhere. Try it—try anything—and my friends will kill your friends. Are we clear?"

Tears spilled down Sha'dae's cheeks, but Tim stood silent. Stoic.

I won't let them hurt you I won't let either of them hurt you even if it kills me I won't let it happen.

Sha'dae's face changed. Her tears stopped flowing. Janey was sure this time: something had flashed in Sha'dae's eyes, some sort of violet light, just for a fraction of a second, just as the thought about protecting her and Tim had raced through Janey's mind.

Aphrodite Lupo put a hand on Janey's shoulder and turned her around. Janey didn't resist, and found herself no more than a foot from Aphrodite's face, her own gray-blue eyes boring into the deep, sapphire-blue of Aphrodite's. Janey swallowed hard. "Who are you? Why are you doing this? Tell me what you want."

Aphrodite smiled. It looked more genuine this time. She was beautiful—unnaturally so. In the same way Anna Grove was, Janey thought, except...too much. She didn't look real. Like an alien pretending to be the world's most beautiful woman.

"I am in Command," Aphrodite said, as if that were the answer to every possible question. When Janey frowned, Aphrodite lost the smile. "The War. The War that's coming. I am in Command, and I need to fill out my ranks."

"Okay," Janey said slowly. "But I don't know what that means. I don't understand why you have to threaten my friends. Threaten me."

"You're my MVP, aren't you?" Aphrodite put a finger to Janey's lips, and walked in a lazy circle around her, the fingertip trailing along

Janey's jaw, around the back of her head, along her other cheek. "I can't fight the War all by myself. I have to have other soldiers. Good soldiers. Powerful soldiers. And that's what you've been doing, isn't it? Demonstrating to the world—to me—what a powerful soldier you are. You and your gray armor, and your spider eyes. 'The Eyes of the Widow.' Has that been working? Do the people of Atlanta really feel safer?"

Something like an arctic crevasse opened in Janey's stomach as Aphrodite spoke. This was her fault. Because of her actions, people she loved were in danger. Anger made her cheeks turn darker. "If you wanted me to be your 'soldier,' you should've just asked. There was no need to threaten my friends."

"I had to make sure you'd play along," Aphrodite purred. "You're powerful, yes. You're my prize. But you're not as powerful as I am. These two..." She gestured at Trent Davis and Julian Roth. "They understood that as soon as they met me. But you'll be harder to persuade. I could tell as soon as I stepped out onto this roof. I have to prove to you that while, yes, you're valuable, I am your superior."

Janey's mind filled with whispers.

Hundreds of hushed voices, thousands, millions, an infinity of tiny ghosts. She took an involuntary step backward and put both hands up, in as peaceful a gesture as she could manage. "Look...Ms. Lupo...there's no need for any of this. The threats, the violence, if you just want to try to convince me of something, then let's talk! I don't understand what you're saying, not yet anyway, but..." She looked Aphrodite in the eye. "It's obvious you're like me. You and, uh, Mr. Davis and Mr. Roth. I don't know how I got this way. Do you? Can you tell me? Can you help me understand why we're like this?"

The whispers grew louder, and Aphrodite's eyes turned a brilliant yellow. Janey tried not to shiver—*They look like Simon's eyes.* Aphrodite's deep-blue irises turned blood-red and...Janey squinted, trying to understand what she was seeing...they *came apart*, exploding into fiery swarms of sparks that floated in the glowing yellow, and somewhere in a deep recess of her mind, in a place Janey had never known existed, she felt something rumble and crack. As if a wall had just broken open, leaving a gap in the defenses of her brain.

The whispers came flooding through that gap.

The fire-sparks in Aphrodite Lupo's eyes intensified, burning, casting red-orange flickering light across the roof, across Janey's face, and Janey understood what the voices whispered: *Let me in. Let me in. Let me in.*

Janey snarled. She never took her eyes away from Aphrodite's. Never blinked. It felt abnormal, unnatural, the kind of energy she had to expend, like using muscles she had never used before in her life, but Janey focused on the crack in the walls of her mind and slammed it violently closed.

Aphrodite took a step backward as if she'd been struck. She cocked her head. "I see. Yes. ...Yes. It's too late for courtesy now, isn't it?"

Janey's head rocked back on her neck, blood spraying from a split lip, and the back of her head cracked hard into the roof, and Aphrodite Lupo leapt onto her, fist drawn back for another punch.

Janey bucked and twisted and threw Aphrodite off of her, but the blonde woman snarled like an animal and charged her again as Janey rolled backward and came up to her feet. *God, she's fast.* Janey slipped a punch, dodged another as she pivoted, and brought the entire weight of her body up from the ground and into her right shin as she kicked Aphrodite square in the solar plexus. The force of the blow took Aphrodite off her feet, and Janey expected to hear the *whoosh* of the woman's breath forced out of her lungs, but Aphrodite landed on her shoulder and flipped over and came up to one knee.

And grinned.

Aphrodite's skin rippled and flowed, only for a second, but Janey's breath locked in her throat as Aphrodite *became her.* A flash and then gone, but she knew she'd seen it. Aphrodite had transformed into an exact replica of Janey.

Sha'dae saw it too. Janey could tell. She wasn't exactly sure how she could tell, but she knew Sha'dae recognized this woman as the one she'd seen in Janey's apartment. Janey shook her head, flinging away unwanted, distracting thoughts, as Aphrodite Lupo charged again.

Aphrodite was strong—*God, so strong*—and fast, but untrained. Janey didn't want to let another of those haymaker punches land, didn't know how many of those she could take, so as Aphrodite attacked, Janey concentrated on redirecting the other woman's energy. A fist rocketed at her face, and Janey tapped the wrist, changed its course so that it shot past her cheekbone, and drove a knee into Aphrodite's ribs. She felt something break, cave in, but Aphrodite spun away, laughing, her eyes like liquid rubies on the surface of the sun.

Another charge, this time coming in low, trying to tackle, and Janey twisted to the side and took control of Aphrodite's head. Strong and fast or not, Janey knew it to be true that where the head went, the body would follow, and she hauled back and torqued Aphrodite's neck and slammed the woman to the roof face-first. The pain to the spine and the shock of the impact should have left Aphrodite reeling, ready to comply, but the laughter continued—louder, shriller—and something that felt like a dog bite tore into her thigh muscle just above the knee. Janey saw Aphrodite's fingers digging into her leg, and knew that if she let her, Aphrodite would tear all the way through the muscle and grind into the bone. Janey turned loose her hold and teleported ten feet away.

Aphrodite rose, loose bits of gravel falling from her face. Janey stared, expecting to see the small cuts and abrasions heal the way Simon had healed...but they didn't. The gravel had never broken the skin. As Aphrodite smiled, her face simply re-shaped itself, dislodging the bits that should have torn and cut her.

"That's hardly fair," Aphrodite said. "How can I beat some sense into you if you're going to do that?"

"This is crazy." Janey had come to rest near an air conditioning unit, and though the entire roof was dark enough for her to flicker, the shadows beside the unit's housing were especially dark and deep. "I don't know anything about any war, I don't know what you mean with all this 'command' shit, and I don't want to fight you. But I've dealt with people like you before. I'll go hard on you if you make me."

Aphrodite cocked her head again. "Oh, you're going to go *hard* on me, are you? I'd say you need an object lesson...hmmm..." Her red-in-yellow eyes tracked around and settled on Trent Davis and Tim. "That cripple is hardly of any use to us. Tell you what. Mr. Davis, if Ms. Sinclair doesn't cooperate, you can kill him."

Trent Davis said, "It don't look to me like she's gonna cooperate no matter what you say."

Aphrodite shrugged, and said, "You may be right," and before Janey could draw another breath, Trent Davis planted a knee in the small of Tim's back and broke him in half.

Tim never made a sound with his voice, but the cracking, shattering crunch of his ruined bones rolled across the roof like brittle, agonizing thunder, and Janey heard Sha'dae screaming as Tim's body collapsed, folded grotesquely backward, his shoulders touching his calves, and Davis's grin flashed out at her, and Janey vanished in a burst of heat.

She reappeared right behind Julian Roth and kicked him in the side of the head as hard as she could, but at the micro-second of impact Roth vanished, leaving Sha'dae standing there alone. Janey clapped a hand onto Sha'dae's shoulder and, in another, much more intense wave of heat, teleported both of them to the Basement.

"You're safe," she barked, regretting the necessity of having to leave Sha'dae alone in the darkness. "I'll come back for you."

Janey leapt away, grabbed an item from her work bench, flickered straight up from the basement to the ruins of the Hargett Theater, and from there straight back to the roof of the La Croix. She had been gone for just under four seconds. A broad, circular section of the roof bore a scorch mark where she and Sha'dae had left it.

She didn't think Trent Davis had even seen her go, or if he had, she didn't think he understood what she'd done. Davis still stood there over Tim's body, a tobacco-stained grin plastered on his face, and she gripped the katana she'd taken from the Basement with both hands and charged him.

Aphrodite Lupo came hurtling out of the darkness from her right and smashed into her as if fired from a cannon. Janey spun with the impact and rolled back to her feet, the katana still in her right fist, and when Aphrodite closed on her, Janey thrust the tip of the blade straight through the center of the woman's chest. The back of her shirt tented as the katana punched through.

Aphrodite looked shocked for a moment. The shock turned to bemusement...then pleasure. "Now *that* is what we wanted to see from you! True spirit! No holding back!" Aphrodite grabbed the blade with both hands, turned it sideways and...*stepped out of it.* Janey couldn't think of any other way to describe what she saw. Aphrodite Lupo's body seemed to create a channel for the blade to pass through, a lateral opening from her heart straight out to the side of her ribcage, and as soon as the blade had cleared her torso, the channel simply re-sealed itself.

Just like her face, pushing the gravel out of it.

Janey stepped backward and yanked the blade free of Aphrodite's grip, and Aphrodite held up her hands, where the sharp, narrow channel the blade had caused in her palms simply filled back in.

"I guess I shouldn't have chided you about fairness," Aphrodite said, the sparks in her eyes dancing crazily. She wiggled her undamaged fingers.

Janey readjusted her grip on the katana's hilt. "I'm going to kill you." She realized as she said the words that she meant it.

"Straightforward! We appreciate that. But you're going to have to learn to take orders. Oh, I'm getting ahead of myself. First I have to make you listen. Make you *understand.*"

Trent Davis had turned and seen Janey as soon as Aphrodite had crashed into her, and now he made his way across the roof toward them, and Janey flickered behind him and drove the hilt of the katana into his temple with every ounce of strength she could muster.

It was like striking a telephone pole. The impact almost knocked the sword from her hands.

Oh God, he's like Ned Fields.

Davis staggered and dropped to a knee, cursing, and Janey wondered if the katana's blade could even penetrate his skin.

Aphrodite Lupo stalked toward her across the rooftop. She

stepped over Tim's inert body, and Janey knew a tsunami of pain and tears waited inside her, waited to flood her and drown her.

Not yet. Not yet.

"This is disappointing, Ms. Sinclair. A woman like you should know her place. Your place is at my side. Obeying my commands. Don't you see that I am your best chance at survival? Don't you see that when the War starts, the only way for us to win is to work together?"

Aphrodite's eyes left trails of red light in the air as she moved, and with a horrible clenching in her heart and stomach, Janey's memories of Simon Grove slammed into the forefront of her mind. Nothing about Simon had made any sense to her, and she got the same sensation washing off of Aphrodite Lupo, as if she were looking at Simon's cousin, or some other kind of blood kin. Aphrodite moved to Janey's right, and Trent Davis, recovered from the blow to his skull, circled around to her left, flanking her.

"Run away," Davis said. "That's what you do, isn't it? That's what your power is. You disappear." He spat at Janey's feet. "Run, then. Fade into the shadows. Live to fight another day, you worthless little *cunt.*"

Two things happened simultaneously.

With a sound of crunching bricks and mortar, Nathan Pittman heaved himself up over the low wall surrounding the building's roof.

And Janey's anger finally got the better of her.

She'd tried to keep it under control. The blind rage erupting inside her chewed at her brain, wore away at the tethers and ground-wires attached to her heart. She'd never before let herself lose control, never let the fury fly free, because she didn't know, honestly didn't know what she was capable of, and the thought of the destruction and carnage she might leave in her wake had always terrified her.

But Aphrodite Lupo moved away from Tim's body, and Janey's eyes flew to his mangled, ruined corpse, and Janey grew vaguely, dimly aware of the waves of power flowing out of her body, thrumming through the air across the rooftop, and she saw Aphrodite's and Trent Davis's hair begin to stand on end, and Janey flickered just close enough to Aphrodite Lupo for the rainbow blade of the katana to connect with the blonde woman's throat.

Janey dreamed of Simon Grove's head leaving his body at least every third night. She had never taken a life before she killed Simon, and in her quiet, private moments, she tortured herself for taking his. *There had to have been some other way.* The thought ran on a loop in her mind, both awake and asleep, and Janey had spent the last six months vacillating between crushing, soul-shredding guilt for killing another human being and a sense of vindication for having eliminated such a savage threat.

Now, on the La Croix's rooftop, the katana singing through the air faster than Aphrodite had any chance of avoiding, Janey felt none of that guilt. She knew she would later, but at that moment, she wanted nothing more than to see Aphrodite Lupo's head roll and bounce away, past Tim's body. She had already begun to plan how she would dismember the rest of Aphrodite's corpse...

...when the katana's blade passed through Aphrodite's neck and exited the other side, leaving the woman's head still firmly attached.

Janey stumbled backward.

Aphrodite eyes shimmered and glowed as she grinned. "Not what you were expecting?"

The blade had entered Aphrodite's flesh...traveled through it...but the skin and muscle and bone had sealed behind the blade as fast as it had cut. *Like trying to slice water.* Trent Davis laughed, and said, "That's power, right there. That's real power. Can't do nothin' 'bout it."

Janey growled, low in her throat. She said, "Back up, Nathan," and when she saw the boy stop and return to the edge of the roof, Janey grabbed Aphrodite Lupo, flickered the two of them right next to Trent Davis—a good thirty feet from Tim's body, and fifty from Nathan Pittman—and in two quick hops, one of roughly a hundred feet and the other one much farther, teleported Aphrodite three miles straight up into the sky.

Night surrounded them. True night, not the light-suffused twilight most people were accustomed to seeing. That far into the sky, Janey felt as if she'd been swallowed by a vast, black ocean. That the stars overheard could only be seen by peering through incomprehensible depths. Far, far below them, Janey thought she could see the pinpoint of red-orange light left behind when she'd flickered this far up, but she couldn't be sure.

As they plummeted, Aphrodite Lupo clung to Janey's shirt, to her hair, and for the first time Janey saw the woman truly rattled. "What are you doing?" Aphrodite screamed. "You'll kill us both!"

Janey said, "Nope," and teleported two hundred miles due west.

Alone.

Falling like a rock, Janey twisted in the air to look east, and saw the spherical blossom of yellow-white flame that marked her point of departure. She concentrated on the roof of the La Croix, flickered, and landed softly on the roof in the same spot from which she'd left. Tim still lay where he'd fallen, and now Nathan Pittman knelt next to him, one hand on Tim's throat. At the far edge of the roof, Trent Davis sagged against the low wall, his clothes blackened and his skin blistered and charred.

Nathan said, "Janey—" but she didn't stop to listen. A flicker put her right in front of the man who'd killed Tim, and a hand around his throat let her repeat what she'd done with Aphrodite. Another wave of heat washed out across the rooftop as Janey and Trent Davis vanished...

...and Davis screamed as he reappeared far above the Earth's surface. No words from him. Just a pure, brutal, throat-ripping howl of terror, but Janey couldn't truly appreciate it, because far below her, barely a speck, was Aphrodite Lupo, plummeting toward the earth. Janey flickered another hundred miles away, leaving Trent Davis at the heart of a miniature star—

—came back a mile closer to the ground and fastened her hands around Aphrodite's throat—

—carried the blonde woman another two miles higher in the air—

—and another star-hot inferno lit up the night sky as Janey vanished, traveling the hundreds of miles it took for her departure to encase Aphrodite Lupo in the heart of a tiny sun.

Just before Janey vanished again, Aphrodite shouted, "Wait!"

But Janey was in no mood to listen. She fell into a rhythm. Using that two-hundred-mile-distant spot high above the Earth as her point of reference, she caught Trent Davis, carried him two miles into the night sky, teleported away, zeroed in on Aphrodite Lupo, carried her up past the falling, screaming, charred Davis...and repeated. Three times. Five times. Seven times. Her lungs burned from the lack of oxygen in the thin reaches of the stratosphere, ice gathering on her eyelashes, but Janey didn't care.

She wanted Davis and Lupo to burn. Burn for killing Tim.

Fall, and scream, and burn...

...and burn they did.

With each flicker Janey heard the grinding fracture of Tim's bones.

Each time she grabbed Aphrodite Lupo or Trent Davis and flung them high into the sky, she saw the man she loved dying right in front of her.

Just like her mother. Just like her father. Just like Adam.

Janey traveled farther and farther, and the heat discharges grew and grew, and ear-splitting booms and cracks of thunder sounded out with each one, so that explosive waves of sound filled the sky and rolled across Atlanta and rattled windows and set off car alarms city-wide. Blood-red lightning arced from cloud to cloud as Janey let the fury settle into her.

Trent Davis quickly fell to begging. Each time she grabbed him and carried him upward, he whimpered and sobbed, and said, "Please, stop...please, please stop," and he said it through blackened, split lips, his hair burned off, his clothes charred to dust.

But Aphrodite Lupo never begged. Never cried out. Her red-in-yellow eyes just burned brighter and brighter each time, and though her clothes disintegrated and her blonde hair blackened and fell away, Aphrodite's skin never sustained any damage.

Janey decided to take Aphrodite as high as she possibly could and simply let her fall. *If heat won't work, let's see what gravity can do.*

But when Janey dropped Aphrodite, a convulsing, writhing cloud of darkness appeared directly below her, and Aphrodite fell into it and disappeared. The cloud vanished, materialized below Trent Davis, and took him away as well. Julian Roth's eyes flashed at Janey for the space of a rapid heartbeat before the night swallowed him up. Janey dropped, in free-fall, the earth rushing up to meet her as she realized Trent Davis and Aphrodite Lupo had escaped her.

One last spherical explosion of white-yellow flame, followed by a final deafening clap of thunder, took Janey out of the night sky and deposited her on the roof of the La Croix. Nathan still knelt there, over Tim, and when Janey arrived he shot up to his feet and rushed toward her.

"Janey, I'm sorry, I'm so fucking sorry, I didn't know, I didn't know she was going to hurt anybody, I didn't know she had those other guys with her, I didn't mean for anybody to get hurt, I swear to God, I'm so sorry!"

Janey stalked past him without a word. She sank down onto the roof next to Tim.

The tsunami was about to arrive. Janey could feel it coming. She felt Nathan kneel beside her. She said, "I tried to stop them. I tried... but I couldn't. And now he's gone. Tim's gone." The tsunami was almost there, and Janey knew that once it started, she wouldn't be able to stop it until it had run its course.

That's when Nathan Pittman said, "Actually, uh...he's breathing. His pulse is kind of...well, normal. Janey, Tim's not dead."

1 2

Janey flickered into the Basement to see that Sha'dae had lit half a dozen candles and was sitting with her back to the wall, staring at one of Janey's "nightmare" paintings.

Oh shit.

Sha'dae looked up, the whites visible all the way around her deep-brown irises. "Janey. Don't leave me here."

Janey didn't bother trying to hide anything. Not now. She flickered around the Basement, grabbing what she needed, and in between tele-portations said, "I'm sorry, I have to, only for a minute, I have to help Tim. I'm sorry, I'll be right back."

Sha'dae stood, reached out for her, and Janey heard her say, "Wait —" but Janey flickered away again.

Nathan still knelt next to Tim on the roof of the La Croix. Janey materialized on the other side of Tim's somehow-still-breathing body with a couple of PVC pipes, a length of canvas she had intended to stretch and use for paintings, and a roll of duct tape. Without speaking, she set about constructing a litter.

In much the same tone Sha'dae had used, Nathan said, "Janey—"

She shook her head, ripping off strips of tape. It was hard enough to work while keeping the tsunami at bay. She had no energy for talking.

Nathan said, "Janey, something happened. Before Aphrodite and, and those other guys showed up. Something happened up here."

Janey finished the litter. It wasn't strong enough to carry anyone for any real distance, but she only meant to get Tim to the Basement. "We can't stay here. They could be back at any second. Help me. Help me move him."

Nathan nodded, and stayed silent, and he and Janey gingerly maneuvered Tim's horribly contorted body onto the litter. Nathan stood, and Janey said, "You'll want to move back a few feet." Nathan obligingly backed up, and Janey put one hand on Tim's shoulder and the other one on the litter. "Don't go anywhere." With an intense burst of heat she left Nathan alone on the rooftop.

This time Sha'dae shrieked when Janey and Tim appeared out of nowhere in the middle of the Basement's shadowy expanse. Janey moved to the end of the litter above Tim's head, and had drawn breath to say, "Get the other end," but Sha'dae's cry cut off immediately. She grabbed the exposed PVC pipes without being asked. They lifted him and carried him over to Janey's work bench, and with a start Janey realized she'd begun crying.

Not yet, not yet, keep it together!

Sha'dae cleared her throat.

Janey turned to face her, all but snarling as she wiped the tears away. "Look, I know you've got questions, probably more questions than I've got answers, but you've got to bear with me for a second longer."

Sha'dae said, "But—" just before Janey took three steps away and flickered into the darkness.

Nathan still stood in the same place when Janey got back. Scanning the area, she barked, "Any sign of them?" and when Nathan shook his head *no*, Janey flickered to his side, grabbed his wrist, and took them both to the Basement.

Nathan staggered a couple of steps to his left and clapped his hands to his head. Janey's world wrinkled and distorted, and she sat down heavily in the floor, her vision pounding in and out of focus. She stared up at Nathan, who had begun making gagging sounds. "What the *fuck*, Nathan? How much do you *weigh?*"

Nathan gagged one more time, but didn't bring anything up. He squinted around through the darkness, shapes barely visible in the candles' soft orange glow, and actually smiled when he caught sight of Sha'dae. He waved—"Hi!"—but his smile vanished again when he saw Tim laid out on the work bench.

Janey got to her feet. Sha'dae said, "Uh...anybody else feel like they're about to go into shock?"

Janey went to Tim's side and took his pulse. Checked his breathing, and then his pulse again, and shook her head as she said, "How is this possible? This isn't possible. You can't survive trauma like that. *How is this possible?*"

Sha'dae came to stand next to her. "I don't know. I don't know. But he *is* alive. And that means we need to get him to the hospital."

Janey nodded. "Right. Right! Get him there, get him to Dr. Gates." Agonizing memories flooded her mind of the night she'd killed Simon Grove. Weeks later, Tim had told her, haltingly, what Simon had done to him before Janey got there. She considered it a miracle he'd survived at all, and believed that he wouldn't have if she hadn't delivered him into Dr. Carla Gates's hands as fast as she had. She smoothed Tim's hair back from his forehead and whispered, "Don't worry, Tim. Don't worry. I've got you."

And she froze.

From her left, Sha'dae's voice held clear notes of trepidation. "Uh...Janey? Why aren't you taking him?"

Janey turned around and leaned against the work bench and covered her face with both hands. "Shit. *Shit.* I can't take him to a hospital! It's a public place. Those freaks would find him there and kill him for sure." She dropped her hands, and Nathan, who had approached her, took a rapid step back. The thudding sound of his quick footfall echoed around the Basement. Janey frowned at that, but didn't have the mental space to process it. "All right. Fine. I'm going to go get Dr. Gates and bring her here. She'll know what to do, she can tell me what medical gear I need to get."

Sha'dae put a hand on Janey's arm. "Wait! Wait. Don't go yet."

Janey pulled her arm free of Sha'dae's grasp, but not roughly. "What?"

Sha'dae made a wide gesture around her. "All of this—I get why you brought the three of us here. I don't know where *here* is, but wherever we are, you brought us here because it's safe, right? Okay. I get that. But now you're talking about kidnapping someone."

Janey's eyes flashed. "I'm talking about saving Tim's life! Can I please stop wasting time?"

Sha'dae persisted. "Just *think* for a second. The police already know the Gray Widow saved Tim's life once, right? You guys told them he got mugged. But if you bring some doctor here, to this place? If they see this—" She pointed at the peg board festooned with weapons. "Or those—" Sha'dae nodded toward the paintings, and shuddered. "I need to ask you about those. I know, I know, later. But still, my point is, the doctor will tell the police, no matter what happens. And the police will investigate, and that'll lead them to you. If Nathan and I are still here, we'll get pulled in, too, but if you take us someplace else, who's to say those...those *people* from the roof won't kill us both?"

Janey's face creased and bunched in rage, and she clenched rock-hard fists. "Then what do you want me to do? He's broken in fucking half, Sha'dae! You want us to just sit down here and see if he gets better?"

From behind her, Tim said, "That's actually not a bad idea," and Janey came very close to wetting her pants.

She rushed to him. "What's, how're you, how—" She paused for breath. "How are you alive?"

"Not a bad question." His voice came out calm and smooth, which made Janey want to scream. Tim said, "I think, though...if you wouldn't mind...maybe you guys could try to straighten me out?"

"Whoa, dude, wait," Nathan said. "In Health class they told us you never move somebody who's been in a bad accident, right? 'Cause if you've got something broken, if you move, it could shift and, like, puncture something. Or cut something. Y'know?"

A slight frown lined Tim's face, and his right foot—up behind his head—wiggled from left to right. "Look, I don't know what's going on myself, but…" He reached up and scratched his nose. "Unlikely as it sounds, I don't think anything's broken. I'm just kind of uncomfortable. Kind of *really* uncomfortable. So if you could?"

Janey looked from Nathan to Sha'dae to Tim.

Sha'dae moved closer to the work bench. She couldn't seem to decide what to do with her hands. "Janey, something happened back there on the roof. And I'm thinking Tim's, uh, his condition is connected to it?"

Janey took Tim's hand. He looked her in the eyes with astonishing calm. "I really think I'll be all right. I'd just very much like not to be folded in half anymore."

The star in the sky. The star Anna Grove saw…that my father saw. The star that changed us all.

Tim said, "Janey. Please. This is actually starting to hurt. *Please* give me a hand here."

Janey nodded, mute.

If that was the same star, the one that made me…able to do what I do… why don't I feel any different?

Janey motioned Sha'dae and Nathan to help her. Together, they lowered the litter onto the cool concrete floor, and try as she might, Janey could not help the cascade of thoughts crashing across her brain. Some part of her wondered if she might trade in the tsunami of tears for a good, old-fashioned panic attack.

Gently, Janey moved Tim onto his side, and when he didn't protest, she rolled him all the way over to his stomach, his chin propped on the floor.

Janey found her voice enough to say, "Okay, you two. Get on either side of him and…get a good hold on his knees. I'll brace his shoulders." Sha'dae and Nathan did as she said, and Janey said a fast, silent prayer. "Okay. I don't know if this should be fast or slow, but I'm gonna go with slow, and Tim, for God's sake, *tell us* if it starts to hurt, okay?"

"You got it," Tim said, and Janey nodded to Sha'dae and Nathan.

Slowly, firmly, while Janey kept his torso in place, they pulled up and back on Tim's legs. When they reached ninety degrees to Tim's torso, two *pops* sounded out, loud as rifle shots, and Janey stifled a scream, but only barely. "Are you okay, did that hurt, are you in pain?"

Tim's eyelids slid closed. "I'm fine. That felt like...like when you crack your knuckles. Keep going, guys."

Sha'dae and Nathan kept up the pressure, and thirty seconds later Tim rolled over onto his back under his own power, his body once again in a straight line. Janey crouched beside him, hovering over him, and as soon as she realized what she was doing, she backed off. But that made her feel as if she weren't paying him enough attention, and she leaned in close again. "Tim. Talk to me. Tell me how you're feeling. Is there pain?"

Tim turned his head to look at her. A slow, sparkling grin spread his lips.

Wait. He turned his head?

HE TURNED HIS HEAD.

Tim sat up. He looked to his left, and his right, and tilted his head up toward the ceiling and all the way down till his chin touched his chest. "Janey," he breathed. He turned to face her.

Janey felt sure she knew how to breathe, but for the life of her, she couldn't remember.

Tim got to his feet. He took a few steps. Stopped and touched his toes. Rotated his hips. His brilliant white teeth flashing in the candlelight, he let out a full-throated *whoop* and sprinted to the far end of the basement, laughing as he came back. "Oh my God! Janey! Guys! I'm, I'm..." He waved his hands in the air as if clawing for words. "I'm not *fucked up* anymore! Look at this!" Tim did a clumsy pirouette, and ran to Janey and gathered her up in his arms.

Before she knew what was happening, Tim's mouth found hers, and his hand cradled the back of her head, and she pushed her fingers into his hair and let her body mold itself to his. Tim's tongue slipped between her lips, and in between the irrational bursts of heat pulsing in her groin, her hands slid up and down Tim's back, touched his shoulders, cupped one cheek of his ass.

"Oh God," she whispered, as Tim lowered his head to kiss her neck. "Oh, God, Tim...you're *healed.*"

He snaked an arm around her lower back and pulled her more tightly to him, and she felt how hard he was, and at roughly the same time that Sha'dae made an uncomfortable *ahem* sound, Janey's eyes flew open and she put both hands on Tim's chest and pushed him away.

On a base, primal level, Janey wanted nothing more than to grab Tim, teleport them to some remote hotel, and ride him until he couldn't walk again. "Tim. We need to focus. We've got to understand what's going on."

Nathan shuffled closer. "Yeah, uh, about that—that thing? That happened on the roof? I started feeling super-weird right after I woke up. And, you said it yourself, right, like how much I weigh now? Well, I've been going back over everything. In my head. And it's kind of like when you remember parts of a dream, like, hours after you wake up? But, yeah, anyway—watch this."

Nathan knelt, pulled a bony fist back, and drove it into the Basement floor. The concrete shattered. Cracks radiated out from the point of impact. Nathan stood back up and showed them all his fist, unclenched it, wiggled the fingers. His skin wasn't even bruised. Nathan's wide eyes glistened.

"Janey...what happened to us?"

Tim spread his arms wide and gave Janey that sparkling grin again. "I, for one, don't *care* what happened! I'm healed! I'm not fucking crippled anymore, and I want to celebrate!"

She took both his hands in hers. "And we will. But I need to know if you're thinking straight. What happened, up there on the roof—it healed your body, but what happened to your mind? Are you okay...mentally?"

Tim looked as if he wanted to give her a flip retort, but after a second his grin faded, and he dropped her hands. "I'm fine. I'm fine. I just...I mean, it *is* a kind of a miracle, isn't it? I swear, Janey, it feels like my blood's been replaced with endorphins."

Sha'dae spoke up. "Except the people who tried to kill us are still out there, right? Out there somewhere? Unless..." She dropped her gaze to the floor. "Unless you killed them, Janey?"

Janey winced. "No. I didn't." *I tried to, though. Tried my damnedest.* "They got away from me. So yeah, they're out there." She turned to Nathan and took a breath to say, *Which means it's time for you to tell us everything you know about this Aphrodite person,* and a wave of noxious whispers came flooding through the crack in her mind. She'd been so caught up with Tim, Janey hadn't noticed that mental rift opening again. Just a hair. Less than that. But less than a hair was all it took. She slammed it closed again, just as she had on the roof, yet even as she felt it seal off, she knew it was too late.

The entire Basement shook with what felt like a seismic tremor.

Faint, and far away, but clear enough to be understood perfectly, Aphrodite Lupo's voice reached them in a crazed sing-song. *"I know you're there, Janey Sinclair! I'm coming for yoouuu..."*

13

Janey was rattled enough that it took fifteen seconds to get into the Vylar suit, rather than the ten she'd gotten it down to, and in those seconds what sounded like a series of explosions crashed out from the far end of the Basement. As Janey pulled on the helmet and secured it under her chin, the cinder-block wall shivered, cracked, and burst outward, and Aphrodite Lupo walked out onto the concrete floor.

Janey's eyes watered, and she blinked furiously, trying to understand what she was seeing. It *was* Aphrodite, there was no question, her face was the same, and the straight, ice-blonde hair still fell around it like a pale gold curtain. But the young woman who'd attacked her and her friends on the La Croix's roof had stood five-feet-eight, maybe five-nine. Now Aphrodite topped out at at least six-feet-two. Her clothing hung on her in ragged tatters, split at the seams, and…her hands…

Janey stifled a scream.

Aphrodite's hands had become huge, scoop-like talons. Like something a giant mutant mole would use to tear through the earth. Janey flashed back involuntarily to the sight of Simon Grove's hideously mutated fingers, long and writhing and barbed, and her guts turned to ice water.

Beyond Aphrodite, a rough tunnel angled up toward the surface, and something flickered behind her. *Oh no, oh shit, Roth—*

Janey didn't have time to complete the thought. Twin hammers clicked behind her, and she spun to see Roth standing between Tim and Sha'dae, a gun in each hand, leveled at their hearts. The darkness spread out from him, contracting and expanding like a ragged, erratic heartbeat, and Janey couldn't tell from one instant to the next which way he was looking.

"No running this time," Aphrodite said, strolling toward Janey. Her hands vibrated and pulsed as they shrank back to a normal human appearance. She used them to brush the dirt from her face and her chest. Trent Davis emerged from the tunnel and stepped up to walk beside her. "If you teleport, Mr. Roth there will pull the triggers on those guns, and I'm betting at least one shot will find its target."

Nathan jumped in front of Sha'dae, and Aphrodite Lupo laughed. "Nathan, you never stop surprising me, do you know that? Haven't you had enough of being shot in the chest? Didn't you spend enough time in the hospital? Do you *really* want another scar...or is it a death-wish? You've realized you can't have me anymore, and now life's not worth living?"

In Nathan's ear, Sha'dae hissed, "What do you think you're doing?"

Nathan's voice rose, filled with tension and approaching panic. "I'm trying to protect you. Don't tell me you've got a problem with that."

Janey clenched her fists, eyeing the distance between her and the weapon-covered peg board, and Aphrodite shook her head. "Ah-ah-ah, don't you do it, Janey. I meant what I said. Julian *will* fire. And while I can't speak to what effect a bullet will have on the surprisingly upright Mr. Kapoor over there, Nathan really will die."

Trent Davis cleared his throat. "Yeah, about that. Can't say for sure, but I'm thinkin' he's like me. Felt awful heavy when I grabbed him out there on the street."

Tim pitched his voice low. It still echoed around the Basement.

"Janey, you've got to get Nathan and Sha'dae out of here. They're going to kill us all. One way or another."

Aphrodite Lupo's eyes flared brilliant, luminous yellow, and her irises turned blood-red and burst apart, embers above a fire. "Oh, we're not going to kill Janey. No, no, no. I want Janey. I *need* her. There is a war coming, you see, and she's going to play a vital role...as one of my lieutenants. So, really, whether or not the rest of you live or die depends on her. Will you let me recruit you? Or do you want to shut me out again, and watch your friends die?"

Nathan said, "Oh, fuck this shit," and took a step toward Julian Roth, and the report from Roth's gun in the confines of the Basement sounded like artillery fire, and the bullet struck Nathan squarely in the center of the chest and bounced off.

Janey heard a sound like *splack*.

Tim grunted. Janey turned and saw that the ricocheting bullet had hit Tim in the left eye, and punched through his skull and out the back of his head, and now instead of an eye, there was a hole that Janey could see all the way through, and Tim fell to his knees and Janey wasn't sure if Sha'dae was screaming or Nathan or if she was herself, and sanity abandoned her entirely.

As Janey flickered and disappeared in a burst of heat and stepped out of the shadows directly behind Aphrodite Lupo, a detached part of her marveled at the physical sensation of losing her mind. Janey's consciousness had just fractured, she had clearly felt it split into three separate parts, and as she jerked Aphrodite backward by the shoulders and clamped the woman's throat into her armpit and wrenched upward to shatter her spine, Janey also saw two other things happening simultaneously.

She saw Julian Roth lunge toward her, gun blazing, his skeletal face creased and horrible in rage—

And she saw Trent Davis charging at her, his mouth wide in a scream, his fist drawn back—

And a sharp, burning pain pierced Janey's mind because Roth and Davis *weren't attacking her, they were attacking Sha'dae and Nathan why am I seeing this how am I seeing this*

The triple-vision distracted her so much that she barely had time to react as Aphrodite twisted and convulsed in Janey's grip, and where there should have been the wet crunching of broken vertebrae, instead the bones of Aphrodite's neck and skull *bent*, warping, and Aphrodite slipped out of Janey's killing clutch and a fist like the head of a sledgehammer pounded into Janey's armored chest so hard she knew it was a miracle her heart didn't explode.

Janey sucked in as much air as she could, and while Aphrodite thundered toward her, she tried to pinpoint everyone's location so that she could flicker to each one in turn and teleport them out of there, out of harm's way. Out of Aphrodite's reach. But something had gone wrong with Janey's brain, so wrong, and while the triple-split-screen in her mind showed her Roth and Davis attacking, and she heard the sounds of Davis's fists as they connected with flesh and bone, she couldn't see Nathan or Sha'dae with her own eyes.

There was Tim. Lying ruined and dead. *Again.* Janey knew she was about to start screaming, but when she tried to focus on either Sha'dae or Nathan, her eyes slid past where she thought they should be.

Aphrodite shrieked and leapt into the air, dropping with a knee aimed at Janey's face, and Janey flickered to the peg board.

She knew everything she had there was useless. If the katana did nothing, neither would batons or staves.

Aphrodite finished her strike, flashing through the space Janey had just vacated, and drove her knee into the pavement. The knee flattened out and re-formed itself as soon as she sprang up again. Aphrodite spun and launched herself at Janey, and Janey had no choice but to flicker out of her path once more. She had no idea how long she could keep it up, how long she could evade Aphrodite before the woman caught her and broke her and ripped her apart. Or worse —"recruited" her. Janey knew she had to grab Nathan and Sha'dae and get the hell out of there, but she couldn't do that if she couldn't fucking *see* them.

Aphrodite's screaming grew louder. She zeroed in on Janey and pulled a gun from inside her jacket. Janey's frantic flickering took her out of the line of fire, waves of heat washing out across the Basement with each teleport, but Aphrodite anticipated Janey's path and a round caught her in the ribs, just to one side of the chest pad.

The Vylar held. The bullet didn't penetrate. But the impact flipped Janey around as the pain blasted through her and made her vision dim —except that the two other sets of eyes connected to her brain didn't dim at all, and in that moment of agony, Janey realized what was happening: she was literally seeing through their eyes. Nathan's and Sha'dae's. Janey was seeing Davis and Roth trying to kill each of them. But why couldn't she *see* Sha'dae or Nathan?

As Janey's consciousness wavered on the edge of the brutal pain from the bullet, Nathan's portion of the triple-split-screen in her mind expanded, and the sight of Trent Davis filled her field of vision. Davis's dirty gray hair and acne-pitted, leathery skin and eight-pack-a-day-stained teeth and bloodshot eyes and rancid breath became her whole world.

His face, and his fists. His fists crashed down like wrecking balls, over and over, and Janey realized Davis had Nathan pinned to the floor, and Davis spat out his words along with flecks of saliva. "Kill you I'll kill you smash your skull you think you're like me you think you're tough I'll break you open you little piece of dog shit."

Janey's consciousness *slid.* She had no other way to describe it. Nathan's pain and helplessness moved off to one side, replaced with Sha'dae's, and Janey found herself staring at Julian Roth, who flickered and pulsed and flowed across the floor of the Basement, shouting. "Where are you? I know you're still here, bitch! Why can't I see you?"

Thoughts danced across Janey's mind faster than words, faster than her active consciousness.

Sha'dae, what the hell are you doing?

The image of Sha'dae's eyes, with that otherworldly gleam in them —the violet spark Janey had seen on the La Croix's roof—floated in front of her, and with a shock like being plunged into a pool of icewater, Sha'dae's voice entered Janey's mind, carried on a smooth, silver stream.

I don't know, Janey, I don't know what's happening, I don't know how to make it stop!

Hands like steel vises dug into Janey's shoulders and hauled her to her feet, and Aphrodite Lupo's teeth gnashed as the blonde woman tried to tear through the face of Janey's helmet, and Janey fought down panic as Aphrodite's fingers broke the skin underneath the Vylar.

And the whispers. The whispers came roaring back, a tsunami in their own right, and Janey felt the pounding and tearing at the walls of her mind as the ghost voices tried to smash through it.

She teleported Aphrodite and herself across the Basement. Anything to disorient her. Both of them crashed to the floor, and Janey expected her muscles to begin shredding apart beneath the inhuman strength of Aphrodite's fingers, but the grip disappeared from her shoulders. Janey rolled away and came up to a crouch...

...and saw Aphrodite, on her knees, staring.

Staring at one of Janey's nightmare paintings.

Aphrodite's chin quivered. Tears started from her eyes, and she made a high, thin, keening sound that cut through the wispy, invasive waves of whispers. "No," she said, in a voice that sounded more like a little girl's than a grown woman's. "No, don't let it through, don't let it come through, don't!"

Janey rolled away from her, ready for another attack, but Aphrodite didn't move. She just stayed there, on her knees, eyes glued to the work of art.

The painting that had taken hold of Aphrodite was called "Door to the Earth." It depicted a fog desert—a savagely barren landscape of dry, hard-packed soil, so dry it was more like concrete than dirt or sand, with a fine, smoky strata of fog drifting above it. In the center of the image, a rectangular hole the size of a racquetball court yawned wide, with broad, shallow steps leading from one edge down and down and down into the darkness. Janey had never shown it to anyone before. She knew the effect that imbued her nightmare paintings, the negative power transfer that she still didn't fully understand, was especially strong in "Door to the Earth."

But similar paintings in the past had done nothing more than cause nightmares in the viewer. She had never witnessed an effect as profound as this. Aphrodite sat, frozen, crying, and her glowing yellow-and-red-spark eyes returned to the normal deep blue that Janey had seen before. Aphrodite slowly hugged herself. She swayed side to side, only a fraction of inch in either direction, and her trembling grew more pronounced.

Janey stood and backed away from her. Staring. She gasped as the pain from the bullet impact fully registered on her, combined with the growing ache from where Aphrodite had tried to tear her arms off. She couldn't seem to suck in enough air, and the triple-vision still played in her eyes, and some part of her was aware that Nathan had wriggled out from under Trent Davis and was now kicking the older man in the ribs, over and over, and though she still couldn't see Nathan with her naked eyes, she heard the impacts, like a baseball bat hammering into a side of beef. Janey started and yelped and almost flickered away when a gentle hand closed on her wrist—

And she cried out again when she realized Tim stood beside her. His hand grasping her arm. The weak glow of the candlelight dancing in his eyes.

Eyes.

Fully whole, Tim said, "Janey, I don't understand *any* of this. But I know we have to go."

Aphrodite sobbed. Janey didn't think the woman had blinked at all in the last thirty seconds. Desperate, Janey searched out the flowing silver stream in her mind, and tried to push her consciousness into the flow. It was a sensation she had never felt before. She dimly wondered if any human ever had prior to this moment. *Sha'dae. You're making it so I can't see you or Nathan. I need you to stop. I need you to let me find you.*

Sha'dae's voice came back instantly. Clearer now. *If I stop, this ghost freak will kill me!*

Janey never took her eyes off Aphrodite Lupo, but she twined her gloved fingers through Tim's. *If I can find you, I'll get us all out of here. Sha'dae. Please. Trust me.*

A long heartbeat passed. Another. And Janey's sanity returned in a rush that left her light-headed. The triple-vision that she had almost become accustomed to vanished, and across the candle-lit Basement floor she saw Nathan and Davis, wrestling on the ground in a pile of limbs, and Julian Roth standing ten feet away from Sha'dae, his back to her, head pivoting, eyes seeking.

Janey could only think of one thing to do. She had never tried it before, but she had learned to have faith in her teleportation ability, even if she understood nothing about it other than how to trigger it. She remembered the debilitating strain of flickering with Nathan when she hadn't realized how much he weighed, and wondered if it were like trying to pick up a box that was supposed to be empty, only to find it filled with bowling balls. She hoped so, and tensed every muscle she could, both mental and physical.

To Tim, she said, "Hold tight." He nodded, and gripped her hard, and Janey took him with her as she flickered across the room. Between one second and the next, they reappeared right next to Nathan and Trent Davis, and Janey reached down and grabbed Nathan's upper arm as the heat from the first flicker washed over them, and Tim gasped as he and Janey and Nathan materialized right behind Sha'dae, and Davis shrieked in pain and slapped out the flames that had erupted along his shirtsleeve, and before Julian Roth could turn around and see them together, Janey said a fast, silent goodbye to the Basement. She slipped an arm around Sha'dae's waist, pulled her close—

And teleported all four of them blind.

The fight on the La Croix's roof had pushed Janey further than she'd ever taken her power before. By flickering two hundred miles away, she had set off fireballs that would have incinerated any normal humans, left nothing but traces of ash hanging in the air. But those journeys were nothing compared with what she attempted this time.

Janey didn't know if it would even work, and beyond that, what effect it would have on her or the people she carried with her. She had never teleported more than one person at a time before, let alone three...

...and she had never traveled a thousand miles in one flicker.

But the power lived within her. She could feel it if she concentrated, the way someone meditating can hear the rushing of their own blood through their veins and arteries. Janey isolated the power, gripped it, demanded that it cooperate, and a sound like every thunderclap of a vicious storm combined into one blasted against her, and she and Tim and Sha'dae and Nathan all materialized a mile above the Earth's surface.

Over Nebraska.

How much time had passed? Janey wasn't sure. She had dealt with the falling, and the screaming—there had been a lot of screaming—and her own convulsing, wracking heaves at the effort of traveling that far with that many other people.

But now...

Now I have to find out exactly what I did.

As Janey flickered back across the country, she thought she might pass out sooner rather than later. She didn't dare travel high in the sky in this state, and not only did she not want to start a series of fires as she traveled east toward Atlanta, she also couldn't afford to leave a trail of scorch-marks delineating her path. So in a long series of short hops, never fully materializing and moving mostly along the shoulders of freeways, Janey made her way back to the city she had sworn to protect. She arrived at the site of what had once been the Hargett Theater and sagged, hands on her knees, trying desperately to fill her lungs.

Two cross-country trips in...what? Four minutes? Five? She half-expected to start hallucinating.

Sirens sang from what sounded like every direction. Getting closer.

No wonder. Janey marveled at the sheer destruction she had caused.

The half-destroyed theater, along with the partially collapsed parking structure Janey had called the Basement, had been replaced by a broad, deep, perfectly hemispherical crater fifty yards across at its widest. Fires burned around its edges. Numbly, Janey considered the stash of weapons she had amassed over the last year.

Her insides twisted and tightened at the thought of all the paintings she had just destroyed. She wondered just how wrong that was, how morally reprehensible, that she felt worse about losing four dozen paintings than she did about killing three people. She figured the full emotional impact might hit her later on, but just then she felt numb.

Janey sat down on a chunk of overturned concrete to wait for her breath to even out. She saw no sign of Trent Davis or Julian Roth or— thank God—Aphrodite Lupo. It might have been worth destroying years of creative output if it meant getting rid of her.

She felt a pang of shame at the thought, which seemed to have sprung into her mind out of nowhere, from some disconnected, trauma-ridden place she couldn't quite focus on. Still, she couldn't see any way around eliminating Aphrodite...and hadn't thought of any other way to do it. If the katana hadn't hurt her, bullets wouldn't have either.

The katana!

Janey knew she could produce other paintings, but that katana had been a one-time find. Even if it hadn't done Aphrodite any damage, she hated the thought of losing it. Plus, if it were still down there in the rubble and the police ran across it, it might set off even more of an investigation than was already centered on her. Janey stood, dusted off the seat of the armored suit, and flickered down into the crater.

She knew approximately where the peg-board had hung, and after a couple of minutes of moving more bits of concrete and sifting through ash and dirt that was almost too hot to touch, she turned up the melted shafts of a couple of aluminum police batons. *That means the katana should be...right over here...*

Janey had to sink her hand into a bank of ash up to her wrist, but it closed around the katana's hilt, and she laughed in tired delight as she pulled it free. The leather had disintegrated, but she could find another way to wrap the hilt. The tang and the blade seemed untouched, and when she wiped off the fine layer of ash, the sword's rainbow sheen winked at her, its colors rendered gray and gold and green in her night vision.

"Things around you seem hard to damage," Aphrodite Lupo said from behind her.

Janey screamed as she whirled, and screamed again at the sight of the creature pulling and heaving its way out from underneath a pile of melted cinder blocks.

Aphrodite's hair was gone, an absence that only accentuated the horror that revealed itself bit by bit as she climbed out of the rubble. Aphrodite's eyes had gone a pale, luminous gray, like low-wattage light bulbs, and her skin had sprouted dozens upon dozens of small, thorn-like protrusions.

Janey couldn't breathe.

Just like Simon she looks just like Simon did right before I killed him

"I believe Julian got himself and Trent to safety," Aphrodite said, and ran a long, forked tongue out between sharp, spine-like teeth. "I wasn't so lucky."

The whispers slammed into Janey, and she staggered backward, the katana dangling from one hand, useless. Aphrodite stood and, as Janey watched, the thorns on her skin withdrew, and long, pale-gold hair cascaded down from her head, and as the temperature of the air around them plummeted and patches of ice spread out along the ground from Aphrodite's feet, her eyes returned from their luminous, hollow gray to yellow-with-red-embers. Aphrodite's jaw rippled, and her teeth shortened, and when she took a step forward, fully human again and utterly undamaged, Janey screamed and flickered away into the darkness.

14

Janey stepped out of the coat closet in her apartment, unable to keep from feeling like the Bruce Willis character in *Pulp Fiction*. Aphrodite Lupo and her pair of...what? What were Julian Roth and Trent Davis to her? Had she "recruited" them, the way she kept talking about recruiting Janey? Were they under the same kind of mind control Brenda Jorden had used on so many people? Janey wondered if that was why she'd been able to resist Aphrodite—for the same reason she'd resisted Brenda.

Whatever that reason was.

More to the point, since they knew where she lived, was one or more of them waiting there in the apartment to ambush her?

Janey kept her apartment dark for a reason. She flickered from room to room, listening, watching, hidden deep in the shadows, the distance of each teleport so short the heat didn't register at all on the thermostat. She saw and heard nothing. No one hiding behind any doors. No boogeymen under the bed.

Janey went to her closet and grabbed every item of clothing on every hanger in one huge double-armful—shirts and hoodies and jeans and a heavy-duty winter coat—and stooped to snag a pair of high-top sneakers. She turned from the closet...

...and froze.

Was that a footstep?

The sound, if there had been a sound, seemed to have come from the living room. Janey didn't move. Didn't even breathe, the air locked in her lungs, waiting to hear the sound again.

Janey stared through the black mesh of the helmet's eyepieces, wishing she could see through walls, and on top of the fear and tension, she realized how ridiculous she must look, standing there in the gray spider-themed body armor, holding an entire clearance rack's worth of clothes. She wondered how quietly she could set down the bulk of her wardrobe—quietly enough not to alert anyone?—and considered which corner to flicker to, to get the best view of the living room, the best angle of attack.

If someone had just appeared in her living room without opening the front door, which she *would* have heard, it could only be Roth. But was he alone? Janey circled a dark, unwelcome thought. If she could take him by surprise, which she had before, barely, what would the best way be to take him out? She'd need to do it fast and silent. Give him no time to react. With Roth gone, it would cripple Aphrodite's ability to move around.

Standing there, motionless as a sculpture of gray and black marble, a wave of nausea rolled through Janey's stomach and up into her throat. When had she started thinking about "taking people out" like this? She hadn't even hesitated, back in the Basement. She'd made it such a point not to kill, such an integral part of the Gray Widow, that she didn't even own any firearms. To date, the only person she'd ever actually killed was Simon Grove.

The image of Aphrodite Lupo, her skin alive with thorns and her eyes gray and hollow, swam in front of Janey like the remnant of a nightmare. Tim and Sha'dae and Nathan were alone, in the middle of nowhere, and Janey was a *protector*, damn it. Not an assassin. Not a murderer. Maybe she could surprise Julian Roth and shove the katana through his skull.

But not if she didn't have to.

Without checking to see whether or not anyone actually stood there in her living room, Janey clutched her clothes to her chest and flickered out.

The sky had begun to gray along the horizon when Janey left Atlanta, but as she traveled west it grew dark again, for which she said a quick prayer of thanks. She wondered if anyone along the freeways she followed spotted her, and what she must have looked like—a semi-translucent, smoky specter, a closetful of clothes clutched awkwardly in her arms—but the hour was punishingly early enough, and the stretches she traveled sparse enough, she was pretty sure her journey went unseen. Janey traveled northwest, up through Nashville and St. Louis, then due west toward Kansas City. Halfway there she stopped on the outskirts to pant and catch her breath, leaning against the rusted hulk of an abandoned car thirty yards off the freeway.

Janey lifted her head and gazed up at the unbroken vault of stars above her. No one in Atlanta ever got a view like this. Janey hadn't spent much time outside cities, and Georgia was densely populated enough, with enough cloud cover, that even in the rural countryside views like this basically didn't exist. But here, deep in the vastness of the Midwest farmland, between her and the million billion stars overhead there was...nothing. No light pollution, no clouds. Just darkness. Janey's breathing calmed and slowed. She felt tiny. Insignificant.

I wonder if one of those stars is the one Anna Grove told us about.

The thought led her down a familiar mental path.

I wonder if using a weird superhuman ability that I don't understand might have unintended consequences.

I wonder if I'm going to turn up with some bizarre, never-seen-before kind of cancer. And the doctor will say, "Well, if you hadn't been teleporting fifty times a day for the last five years, you might be in better shape."

It was a conversation she'd had with herself more than once. Janey straightened up and flickered back to the freeway, leaving a scorch mark on the wreck's rust-red surface.

She headed northwest again, up I-29 to Omaha, and veered west onto I-80, where she passed through Lincoln. From there, getting back to Tim and Sha'dae and Nathan was a matter of spotting the right "Exit" sign. The engineers responsible for the construction of

Interstate 80 had apparently been unconcerned with taking the highway through any actual townships, and seemed content to follow the course of the Platte River instead. Janey passed signs pointing north or south to places such as Giltner, and Wood River, and Odessa, before spotting the one she needed: Lexington. She swung north on Route 283 and soon arrived at the Barlow Motor Court, a tiny motel across from a Subway on Lincoln Highway. Two quick jumps took her around to the rear of the building, where she peered through a high window into the bathroom of Unit 7.

One more flicker and Janey stepped out into the motel room proper. Tim paced back and forth in front of the curtained window, Sha'dae perched on a straight-backed wooden chair next to a tiny circular table, and Nathan sat on one of the two queen beds, staring at Tim's phone. Janey said, "I'm back," and dumped all her clothes on the other bed.

She'd expected some startled exclamations, or at least a word of greeting. Instead, Nathan didn't even look up from the phone. Tim turned and stared at her, but said nothing. Sha'dae sprang up from the chair and, as Janey pulled off the helmet, crossed the room and took her hand. "Could I talk to you? In private? For a minute?"

Tim peered out between the curtains, still wordless. Janey nodded, grabbed up a pair of jeans and a T-shirt, and let Sha'dae lead her into the bathroom.

Sha'dae shut the door and leaned against the counter as Janey wriggled out of the Vylar suit. "What's going on? Mutiny so soon?"

Sha'dae managed a grim smile. "We'd have to be some kind of crew to have a mutiny. Right now we're just three people who are, pardon my language, scared shitless."

Janey tugged on the jeans. Before slipping into the T-shirt she surveyed the damage in the mirror: bruises ran across her arms and torso, and Aphrodite Lupo had blackened her left eye. She pulled the T-shirt on and faced Sha'dae. "You're not acting scared shitless."

Sha'dae's eyebrows quirked. "Yeah, well, that's part of what's scaring me. I, uh, I think you'd better address the group."

"And try to explain what the hell is happening?"

Sha'dae nodded.

Janey sighed. "I'll give it my level best."

When she opened the door, Tim was standing there, and as Sha'dae got out of the way, Tim wrapped Janey up in his arms and held her. He didn't try to kiss her. Janey got the impression it was more to convince him that she was actually there, and whole, and real. After half a minute he pulled back. "Are you all right?" His fingertips skimmed along her cheekbone, hovered near the black-and-purple bruising.

"I'm fine. I've been through a lot worse." She raised her hand, her turn to touch him, gently probing his temple and orbital ridge. "Not as bad as you, though."

Tim recoiled, and Janey instantly regretted her choice of words. Janey said, "Sorry, I'm sorry, I didn't mean—" but Tim shook his head.

"No, no, it's okay. I guess some of the endorphins have worn off, is all. Reality starting to set in. For all of us, I think. Well, reality or whatever this is, anyway."

Sha'dae cleared her throat, and said, "Maybe we could gather over here?"

Nathan hadn't moved from the bed, where his back was against the headboard, his feet tucked underneath him. Sha'dae went back to the chair she'd been sitting in, but moved it over next to the bed, and Janey noticed with a tiny bit of relief that Nathan gave Sha'dae a brief smile. Tim leaned against the edge of the small, round table next to the air conditioner mounted under the room's front window. Janey didn't know whether she should sit or stand or what, and decided to stand, but immediately grew self-conscious and shoved her hands in her pockets. She absently kicked the floor with the toes of one bare foot.

"I don't know where to start, guys. I've never been in this position before. The things that happened tonight have never happened to me before. I guess...do any of you have any questions?"

She looked from Tim to Sha'dae to Nathan and back. After the longest fifteen seconds of Janey's life, Nathan raised his hand. "Nathan, that's not necessary. Just speak up."

Nathan's voice struck Janey hard. The few times she had heard him speak, he'd been full of energy, full of the kind of enthusiasm that only truly lives in the very young. Now his words came out strained, with a trace of quiver. He sounded...damaged, which Janey found ironic, considering what she'd seen happen to him. Janey squeezed her eyes shut, an internal wince for such a cynical thought.

"I got shot tonight," Nathan said. "Again. Except this time it bounced off of me. And it hit your boyfriend." He pointed at Tim. "It hit your boyfriend and *blew a hole in his head*. Except he's standing there now like nothing happened." Nathan rubbed both his eyes. "Before...before Aphrodite and, and those other guys showed up, you took us up to the roof. Because you're the Gray Widow. And you've got. Y'know. Abilities and shit. But now..." He rubbed his eyes again, and Janey realized he was trying to halt the flow of tears. "It happened to us, didn't it? Me, and Tim, and..." He glanced at Sha'dae, his words faltering, and she put a comforting hand on his. "And Sha'dae. All of us. What happened? What was that?"

Janey couldn't take towering over everyone. She sat down on the other bed and crossed her legs. It made it easier to slump forward with her face in her hands. "Okay. Okay. Let me try to start at the beginning." She looked up at Tim. He gave her a nod of encouragement. "Tim already knows a lot of this. I...had some trouble...as a child. That's not really germane to this discussion. But when I was nineteen, one night, something happened to me. I couldn't explain it then, and I can't really explain it now, either, but I was in my room, and I decided I wanted to be outside, and—bang. There I was. Out on the lawn, in my pajamas."

Sha'dae said, "You teleported. For the first time."

Janey nodded. "In my head I call it 'flickering.' I can only do it in darkness. Bright light, direct light, shuts it off."

Nathan frowned. "You've been the Gray Widow since you were nineteen?"

Janey drew a long, slow breath. "No. No, I decided to do something...I...I was married. And my husband got hurt. Hurt really bad. He's still alive, but...he suffered catastrophic brain damage."

Sha'dae said, "Oh, honey—" but stopped herself with a glance at Tim.

"I decided, if I couldn't fix what happened to Adam—my husband —I'd set things right for as many other people as I could. So I spent some years learning how to fight, and I got my hands on a suit of body armor, since I didn't want to get shot or stabbed. And I started sticking my nose in a lot of other people's business."

Nathan had put Tim's phone down, but now he just stared at the bedsheets. "So what happened? What made you like this?"

She heard the further question in his voice: *What made us like this?*

"No idea. I only know a little bit more about it, really. One: there are other people out there who've been 'Augmented.' Not my word. You've, uh, encountered some of them. Two: one of the other Augments, someone I trust, said that there might be some connection to an object that NASA spotted in orbit."

Sha'dae said, "What, you mean a satellite? Did the government do this?"

Janey shrugged. "No way to know. They couldn't tell what the object was. Just that it might have emitted some kind of signal at some point. Three: Tim and I talked to the mother of one of the other Augments. She had a little bit of the same kind of ability he did. But here's the thing...my father could teleport small objects. So we're thinking maybe some Augments are, uh, 'second generation,' for lack of a better term."

All three of them eyeballed her. Waiting for her to continue. She opened her mouth, but hesitated. She didn't know if she should tell them all at once, or pull Tim aside and tell him separately first, though she leaned toward the first option. Especially since they didn't know when Aphrodite might find them again.

Tim's brow furrowed. "Janey. You've got something else to say?"

Janey ran her hand over the short, springy curls on top of her head. "About six months ago, Tim and I ran into an Augment named Simon Grove. It was his mother we went and talked to. Simon...I think he might have been meant to be a shapeshifter. But it must have gone wrong somewhere along the way. His hands, his fingers, he could *lengthen* them, turn them into these tendrils, like whips. And his jaw, his teeth, got kind of...predatory. Teeth like needles."

Sha'dae sucked in a short, hissing breath.

"I never told anyone this. Not even you, Tim, I'm sorry. I had to kill Simon Grove, he would have killed me if I hadn't. He *tried* to kill me. Really damn hard. But in the process, when he was hurt bad, his body got even weirder. He got these, these things like *thorns* all over him, little sharp, hooked thorns, and his eyes... Aphrodite Lupo's eyes are freaky enough, but Simon's turned white, and they glowed, and they looked *hollow*."

Nathan had taken the bedspread in both hands, crumpling it in his fists. "Okay. So he got weird. Why're you telling us about a dead guy?"

"Because I went back to the Basement. Just now, I mean, I was there right before I went back to my place to get clothes. The place with the candles and the paintings. I called it the Basement."

"The place where those people tried to kill us," Sha'dae said softly.

"Yeah. When I—when I flicker, it leaves heat behind. And the farther I go, the hotter it gets."

Tim had had his arms folded. He dropped them to his side and pushed away from the table. "Janey—the Basement—all your paintings?"

Nathan still looked confused. "What? What're you saying?"

Tim said, "Nathan, Janey took us from Atlanta to wherever-the-hell-we-are, Nebraska. In one teleport. Janey—what happened?"

Janey tried for a resigned smile. She wasn't sure she pulled it off. "The whole place is gone. It's literally a crater."

"Okay," Sha'dae said, "so what happened to Crazy Buff Chick and Redneck and Shadow Guy? Are they..." She circled the words. "Did you *kill* them?"

Janey hung her head. "I tried to. But I don't think I did. I *know* I didn't kill Aphrodite, and she said Roth and Davis got away, too." She raised her head again, and locked eyes with Tim. "She was there. When I went back. She was there, she'd survived the explosion, but her body had changed." Janey swallowed hard. "She had the thorns all over her. And the hollow eyes. Just like Simon."

Janey could see the wheels turning in Tim's head. He was smart, and he'd been through a lot of what she had, and he'd just survived a shattered spine and a lethal bullet wound. Not just survived—healed completely. Janey watched as Tim traveled down the same thought paths she had herself. Watched his beautiful, chiseled face and his mesmerizing, ink-black eyes as the realization set in.

Tim said, "I need a minute," and before Janey could say anything in response, he had flung open the door and stalked out of the room. Away from them.

Away from her.

Janey slid down off the bed to sit on the floor, her back to the flimsy mattress. She crossed her arms over the tops of her knees and pressed her forehead against them. She didn't look up as she felt Sha'dae come and sit down beside her.

"Do you know why he stormed off like that?"

Janey was pretty sure she did know, yes. What she didn't know was whether or not to voice her concerns to Sha'dae and Nathan—her possibly unfounded concerns. Why cause them more trauma if she didn't have to?

Janey peered over her forearms at Nathan. "Hey. Nate. I realize the circumstances may not lead to a rational answer, but...how are you? How're you doing with all this?"

Janey didn't know what to expect. Nathan was still a kid, worse yet, a *boy*, and Janey figured he was likely as not to scream at her and tell her to go fuck herself as he was to shut down completely. Or maybe just answer with a grunt. She felt a rush of relief when he started talking in a normal tone of voice.

"This is all my cousin Rory's fault," Nathan said, leaning his head back against the wall above the bed. The shifting of his weight made the mattress and box springs creak, and Janey noticed for the first time how far down the mattress sagged with his weight.

Sha'dae said, "Your cousin? How so?"

"He's like five years older than me. And last year he was telling me about when he was a sophomore in college, and this thirty-three-year-old nurse named Sheila saw him on campus and picked him up.

Said she 'liked 'em young.' They went back to her place and, uh..."
Nathan's cheeks turned pink. "She sort of. Y'know. Educated him."

Janey had zero responses for that, but Sha'dae let out a small,
snorting kind of laugh. "So you're saying you thought Aphrodite was
going to give you the same kind of education? Before you realized she
was—"

"A gross shape-shifting freakshow, yeah." Nathan's face clenched
like a fist. "Before I found out she was using me to get to you, Janey.
I'm sorry. I'm really, really fucking sorry." The pink in his cheeks
turned darker, and spread down into his neck. "God, how could I have
been that stupid?" He punched the bed, and the frame squealed and
shifted half an inch to the left. "I almost got you guys killed! *Fuck!*" He
slapped both hands over his face.

Janey caught Sha'dae's eye, and tried to convey "I have no idea
what to do here" in a wordless look. Sha'dae seemed to understand.
She gestured with her chin toward the parking lot, which Janey took
to mean, "You should probably go talk to Tim." While Janey got to her
feet and headed for the door, Sha'dae lightly patted Nathan's knee.
"Nathan. It's okay. I don't think anybody can blame you for not seeing
this coming."

Nathan groaned as Janey slipped outside.

A piercing wind blew through the parking lot, and almost took the
door out of Janey's hand. She realized how much she'd come to
depend on the Vylar suit to protect her from cold winter nights, and
considered going back inside for her coat, or at least a hoodie, but she
spotted Tim at the far side of the parking lot and decided not to
bother. She wondered idly what it said about her life that she spent
more time at night wearing body armor than not.

Janey hurried across the small, cramped lot, past battered sedans
and pickups, and came to a stop at Tim's side. She didn't touch him.
Tim stood there, unmoving, staring out across the pancake-flat landscape. After a minute, maybe a minute and a half, and still without
turning his head to look at her, Tim took Janey's hand. Her heart
thumped in her chest.

"I've pretty much always felt like an outsider, to one degree or another," Tim said. "I mean, there was the whole 'son of immigrants' thing to begin with. Then 9/11 happened, and everybody with brown skin got a target slapped on their backs. Didn't matter that I sounded exactly like they did, watched all the same TV shows, listened to the same music. I even went to their churches. But that feeling has stayed with me, right up to tonight. You know the kind of looks we got from the desk clerk here, while you went back to Atlanta? A skinny white boy, a girl in a hijab, and me, renting a shitty motel room in Lexington, Nebraska?"

Janey slipped her arm around his waist. "I'm a mixed girl who grew up traveling around the Southeast. I know a thing or two about side-eye."

Tim turned and pulled her more tightly against him. Janey's heart thumped harder and louder, and Tim slid his hand up her back, grazed his nails along her neck, cupped the back of her head as he kissed her. Heat flooded her, and she forgot the cold as she melted into him. Her hands gripped and kneaded his ass as their tongues swirled against each other.

Janey broke the kiss, breathing hard. "I know we could find a better place...but this parking lot's pretty deserted..."

Tim laughed. It sounded sorrowful. "Janey. I promise you. I want you in my bed more than anything else I've ever wanted in my life. Tonight's the first night in six months that I haven't been in constant pain, and I want to take full advantage of it, multiple times. But..."

Janey bit her lower lip. "*But...*"

"I think you know what I'm about to say."

Her hands had moved up to Tim's lower back, and she glided them forward, along his forearms to his hands. Stepped back just enough to look him in the eye. "I know. I know. I didn't tell you about Simon...*changing* before, because I didn't think it had anything to do with anything. But if Aphrodite did it, too..."

Tim lowered his gaze to the ground between them. "What if that's something that happens to everyone who's been Augmented?"

There it was. The thought that had taken up so much space in her mind, brought out and laid bare.

"There's no reason to think it is. I've never changed that way. Not at all. Mr. Vessler never said anything about it, and he's dealt with a lot more people like—um…"

"You can say it. 'People like us.' I'm like you now, right? We all are. For good or ill."

Janey tried for a smile, but it came out bitter. She shivered, gooseflesh rising along her arms, and with a downward glance realized her nipples were visible even through her heavy-duty sports bra. Wondering how silly it was to be embarrassed about that when, moments earlier, she had basically suggested that she and Tim could fuck in the back of some stranger's pickup, Janey embraced him again, hiding her breasts against his chest. Tim wrapped his arms around her. His fingertips lightly massaged along her spine as if by instinct.

Tim sighed. "Part of me wants to kick myself."

"Why?"

"Because I'm *healed*. All the damage Simon Grove did to me…the damage I thought was permanent. The damage the *doctors* thought was permanent. It's just gone. I mean, hyperbole aside, I have never felt better in my life." His stomach growled. "Okay, I'm really freaking hungry, but aside from that, I've never felt better."

"You do look pretty good for somebody who's been shot through the head."

He laughed. Not strained this time, and not for very long, but it sounded genuine. "I know, right?" His lips moved to her ear. His voice dropped to just above a whisper. "I never thought I could be with you. I thought I was too…y'know. Damaged. And now I'm not."

Janey nuzzled against his neck. "So you're wondering why it feels like everything in the world just got a lot worse?"

"Is that stupid of me?"

Janey's hands drifted down to Tim's butt again. It really was an amazing butt. "It'd be stupid *not* to be worried. Whatever's happening to us—and however Aphrodite Lupo's involved—I don't even have the words to describe it. I'll tell you one thing, though." She nibbled on his ear lobe, which prompted a low, quiet groan. "I'm tired of feeling powerless."

Janey couldn't see his face, but she heard the grin in his voice. "Oh yeah? Feel like you want to take control of something?"

"There are other rooms in this motel. The Vacancy sign's still lit." She moved one hand around and pressed it against his groin. Her fingertips traced his outline, and she grinned as he grew harder at the touch. "And I'm pretty sure you're happy to see me."

Janey didn't resist when Tim turned her to face away from him. The iron-hard length of him pressed against her ass, and she ground into him as his lips and tongue found her neck. She lifted an arm and reached back, her fingers twining through the thick curls of his hair, and it was her turn to groan as he cupped and caressed her breasts, tweaked her still-hard nipples, and his right hand moved down, across the ridged plane of her stomach, pushed inside the waist of her jeans and

JANEY!

"Gaah!" Janey staggered away from him.

Tim came after her. "What, what, what's wrong, did I hurt you?"

She bent double, hands clamped to her temples. "No, no, it's—"

The motel room door sprang open, and Sha'dae came pelting across the parking lot. "Janey! Tim! It's Nathan!"

Sha'dae reached them, and Janey managed to straighten back up, her whole brain ringing like a bell. "Sha'dae...listen...we have *got* to work on some control for whatever this is you can do."

Sha'dae blinked. "Huh?"

Tim said, "What about Nathan? What's the problem?"

Sha'dae pointed frantically back at the room. "He's gone, that's what's the problem! He said he had to use the bathroom, but I waited and waited, and I finally knocked and went in, and the window's open! He took off!"

Janey let out a very different kind of groan. "Shit. Great. I'm going to go find him, okay? You two head back to the room and wait there. And neither of you go anywhere, all right?"

Sha'dae nodded mutely and started back across the parking lot. Janey let her get a couple of steps ahead, and leaned over to whisper in Tim's ear. "Rain check?"

He squeezed her hand and whispered back, "Rain check. Go bring back the prodigal." In his normal volume, he added, "But if you need us, either one of us, you come get us. Deal?"

"Deal."

Janey's phone rang. Tim and Sha'dae paused as she hauled the phone out of her jeans pocket. "It's Vessler."

Tim said, "Want me to take it?"

Janey shook her head and answered. "Hey. I've got kind of a situation right now, can I call you back?"

Vessler's gravel-thick voice rumbled over the connection. "Handle your situation and get back to me ASAP. I have information."

"Will do." Janey ended the call, gave Tim a quick kiss and Sha'dae the kind of grin that meant *Wish me luck*, and darted into the shadows at the end of the building.

Janey began flickering from shadow to shadow, spreading out in a cone from the back of the motel. It didn't take her long to spot a series of widely-spaced, freakishly deep footprints, leading south across some train tracks.

As she followed the prints, which looked more like something that should have been made by a four-hundred-pound giant than by a stick-skinny seventeen-year-old, Janey wondered about the wisdom of going after him like this. *What if he's just hanging out with some other kids? I'd make things ten times worse, blundering in like some over-protective parent. Haven't I learned from dealing with Tim why that's a bad idea?* She knew she had no choice, though. As newly-powerful as Nathan was, and as angry as he'd been when she last saw him, leaving him alone in the wild could lead to nothing good.

Janey followed the tracks about half a mile, first due south and then southwest, and found Nathan at the outer edge of what appeared to be a sprawling mobile home park. Nathan and three men stood near a barrel fire, not far from a battered old Jeep blasting country music from the stereo.

Janey figured the time to be somewhere around 3:30, maybe 4:00 a.m. The three men surrounding Nathan, if Janey had had to guess, had probably been drinking since 8:00 or 9:00 the night before. Two of them wavered on their feet, but the third—*Of course it's the biggest one*—looked rock-solid. He also looked like the kind of man in whom alcohol brought out the most vicious streak possible.

"You get your ass outta here," the big man said to Nathan. Janey caught a glimpse of a broken beer bottle in his fist. "Get back to wherever you come from. Or I'll fuck you up good."

Nathan Pittman, the sweet-natured, sunny-dispositioned kid, said, "You can *try*, you corn-shucking redneck sister-fucker. Why don't you give it your best shot, and we'll see what happens?"

Someone had been stoking the barrel-fire all night, because it threw off more light than a streetlamp. The shadows thrown by the men, and by Nathan, were deep enough to flicker into, but narrow and unpredictable enough that Janey didn't want to try hitting that kind of moving target. She got as close to the group as she could and simply walked out into the light. "Nathan. It's time to go."

Nathan turned his back on the drunk. "I'm not going anywhere. Not until I pound on this asshole for a while." He winced. "That didn't come out right. But I'm still not going anywhere!"

The drunk took a step forward, while the other two men just stood in place, wide-eyed, staring at the woman who'd just appeared out of the shadows. Janey turned her head and sized up the dangerous one. He was big, six-five, maybe six-six, with straw-blond hair, thick arms, and a massive beer gut. He slurred his words as he pointed a finger at Janey. "You. The fuck're you? An' what the fuck you doin' here?"

"Not taking up any more of your time," Janey said, and put a hand on Nathan's shoulder, but he batted it away. Janey hissed. Nathan hadn't put much force behind it, but it felt like getting struck with an aluminum baseball bat. She leaned close to him. "Nathan, if you get into a fight with this guy, you'll kill him."

Tears glowed red-orange in the light from the fire pit as they welled up in Nathan's eyes. "It's my fault." His words quavered. "It's my fault she knew where to find you. Knew who you were."

"The fuck you mean, he'll end up killing me?" The drunk lumbered forward, looming over Janey and Nathan. "Little shit couldn't kill fuck-all. You wanna see what'll do the killin'? I keep this special. Fer 'mergencies." He reached behind him and pulled a snub-nosed revolver out of his waistband. Janey stepped forward and took it away from him before he could even lift it, and as he said, "Hey, that's mine," she emptied the rounds onto the dirt at her feet.

In the distance, a single siren rang out. Getting closer. One of the other drunks said, "Shit, somebody done called the fuzz."

Janey focused on Nathan again. "Look, I know you're hurting. But it's not your fault. And we can talk about it, but not here and not now. It's time to go."

Nathan swiped at his nose with his sleeve and nodded. He reached out for the empty handgun. "Okay. Let me see that for a second?"

"Why?"

Nathan pouted. "I'm not gonna pistol-whip him. Just let me see it."

The drunk wavered on his feet, and repeated, "Hey! That's mine!"

Nathan took the pistol, put most of it in his mouth, and bit it in half.

As Janey stifled surprised laughter, Nathan spat out the barrel and part of the cylinder and handed the rest of the mangled weapon back to the drunk. "There you go." To Janey, he said, "Okay. I guess we should leave?"

"You wait just a minute, you little shit!" the big drunk bellowed. "I paid good money fer that piece! And I'm'a take it out o' yer hide!" He balled up a huge fist and swung it at Nathan's head, but Nathan put up a hand and caught the fist as if it carried no more force than a viciously thrown wad of paper. Nathan closed his hand around the fist, and as the big drunk howled in pain, Nathan let his lips peel back into a snarl.

"Come with me, fat boy."

Janey stepped forward. "Nathan, let him go! You'll break his hand!"

Nathan shook his head. "Nah. I'm just gonna make a point." Nathan pulled the big man over to the Jeep. "This rustbucket belong to you?"

The drunk nodded between pained grunts.

Nathan said, "Be more polite to people," and drew back a foot and kicked the Jeep just below the driver's side door. The entire frame buckled, and the stereo died with a whimper. Janey's jaw dropped open. The Jeep looked as if it had been T-boned by an SUV. Nathan let go of the man's hand and stomped back over to Janey. "Okay. We can go now."

Before they flickered back to the motel, Janey heard one of the other men say, "Well, ain't nobody gonna believe this."

Five minutes later, back at the hotel, Janey and Nathan stepped out of the bathroom and into a pair of half-accusing, half-concerned glares from Tim and Sha'dae. Nathan ducked his head. "Sorry. I shouldn't have run off like that. Sorry. Sorry." He sank down into one a wooden chair, which creaked alarmingly under his weight.

Sha'dae gave him a patient smile. "I'd say freaking out is acceptable under these circumstances. Or at least understandable. You had your suspicions confirmed, your heart broken, and your DNA messed with, all in the space of one night."

Nathan looked up at her. "My DNA messed with?"

Sha'dae made vague, sweeping gesture. "I'm guessing. But something affected us all, didn't it? We gained something...or were changed. Somehow..." She flicked a glance at Janey. "And we have no way of knowing exactly what happened, do we?"

Tim came over to stand beside Janey. She leaned against him, and put her head on his shoulder. He took her hand and kissed it, and to Nathan, said, "I'm glad you came back."

Nathan attempted a smile, and mostly succeeded. "I, uh, I'm sorry, guys. I don't know what to do. How to handle this. I just sort of...I guess I wanted to pick a fight?"

Janey couldn't help but chuckle. "You picked a hell of a fight with that Jeep."

Tim said, "Jeep?" and Janey's eyes went wide. She smacked herself on the forehead.

"Vessler! I forgot he called!" She let go of Tim's hand and hauled out her phone.

Sha'dae said, "Who's 'Vessler'?"

Janey punched in a number. "He's an Augment. The one I mentioned before, like, uh—like us. Plus, he's the guy who's had some answers for me in the past, and he said he had some information." The line only rang once before Garrison Vessler answered. Janey said, "Hey. It's me. This line is still encrypted, right?" She paused. "Well, I'm here with three brand-new Augments. ...No, I'm serious. Let me put you on speaker."

Janey hit a button and held the phone out, and Sha'dae and Nathan moved closer. Garrison Vessler said, "To whom am I speaking?"

Janey answered him. "You know two of them already. Nathan Pittman and Tim Kapoor. The third is my friend Sha'dae Wilkerson."

"Nathan Pittman—the boy who got shot trying to imitate you?"

Ruefully, Nathan said, "That'd be me."

"So what kind of Augmentations are we looking at?"

Janey said, "Near as I can tell, and I'm guessing here, because it just happened last night, Nathan's like Ned Fields. Except stronger, I think. Tim seems to be able to heal...well, so far, pretty much any injury he gets. And Sha'dae has some kind of telepathic thing going. She hasn't figured it all out yet."

"Sorry," Sha'dae said to no one in particular.

Vessler's voice grew sharper. "This happened last night? What time last night?"

Tim spoke up. "About eleven forty-five."

"Fucking hell. Pardon my French." The sound of shuffling papers came over the phone. "Janey, you remember I said we were tracking an object in low orbit? Well, it released another pulse of energy last night. So far off the known spectrum it was barely even detectable, much less identifiable. You can guess where this happened."

Janey's eyelids slid shut. "Directly over midtown Atlanta?"

"Correct in one."

She took a deep breath. "Where is this object now?"

"That's the thing," Vessler said. "Its orbit finally decayed. That pulse—whatever it hit you all with—that was its last gasp, so to speak. It hit the ground in North Carolina. The Army has it now."

Janey's eyes settled on Tim's. "Where? Where'd they take it?"

Vessler hesitated. "Janey, it's in a secure military facility. It's gone. I just wanted to compare notes and see if you'd witnessed anything to do with it. Whatever that thing is, it's beyond our reach."

In that instant, hearing those words, Janey Sinclair achieved a moment of clarity.

As soon as Aphrodite Lupo entered her life, Janey lost control of... well. She took stock, and had to admit: everything. She'd done nothing but react, and run, and suffer loss. Only by the grace of forces none of them understood had she not lost Tim, since he would have been dead twice over if not for his unexpected Augmentation. Her apartment wasn't safe, the Basement was gone, and now she and the few friends she had sat huddled in a hole, hiding in fear. And Janey had had enough of it.

"I hate to contradict you, Mr. Vessler, but...it's not beyond *my* reach."

Sha'dae's eyes widened. "Janey, what're you saying?"

Janey's jaw clenched and unclenched. "I'm saying there's an Augment out there who wants us dead, and so far, I haven't come up with a way to stop her. I've cut her, broken her bones, and put her in the heart of an explosion that melted concrete, and nothing's worked. None of us has any idea what's been done to us or who's behind it. And right now, as I see it, the only way we're going to survive is if we get some actual answers to those questions. So. I'm going to go to this 'secure military facility,' figure out what it was that fell out of the sky, and try my damnedest to figure out what's happening to us. To all of us."

Tim and Sha'dae and Nathan all started chattering at once, but Janey silenced them with a decisive gesture. From the phone, Garrison Vessler said, "Janey, you're talking about getting into a place that's crawling with armed, well-trained soldiers and intelligence operatives. Dozens of them. Maybe hundreds at this point."

Janey narrowed her blue-gray eyes, and her voice came out like frost-covered metal. "Meaning no disrespect, sir. But the lights go out everywhere, sooner or later. Now. Please. Tell me where this place is."

Vessler sighed. "Fine. Grab something to write with."

15

At 9:30 the following morning, while a white-yellow sun glared down through a wide, cloudless Nebraska sky, Janey sat on the floor of the motel room's bathroom and meditated. Or at least, she thought of it as meditating. It was more like memorizing. The process took much less time in such a confined space than it had in the Basement.

Tears welled in her eyes and spilled down her cheeks. She wiped them away and tried to ignore them, but she couldn't stop them. They came in waves. Punches to her heart, like the pulsing pain of an earache, random enough and sharp enough to make her breath catch in her throat with each impact.

On the other side of the door, Tim and Sha'dae and Nathan all slept. Not well, probably, not after the events of last night, but sheer exhaustion had overcome the mind-wrenching truth that Janey herself had faced years before: in one way or another, they were no longer technically human. She knew facing that, truly acknowledging it, would take time.

Janey had stuffed an unused blanket into the small window, so that the pure morning sunlight barely reached the bathroom, coming in only as faint bright lines glowing around the edges of the frame. It rendered the room dark enough for her to use her night vision. Every corner and contour of the tile floor, the chipped bathtub, the too-small pedestal sink, all of it stood out to her in vibrant shades of green and gold and softly shining gray. She took in the scents, the sounds. Ran her fingertips across the grouted joints between the floor tiles. Faint traces of a bleach-based cleaner reached her nostrils, along with the slightly stronger smell of mildew from behind the toilet. A lingering curl of perfume, somewhere near the mirror with the crack in the lower right corner—the scent a tiny signature, left by a former guest. Janey concentrated on it. The perfume smelled expensive. She wondered what someone who could afford a fragrance like that would have been doing in a motel this cheap.

Janey drank in the sensory input. She opened her mouth and drew in great breaths, letting the totality of the room settle in.

Another wave of pain crashed into her. She stifled a sob, just as a quiet, polite knock sounded at the door to her right. Janey blotted her cheeks on her sleeve, reached up and turned the knob, and the dim light flooding in when the door opened was enough to send her night vision skittering away in shreds.

Tim stood there, half of his face visible in the crack between the door and doorframe. "You all right?"

Janey pushed the door open wider and motioned for him to come in. He did, leaning against the sink, and she closed it again. Her night vision started back up, allowing her to see Tim as clearly as if he had flicked on the overhead light. The difference in him still startled her—after six months of recovery, six months of watching him go from bed rest to a wheelchair to the ever-present set of crutches, now to seeing him stand there, casual, arms folded, head cocked to one side. It felt like a miracle.

"If you don't mind me asking...is there a reason you're sitting in here in the dark?"

Janey patted the floor next to her. Tim put his back to the door and sank down to sit beside her, and Janey moved close enough to him to rest her head on his shoulder. "I had a...a bond with the Basement."

Tim nodded. "When you reach into a shadow. That's where you were reaching to, right?"

"I can do it with my apartment, too, but…it's not safe to go back there now."

Tim took a moment. "So, it's places you're familiar with?"

Janey took his hand. Laced her fingers through his. "*Intimately* familiar with. Places I know like the proverbial back of my hand."

He traced a line across her scarred knuckles. "Is that what you're doing in here? Becoming intimately familiar?"

"I can't use this place the way I did the Basement. To store things, I mean—it's too small, not to mention too temporary. But if I needed to get out of a situation…the flickering, the…it still sounds weird to say the word 'teleportation' out loud. It works by line of sight. Except with places I know really, really well."

"So if somebody shoved a bag over your head, or blindfolded you?"

"Right. I could always flicker back to the Basement. Or the apartment. If it was dark enough, I mean." She gestured around them. "Now I'm getting to know this place. In case I need to make a quick escape tonight."

Tim raised her hand to his lips and kissed her knuckles, then her palm, then each fingertip. "Are you sure I can't talk you out of this?"

Janey sighed. "I don't have a death wish. I don't *want* to make myself a target for however many armed Marines. But the simple fact of the matter is that we don't know what we're dealing with. With Aphrodite, I mean. She's a little like Simon, but she tried to use the same kind of mental whammy on me that Brenda Jorden did. Well, not the way Jorden did, but it would've had a similar effect, I think. Anyway, try as I might, I can't put her down. I can't even hurt her. She's worse than a damn Terminator. If we don't figure out what's behind all this, Aphrodite and Davis and Roth are going to find us. I know it. And no, I don't want to die, but I have to do this. Because if anything happened to Nathan, or Sha'dae, or…or you…"

Tim put a finger to Janey's chin and turned her face to his and kissed her lips. She leaned into it—and another burst of agony exploded in her chest. She pulled away, and this time couldn't stop the sob that escaped her as more tears flowed.

He shifted toward her, put his hands on her shoulders. "Hey, hey, what is it? What's wrong?" Janey collapsed against him, her cheek against his collarbone, and now that the first hitching sob had come out, she couldn't stop the rest of them. Tim held her, and stroked her hair, and said, "Baby, please, tell me, what's the matter?"

For a long moment Janey just held him, and loved the warmth of his body, the smell of his skin, the feel of his hands on her back. When she thought she could speak, in a tiny voice she said, "It's stupid."

Tim rested his chin against her curls. "Nothing you're feeling could be stupid." He lifted her face to look into her eyes. She almost pulled away, because she didn't want him to see her all swollen and puffy, but she realized it was too dark in the bathroom for him to get a good look at her. "Janey. If you don't want to talk to me about it, I'm not going to push you. I just want you to know that I *want* to know. I'm here to listen."

Janey let out a long exhalation. She unspooled a length of toilet paper and dabbed at her face. Blew her nose. "Sorry," she said, as she dropped the wad of paper in the plastic garbage can. "I know how sexy that sounded."

He ran a hand lightly down her arm. "About as sexy as a guy sitting on the floor of a motel bathroom, squinting in the dark." She could have heard the smile in his voice even if she hadn't been able to see him.

"It's...it's the Basement. And my paintings."

"Ah. Okay. Yeah...is it finally hitting you?"

Janey wanted to sob again. She fought the urge down, but put her face against his chest. Even in the dim light, she didn't want him to see her. "I spent y-years on them. And, and I know it had to be done...or at least, I *thought* it had to be done. I thought it would get rid of Aphrodite and the other two."

He stroked her hair some more. "You were trying to save our lives."

She nodded. "I didn't even think about it at the time. Well, I mean, I did, but...you know what I thought? 'I was never going to sell those anyway, I'll just paint more.' But now...now that it's sunk in? They were *part* of me. I spent days on each one. Sometimes more. Weeks. And no, I wasn't going to sell them, or even show them to anybody, but they meant something. To me. I did them all for me, for myself, they were...a kind of therapy, maybe." She slid a hand along the length of his thigh, and rested her palm on his knee. "Imagine if you'd spent two or three years writing a novel. You had only one copy, in your desk. And then your house catches fire, and to save the other people in the house, you have to let your novel burn."

Tim groaned. His head thumped softly against the door as he tilted it back. "Are you kidding? I'd have to move into my shrink's office."

"You have a shrink?"

"No, but if I lost the only copy of a novel I'd written, I'd have to get one. And maybe a hostage negotiator." He hugged her more tightly. "Janey, I am so sorry. I can sort of imagine what you're feeling, but that's all I can do. Imagine. And try to sympathize."

She sat up and stretched, arching her back. "It's pitiful. Letting it get to me like this."

"What? Why?"

"Because three Augments who want to kill us are still out there looking for us, and tonight I'm going to try to break into a place that might as well be Fort Knox, and you and Nathan and Sha'dae have some really fucking serious adjusting to do, and I'm sitting here crying about lost paintings."

Tim shook his head. "You can't beat yourself up. Not for that. We're in the middle of a shitstorm that, I'm willing to bet, no one has ever been in before. I say, if you've got some emotions? Don't keep them pent up." He leaned over and kissed her mouth. "That's my philosophy, anyway."

So gentle.

Their encounter the night before in the parking lot suddenly roared back to the forefront of Janey's mind, and she felt a flush of heat that started in her abdomen and rushed lower.

Maybe I don't want to be gentle now.

Janey considered how rough she could be with Tim, since he

seemed determined to heal from every single injury done to him, and had planted one hand on the floor, about to swing over and straddle him, when a plaintive knock rapped out.

"Are you guys in there?" came Sha'dae's voice. "I kind of sort of really have to pee really bad."

Janey let out a groaning sort of chuckle, and touched her forehead to Tim's, and allowed her night vision to fade as she clicked on the overhead light. "Just a second."

Zach Feygen loaded another 45-pound weight plate onto the barbell, extra-careful not to drop it. He couldn't stand the thought of the floor of his new garage getting cracked. He kept meaning to get some of the thick, interlocking rubber mats like he'd seen on the floors of gyms, but hadn't gotten around to it yet. Heavy muscles bulged under the smooth, dark brown skin of his arms and shoulders.

He had the garage door open. Heather would've been too cold, since it wasn't supposed to get above 50, but he liked the Atlanta spring weather just fine for working out.

Feygen sat down on the weight bench—he had another thirty seconds before his next set—and stared around at all the still-unopened moving boxes. He'd promised Heather he'd unpack at least some of them today, and he meant to, right after his workout. For the next thirty seconds, though, he planned to just sit and bask in the pride of homeownership.

Heather had been very clear on one thing. Well, she'd been clear on a lot of things, but the primary one for the last several months was this: "If you've got a choice between putting up money for a ring, or putting up money for a house? Buy me a damn house." Feygen chuckled. He hadn't exactly "bought her a house." He and Heather had pooled their resources and put together a pretty decent down-payment. So now he sat on a weight bench in the one-car garage of their small two-bedroom condo in North Druid Hills.

King and his castle.

The place didn't feel like a castle in his eyes. It felt like some kind of imperial palace. And so what if that hadn't left any money for a big-ass diamond engagement ring? Heather wore the cubic zirconia she'd picked out with just as much pride as she would have something from the Shane Company. And he figured they were every bit as engaged as if she had a two-carat princess cut.

Feygen ended his reverie, lay back on the bench, grabbed the barbell and did eight slow reps, count of five down to the chest, count of five back up. A shadow fell across him just as he set the barbell back on the rack, and he sat up and mopped his brow with a ragged hand towel for a moment before he spoke. "Help you with something?"

A tall, angular Caucasian woman with iron-gray hair and an iron-gray business suit stood there staring at him. Before she spoke, she held out an ID case. "Major Nicole Grassley. Army Intelligence."

Feygen's adrenal gland dumped what felt like a quart of adrenaline into his blood, but he kept his composure as he slowly stood up from the bench. He'd been wondering how long it would take for something like this to happen. "All right. Guess you already know who I am. What do you want, Major?"

She put her ID away. "I want to talk to you about the association you have with the vigilante commonly known as the Gray Widow."

Feygen cocked one eyebrow up. "What makes you think I'm associated with the Gray Widow?"

Grassley folded her arms. "I'll give you time to get dressed, Detective. You need to come with me."

At ten minutes to midnight that night, in full armor and with the dark pouch strapped to her back, Janey crouched on a high tree branch and peered down at her target. She would have gotten there faster if the place had been on any maps. For the fiftieth time she thanked Garrison Vessler for what directions he'd been able to provide. Janey pulled her phone out of the pouch and checked it, and to her complete lack of surprise saw the words "No Service" in the top left corner of the screen. She put the phone back—placing it carefully on the corner of the sink in the motel's bathroom—closed her eyes, and concentrated. Looked for the cool, smooth rush in her mind.

I'm here. About to try to get inside.

Janey listened. She got no reply. That didn't surprise her, either, since Sha'dae still had zero control over, or understanding of, her unique form of communication. Janey replayed the conversation she and Tim and Nathan and Sha'dae had had before she left, the highlight of which had been a full-throated objection from Nathan.

"Why wouldn't you take me with you? I'm freaking bulletproof! I'm like a skinny white Luke Cage!"

"Because if we got separated and you got captured, you wouldn't have a built-in escape route."

She'd countered the rest of their protestations the same way. Even if Sha'dae stayed out of sight and just served as a telepathically-connected lookout, she was vulnerable because she could be physically held. Janey couldn't. Tim already understood her reasoning, so the only thing he'd said was, "Just promise me you'll come back, all right? Can we agree on that?"

Janey left him with that promise, and whispered in his ear several other promises to keep when they had they chance. She held on to the lingering image of his half-embarrassed, half-lusty grin.

Now, crouched in the tree, Tim's huge, dark, sparkling eyes so fresh in her memory, an image of Adam appeared unbidden before her. Janey clenched her teeth.

I won't feel bad for pursuing my own happiness. I won't. I will not.

When that failed utterly to make her feel any better, she decided to concentrate on the scene spread out below.

Janey's target lay in a remote area of West Virginia, accessible on land only by way of a single, winding, one-lane road, or by air thanks to a small helicopter pad. The United States military, she presumed it was the Army, had sliced off the top of a mountain and installed a missile silo. Vessler had said the airspace above it was a no-fly zone, and the access road boasted a rusted "Road Closed" sign at its other end, so the only way anyone could know this place even existed was to be directed to it specifically.

A twelve-feet-high chain link fence topped with loops of razor wire surrounded an area roughly the size of a football field. Janey had spent a little better than two hours googling missile silo plans earlier that afternoon, and while there was of course no way to know what really lay beneath the surface, from the structures she could see, she thought it was probably a Titan II complex. Farthest from where she crouched, a broad, shallow, convex dome protruded a couple of feet from the ground. She figured that for the top of the silo itself. Closer, a blocky concrete platform sported a metal handrail beside a staircase that descended into the mountain: the main entrance. And right on the other side of the fence, about twenty yards from where she perched, an eight-foot-by-eight-foot square built of concrete and steel poked up above the rocky soil.

That's my target.

If this complex bore any resemblance at all to the ones she'd seen online, that metal-and-concrete housing was the top of a dual-purpose air vent and escape shaft. If she hadn't turned the Basement into a smoking, fire-rimmed crater, she could have reached back there and grabbed a pair of high-powered binoculars to get a better look at it. As it was, she had taken a number of steps to prepare for this excursion, but getting her hands on binoculars hadn't been one of them. Janey concentrated on the complex's lighting.

Something that looked for all the world like a regular streetlamp rose next to the entrance, flooding the scene with unpleasant yellow light. Long after the complex had been built, someone else had installed two more towering lights, one beside the silo proper and another halfway between the entrance and the top of the escape hatch. Those were much more modern, and banks of powerful LEDs threw off harsh, glaring white light, rendering the whole scene almost as bright as day.

Janey said a quiet prayer of thanks that the starkness of the light made the escape hatch throw an equally stark shadow on the ground.

She'd have to fling herself fully prone on the grass not to be seen, but it could be done.

If no one was looking right at the escape hatch at that moment.

If there weren't any cameras or motion-detectors she had missed.

If neither of the dogs smelled her.

Two armed patrols roamed the perimeter of the complex, one inside the fence, one outside—two Marines and one formidable-looking German Shepherd per patrol. Janey had no doubt that the dogs had been well and thoroughly trained to sniff out interlopers, and she qualified as an interloper in every respect.

"All right," she breathed. "Desperate times. Desperate measures."

Janey pivoted on the branch, let her night vision come up to full strength, and flickered away into the forest.

Several minutes later, Janey and a confused, one-hundred-twenty-pound white-tail buck materialized four feet off the ground, outside the fence, at the farthest point from the escape hatch. Janey dropped him and vanished back into the trees. The buck thudded solidly onto all four hooves and let out an eardrum-bursting bellow before crashing away through the woods.

Both dogs lost their minds.

The Marines on patrol kept hold of the leads, barely, and three more men in uniform came barreling up the stairwell at the entrance, but all of their attention was focused on the fleeing deer, and no one saw Janey flicker into the dense shadow on the far side of the escape hatch. She lifted her head just enough to get a good look at the top of the housing.

At one point, this structure actually had been an escape route, with a circular hatch affixed to the top on a heavy-duty hinge. Now, as far as Janey could tell, it served strictly as an air vent, and the round hatch and hinge had been replaced with a stainless-steel rain cover bolted into the concrete. Wire mesh stretched across the opening, effectively keeping out any woodland creatures who might have gotten curious about what lay below. Through the mesh, Janey could see metal rungs screwed to the side of the three-foot-wide shaft.

As the German Shepherds' barking died down, Janey flickered into the darkness of the shaft, her gauntleted hands gripping the rusted rungs as her feet found purchase farther down the ladder. Janey hurried down, moving as fast as she could while making no noise, and hoped her scent wouldn't linger enough on the surface to alert the dogs.

A steady stream of air pushed its way past her, filling her nostrils with traces of stale water, mold, and machine oil. Her night vision showed her the interior of the shaft in grays and greens, and less than a minute of furtive descent brought her to a circular opening on her right the same diameter as the shaft, with another, identical opening set fifteen feet below it. The first opening led into a horizontal tube, just large enough to crawl through. Its far end appeared to be blocked, but she couldn't tell by what, so she left the ladder and crept along the crawlway, moving on fingertips and toes, only the occasional soft scuff betraying her movement. She cursed each tiny sound as it echoed around her.

The end of the horizontal tube terminated at what Janey was pretty sure was the kind of hatch that used to cap the vertical shaft at the surface, with a ring-shaped handle set into its center. It made her feel as if she were in a submarine's torpedo tube. She couldn't tell if it was locked or not, and when she pressed her ear against it, she heard nothing. Did that mean nothing moved on the other side? Or just that the metal was too thick to let her hear anything?

Janey held still, imagining the God-awful squealing the hatch might make if she tried to open it. After several seconds' hesitation, she ferreted around in the tube and headed back to the vertical shaft. Another dozen rungs' descent brought her to the lower of the two circular openings off the main shaft, and she held her breath at the sight of dim light filtering in from the second crawlway. Instead of another locked hatch, this one seemed to be blocked by a mesh screen like the one across the top of the vertical shaft.

Janey left the ladder and crept along the length of the crawlway toward the screen, moving even more carefully than she had in the first one. Any sound reverberating through the tube could alert someone on the other side, and if she had her way about it, no one would ever know she'd set foot inside this complex. As she crawled, alert for any movement or shadows from the tube's far end, she ran back over the thought that had haunted her as she'd made her way here.

Does the military know about Augments? If so, have they taken steps to "Augment-proof" this place?

What Janey could do, what other people like her could do, rendered the bulk of human systems and precautions useless. She recalled the horror and sharp stab of hopelessness she'd felt when fighting Simon Grove. None of the martial arts techniques her instructors had driven into her even mattered if the body of the person she was fighting didn't behave the way human bodies do. The most highly-trained combatant, someone of legendary skills, still had the same muscles and nerves and bones as everyone else, and could still be damaged in known, predictable ways. Simon Grove had thrown all of that wisdom, all of the training predicated on the consistency of the human body, out the window and pissed on it. Even when Janey had used her father's katana to cut Simon's head off, she hadn't been convinced it would kill him.

Now, with Aphrodite Lupo, Janey knew that hopelessness would come rushing back worse than ever if she let it. How could she fight someone who couldn't even be hurt, much less killed?

But that train of thought led her back to the missile silo. If it were designed to keep out normal humans, fine, that was one thing. But the soldiers here were guarding something that fell from the sky. Something that, for all she knew, might not have originated on Earth at all. Would the security here have taken that into account? If so, was she walking right into her own death?

Janey kept her breathing soft and silent as she arrived at the mesh screen. Through it, she looked out into a broad, circular room about thirty feet across. A metal stairway close to her led up out of sight, and a handful of computer stations lined the far wall, though no one used them at the moment. The floor and walls bore holes and outlines indicating where other, older equipment had once been installed, presumably ripped out when the silo was first decommissioned. Rows of long fluorescent bulbs shined and buzzed from fixtures in the ceilings, but behind the metal stairs was a shadow big enough and deep enough for Janey to use. With a tiny burst of heat she flickered out of the crawl-way, through the mesh screen, and onto the floor. She decided to try Sha'dae again, though if the connection hadn't worked up in the trees, she doubted it had any better chance down here.

So far so good. Nothing more than an ordinary military facility—

Voices echoed from the floor above. Masculine laughter boomed down the stairs.

An ordinary military facility staffed with armed Marines trained to kill people who try to break into it. What am I even doing here? She hoped that last thought hadn't gone through.

Janey shook her head. This wasn't something she could walk away from. Not with Aphrodite still out there, and not with whatever had fallen from the sky still in here, maybe holding the answers that would keep her friends and herself alive. She left the shadow and silently crept up the stairs.

The floor above was laid out exactly like the one she'd come through below, but with more computer stations and—she allowed herself a tiny smile—a broad doorway set into the wall on the side farthest from the escape shaft. It was a Titan II complex, constructed just like the schematics she'd found.

Directly in front of her were two Marines, one seated at a computer station in a folding metal chair, the other standing right behind him. Both of them watched something playing on the computer monitor. Both of them carried sidearms, too, and the one standing held a rifle. Janey couldn't tell for sure what model, since the Marine's body hid most of it, but she figured it was most likely an M4. She had no interest in getting shot again by any firearm, and no desire whatsoever to be on the business end of an M4 carbine. The Vylar would keep her from getting killed, probably, but she had taken a spray of rounds from an Uzi across the chest before, and that wasn't the kind of pain she wanted to re-live if she could help it. Janey held her breath and stepped from the stairway out onto the floor, her head pivoting between the soldiers and the doorway.

The doorway opened onto a long, straight corridor punishingly well-lit with more fluorescent lights. Thick power conduits ran the length of one wall. *No chance of flickering in there.* At the far end she saw only darkness, and heard a deep, steady, machine-like hum. She couldn't tell what was down there, and wasn't about to teleport blind again. Aiming high in the sky was one thing. Down here, she was liable to end up with a filing cabinet lodged in her ribcage.

Janey glanced around, and frowned behind the faceplate at the lack of shadows. Her shoulders slumped a little as she swung the steel bands around from the sides of her gauntlets and fastened them into place across her knuckles.

The standing Marine said, "How'd you even get this to feed down here?"

The seated one said, "Hey, that's why they pay me the middle bucks," and as the standing Marine laughed, Janey spun him around and punched him in the jaw. The blow wasn't hard enough to break bone, but it was more than hard enough to knock him senseless, and as he crumpled to the floor Janey snaked her arms around the seated Marine's neck and applied a blood choke. His hands flailed and clawed at her, and then drove toward the keyboard, but Janey pulled him backward in his chair so that he couldn't reach it. Once he had collapsed, she laid him on the floor next to the first Marine, folded the steel knuckles back, and climbed up onto the metal chair. A quarter-turn for each of the four fluorescent bulbs above the computer station cut their power, but let them remain in the fixture, so that at a glance it would appear that they had simply been switched off. This created a deep, dark pool of shadow in the room, which Janey used to take both Marines back to the floor below, along the crawlway, and into the bottom of the escape shaft, where she propped them up in seated positions.

Janey had hoped she wouldn't have to interact with anyone here, but had planned for it anyway. She reached through the darkness, back to the motel bathroom, and grabbed the stack of zip-ties and hand towels she'd placed on the floor next to the sink. Before the Marine she'd choked out began to come around, she had zip-tied both men's hands behind their backs, their ankles together, and then bound the first Marine's right ankle to the second one's left. She finished up by stuffing a towel into each of their mouths, held in place by zip-ties around their heads, before checking their pulses and breathing.

She was about to flicker away again—she'd have to be careful not to travel too far, since she didn't want to burn either of them—when she saw the Marine she'd punched staring at her. Or rather, she saw that his eyes were open. It was pitch-black in the escape shaft. He couldn't see a thing.

For a second or two, Janey considered messing with them. Leaning in close and whispering something along the lines of, *"I'll be back to eat you later."* The Marine with the rifle might not have had time to process what she looked like before she'd knocked him unconscious, and the seated one had never seen her at all, so it wasn't as if they both knew they'd been assaulted and subdued by a woman in a suit of body armor. She could tell them anything.

She did whisper. But she waited until they were both awake, and tried to keep her voice as non-threatening as possible. "Listen, guys. I know you're both just doing your jobs, and I apologize for the rough treatment. I'll make sure you don't stay down here for too long, okay?"

Both men tried to talk—Janey felt gratified that the towels stuffed in their mouths did a good job at muffling the sound—but she flickered up to the crawlway entrance and back out into the complex instead of listening to them.

On the second floor, Janey pressed her back to the wall next to the hall doorway and concentrated. She couldn't hear anything from the far end, so she hurried down the length of it, pausing twice to disable more fluorescent bulbs, so that half the hallway's length was draped in shadows.

The hallway opened up into a large, dimly-lit, square room so densely packed with bulky generators that there was barely room to walk. Off to her right stood a set of double metal doors that, if her sense of direction was right, would lead to the stairway that climbed up to the main entrance topside. That wasn't where she needed to go, though, and she followed another set of power conduits to the far corner, where another metal door stood, rusting, set into the cinder block wall. Janey folded the steel knuckles back into place, took a deep breath, and opened the door—

—just as a young woman in the same pixelated camo fatigues as the first two Marines, carrying another M4, pushed the door open from the other side. The woman took in a breath to scream as she raised her rifle, and Janey spread her thumb and forefinger wide and hit the woman in the throat with the webbing between them at the same time that she wrenched the rifle out of her grip. The woman staggered backward and fell against a set of concrete steps, gagging and clutching her throat, and Janey lunged forward and gave her the same knockout blow that she'd given the first Marine.

Janey's breath came fast and ragged, expecting to be discovered at any second, but the woman seemed to be alone, so with rapid-fire bursts of heat Janey teleported her back across the generator room, down the hallway, back to the computer rooms, and down to the bottom of the escape shaft again. Neither of the first two Marines had gotten loose, but they both made a lot of muffled noise when Janey and the young woman materialized between them, especially when Janey accidentally stepped on one of their legs. She propped the woman up beside the Marine she'd choked out, reached back to the bathroom, and bound and gagged her with the same technique she'd used on the men—except that, before she could get the towel in her mouth, the woman regained consciousness and said, "Who are you? What do you want?"

Janey sat back on her haunches. Hesitant. She hadn't considered actually talking to anyone here. Janey peered at the woman's name stitched into her uniform, and didn't want to try to pronounce it. She whispered, "What's your name?"

Janey's night vision was in full effect, and she saw the emotions play out across the woman's face. Fear first, yes, but only a fleeting glimpse of it, followed by anger and determination. "Strandjev. Sergeant Ashley Strandjev." She pronounced it *strahn-jeff*. Sergeant Strandjev listened as the men tried to talk through their gags. "Who else is in here?" She turned her head, staring wide-eyed through the utter darkness. "Where did you take us?"

Janey whispered, "You're safe, Sgt. Strandjev. So are the two men I found in the computer room." She weighed the pros and cons of this. "Listen. Something was brought here yesterday. Something you're guarding. Where is it?"

Sgt. Strandjev leaned her head back against the wall, and Janey watched as Strandjev's face, a rich gold in Janey's night vision, faded to a pale yellow. Her voice betrayed a slight quiver. "Go to hell. Whoever you are. You're not getting shit from me."

Janey's thoughts raced. Whatever they brought in, whether she was willing to admit it or not, Strandjev was terrified of it. Janey wished she had enough time to press her for information. She also wished she had any idea how to carry out an effective interrogation.

Janey shrugged. "It was worth a shot." She jammed the towel into Strandjev's mouth, zip-tied it securely, and in another ten seconds had flickered back to the concrete stairwell. Janey followed the conduits up the stairs and along another hallway identical to the one between the computer room and the generator room. She knew it had to lead to the silo proper. Another rusted metal door hung there, and Janey kept a close watch on it as she disabled the lights along the hallway's length. She half-expected to find some sort of security measure beside the door, a card-swiper or retinal scanner or something, but it was just a door.

Just a door in a re-purposed missile silo that no one was supposed to know about in the first place, in a location so remote no one in their right minds would go looking for it, guarded by armed Marines. She chastised herself about looking for trouble.

Janey folded the steel knuckles into place and gripped the lever-style door handle.

The absurdity of what she was attempting reared up and snapped at her. She grew acutely aware that she had zero military training, zero knowledge of military procedure, and zero knowledge of what sorts of security measures the military would put in place when guarding a questionable object that had fallen from orbit. Would there be one or more high-ranking officers watching the thing? A team of scientists? CIA operatives? No, it wouldn't be CIA. More like...what? Homeland Security? National Security Agency?

Janey took a long, deep breath through her nose and just as slowly exhaled through her mouth. The issue was a simple one, really. The only lead she had for understanding what Aphrodite Lupo was—what they *all* were, all the Augments, herself included—lay beyond this door.

Janey turned the handle and opened it, just a crack, just enough to peer through—

—and the half-dozen armed Marines standing on the platform beyond the door all turned and looked as the door let out a piercing, metallic squeal. The closest one locked eyes with Janey, and she had just enough time to throw herself flat to the floor before a deafening barrage of bullets slammed the door the rest of the way open. In a burst of heat that left scorch marks on the floor and wall, she flickered back down the hall to the stairs where she'd subdued Sgt. Strandjev.

Janey rolled down the stairs, into the generator room, as what sounded like twenty voices started bellowing, and more bullets screamed down the hallway, slamming into metal and concrete and ricocheting down the stairs.

Janey ripped the conduits off the wall, gathered them into a thick bundle with both hands, and heaved. The conduits and the heavy power cables inside ripped free of their metal moorings with a series of *pings*, and one more heave tore them loose from the nearest generator.

The entire complex plunged into total darkness.

Janey hadn't seen any night-vision goggles on any of the Marines beyond that last door, and dearly hoped they didn't have any. She turned her own night vision up to full power and, no longer encumbered by any ambient light, became a smoky, blistering wraith.

All six of the Marines she'd seen at the end of the hallway had charged through the door, and three of them had high-powered flashlights in their hands, ready to send piercing beams down the corridor.

That won't do.

Janey took all three flashlights away and, as efficiently as she could, beat all six men senseless. She felt bad doing it, just as she had felt bad stashing the first two Marines and Sgt. Strandjev in the bottom of the escape shaft. She also knew that, if she had been an ordinary woman, with no teleportation, no night vision, and no enhanced strength, she wouldn't have lasted two seconds. But she *could* teleport, she *could* see in the dark, and she *was* as strong as three beefy men combined. The Marines fell like dominoes.

Janey had no time to give them the zip-tie-and-hand-towel treatment, now that she had alerted the rest of the complex to her presence. She took small comfort in the knowledge that, since she was still breathing, the place did not appear to be Augment-proofed after all.

She also took the few seconds necessary to grab their sidearms and rifles and push the weapons through the darkness back to the bathroom, where they clattered on the chipped ceramic tile in a heap. She made a mental note to tell Nathan not to touch any of them.

Janey flickered through the door at the end of the hallway, slammed it shut, and jammed another folding metal chair under the handle. She didn't figure that would hold more than a few seconds if anyone got truly determined to come through the door, but those seconds might be important. Turning, she finally took the time to absorb the sight that confronted her.

The cylindrical silo seemed to be about as wide as the computer rooms she'd come through initially. A ten-foot-wide platform hugged the walls and curved all the way around. A space in the center of the floor, she felt sure, had at one time been vacant, making room for a massive-as-all-hell Titan missile to sit there, ready to launch. That center space, however, had been filled in with a corrugated metal plate, so that the only break in the floor came in the form of another rusted metal staircase to her left, leading down.

A wall-mounted emergency light came on near her. Janey smashed the bulb with one of the flashlights she'd taken off a soldier in the hallway—

—and almost fell on her ass as the entire silo trembled. From somewhere below her, a rumbling, crashing explosion boomed out, and for half a heartbeat Janey was convinced that an actual missile was there below her, about to blast off.

That thought quickly left her, though, as the screams of multiple men and women echoed up the stairwell, replacing the din of the explosion and accompanied by gunfire and a long series of wet, meaty impacts.

Janey sprinted down the stairs, smashing emergency lights as she went.

More metal plates had replaced the missile shaft in the levels below, so that Janey found herself descending through a series of mostly empty circular rooms. She wasn't sure how far down the silo went, but when she got to the fourth "floor," she paused at the sight of a yawning gap in one wall—a gap beyond which Janey saw, as she stepped over the shattered cinder blocks littered about the floor, a perfectly round shaft tunneled through solid rock, leading away to what she thought was the west.

So that was the explosion. But what the bloody hell tunnels through solid rock like this?

Two more screams reached her from below. Janey smashed out three more emergency lights as she made her way farther and farther down the stairs, exercising more and more caution the deeper into the earth she went. Immediately below the floor with the hole in the wall, she started finding bodies. Marines, male and female alike, every one of whom looked as if they'd been hit by a car. Janey went from form to crumpled form, checking for a pulse, but found none. She counted twelve Marines, all of them with what appeared to be some sort of immense blunt force trauma to their heads and torsos.

One of the demolished bodies had been hurled into the last emergency light, destroying it. Janey crept over to the stairs in what should have been total darkness.

But below her, the darkness was far from total. She moved halfway down the eighth and final flight of stairs, peering under the hand rail like a child sneaking down to watch her parents wrap holiday gifts. She might have been breathing. She wasn't sure.

In the center of the floor, there on the bottom level of the silo, lay a skeleton. Or Janey thought it was a skeleton. Her first thought was, "Is that some kind of baby whale?" But there was no tail, just an oblong, asymmetrical collection of charred, blackened bones.

No. Not bones.

Bones weren't made of metal.

The staircase trembled as the gigantic figure standing next to the skeleton took a staggering step backward…and Janey gasped as she realized the source of the swirling red and blue light that filled the room and cast bizarre, moving shadows on the far wall.

The gigantic man's skin was molten silver. The red and blue lights swam and danced under its surface.

16

In a house off Whittle Springs Road in northern Knoxville, Tennessee, Aphrodite Lupo sat in the master bedroom with her head in her hands and rocked slowly back and forth. "I don't want this," she said, the words taut as high-tension cables. "I don't want to do this."

Aphrodite's breath came out in long, ragged plumes. The temperature inside the house had plummeted after she'd taken the man and woman who lived there. The soundproofing in the man's private recording studio had trapped her unrestrained screams and prevented the neighbors from hearing the throes of her latest transformation, but had done little to keep the heat from fleeing or the ice crystals from collecting on every surface. Now, hours later, the ice had finally begun to melt, soaking into the thick shag carpet that layered every floor except those in the kitchen and bathrooms.

The seat of Aphrodite's pants was wet and cold because of it. She didn't care.

"Just get them out of my head."

The whispers churned and beat their way around the room like a frenzied swarm of locusts before coalescing into words.

If we know their secrets, we can use them as motivation. Do not reject this gift.

Aphrodite rocked back and forth. A thin keening made its way out of her throat. She knew Julian Roth and Trent Davis waited for her downstairs. Down there next to the studio, where the skeletonized bodies of the husband and wife lay, their muscle mass taken and utilized, now cladding Aphrodite's frame with even greater strength and vigor. Aphrodite could smell Roth and Davis. Even over the fresh corpses, traces of their individual scents made their way up the stairs and into her nostrils and soaked into her brain and—

Aphrodite clutched her head even more tightly as another burst of images exploded behind her eyes.

Julian. Thirteen years old. Chubby, awkward—not a stutterer, not clinically, but so shy he might as well have been. Too shy to do more than sneak the occasional furtive glance at Angel Hilliard, the pretty, smart girl with the glasses and the backpack stuffed so full of books Julian didn't know how she could stand up straight.

He wanted her to know who he was.

He wanted to carry her books for her.

He wanted to kiss her.

None of those things happened.

They might not have happened even if he'd been brave, but he wasn't, he was the opposite of brave, and he didn't want to admit that, not even to himself, because his father hated cowards, hated them, said any man who was a coward wasn't a man and didn't deserve to live. His father played football when he was in high school, and the girls loved him, and he stood up to anyone who gave him any kind of shit. Julian's father never let anybody look down on him, nobody, not black, not white, no one.

And Julian was scared to talk to a girl. He hoped his father never found out.

But Antonio found out. Antonio and his...his...

Julian had learned a word. "Troglodyte." Antonio had two cave-dwelling goblins, two troglodytes, who did whatever he said, and Antonio saw him looking at Angel one day, and when he and the troglodytes stopped laughing, they went straight to Angel and told her about Julian's crush.

Julian didn't hear what she said.

He just saw her shake her head, emphatically, and turn and walk away. Fast.

That was how Antonio and the troglodytes started with Julian. That was in eighth grade. They hadn't stopped. He knew they would never stop. They tripped him and pushed him, so that he fell hard in the halls and in the parking lot. They made up whatever rumors about him they could—Julian is gay, Julian jacks off in the boys' bathroom, Julian keeps naked pics of his mom on his laptop.

They keyed his parents' car the one time Julian drove it to school. Julian was too scared to tell his father the truth, so he made up a lie about side-swiping a mailbox, and his dad screamed at him and grounded him and took away the license he'd just gotten.

They poured Coke into Julian's laptop, the day before a massive term paper was due. Julian's grades weren't great to begin with, and he failed the course because of what they did and got held back a year. His guidance counselor told him he should stop thinking about college.

They found him on Facebook, and followed him to Instagram and Twitter. That was where they truly hit their stride, Antonio and his troglodytes, because there Julian couldn't get away from them. One of the troglodytes Photoshopped an image of Julian having sex with a pig, and it circulated through the entire student body overnight. Everyone laughed at him when he came to school the next day.

Even Angel Hilliard.

Julian didn't walk at graduation with the rest of his one-year-younger classmates. Antonio and the troglodytes had made sure Julian knew he wasn't welcome at the ceremony. It didn't matter that none of the three of them were doing anything with their lives after graduation. It didn't matter that both troglodytes just stayed in their parents' houses, no college, no jobs, or that Antonio got busted for possession and did a month in county. It didn't matter that, despite his stupid, lazy, worse-than-useless guidance counselor, Julian applied and got accepted to a community college. Everyone he knew, everyone he had ever met, laughed at him.

Laughed at him and called him Julian Pig-Fucker.

Aphrodite couldn't take it. Didn't want to take it. She toppled over onto her side and stretched out full-length on the wet, icy-cold carpet, Julian Roth's pain flooding through her.

And since the light in the sky had shined on him...since he had become something Antonio and the troglodytes couldn't laugh at, couldn't fight, couldn't run from...even since then, the pain remained. It simply shifted and became something else.

Because now Julian had to concentrate to stay solid. Like clenching a muscle and balancing a chemistry equation at the same time...and it wore him out. Physically. Mentally. Staying tangible for more than two seconds exhausted him...

...and yet that was the only way he could eat.

Revolting bits of half-chewed food simply fell out of his skull, down through his smoke-like jaw and onto the ground, if he lost his concentration.

That's why the pounds had dropped off of him so fast. That's why his face had gone from round and pleasant to angular and severe. That's why hunger gnawed at his stomach every waking hour.

Aphrodite groaned. "I don't want to know this. I don't want to *feel* this."

But she knew. She commanded them. She was responsible for them. She was part of them, as they were part of her. Aphrodite rolled onto her stomach and drummed her fists and feet against the floor, her nose buried in the wet carpet. It didn't work. A new wisp of scent reached her. Not Julian.

Trent Davis. One of whose earliest memories was hearing his mother say, "Shit, I love niggers! Everybody ought to own one!"

Aphrodite snarled. Her teeth ground together as pain gave way to hatred.

Trent Davis, who followed a black girl home from school one afternoon and forced his way into her house before her parents got there and held a knife to her throat and made her suck his cock.

Who bragged about it to his friends the next day.

Who saw that the girl committed suicide eight weeks later, and made jokes about having one less darky around town.

Trent Davis, whose success as a salesman at the boat dealership relied on telling racist jokes to his customers, and who eagerly accepted an invitation to a Klan rally, and who marched through the streets of his hometown with a white hood covering his face every chance he got.

Trent Davis, who screamed at the realtor for selling the plot of land next to his to a Black family named Lerandus. Who shouted taunts at his new neighbors and knocked down their mailbox and poisoned their dog.

Who ran their sixteen-year-old son off the road when Davis caught him riding his bike home one night. Who was disappointed that the boy lived, and relieved that he couldn't identify the motorist who'd caused him to crash.

Trent Davis, whose wife left him after decades of bitterness and abuse. Who watched as Mr. Lerandus's wife withered and died of cancer. Who secretly celebrated the neglect shown their father by his neighbor's children, as they moved away, never to return to the small, hate-filled town of their birth.

Davis hadn't intended Lerandus to see him on the late summer evening when he'd gone to get a closer look at what his neighbor was up to. Davis had been hiding in the thick treeline that separated their properties, and would have stayed there, unnoticed, except for the star above that looked down on him and opened its eye wide and bathed him in its glare.

Davis staggered out of the trees, dazed, baffled as to why his body suddenly felt so heavy, why his feet sank so far into the grassy soil, and that's when Lerandus saw him and screamed at him. "Get off my property! Get! Go on, get! You don't belong here!"

Davis didn't know what had happened to him, but he knew damn sure he wasn't about to let any nigger talk to him that way, and he followed Lerandus into his house and balled up his fists and swung them and...

...and Lerandus just...

...came apart.

Davis had holed up in his own house every second of every day since then. Only used his phone to order groceries delivered. Unplugged it when he wasn't using it. Never stopped watching. Waiting for the sheriff to come and accuse him of murder and drag him out of his house.

But the sheriff never came. Davis heard talk from the grocery delivery boy that Lerandus had been killed by some sort of wild animal. Told Davis to be careful, since he lived out here by himself.

Careful. Yeah. He'd be careful.

Davis huddled there, alone in his house, staring out at the world, until a shimmering black cloud appeared in his living room and a pretty blonde girl stepped out of it and made him an offer.

"Oh God," Aphrodite whimpered. "I don't want this, I don't want this in my head!"

We must use his hate. Understand it, channel it, direct it. Give him a target. He is our footsoldier. We must use him as such.

Aphrodite rolled onto her back and stared at the ceiling. The air had warmed up just enough that she could no longer see her breath, but the chill atmosphere inside the house had produced fat drops of condensation on the skylight directly above her.

"Do I have to recruit Janey Sinclair?" she whispered, the terrible, searing heat fresh in her mind. "Can't I find another like her?"

But she knew the answer. There was no other like Janey Sinclair. Aphrodite had to bring Sinclair to heel. Make her serve the cause. Aphrodite got up and threw open a window. Leaned out into the humid night air and drew in breath after breath—as much to get Roth's and Davis's scents out of her nose as anything else. But after a few moments, her breathing slowed, and the channel she had so briefly opened into Sinclair's mind came into focus. She'd been trying to establish this connection for long, frustrating hours. Why now? What had changed? The channel felt...different. It echoed, like a tiny voice suddenly moved next to a megaphone.

"Yes. Yes. The connection is still there. Amplified...somehow..."

Aphrodite closed the window and made her way down to the first floor. Along the way, she passed a full-length mirror, and paused to admire her new shape. The long, fine blonde hair remained, as did the blue eyes. But now her pale skin stretched over a six-foot-six-inch frame rippling with muscles like plates of iron.

She would make Janey Sinclair see the error of her ways.

Or rip her head off her shoulders.

J aney couldn't decide what to stare at—the thing that looked for all the world like some kind of metal monster skeleton, or the giant with lights floating in his silver skin. She became, in effect, a part of the rusted staircase she crouched on, one gauntleted hand affixed to the rail, eyes wide behind the black mesh eyepieces of her helmet.

The giant wore rough work boots and threadbare jeans, and a long-sleeved cotton shirt under a thigh-length leather coat. The plain clothing made his opalescent skin that much stranger. Janey sucked in an involuntary, gasping breath as the giant spoke.

But it wasn't *words* he said. Not exactly. He took a step closer to the charred, whale-like skeleton, and one massive hand ran across a scorched, metallic bone, and a sound rushed out of him like the crashing of violent ocean waves. He bowed his great head, and sank to his knees, and he *roared*. Roared like the fury of a hurricane, roared so loud and so long that Janey feared she might go deaf. Roared with a pain and a boiling grief that washed over Janey's skin and sank down deep into her marrow.

The giant's rushing, blasting, devastating howl of rage and sorrow built and built, and he slammed his silver fists into the floor of the silo, cracking and cratering the concrete, and the hurricane continued until Janey felt as if the sheer anguish of it would knock her loose from her grip on the rail and send her tumbling and flailing back up the stairs.

Finally, the pounding of the storm dwindled and died. The giant stayed on his knees, his head still bowed, his hands slack and resting on the floor. Janey fought down the fear, the urge to run that threatened to overpower her, and stood up. This was what she had come for. To understand, to know. This was her chance.

The lights twisting and shimmering under the giant's skin had settled into a deep, intense violet that left the broad, circular chamber just dim enough for Janey to flicker away if she needed to. After a long moment's thought, she folded the steel knuckles away, undid the catch of her helmet, and pulled it off. Her booted feet thunked softly on the stairs as she walked down to the silo's floor. She had no idea what to say in a situation like this, especially given the corpses of Marines littering the silo's upper floors. *"I come in peace?" "Please don't kill me?"*

Janey cleared her throat. "Excuse me? Sir?"

The giant's head whipped around, every light beneath his skin went out, and his hand wrapped around Janey's throat and slammed her against the wall at the base of the stairs. The giant had moved so quickly that her brain couldn't process what she'd just seen, or hadn't seen—one second he'd been twenty feet away, the next he'd crossed the room and grabbed her.

But the colossal metal hand wasn't crushing her. Her feet hadn't even left the floor. She was simply pinned, as effectively as if she'd been locked into metal shackles. Gripping the giant's hand and arm felt like clutching at a bridge abutment. The giant leaned in until his nose almost touched Janey's, and this time the wave-crash voice produced words in English.

"Are you responsible for this?"

Janey held still. The giant didn't seem to want to hurt her, not yet anyway, and it was still dark enough to teleport out. Her night vision had come up to full power, and with a minor shock she saw that the giant's skin had turned opaque, now deeply tanned and leathery and unquestionably human, instead of translucent silver. "Responsible for what, exactly?"

He didn't move the hand pinning her to the wall—it was so huge, his thumb and fingers had driven into the cinder block on either side of Janey's neck, with enough room left for her to breathe comfortably—and he didn't take his eyes away from hers, but he gestured toward the charred skeleton with the other hand. "That. Bringing him here. After he crashed."

"Sir...my name is Janey Sinclair. I didn't have anything at all to do with that—with *him*." She swallowed hard, sharply aware that if she thought about this too much, she ran the risk of panicking and screaming. "But I think he had something to do with me. With changing me. Me, and some other people."

The giant pulled his hand away from Janey's neck—tiny bits of concrete from the wall pattered down on Janey's shoulders—and rose to his full height, which made Janey feel tiny and petite and fragile. She was pretty sure she had never felt that way before in her adult life. His voice still carried the crash and rush of ocean waves, but changed as he spoke, getting closer and closer to that of a normal human. "You...you were a subject." He turned his back on her. Faced the skeleton again, an eloquent statement as to how much of a threat he considered her.

Janey walked around to his side, craning her neck to look up at him. "A subject? What do you mean? Please forgive me, I have a million questions."

The giant looked down at her, and his eyes had turned the same glowing violet that had danced and floated in countless pinpoints of light when he was collapsed on the floor. "You were a subject in his experiment."

Janey made a vague motion toward the skeleton. "And what is—who, um, who was...this?"

The giant closed his eyes. "This was my brother."

Janey would have said something else, but a chorus of whispers like fingernails scraping across the surface of her brain filled the room, and on the other side of the skeleton, Aphrodite Lupo, Julian Roth, and Trent Davis appeared in a rippling, static-filled cloud of darkness.

Aphrodite had *grown*. She towered over Janey now—towered over everyone in the room, except the metal giant—and massive knots of muscle rippled and rolled under skin stretched so tight Janey could count the striations in the tissue beneath it. Aphrodite's eyes already glowed yellow, the flying-cinder specks of red shooting through them, and they locked with Janey's—for all of two seconds. Aphrodite's gaze traveled from Janey to the giant to the skeleton and back, and her face distorted with a grin much too wide for a human skull to accommodate.

"I hate to engage in clichés, but in this case I feel it's appropriate." Aphrodite stepped forward, locked on to the skeleton now. *"What have we here?"*

The giant said, "More subjects," and his skin turned translucent again, the pinpoints of light beneath it flaring red and orange.

Aphrodite took in that change, and clapped her hands together. "Oh, this just gets better and better! Janey, you didn't tell me you had such interesting friends!" She snapped her fingers at Roth and Davis. "You two. Take this...pile of bones. Whatever it is. Haul it back to the house while I talk to the adults in the room. Also, Trent, if you would?"

Trent Davis took a magnesium flare out of his jacket pocket and, before Janey realized what was about to happen, struck it into blinding, glaring light. He tossed it at Janey's feet, and she backed away from it, shielding her eyes with one arm. Hurriedly she put her helmet back on and strapped it tight, as Davis took out another flare, and then another. In seconds the room was awash in painful white radiance.

What is she doing, this will shut down Roth's teleportation just like it does mine—

Janey's breath caught in her throat as Roth glided toward the skeleton. The dazzling brilliance of the flares fell into the cloud of darkness he carried as if they were rays of light plummeting into a black hole. The giant took a thunderous step toward him, and the hurricane fury crashed out again: *"NO!"*

Roth's darkness expanded, enfolded the skeleton, and in the space of a heartbeat both disappeared.

Aphrodite said, "Keep the big guy busy," to an answering grin from Davis, and almost as fast as the giant had moved earlier, Aphrodite launched herself across the room and slammed into Janey. The impact drove them into the metal staircase, and the edges of the treads bit into Janey's back and buttocks and thighs. Aphrodite slammed a brick-like fist across Janey's face. Janey's vision went red for a second, and vaguely she thanked God for remembering to put her helmet back on.

Aphrodite drew her fist back, and Janey tried to get her arms up to defend herself, but she was too slow, knew she was about to get drilled again and that the helmet wouldn't hold and her skull would crack—

—and the silver-skinned giant staggered backward and crashed into Aphrodite, knocking her off of Janey and pinning her against the handrail. Trent Davis charged the giant again, his own fists hammering at the enormous man's mid-section, and Janey heaved herself up and ran up the stairs as fast as she could manage. It was dark up there, and she only needed a few seconds to get her bearings back, and—

Horrible piercing agony spiked through Janey's left ankle, and she slammed down into the stairs face-first. Booms and cracks like a wrecking ball demolishing a building rolled up the stairs from the fight between the giant and Davis, but Janey had no time to think about that. She could only stare in horror at Aphrodite's fingers, which had lengthened and hardened into knives and pierced straight through the top of Janey's boot and into her leg.

Aphrodite gave Janey a grin like a barracuda's and struck another flare with her free hand. Her jaw distended, dropping down near her chest, and she set the flare between her teeth. Just before she clenched them on it, holding the blinding light source in place, Aphrodite hissed, "Didn't think I'd figure out your gimmick? Fuck that. Let's see you teleport away now."

In answer, Janey twisted and kicked Aphrodite in the face as hard as she could. The woman grunted, and as teeth broke out of her mouth, the flare spun away and thudded down the stairs, draping both of them in sweet, blessed darkness. Janey flickered away, traveling up and into the center of the floor above them—

—and collapsed to the floor, screaming, writhing.

She had teleported Aphrodite with her. The knife-fingers ground deeper into Janey's ankle.

"Wow." Aphrodite crouched and dragged Janey closer to her. "Guess you can't get away from me if I'm inside you, huh? How carnal." Aphrodite's free hand grew larger. The fist curled into a ball, and spikes of bone emerged from it. "Anyway. Let's see how many more holes I can put in that armor, yeah?"

Janey flickered blind, two hundred feet straight up.

The pain in her ankle almost made her pass out, but she looked down to see Aphrodite Lupo, still attached to her, still digging finger-tips like diamond drills through her skin and flesh and bones. Some tiny, distant part of her mind registered that the four soldiers and both patrol dogs lay dead near the main entrance below, and as she and Aphrodite began to free-fall, Aphrodite shouted, "*Whooo!* What a ride! Take me higher!"

Janey didn't hear Aphrodite's words. She knew, as well as she knew her own name, that if she didn't do something, something dras-tic, something *right now*, this muscle-bound woman was going to tear her apart. Janey twisted her head around, found a spot beyond the fence, out past the reach of the complex's lights, out in the comforting darkness.

And she teleported Aphrodite into the ground.

The fireball above her filled the sky with white-orange light, and the heat smashed down against her, withering leaves and scorching grass, and she felt Aphrodite's knife-fingers slide out of her as Janey rolled away. Janey curled into a ball, gripping her pierced, mangled ankle with both hands.

Teleporting *into* a solid object had been one of Janey's greatest fears, ever since she first realized she could move from one patch of darkness to another. It went back to reading *X-Men* comics, when the teleporting character Nightcrawler talked about the ungodly damage it would do to a living body if that body suddenly occupied the same space as, say, a concrete wall. That was why Janey tried her best never to teleport blind, except straight into the sky, and she'd only just begun doing that. It was why she stuck to what she knew would work —line of sight, or an intimately familiar space like the Basement. The blind leaps she'd taken over the last thirty-six hours had been some of the most reckless behavior she'd ever engaged in. What she had done to Aphrodite Lupo was a death sentence.

Janey struggled up to a sitting position, still keeping pressure on her ankle, and looked to see the results of her desperate measure.

Her mouth went dry as dust.

Aphrodite had disappeared into the ground up to her waist. Her body convulsed, and the thorns emerged from and reabsorbed into her skin. Her eyes flared yellow, shifted to normal human blue, and blood leaked from the tear ducts. She clawed at the earth. Bits of her teeth broke free and flew in tiny arcs from her mouth as she ground them together.

The worst part was that she made no noise.

Janey would have felt better if Aphrodite had screamed. If she had indicated, in any way, that she was still human. Instead her head twitched from side to side, her impossibly-muscled arms tensed and thrashed, and the claw-fingers dug into the earth around her.

Dug in...

...and pushed.

Tears started from Janey's eyes. "No."

Aphrodite pushed. And her body began to emerge from the earth. Inch by inch, her torso slid up out of the ground, and sand and rocks and bits of decayed plant matter slid out of her, raining down around her hands as her fingers dug for greater purchase.

Janey flickered away. Back to the escape hatch, inside, down into the dark.

Rational think rational don't panic you can't panic not yet.

She couldn't stand, not with the damage to her ankle, and she wondered what kind of blood trail she must have been leaving behind, but that didn't stop her from verifying that Sgt. Strandjev and the other two Marines were still alive. She was truly grateful for the towels jammed into their mouths so that she didn't have to hear them scream when she dumped them in the woods several hundred yards from the silo complex. Janey tried not to scream herself as another blast of pain crashed up from her ankle. She clenched her jaw and snapped the zip-ties, and before the soldiers could work the towels loose, Janey said, "Really sorry for the inconvenience, but you all need to get away from the silo, run as far and fast as you can, or there's a really good chance you'll get killed." She left them there, flickering straight up above the treetops, down to the escape hatch, and from there back through the complex. The six Marines she'd beaten in the hallway lay scattered about, broken and shredded and very, very dead.

Aphrodite.

Janey reached the bottom of the silo again. The flares had run their course, leaving everything draped in gorgeous, welcoming darkness. Janey let her night vision come up to full strength.

The bottom level was in complete shambles, and Janey could track the path of damage they'd taken as the giant and Trent Davis had fought their way up the now-twisted staircase. She had just leveraged herself up to her one good leg when she felt the familiar vibration in the air: Julian Roth had returned.

Janey flickered up the stairs to the next level, appeared right in front of Roth, and gave him no time to orient himself. She threw every ounce of weight she had into a lunging Superman punch, and though she hadn't had the time nor the presence of mind to fold her steel knuckles into place, she still felt the satisfying crunch of bone and cartilage as she smashed Roth's nose flat against the rest of his face. Roth collapsed to the floor and lay motionless, and Janey took in the rest of the scene.

She felt her gorge rise.

Trent Davis lay crumpled on the far side of the room. He was still breathing, she was pretty sure, but looked as if he'd taken the kind of beating a bulldozer hands out to a condemned house. He wasn't the reason she'd almost emptied her stomach, though.

Julian Roth had been at the giant. The same way he'd been at the men who'd bullied him.

Enormous sections of the giant's body were simply *gone*. Scooped out, as Zach Feygen had put it, as if by a giant melon-baller. A massive chunk gone from his right hip, another basketball-size hole in his chest, and...Janey couldn't stop herself from staring...about a third of the giant's head was missing.

And he was *twitching*. Twitching the way someone does during a seizure...or right after sustaining the most devastating of traumatic brain injuries. Janey's hands flew involuntarily to her mouth.

Twitching the way Adam did after he got shot.

Trent Davis groaned, and Julian Roth blew blood out of his ruined nose, and from somewhere, Janey wasn't sure if she actually heard the sound or if it was all in her brain, Aphrodite Lupo's whispers reached her.

Janey laid a hand on the giant's broad, leather-clad shoulder and teleported both of them to the motel bathroom in Nebraska.

She knew the resulting explosion would wipe the missile silo off the face of the earth, and if Julian Roth hadn't recovered in time, it might also prevent him from getting himself or anyone else to safety. Maybe he and Davis and Aphrodite would burn, the way Janey had meant them to in the Basement, though she figured that was probably too much to hope for.

Janey winced. Hoping for living, breathing human beings to die in a fire. How heroic.

When she and the unconscious—*Inert?*—giant emerged from the shadows into the tiny confines of the bathroom, the giant's head tore through the cheap drywall, and one nerveless fist smashed the sink and the mirror above it to pieces before he settled in a heap on the floor. The lights swimming beneath his skin flared brilliant fire-orange, and his eyes focused on Janey, and she said, "We can sort all of this out."

Or that's what she meant to say.

Instead, her head smacked into the floor and she passed out.

17

Janey glided along the edge between conscious and unconscious. She couldn't tell for how long. She couldn't tell what was a dream and what wasn't.

Her ankle throbbed. A river of punishing icy water flowed up her leg and into the rest of her body. The water hurt. Screamed at her. Tore at her. But she could feel the current pulling her away, and knew how peaceful it could be to float along with it. If she let it carry her away, the pain would stop.

She dreamed, or thought she dreamed, of Adam and Tim, both of them crouching over her. At some point someone pulled her helmet off, and when the black mesh slid away from her eyes, it took Adam with it, so that only Tim remained, his dark eyes wet with tears above her. "Janey," she was pretty sure he said. Pretty sure it was his voice. "Janey, stay with me."

Darkness around her turned a weak, light gray, and she felt movement, and heard what sounded like grunting and scraping. Someone else said, "Good thing nobody's awake this early." More scraping, and footfalls around her, and a metallic rattling.

Somewhere, an engine started.

The flow of agonizing, icy water from her ankle doubled. Doubled again. Janey tried to dig her fingers into...what was she lying on? Metal?

Someone else's voice said, "Is it dead? If it's not dead...what if it wakes up?"

A hand under her head. Lifting it. She didn't want her head lifted. She wanted to lie back in the current and let it buoy her. "Drink this." Something against her lips. More water? No—sweeter. She couldn't find the strength to argue.

Voices all around her. Impossible to identify. Pressure on her ankle narrowed the channel for the ice-cold current of pain. Made it stronger. Faster.

Janey passed out.

When she woke, the river of pain had diminished to something more like a brook. Janey opened her eyes, and at first could make no sense of what she saw—metal squares high above her, ragged strips of cloth hanging from distant walls. Row after row of...what? Were those chairs? Why were they folded in half?

She thought about trying to sit up, but it seemed like a tremendous amount of work. Plus her mouth was so dry that, when she tried to talk, she discovered that her throat was literally stuck shut. The best she could manage was a faint croaking sound.

"Hey." Tim came and knelt beside her. He held a bottle of water to her lips, and she drank what felt like half of it. The dust in her mouth receded, and her throat opened up again. She didn't think water had ever tasted that good before.

Six months ago, Simon Grove had broken Janey's leg—the same leg that Aphrodite had just brutalized—but back then she'd been able to flicker into the shadows right outside an emergency room, where she'd spun the doctors a story about falling down a flight of stairs. This was no hospital. Janey pushed aside the water bottle and squinted at her surroundings.

All the light came from a battery-powered lantern about twenty feet away, and by its illumination Janey finally put the pieces together: she lay on the floor in front of the first row of seats in what appeared to be an abandoned movie theater. The decorative ceiling, the curtain in front of the screen, the folding chairs, all of that made sense now.

Her understanding of her surroundings took a hit, though, when a craggy-faced man in his late fifties came and crouched on her other side and said, "How're you feeling?"

"Mr. Vessler? How—what—why are you here?"

From somewhere up one of the aisles, Nathan's voice rang out. "Hey! She's awake! Janey's awake!" Rapid footsteps approached, and Nathan and Sha'dae joined Tim and Vessler, crowding around her—along with a pale kid she didn't recognize.

For about five seconds.

Janey struggled up to her elbows, staring. "*Scott?*"

Scott Charles gave her a timid smile and wave. "Hi, Janey. It's nice to see you again."

When Janey had last seen Scott, he'd looked closer to death than life. Frail, emaciated, his waxy skin and colorless hair more like what you'd see on a corpse than an adolescent boy. Apparently whatever living conditions Garrison Vessler had provided had agreed with him in a big way. Scott had grown, Janey estimated, about four inches, put on at least thirty pounds, and though his skin was still very pale, his cheeks had a healthy glow to them.

Janey opened her mouth to say something appreciative, but a stab of pain from her ankle yanked that breath away. She winced, and simply said, "You look good."

Scott blushed. Vessler said, "Amazing what three squares a day will do for a boy. That, and plenty of wood-chopping."

Janey fixed her eyes on Vessler. "Wood-chopping? You really did take him off the grid, huh?"

"As far off as I could manage. He's the reason we're here, though. Whatever you did back at that fleabag motel, it got his attention."

Between flinches at the pain in her ankle, Janey tried to make note of that: meditation apparently made her stand out like a beacon. "Where are we?"

Sha'dae grinned. "Memphis. Always wanted to come here. Elvis and all. My father's kind of an Elvis nut." Her grin faltered, and she picked at the hem of her hijab. "Not that we're here to sight-see."

Janey carefully, slowly, and against Tim's sounds of protest, maneuvered up to a sitting position, her back against the wall below the screen. "How'd we get here?"

To her surprise, Scott spoke up. "Once I saw you, I could see everybody else around you, too." He gestured at Tim and Nathan and Sha'dae. "I told Dad we'd need to bring something big. He got an old box truck."

Pain in her ankle aside, Janey felt her heart swell when Scott Charles called Garrison Vessler "Dad." She said, "Scott, I think that's the most words I've ever heard you say all at once."

Vessler's steely eyes twinkled. "He's a talker if you get him started." Scott blushed again. Vessler glanced over his shoulder. "Janey—we need to talk about the elephant in the room, so to speak." He moved, clearing a line of sight for her, and pointed, and Janey almost choked.

The giant from the missile silo lay draped across four of the theater seats. His skin had returned to the tanned, leathery, "human" appearance, but he still had great, gaping craters missing out of his torso and head. The human-looking skin had covered over the craters, as well, which emphasized his—Janey could think of no better word for it—his *alienness*.

Nathan cracked his knuckles. "You would not *believe* how heavy that guy is. Good thing I was there. Nobody else could've gotten him out of the bathroom and into the truck."

Sha'dae knelt and put a tentative hand on Janey's shin. "Please tell us it was a good idea to bring him. We didn't think we should just leave him for, y'know, for the local cops to find…"

In a tone that made Janey think of a straining dam finally bursting, Nathan blurted, "What *happened*? When you went to that place, what happened there?" He pointed at the giant. "Did he do that to your ankle? Who is he? *What* is he? What happened up there?"

Tim said, "Explanations can wait. We need to get you to a doctor. Your ankle's kind of…well, pardon my language, but it's fucked up."

Scott giggled, and Nathan joined him. Vessler shot each of them a withering glance, and while Scott just shifted his gaze to his feet, Nathan said, "Sorry, sorry, I know it's serious, sorry."

For the first time, Janey gave her ankle a hard look. Someone had taken off her boot and wrapped a strip of cloth around the wound, but blood had already soaked most of the way through it. Her foot had swollen. It wasn't quite purple, but it wasn't the right color, either. She didn't try to move it.

Janey carefully maneuvered around so that she could lean her head back against the wall below the screen. "You always hear people in movies say, 'No hospitals! They'll know I'm there, and they'll come and try to finish the job!' Well, I don't think Aphrodite's that kind of... whatever you want to call her. I mean, I don't think she'd get alerted if my name turned up on a computer database or something. But she *did* find me. At the missile silo, she and Roth and Davis found me, and after she survived what I did to the Basement..."

Into the pause, Vessler said, "What did you do to the Basement?"

Janey shook her head. "It's gone."

Vessler sucked in a sharp breath. "The explosion in Atlanta? Was that you? God in Heaven, Janey, the news has been calling that a terrorist attack."

"Nope. Just me. Unless you count me as a terrorist, which a lot of people would. I'll tell you all about it later. Anyway. On the roof of my apartment building, Aphrodite...she opened a sort of a connection..." Janey poked the side of her head. "In here. A little bit like the way you do it, Sha'dae, except *horrible*. And I'm pretty sure that's how she found me in West Virginia." She looked around at the group. "My point is, I can't let her show up here and put you all in danger, and I sure as hell can't go to a hospital and be surrounded by hundreds of sick, defenseless targets."

"This discussion is irrelevant," the giant said in his booming, crashing, ocean-wave voice, and Sha'dae and Nathan both shrieked. Vessler grabbed Scott and put the boy behind him. Vapor rose from Vessler's body as his skin temperature plummeted.

Tim jumped in front of Janey.

Janey cried, "Wait! Wait! It's okay. I think."

The giant sat up and got to his feet, towering over them, every inch of seven feet tall. His skin turned metallic, opalescent, and the fluctuating, shifting pinpoints of light beneath its surface burned a brilliant yellow-white. A third of his head still missing, he gazed down at each of them in turn with his one terrible remaining eye.

Garrison Vessler said, "Holy God."

Sha'dae had begun quietly crying. Nathan slipped an arm around her waist, and she clung to him, though her gaze never left the giant. No one else moved. A congregation before a resurrected deity.

The giant raised an arm and pointed at Tim. "You." The pointing finger dropped to Janey's leg. "Repair her."

Tim trembled. "What?"

Nathan had laid the giant down on the second row. That left only one row of seats between the giant and everyone else, and he stepped gracefully over it to stand in their midst.

He doesn't move like a human. Graceful. Deliberate. Janey's mind scrounged for a comparison. *Like a praying mantis. Or a spider.*

The giant's eye raked across the group. "Subjects. Every one of you." This close, the giant's voice pulsed through them, like standing in front of a stack of sub-woofers at a concert. "Your Scout is damaged." He faced Tim again. "Medic. Repair her."

Tim said, "M-medic? I don't—I don't understand."

The flame-yellow of the giant's eye shifted to acid green. "The depth of the protocol breach grows. Are none of you aware of your stations?"

Janey couldn't think of anything to say. No one else came out with anything, either.

The giant's eye narrowed and, using that impossible speed Janey had seen in the missile silo, he whipped one hand out and grasped Tim's head. His fingers and palm completely enclosed Tim's skull, and Janey tensed as she prepared to come up off the floor, but just as fast as he'd grabbed Tim, the giant let him go.

Tim staggered. He turned, slowly, and looked down at Janey, and Janey wanted to scream when she saw Tim's eyes. He didn't seem to be hurt, not physically, but…he didn't seem to recognize her. Not her, not anyone else—not where he was. Nothing.

Janey did her best to ignore the grinding, super-nova pain in her ankle as she twisted, reaching up for Tim, trying to take his hand.

Vessler barked, "Tim! Tim, are you hurt?"

Tim said nothing. Instead he dropped to his knees and took Janey's ankle in both hands, lifting it off the floor. Janey cried out in pain, tried to pull the leg away out of pure reflex, but Tim kept hold of it— and the pain began to diminish. He hunched over her ankle, still holding it with both hands, the leg held tight to his chest, and he started *vibrating*. Not like a jackhammer. Just enough for Janey to feel it. The thrumming in Tim's body, in his hands, pushed a delicious warmth into Janey's ankle, displacing the crippling, grating pain. She felt that warmth, that sublime, energetic heat, pulse up from the ankle wound into the rest of her body. The exhaustion she hadn't realized she'd been suffering disappeared.

Janey wanted to stretch. As if she'd just awakened from a deep, dreamless, nine-hour sleep.

The vibrations stopped. Panting, Tim set her ankle back down on the floor, and when he looked up at her, it was him again. The Tim she knew. *The man I love.* Her heart thundered in her ribcage.

Tim's voice quavered. "How does that feel?"

Janey moved her foot—tentatively at first, then with abandon, wiggling it in every direction. She tore the blood-soaked bandage off, and saw her unblemished ankle, exactly as it used to be. Maybe better.

Tim smiled, but then groaned and rolled over onto the floor, on his back. Janey sprang to his side. "Tim! Tim! What is it, what's wrong, are you okay?"

He groaned again. "I am *starving*." He clutched his stomach. "Oh, God. It's like I haven't eaten for days. Somebody get me a cheese-burger. Five cheeseburgers. *Aargh*."

Janey looked up and saw the giant's dancing-flame eye light on Sha'dae. "You. Communications. Come here."

An hour later, after Nathan and Scott had made a swift run to a nearby burger joint—Janey thought it might have burst some blood vessels in Garrison Vessler's brain to let Scott go, but he'd gritted his teeth and done it—everyone sat around in theater chairs, staring at the giant. Or, as he had told them he preferred to be called, "the Plowman."

Sha'dae rubbed the bridge of her nose. "But that's insane. Your... your brother...he was up there, in orbit, and he'd just zap someone? Send a signal down and Augment some random human? What kind of experiment is that?"

The Plowman's skin had gone from translucent, glowing metal to leathery human again. Before he answered Sha'dae, he ripped a theater seat out of the floor and *absorbed* it. That was the only way Janey could think of it, could make sense of what she and everyone else saw. The metal and fabric of the seats narrowed, collapsed, and flowed into the giant's palms, and the great divot that Julian Roth had taken out of his right hip began filling in.

Even though the giant—the Plowman—seemed to be composed of some sort of metal, the process of his self-repair had a wet, organic quality to it that made Janey's stomach roll over. She stared, transfixed and more than a little queasy, as bones, intestines, and flesh emerged from the wound, growing and developing, settling into place. As if nothing unusual were happening, the Plowman said, "There is precedent among your own people. Are you not familiar with Project MK-Ultra?"

Tim made a sound like *ugh*. Nathan said, "No. What's that?"

Vessler stared up at the ceiling. "The CIA decided to see what effect LSD had on the general populace. So they dosed a bunch of people without telling them, and observed the results."

Nathan's jaw dropped open. "Our own government did that? But that's...God, that's *really* shitty."

The Plowman's crashing-ocean-wave voice modulated down, growing closer to normal human speech. "Though my brother's body was badly damaged by re-entry and impact, I was able to glean a few small bits of information from it. He had been wounded. Some sort of impact had negatively affected his cognitive array. I do not know how long he had suffered from this damage. It might have been many of your years." He paused. In the gaping wound at his hip, layers of muscle grew over the exposed organic-metallic organs. "The experiment should have been conducted using different methodologies and parameters. As soon as a subject displayed acceptable reconfiguration, that subject should have been tagged, removed from the population, and stored for export. My brother succeeded in activating many of you. He failed in all other respects."

The cool, silver channel opened in Janey's mind, and Sha'dae's voice came to life in her head. *Can you hear me?*

Janey glanced at Sha'dae. *Yes. Is something wrong?*

Sha'dae's cheeks turned marginally darker. *No. I'm...just sort of... playing. I guess.*

Janey gave Sha'dae a tiny grin, feeling as if they were passing notes in class. Vessler cleared his throat and said, "All right. This is an awful lot to take in. Even though I've known about Augments for years."

The Plowman turned his head to fix his single eye on Vessler. "Janey Sinclair prevented Julian Roth from destroying this body. From killing me. I am in her debt. That is why I am providing her, and the rest of you, with an explanation. But I will divulge nothing that weakens my people's position."

Vessler chuckled. He didn't sound amused. "That's what I'm saying. This has a lot of moving parts. Are we to understand, once and for all, with no room for ambiguity or argument, that you are not from this planet?"

The Plowman stared at him.

Vessler said, "May I take your silence as assent?"

The Plowman said, "You may ask another question."

"Are you telling us, then, that the purpose of the experiment was to see if humans could be turned into military assets? And if so, to take them *off-planet*, and make them fight in some galactic war somewhere?"

The Plowman's eye darkened. "Not to fight. To be replicated."

Sha'dae's face twitched. *So if you had your way, we'd get turned into, what, mutated DNA soldier factories?*

Janey concentrated. *Did you mean to say that out loud?*

Oh. Shit. Oh! I didn't mean to use that word! Sorry!

As if to talk over her own telepathically transmitted thoughts, Sha'dae said, "So what kind of life would that be? Getting 'replicated'? We'd be, what, like prisoners?"

The Plowman tore loose another seat and absorbed it. As he spoke, skin grew over his now-whole hip, and bones began to develop, lattice-like, in the circular cavity in his chest. Beside her, Tim stuffed a fast-food wrapper back into the paper bag it had come from and, just loudly enough for Janey to hear, said, "Jesus, that's gross. Makes me wish I hadn't eaten a fifth burger."

The Plowman's voice turned ice-cold as he answered Sha'dae. "In a sense, yes. If the experiment had gone as planned, all viable subjects would have been exported and utilized. That would involve placing you in specimen tanks and extracting cellular samples as needed. Of course, the experiment did not go as planned."

Silence settled over the group like a cold, depressing blanket.

After a few moments, Tim raised his hand. "You called Janey a Scout, and said I was Medical, and Sha'dae is Communications. What are the rest of us? Do we all...I mean, did we get Augmented to fit specific roles?"

The Plowman pointed a finger at Janey: "Scout." At Tim: "Medical." At Sha'dae: "Communications." At Nathan: "Infantry." At Scott: "Surveillance."

Vessler said, "What about me?"

A pair of lungs began lacing themselves together behind the visible bones in the Plowman's chest. "I suppose the closest term would be 'sapper.' One specializing in sabotage. You were one of the earliest attempts at a fully-utilizable activation, Mr. Vessler. The technique at the time—and your ability, as a result—were and are imperfect."

Vessler snorted and folded his arms across his chest. "Story of my life."

Janey said, "Brenda Jorden?"

The Plowman closed his eye briefly. She imagined him consulting an internal database. When he opened the eye again, he said, "Interrogation."

Scott Charles spoke up, and his voice cracked on the first word. Janey found him adorable, and wanted to give him a bowl of hot soup and help him with his homework. "Okay, Mr. Plowman, but...what about Simon Grove? And, and Aphrodite Lupo? What kind of roles could they possibly fill?"

The Plowman's partial face creased with pain, or disgust, or maybe pained disgust. "Aberrations. The result of my brother's cognitive damage. Simon Grove's physical distortion was a highly imperfect result of what should have been an infiltration skill."

Janey turned that over in her head. "Infiltration—so he was supposed to be able to make himself look like other people?"

"Correct."

"And the...the blood stuff? His, um, vampiric tendencies?"

The Plowman shook his head. "Unintended. Disgraceful. He should have been rejected and neutralized."

Sha'dae put a hand on Janey's knee. *So when Aphrodite was in your apartment, looking like you! That was what Simon Grove was supposed to do? Infiltrate?*

To the Plowman, Janey said, "No argument there. But Aphrodite Lupo *can* make herself look like other people...and she has, I guess, some Interrogation abilities. And she keeps getting bigger, and I'll be damned if I can figure out how to damage her. What the hell is she?"

The pained expression returned to the Plowman's face. He ripped out another seat, absorbed it, and a thick sheet of muscle covered his metallic ribs. "She is difficult to classify. Something in her activation kept her partially cloaked from my brother's sensors."

Tim frowned. "Okay, I get the whole Infiltration thing. I get somebody turning into somebody else. That's like a spy's dream. But what's *wrong* with her? It's like she hears voices. I mean, I know that's a human disorder—schizophrenia—but her voices, near as we can tell, are ordering her to 'recruit' other Augments. She's already got two, the two you saw, and she keeps trying to do the same thing to Janey."

The Plowman lowered his head and stared at the floor, instead of meeting anyone else's gaze. "She may have had a dual activation, then. Infiltration and Command. The voices could be the result of a pre-existing human disorder, as you say. It is equally possible that she may have had a Command module imprinted on her brain."

Scott Charles spoke up. "What's a Command module?"

Skin crawled across the Plowman's chest wound, sealing it shut. "You would call it...something like an on-board strategic advisor. A knowledge base. A guiding resource that aids in the implementation of missions. From what I have observed, it seems likely that Aphrodite Lupo is attempting to construct a combat unit. Recruiting other Augmented humans to serve under her." His eye shifted to Janey. "She either does not realize, or does not accept, that you are part of a pre-existing combat unit."

Vessler let out a long, low whistle. "You're telling us that Aphrodite Lupo is taking orders from some sort of alien military officer riding around in her head?"

The Plowman pointedly ignored Vessler's question. "Her real name is Agnes Lorch."

Janey stood. "Wait. Wait a minute. Back up. You just said I was already part of a combat unit? What's that supposed to mean?"

The Plowman blinked. It was a disconcertingly human gesture, especially coming from his truncated face. "I pointed out your stations earlier. Scout, Infantry, Medical, Communications. Given my observations, and what scarce data I was able to glean from my brother's remains, it is hardly surprising that you were drawn together. Helped along, no doubt, by the human pack mentality retained from previous evolutionary iterations."

Tim got to his feet next to Janey. "I'm sorry, you said we were drawn together?"

The Plowman tore another seat out of the floor. As it disappeared, his skull began re-growing itself. "You would have sensed the other members of your unit. A subconscious urge, if I understand your neural processes correctly."

Janey's guts turned to ice. She glanced at Sha'dae, and Nathan, and slowly turned to face Tim.

Tim still stared at the Plowman. "But...some of us were *drawn together* before we got Augmented."

The Plowman's missing eye socket writhed and settled into the proper shape, the dark, empty space inside it focused on Tim. "Irrelevant. You possessed the potential for Augmentation. You would have found your way to Janey Sinclair eventually. You all would have. Just as Julian Roth and Trent Davis would eventually have found their way to Aphrodite Lupo."

Silence fell across the theater.

It made Nathan's voice sound even louder than usual. "Wait, you mean I was *destined* to get superpowers? Fuck *yes!*"

Janey barely heard him. She figured the look on her face must have been some sort of giveaway, because Sha'dae put a hand on her wrist. "Janey? Honey, what's wrong?"

Janey fixed her eyes on the ceiling. "If we...if we were all drawn to each other because of this...this predisposition. This..." She scrubbed her face with both hands. "This *artificial* predisposition..." Janey didn't dare look at Tim. Not yet.

Sha'dae put herself in front of Janey and gripped her shoulders. "Don't you go there. Don't you do it. Don't you even think about it."

Janey tried to keep the emotion out of her voice. The only way she could do it was to whisper. "But...Sha'dae, what if our friendship, what if the, the, the *bond* we have, what if none of that is real? What if the only reason you moved into my building was because of this...this *thing* in our genes?"

Don't look at Tim. You can't look at Tim.

Sha'dae glanced up, over Janey's shoulder, and Tim spoke into Janey's ear. "Can I talk to you? In private?"

Janey still didn't look at him. She nodded, and quietly followed Tim up the aisle and into the lobby. She didn't want him to see what was in her face, in her eyes, in her soul—the sudden doubt, the torturous guilt—but when she finally gathered the courage to meet him eye to eye, what she saw in his face was so, so much worse. Janey's heart dropped out of her. Left her hollow. Cored.

Tim said, "Janey," and the ache was too much. She couldn't take it. She turned away, and had to brace herself against a wall, because her world had pivoted and gone out of balance and she knew she was about to fall. Tim came after her. Steadied her. "Janey, I've been thinking about something."

"Don't." Her stomach rebelled against her. Demanded that she empty it. She swallowed hard, and again, and tried to breathe deeply, but her lungs had joined the rebellion.

"You need to hear it, though."

"Tim, please."

"Janey—"

"*Please.*"

He came around to stand in front of her, but didn't touch her. She wanted him to. God above, she wanted him to pull her into his arms, so she could wrap hers around him and never let him go. But she knew he wouldn't. Not yet.

"I've been trying to figure out how to bring this up, but...after what the Plowman just told us. I mean, assuming it's true. But even if it isn't true, it doesn't change anything."

Janey held up a finger: hold on. Tim went quiet. A few more deep breaths, and Janey straightened up, her stomach and tear ducts under control. She folded her arms across her chest. She couldn't help it. It was a defensive posture, the kind of body language that did no good in this kind of discussion, but she couldn't help it.

What kind of discussion are we having, anyway? The man I love is about to dump me because of what a giant alien said. And he might be right to. There are no therapists equipped to handle this.

"Tim. I know I've said this a lot. But it's still true. No matter whether we're a...I can't even process this. Whether or not we're a 'combat unit.' I can't...I *don't want* to lose you. I don't care what Alien Yao Ming in there says. And, and maybe I don't say it enough, maybe I haven't shown it enough, or in the right ways, but..." Her eyes began to swim, and she blinked the tears away. "*Damn it.* Tim, I love you. I want to spend the rest of my life with you. And once we don't have to worry about creepy homicidal blonde freakshows trying to kill us, I swear to you, I *swear*, we're going to have the kind of life we both want."

Tim still didn't pull her to him.

He folded his own arms, and put his back to the wall, and bounced the heel of one shoe on the floor. "Janey..." He closed his eyes. Wouldn't even let her have that much of him. "Janey, I love you, too. I think you know that. I hope you know that." He sighed. "If I hadn't spent the last six months wallowing in a giant heap of self-pity and non-existent self-esteem, I..."

She waited. "What? You what?"

He opened his eyes again, but studied his shoe instead of looking at her. "What I wish could happen? I wish I could propose. I mean, you know I'm flat broke, but Mom has a ring that belonged to her grandmother, and—"

"Tim."

"You've got to let me finish."

"Tim. That's what I want, too. It is, I promise you it is."

Tim thumped his head back against the wall and groaned, and took a few steps away from her. Janey felt as if she'd just tried to put out a grease fire by pouring water on it. She went after him.

"What is it? What the Plowman said? I told you, I don't care about that, I love you, I want to be with you! Tim, we—"

He spun around to face her, and when she saw the pain in his eyes, the words turned to sawdust in her mouth.

"Janey. I healed myself of all the injuries Simon Grove gave me. I healed myself of a bullet hole through the skull, for God's sake. And when you showed up with your ankle looking like raw hamburger, and the bones all splintered out of it, I healed that, too."

"What's this got to do with, with anything?"

He stepped closer to her. Pain and sorrow and guilt and yearning etched across him. "I should've said something sooner. I'm sorry. I was being selfish. Janey...I can heal Adam."

1 8

Several hundred miles from the abandoned theater, Derek Stamford rode with Anastasia Capelli and two other passengers in a heavily modified Bell 525 helicopter. No headphones were necessary, since only a whisper of the rotors' noise made its way into the cabin. Stamford sat with his good leg crossed over his bad one, the silver-headed cane propped against the side of the chair, and watched Anastasia. She seemed more...withered...than usual.

"How old are you now, Ana?"

Tendons stood out in her neck. "Please, sir. I need to concentrate." She had a tablet in her lap, her fingers moving deftly across the topographical representation of the ground below. The deep brown of her irises faded to a near-colorless yellow and back again with each of her breaths. He knew she wasn't actually looking at anything. Not in the cabin, in any case.

"We picked you up...how long was it before your eleventh birthday? Four days? Three? And you've been with us...I should look at a calendar. Three years now, isn't that right?"

Anastasia's breathing grew shallower. Faster. Her eyes faded to pale gray-yellow and stayed that way. "It's coming up. I don't...don't think I can pinpoint it, but...it's in front of us. Coming up fast."

Stamford touched a button on a console near his head. "Rodney. Tell us what you see down there."

The pilot's voice crackled back to him. "A whole lot of nothing, sir, except—okay, got some lights about three miles ahead. Small cluster. Looks like a ranch."

Stamford watched as a few strands of hair turned loose from Anastasia's head and drifted down to the surface of the tablet. She said, "That...that should be it. Sir."

"Rodney. Circle that ranch a couple of times. Let's see what we can see."

"Yes, sir."

The helicopter turned in a series of wide arcs around the farm. Stamford activated an array of cameras and sensors on the craft's belly, feeding into a bank of monitors mounted on the wall in front of him, and peered out the window with his naked eyes, but nothing seemed out of place. The only thing that did stand out was that there was no livestock of any kind in evidence. Stamford murmured, "Plenty of fenced-in land, no animals. What kind of ranch doesn't bother to raise livestock?"

The woman sitting behind Anastasia, a thirty-year-old beauty with copper-brown skin and dark red hair, said, "I'm sorry, Mr. Stamford, did you say something?"

Stamford favored her with a patient smile. Fasolo had found Kay Bacigalupo six months ago, and had subjected her to the most stringent course of mind-altering drugs and behavioral conditioning Redfell had ever engaged in. Unlike a few other, less cooperative finds, Kay had responded beautifully, and now obeyed and served without question. Unfortunately, the treatment had also lowered her IQ by about fifty points. If not for her Augmentation, Stamford would have had her put down already. "I was just talking to myself, Kay. Nothing to worry about."

Kay gave him a wide, peaceful smile. "Okay, Mr. Stamford."

Anastasia's lower lip trembled. "It's there, sir. I'm sure of it now. That ranch. That's what you're looking for."

Stamford hit the button again. "All right, Rodney. Set us down."

The helicopter kicked up great swirling clouds of Texas dust as it settled onto the ranch house's gravel driveway. Stamford could see nothing out the front windows. For all he knew, something could have come out of the ranch house, or the barn, and using the dust for cover, maneuvered right up to the helicopter unnoticed. But Anastasia had slumped back in her chair, her eyes brown again, and since she didn't seem overly bothered, Stamford didn't figure he should be, either.

Ten minutes later, once the dust had settled enough to reveal the vast starscape above them, as well as the utterly mundane house and barn, Stamford followed Kay Bacigalupo out of the helicopter. The Texas wind ruffled Stamford's collar-length hair.

Anastasia had stayed aboard the aircraft with the pilot. Stamford touched his earpiece. "Ana. Where do you see the signal coming from? The house?"

Anastasia's voice sounded even thinner and weaker in his ear than when she spoke to him face to face. "The barn. I think. I'm pretty sure." She paused. "There's nothing in the house. Nothing living, I mean." Stamford pointed toward the barn, and he and Kay approached it warily. They both held powerful flashlights, and soon their broad beams of light settled on the door of the barn.

Stamford wasn't sure what triggered it.

The helicopter landing had certainly not been silent. Neither had he tried to lower his voice since stepping out onto the Texas dirt. Stamford figured it must have been the act of shining their lights on the barn's entrance that provoked the wave of huge, translucent, metallic sidewinders to come pouring out of the barn and writhe toward them, a terrifying horde of attackers so bizarre Stamford's brain balked at processing what he was seeing.

Kay Bacigalupo didn't move. She only turned her head to look at Stamford, the question plain on her face.

Stamford's will to survive was strong. *Very* strong. He said, "Burn them all."

Kay smiled and dropped her flashlight. "Yes, Mr. Stamford."

Blue-white flames sprang into being around Kay's hands. She

gestured at the metal serpents—which, as they drew closer, Stamford realized were filled with tiny, floating pinpoints of ruby-red light—and a broad sheet of white-hot fire engulfed the sidewinders. They made no noise as they died. But die they did, their metal bodies twisting and bursting, the tiny sea of light within each one winking out as the serpents melted into oblong pools of molten ruin.

Moments later, only the ever-present Texas wind moved on the ranch.

Stamford followed Kay into the barn. They encountered no more of the metal sidewinders. Kay's lake of fire seemed to have destroyed them all. Stamford said, "Careful. That may have just been the first line of defense."

Kay pushed open the barn door. Nothing inside moved. Stamford walked past her, looking around, and within seconds his eyes lit on the hole in the floor. He whispered, "Holy shit." Just walking up to the edge of the opening, gazing down at the broad, spiral ramp, he could feel something emanating from below. From down there in the hole. It felt like...

...information.

***

Janey sat alone in the theater's lobby, her back against a wall, knees pulled up to hide most of her face. Tim had tried to talk to her after he dropped that billion-megaton bombshell about Adam, but he'd had no luck. The only thing Janey had said was, "Let's keep this between us for now." After ten minutes of talking to what might as well have been a statue, Tim had given up and wandered back into the theater proper.

Janey sat. Sat and stared.

Once, when she was fourteen, she had accidentally broken a mirror in the rental house she and her dad had moved into. She hadn't meant to do it, and felt terrible about it, and tried to apologize...but the mirror had belonged to her mother, and it meant something special to her father. Something he never explained to her. When that mirror broke, Janey's father got angrier than she'd ever seen him before. *Furious.*

It was the only time she'd ever been terrified of her father. The memory of his fury, the straining tendons in his neck, the bulging vein in his forehead, sprang to mind as clearly as if it had happened yesterday. Fourteen-year-old Janey had wanted to run, and hide, and came very close to losing control of her bowels.

She had felt something very similar when she watched her father die in front of her. That impulse to run. Run away from her life. From the world. Find a hole no one knew about and crawl inside and pull it in after her. Disappear.

Sitting there on the floor of the lobby, she wanted to disappear again. It was only with a monumental effort of will that she forced a word into her mind.

No.

Words her mother had spoken to her—one of Janey's earliest memories, in fact—came bubbling up to the surface. *"When something goes wrong, a lady does whatever is necessary. If you need to have a breakdown, you wait until the bad thing has passed."*

A lady does whatever is necessary.

Janey began building a wall in her mind. Just a foundation at first. Just a few bricks. But the more determined she grew, the faster the wall rose.

I can have a breakdown later.

She made the wall thicker. Higher.

I don't dare go to see Adam now. I can't risk leading Aphrodite to him.

The wall curved around, blocked off Tim's words, blocked off what the words represented.

...I could have Adam back?

No. Unacceptable. Deal with the bad thing first. The wall can come down later.

The thought of Adam restored was...was like looking straight at the sun. Brick by brick, the wall grew until it blotted all the sunlight out.

Janey took a few deep breaths, got to her feet, and went to the doorway leading into the theater proper. Faint sounds of snoring reached her. Sha'dae and Nathan and Scott and, to her surprise, Tim were all stretched out across dusty folding seats, fast asleep.

How exhausted must Tim be to fall asleep after what he told me?

No. No! Don't look over the wall!

The Plowman stood in a corner of the lobby, over to Janey's left, propped against a wall and looking for all the world like an oversized mannequin. His dancing-flame eyes had closed. Janey didn't think what he was doing would qualify as sleeping, exactly, but he did seem to be conserving power. Janey turned and wandered over to the plywood-covered front windows. She was staring out at the broken, weed-choked parking lot when she heard a light footstep behind her.

Garrison Vessler said, "Scott and I are going."

Janey nodded. "I didn't figure you'd want to be out in the open for very long."

"Sorry I can't help you any further. Provide a vehicle or something. I have to move that truck—it'll be reported stolen soon, and you don't want to get pulled over."

"I'd offer to take you back to your home myself, but the sun's been up for a while."

Vessler smiled. Janey couldn't remember ever seeing him do that before. "I appreciate the thought. But even if it were dark, I can't risk anyone else knowing where 'home' is."

"You sure you and Scott'll be okay getting back?"

"I still have a few tricks of the trade up my sleeve. We'll be fine."

Janey stepped forward and gave Vessler a quick, fierce hug. "Thank you. You saved my life."

Vessler took one of her hands in both of his. "You know how to contact me."

Janey watched as Vessler walked down the aisle and shook Scott's shoulder to wake him. Scott nodded and got up, quietly, without saying a word. The boy waved at Janey as he followed his surrogate father to a rear exit door and out of the theater.

When she turned around, Janey jumped and almost yelped at the sight of the Plowman standing ten feet away, in the middle of the lobby, staring at her. She struggled to keep her voice low. "Can I help you?"

The Plowman also spoke in a quieter tone than he had before. "It is possible that Aphrodite Lupo was able to find you in the missile silo because of my presence. The energy you expend may have been amplified by some of the processes this body utilizes. I wanted you to know that those processes shut down when Julian Roth damaged me. And that, since awakening, I have dampened them."

Janey's brow wrinkled. "Okay. Thanks?"

"I explain this by way of letting you know that Aphrodite Lupo will not be able to track you. Unless you initiate contact."

She shuddered. "Not much chance of that." When he didn't move, she said, "Was there something else you wanted to say?"

"The question was asked—what possible use could any army make of someone like Simon Grove. I find the answer to that question troubling."

"Okay. Care to elaborate?"

"The point of my brother's experiment, the experiment he was sent here to conduct, was to assess whether or not humans were genetically malleable enough to be converted into military assets."

Janey waited. "...And?"

"Judging by the data I collected from his remains, humans have proven to be, for lack of a better way to phrase it, *too* malleable. Even the experiment's most notable success does not operate strictly within the parameters set."

"Yeah? And who's your greatest success?"

"You are, Janey Sinclair."

She blinked. "*Me?* Are you serious?"

"The heat generated by your teleportation is an unexpected and, for your position within a combat unit, undesirable phenomenon. You were meant to become a Scout. Undetectable. Designed to move ahead of a combat force, observe, and report, all while leaving no trace for the enemy to find. As it is now, your heat residue makes your presence obvious."

A cascade of possible responses made Janey take a deep breath. *I didn't ask for any of this, you know,* and *You do realize I figured out how to use that heat as a weapon,* and *Well if you could just get rid of the whole tele-portation thing, that'd be fine with me.*

Except Janey didn't *want* to get rid of the teleportation. Even if that were possible. She fought down the rush of defensiveness. "Okay, so, what are you saying? Simon Grove was a, what, an error?"

Slowly, the Plowman nodded. "There have been several such. Simon Grove. Aphrodite Lupo. Julian Roth, the man who…"

"Who almost killed you."

"Roth was meant to be another Scout. He does not have the same irregularities you do, but the ones he does have are far more pronounced. I do not believe he is viable in the long term."

"You mean…wait. He's not viable? You're saying Roth's going to die?"

"Yes. Probably soon."

Janey's mind raced. "Look, I went to the missile silo because none of us had any idea why we got Augmented."

The Plowman nodded slowly. "Augmented. Yes. I approve of that term. I shall retain its use."

Janey pushed on. "And now we've got a pretty good idea of how all this happened, but that's not the only reason I went there. Aphrodite. I can't figure out how to stop her. Nothing I try seems to do her any kind of real damage, and…she tried to control me. She calls it 'recruit-ing'—I think it's in the same vein as Sha'dae's communications, but, I don't know, distorted in some way. I'm betting she used it on Roth and Davis. Except it didn't work on me, and now I'm pretty sure she just wants to kill me. So how do I stop her? How do I keep her from killing me, if she can find me anywhere, and can't be hurt?"

The Plowman slowly shook his head. "That is why I came to talk to you. Thanks to several different factors—my brother's injury, the subsequent lack of data, my own incomplete comprehension of the experiment—I am left ill-equipped to anticipate the results of these Augmentations."

Janey shifted her weight from one foot to the other. "What're you saying?"

"I am saying, Janey Sinclair, that if I fully understood the effects of the experiment, Julian Roth would not have been able to best me. I am saying that you are—humans are—like nothing I have encountered before. I am saying that I do not know how to kill Aphrodite Lupo."

"But…" Janey's throat constricted. "But you *have* to. You, you and your, your people, you did this to us!"

The Plowman attempted a shrug. It came off stilted and artificial, and he frowned at it. "You know that if you mix yellow pigment and blue pigment, you get green pigment. Yes? That is a known quantity."

"What the hell does color theory have to do with anything?"

"I am attempting to employ a metaphor. Our experiment was designed to mix yellow pigment with blue pigment, and see if the two pigments blended into an acceptable shade of green. Instead…we got something else. We got pink with purple spots. Do you see how impossible that is? Do you see how impossible humans are? *I do not know how to kill Aphrodite Lupo.*"

Janey stared at him, eyes wide. Her lips parted, and her breathing grew rapid and shallow. She dug her phone out of her pocket and tapped in a number.

Vessler answered on the second ring. "Janey? Is something wrong?"

Janey turned away from the Plowman as she spoke. She knew he could hear her, but she couldn't look at him anymore. "How far away are you? Do you still have the truck?"

"Yes. What's going on?"

"Come back here, ASAP. I need you to take everyone else someplace safe. …Someplace I don't know about."

J aney spent every minute of the time it took for Garrison Vessler and Scott Charles to return to the theater arguing with Tim about her plan.

"I hate this," he finally said, after she'd explained it for the eleventh

228

time. "I *hate* this. Leaving you here by yourself? When Aphrodite could show up any second? It's nuts!"

He and Janey stood in a far corner of the lobby, out of earshot of everyone else. Janey said, "We don't know what we're up against. Not really. We just know that Aphrodite and Roth and Davis want me dead, and no one knows how to stop them. And I can't live with the thought of any of you becoming collateral damage." She sighed. "Look, the Plowman spelled it out. The answers I went looking for? The way to take Aphrodite down? There isn't one. There's no magic bullet. She's got no Kryptonite."

Tim made a sour face. "Except for what you're going to try. Which might or might not work at all."

"I've got to take this fight to her. We don't have any choice anymore. I don't have any choice."

"And if this doesn't work? What then?"

"I reach out to Sha'dae and she guides me to you. Past that...well, that's more or less where my plan stops."

He kicked at the floor. "And I guess, if it *does* work..."

"If it does work, it'll be problem solved. Well, one problem, anyway."

Don't say anything about Adam. Don't say anything about Adam.

Janey couldn't tell if that silent command was supposed to apply to Tim or herself.

Sha'dae came out of the theater and called out to them. "They're back. Time to go, I guess?" Janey nodded. She strode after Sha'dae, and didn't look back at Tim.

Janey stood at the theater's back exit and watched Nathan and Scott and the Plowman climb into the back of the box truck. The suspension groaned under the Plowman's weight. *Good thing it's not summer, or that'd be like riding in an oven.* As it was, the cargo space was heaped with blankets. Idly she wondered if Scott and Nathan would end up building a fort.

Sha'dae gave Janey a hug and a peck on the cheek. Janey said, "I'm counting on you to look after all these boys while I'm gone."

Sha'dae's eyes glistened. "And I'm counting on you coming back."

She climbed into the truck, skirted the Plowman—who sat like a statue, his eyes closed—and settled down next to Nathan. Janey spotted the color deepen in Nathan's pale cheeks as he snuck a glance at Sha'dae.

Tim came to her. "Do you remember, back when I was first learning all about you, learning the truth about you. At one point I said I felt like I was waiting for a commercial."

"I do remember that. You said something about feeling like your life didn't seem real, and you were waiting for a break so you could come back to reality. Feeling like that again?"

Tim almost reached for her. She could read his body language like a billboard. "Just…don't take any foolish chances, okay? Promise me?"

"I promise."

Tim climbed into the truck, and Janey pulled down the rolling door. She walked around to the driver's door, where Vessler's deeply-seamed face displayed more worry than usual. "Thank you. I know this is asking a lot."

"It's not every day I get a chance to play chauffeur for a seven-foot extraterrestrial." Vessler frowned down at her. "I'll echo Tim's sentiment. Don't do anything stupid."

She mustered up a smile. "You'd better get going."

He nodded and put the truck into gear. Once it had rumbled out of the parking lot and disappeared around a corner, Janey walked back into the theater, closed the door, went to the middle seat in the middle row, and got as comfortable as she could. According to her phone, whose battery was getting awfully low, it was 10:14 a.m. The sun wouldn't set for another seven-ish hours. That would give her plenty of time to absorb this place. She'd never had more than one "home base" before, and wasn't sure if she even *could*, but she didn't think she could do without this one. It wasn't as if the motel bathroom was in any way practical, and now that the Plowman had damaged it, there'd be workers in and out. Not at all suitable. Not even dependably dark.

An abandoned theater wasn't that much better. It could be invaded by drunken teenagers, or building inspectors, or for that matter it might get demolished. The Basement had been so ideal because no one knew about it.

Still. Beggars and choosers.

Janey stretched out across three seats and let the essence of the place sink in.

———

R ight this way, Detective." Grassley held the door open for Zach Feygen. She had about an inch on him, and the more he got to know her, the more she reminded him of his mother. Not that his mother looked anything like Nicole Grassley, who could pass for a retirement-age Norse Valkyrie. But his mother had never, ever accepted "no" for answer. Near as he could tell, Grassley didn't either. Feygen just wished he knew what the question was.

The last time they had spoken, Grassley hadn't taken him to an office or precinct or station of any kind. They'd just driven around in her car for an hour, while she grilled the ever-loving shit out of him regarding anything and everything he might or might not have known about the Gray Widow. Feygen had told her a lot of truth. He stopped short of revealing Janey's name, and Grassley didn't ask him anything about teleportation. Garrison Vessler's name didn't come up at all.

Still, he got the feeling that Grassley learned just as much about him from what he didn't say as what he did.

She followed Feygen into the building she'd driven him to after surprising him again at his house, again when Heather wasn't home. Feygen glanced around. They stood in what could have been any kind of boring, beige office suite, anywhere. It would have looked just as appropriate in Chicago or Los Angeles as it did here, on the southern edge of Buckhead. "Low-key place for Army Intelligence."

"It used to be a copier repair business." Grassley locked the front door and pointed past the small, empty reception desk, down a hall-way. "First door on your right, please."

Feygen did as he was asked. The first door on the right opened onto a room that, again, could have been used for almost anything. If not for the window set in the far wall, it could've passed for an interrogation room, which Feygen figured was probably what Grassley wanted to use it for. A couple of cushy office chairs sat in the middle of the floor. There was no other furniture.

Grassley gestured at one chair as she sank into the other. "Please. Sit."

Feygen did. With his feet he pushed the chair over so that his back was to the corner, allowing him a clear view of the door, Grassley, and the window. A quick scan of the room didn't show him any obvious cameras or microphones, but he knew that didn't mean anything.

Grassley sat with her back ramrod-straight, her hands poised neatly in her lap. He wondered if she'd forgotten how to relax. Or if she ever knew.

Grassley said, "We know about the Augments."

Suddenly glad that he wasn't drinking anything, because he might have sprayed it all over the room, Feygen tried to mask his surprise with a frown. From Grassley's expression, it didn't work. She went on, "We've known about their existence ever since the private security firm known as Redfell popped up on our radar. So it's been several years. We're also aware that the Gray Widow is one such Augment. We'd like your help in contacting her."

Feygen turned his chair slowly back and forth. "What makes you think I know where she is?"

"You misunderstand me, Detective. I didn't say we wanted your help in *locating* her. I said we wanted your help *contacting* her. Once our satellites knew what to look for, those heat signatures she leaves behind readily mapped out her whereabouts. We know where to find her. We know she's had contact with you. And we'd very much like to talk to Ms. Sinclair...with your assistance."

Feygen couldn't help it. He felt his face turn a little gray at the sound of Janey's name in Grassley's mouth. He took a long pause before responding. "Why? Why you want to talk to her? What's she to you?"

Grassley gave him the kind of look a dog owner gives a puppy who pees on the carpet. "Really? Really, Detective? Do I have to explain the vast, profound, society-altering implications of someone who can do what she does? What the other Augments can do?"

Feygen stood and went to the window. The office sat on the corner of two moderately busy streets, and he stared at traffic for half a minute. "So you want me to talk to her because you think she'll trust me. And by extension, you."

"Correct."

He turned around and leaned against the windowsill. "But if you've known about Augments for years...if you know about Redfell. And Derek Stamford. Why haven't you already grabbed up every Augment you could find? Why hasn't this been all over the news? You're the government. The U.S. gets that kind of advantage—like you said, all vast and profound and shit—and no word gets out?"

Grassley cocked her head to one side. "What makes you think we haven't grabbed up more of them and then covered it up? Kept it out of the media? As you say, we're the government. That's the kind of thing we can do."

He crossed the room and dropped back into his chair. "No. No. It doesn't add up. If you pulled this off, started plucking these people out of their lives, then you wouldn't care about...about the Gray Widow trusting me or not. Trusting *anybody* or not. You'd just take her."

A tiny line appeared between Grassley's eyebrows, and she took a breath to speak, but the rush of thoughts forced its way out of Feygen's brain and through his mouth. "You haven't because you *can't!* You're not the government! Who the fuck are you?"

She put out placating hands. "Relax, relax, Detective. All right. Cards on the table? Yes, we are the government. Just not the *whole* government."

Feygen slouched back into his chair. "Okay. So, what? You've gone rogue? Is that why you're talking to me in this nowhere shithole, instead of dragging me in front of some Congressional committee?"

She leaned forward and put her elbows on her knees. It was the most genuine gesture he'd seen her make yet. "Detective Feygen, think about our government. For that matter, think about any country's government. Would you want the kind of power that the Augments represent at their beck and call?"

He snorted. "Fuck no. But this still doesn't make sense. If your little club has this information, surely somebody higher up the chain has it."

A tiny, quiet smile crept onto her lips. "That's, ah...that's a good joke, actually. The current administration received a detailed briefing on the existence of Augments three years ago."

Feygen's eyes tried to bug out of his skull. "For real? Then—why hasn't it gone public?"

Grassley sat back and let the smile get wider. "They denied it. Dismissed the report completely. The Secretaries of Defense and Homeland Security both advised the President that the existence of Augmented individuals was...I believe the term was 'Conspiracy-theory garbage.'"

Feygen blinked a few times. "So...you and whoever else you have working for you...you want to be the ones to bring the Widow and everybody else like her into the fold."

She shook her head. "Not exactly. We don't want anything on the record. There's no fold to bring them into. All we want to do is establish a cooperative relationship."

Feygen crossed his thick arms and propped a knee on an ankle, studying her. "Why start with the Widow, then?" He couldn't bring himself to just come out and call her *Janey*. "And if she cooperates, like you say...cooperates with what? What kind of agenda do you have?"

"We want to start with Janey Sinclair because, of all the Augments we're aware of, here or abroad, she is the first one to put her Augmentation to good use. Serving the public. That's our agenda, Detective. We want to serve the public. And we think Ms. Sinclair would be an excellent ambassador to others of her kind."

Feygen joggled his foot up and down. He could tell that irritated Grassley, so he did it some more. "What would she get out of it? Sounds to me like you just want somebody to do the dirty work you can't do yourself."

"We would be prepared to offer her assistance in a variety of areas.

Keeping her name out of certain databases. Offering her a safety net. We have even siphoned away enough funding from an off-the-books DARPA project to develop a few pieces of technology that could, if we understand her Augmentation correctly, prove useful in the field."

Feygen chuckled. "You want to be the Q to her James Bond, huh?" Grassley didn't say anything. Feygen couldn't tell if she'd just decided not to talk, or if she didn't get the reference. "So that first conversation we had, you were sizing me up in person, yeah? I guess you've already done all sorts of background checks on me."

"Exhaustively, yes."

"So what if I don't play along? You bring up some kind of fake incriminating bullshit and get me thrown in prison?"

"Oh, I don't think that will be necessary, Detective. Though I suppose we could mention the file you put together on Janey Sinclair six months ago, and conveniently forgot to turn in to your commanding officer. Is it still in the bottom drawer of your desk?"

Feygen said nothing. Only glared.

Grassley put up her hands again, palms out. "I joke, Detective, I joke. I told you we were exhaustive. No, we are not here to threaten you with arrest. We are here to, in essence, offer you a job."

He spun around in the chair. "We. We. You keep saying 'we.' All I see is *you*. Do you even have anybody else along for the ride? Or is this a one-woman show?"

Grassley stood. "An excellent segue. Detective Zachary Feygen, please allow me to introduce you to one of our other newly-cooperative assets." She opened the door, and a short, dark-haired, pale woman in her early twenties walked in. She wore casual street clothes, and might have passed for any random girl on the street, except for the United States Marine Corps tattoo Feygen spotted on her forearm, and the huge, livid bruise on the left side of her jaw.

"This is Sgt. Ashley Strandjev."

That night, comfortably encased in Vylar, Janey left a cloud of flickering, smoky, blistering heat along Interstate 40, then turned south on I-24, and finally took I-75 into Atlanta.

Away from Tim, the wall she had built in her mind seemed to tower. Impenetrable. She felt vaguely proud of her denial.

Janey allowed herself a smile as she headed through downtown and caught sight of the Varsity—her father had bought her many a Frosted Orange when she was a girl—before veering off to the east. Janey flickered in short hops along Ponce, moving up to the rooftops to avoid pedestrian traffic, and not far past Mary Mac's Tea Room, she spotted her target: a hardware store that had closed for the night.

Janey knew exactly what she was looking for, and had the brushes and paint gathered up and shoved into a duffel bag in under thirty seconds. She'd been bracing herself for the shriek of the alarms. It never came. A pang of guilt shot through her as she flickered out through a rear window. *They really should have motion detectors in there. ...Not that it would've stopped me.* She promised herself she'd go back later and leave enough cash to cover what she'd taken.

The next part of the plan was trickier than finding the hardware store, but not by that much. Janey headed back toward downtown, the duffel bag heavy across her shoulder, and skimmed through the streets. She recognized a corner as one she'd marked with the Eyes of the Widow, and an entirely different brand of guilt shot through her.

Some protector of the city I am. How many days have I been out of action? How many people have gotten hurt because I wasn't here?

No one stood on the corner. No crimes to prevent, no one to save. Janey flickered on past, and three blocks farther west, spotted her next objective: a fifteen-story building surrounded by chain link, a twelve-foot sign on the metal fence proclaiming the structure to be a brand-new office building, opening in the spring. Janey hefted the duffel bag and, in rapid bursts of heat, flickered past the fence and through the front entrance. She paused and looked around, and whistled softly in appreciation.

Polished marble floors made her footsteps echo. None of the

furnishings had been brought in yet—the builders weren't that far along. But the massive, currently waterless fountain in the lobby supported Janey's initial impression: this place was high-dollar.

She padded down a hallway to a suite fronted with glass doors and flickered inside. Two more doors led to offices, but the third one struck gold. Janey stepped into an oblong conference room that not only didn't yet have any furniture, but also had not yet been carpeted. Builder's beige paint covered the walls, so that when Janey walked out into the center of the floor, she stood in what was effectively a windowless box. Only the door and a number of regularly-spaced wires protruding from rectangular holes—holes that would eventually be electrical sockets—broke the monotony. Even the flat white ceiling was smooth and unmarred, save for a few pot-lights set flush with the surface.

Janey took out the cans of paint and the brushes.

What she was about to attempt wouldn't work at all if it weren't the weekend. But it *was* the weekend, Friday night, and that meant the workers wouldn't come back here until Monday morning.

Surrounded by enormous, inviting, perfectly blank canvases, Janey pulled off her mask and gloves, dipped a brush into a can of satin black, and started painting.

19

Janey stumbled into the lobby, reached through the shadows, and pulled her phone off the armrest of one of the theater seats. It was 4:23 a.m., and when she put the phone away again, she realized a bank across the street had the time flashing on a big digital marquee.

That's how tired I am. As Dad used to say, "If it was a snake, it would've bit me."

Janey sat down cross-legged on the floor and stretched her back. She was hungry. Not as hungry as Tim had been after he healed her ankle, but the last thing she'd eaten, a hamburger from the junk-food run Nathan and Scott had made for the group, seemed long in the distant past. At least two days ago. Maybe more like five days, or a week.

Another quote from her father popped into her head.

Nothing for it but to do it.

Janey slowly stood. She pulled on her gloves. Slid the helmet over her head and fastened it in place. She bent over and touched her toes, twisted sideways to pop her back, tilted her head both ways and got a satisfying crunch out of her neck. Then she pulled the rainbow-bladed katana out of the shadows. Her gloved hands tightened around the haft, which she had inadequately covered with duct tape. She struggled to keep her breathing even...

...and went looking for the crack in the walls of her mind.

It didn't take long, but Janey had to screw her courage up to go through with it. It felt like digging at a fresh scab.

Aphrodite. Can you hear me?

As soon as she formed the words, turning them over silently in her head, the crack opened up—became a rift that led to something like a cave...no. More like the hollowed-out body cavity of a rotting corpse. Janey winced and ground her teeth. Every second the rift stayed open, it seemed to pour noxious gases out into her thoughts, while small, skittering creatures crept out, *tik-tik-tik*, across the surface of her brain.

She didn't have to withstand it for very long. She slammed the rift closed again as footsteps behind her echoed across the lobby, and when Janey whirled around, sword at the ready, she saw the shimmering, roiling, vaporous cloud of darkness disgorge Aphrodite Lupo and Trent Davis. The darkness pulled in on itself to reveal Julian Roth, more gaunt than ever, as if he were in constant pain.

Aphrodite hadn't gotten any bigger since the last time Janey saw her. It was little comfort. Aphrodite had torn the sleeves off her shirt, and her muscles bulged and rippled as she cracked her knuckles. *Turn her green and she could pass for She-Hulk.* Janey winced inwardly at the inappropriate thought. *Sure, Janey, make jokes right before you get your head ripped off.*

The thickening of Aphrodite's neck had lowered her voice an octave. "Where's the rest of your crew?"

Janey glanced around the lobby. The only light came in from outside, and at a quarter past four in the morning, that wasn't saying much. What illumination there was consisted of weak, dim yellow light. Thick patches of darkness lay everywhere.

"It's just me tonight."

Aphrodite laughed. Low and smoky. "Why did you reach out, then? Are you ready to let me take you? Or have you given up, and decided to end it quickly?" Something strange happened with her jaw, a kind of rippling, shifting, sideways movement—just for a second, but long enough to make Janey's gorge rise. Aphrodite ran her tongue along her upper lip. "I can accommodate that. Snap your neck. You won't feel a thing."

Janey readjusted her grip on the katana. "Tell you what. Why don't we settle this gladiator-style? Just you and me? If you can beat me—pin me down, make me tap out—I'll submit. I'll let you recruit me. Won't even struggle."

Aphrodite grinned, but the grin widened into a yawn. "More combat? And with that ridiculous pig-sticker? Please. You already know you can't hurt me. You can't hurt any of us. Or do you plan to try your teleport-into-the-sky trick again? Do we look any the worse for wear thanks to that? No. That barely counted as a parlor trick. Besides, try it this time and Julian will pluck you out of the sky like he's shooting skeet."

Janey shook her head. "Humor me, then. Make me feel like I put up a good fight."

Aphrodite's grin hardened into a snarl. She said, "Trent, light us up again," and took two long strides forward, and as Davis pulled another flare out of his jacket, Janey flung herself backward into a patch of dense shadow—

—and emerged from the darkness directly above Trent Davis. She landed on his shoulders and clamped her thighs around his head from behind, and as he staggered she swung the katana and knocked the flare, not quite lit yet, from his hand. The two of them vanished in a burst of heat.

Janey flipped backwards off of Davis before he could get his hands on her. She and Davis stood in the second-floor corridor directly above the lobby, encased in total darkness, and Janey's night vision rose to full power as Davis blindly swung his rock-like fists. Janey could hear Aphrodite roaring, faintly, from the lobby below. She darted in between flailing swings and sliced Davis's jacket to pieces, so that the four other flares he was carrying hit the floor and rolled, and it only took seconds for Janey to touch each one and send them all to the abandoned theater. As Davis screamed, "*Fuck you bitch I'll fucking kill you,*" she threw herself flat and grabbed his ankle.

Come and get me.

A patch of carpet under Davis's feet scorched and sent a single wisp of foul-smelling smoke upward as they vanished.

Janey had to fight herself to keep from screaming. This wasn't teleporting blindly—not quite—but given how long what she'd done in the empty conference room had taken, she had had no time to absorb even one floor of the building, much less all of them. What she *had* taken the time to do, along with making a few other preparations, was make sure each floor above the lobby was empty, cleared of any construction supplies, and then practice flickering the exact height of each floor. She didn't think she'd teleport herself into a concrete slab. Not if she kept her wits about her.

Oh God please let this work please don't let me stupid myself to death here...

When he and Janey thudded out of the shadows on the third floor, Davis bent double, his stomach heaving. He gasped out, "What the fuck are you doing, you bitch," and Janey slammed the pommel of the katana into the side of his head as hard as she could before grabbing him by the back of the neck—

Come and get me

—and flickering up to the next floor.

Janey did that eleven more times. Materialize, hit Trent Davis in what she hoped would be a vulnerable place, telepathically call out to Aphrodite, and teleport out again. By the time they reached the top floor, Davis seemed so disoriented she thought he might be near tears. He slammed his shoulder into the nearest wall—she wasn't sure if that was a failed attempt to land a blow, or just an effort to steady himself —and screamed, *"Stop it! Stop it! Stop it!"*

Janey flickered around him, a cloud of smoke with a thin, flame-hot edge, striking, stabbing, slamming. She never stayed close enough for him to react. "I knew a man like you once," she said in her best growl. "I knew better than to let him touch me."

Davis sneered into the dark and swung another fist. "Yeah? 'Cause he'd fuck you up just like I'm gonna fuck you up, you little mulatto cunt?"

Janey left Davis there and flickered down, and down, and down, all the way to the basement. She knew this was a gamble. Everything about this was a gamble, but Janey had never claimed to be a strategist. This was simply the best she'd been able to come up with.

Not like I have some alien A.I. riding around in my head, giving me tactical advice.

The thick power cables ran along the basement floor and into the elevator shaft, right up to the work bench and vise that Janey had dragged in there an hour earlier. Janey fastened the rainbow sword in place and screwed the vise tight, flickered over the breaker box and threw the lever marked "basement," and in rapid bursts of heat traveled back up to the top floor where she'd left Davis.

Along the way she caught glimpses of both Aphrodite and Roth, combing the building for her. She didn't think Roth saw her, but Aphrodite did, and shrieked. Janey knew she only had seconds.

On the top floor, a still-disoriented and highly agitated Trent Davis had made it to the stairwell. Janey groaned with effort as she forced the elevator doors open. She thought she felt the trembling air created by Julian Roth's cloud of darkness approaching, and in two heartbeats she grabbed Trent Davis from the stairs, flickered with him to the elevator shaft, shoved him in, and teleported back down to the basement.

Janey was there, watching, when Davis fell screaming directly onto the upward-pointing tip of the katana. The blade pierced his left thigh, and his screams doubled in volume as showers of sparks exploded from the vise, a building's worth of electricity coursing through him and into the walls and floor of the elevator shaft.

Davis screamed like that, writhing, his body smoking, for a good five seconds before the electrical system shorted out. The gray-haired man hung there, impaled, limp as a wet sock, and Janey might have felt bad but for two factors: first, she could still hear him breathing, and second, he wasn't bleeding. She wondered if Nathan was that hard to kill now. She hoped so.

Janey didn't even try to pull the katana out of Davis's leg with her own strength. After turning the breaker back off, she touched the blade with both hands, concentrated, and sent it flickering three feet straight upward, where she caught it as it fell. Janey teleported out of the basement with it.

One down. Two to go.

Janey didn't fully understand the way Julian Roth's version of teleportation worked. She knew it didn't have the same limitation to darkness hers did, since he seemed to take his own darkness with him wherever he went, and he didn't project any excess heat when he moved. But one thing she did know was that she had had her ability for years longer than Roth had had his. Months spent flickering through the city, patrolling, moving from one Eyes of the Widow symbol to another, had given her more than enough practice to carry out a search through the building. Plus, it was much easier to maneuver now that she didn't have to take Davis with her.

Janey had just flickered into the shadows of the sixth floor when she felt the signature tremble in the air. Janey flickered down the hallway and caught sight of Roth gliding through what would eventually become a kitchen. Janey didn't see or hear Aphrodite anywhere. Now or never. She unhooked the small canister from her belt.

Janey had felt sure, when she destroyed the Basement, that the fireball would have incinerated Roth, but instead—as far as she could tell—he had teleported himself and Davis away in the microsecond before the blast hit. Janey didn't think her own reflexes would have worked that fast. And when Janey had been trying her hardest to burn Aphrodite Lupo to a crisp in the sky above Atlanta, Roth had appeared out of nowhere and taken Aphrodite to safety.

She knew she couldn't set a bomb for Roth. She couldn't follow him, either, with no way to track him, and getting close to him was just as dangerous as getting close to Davis. Probably more so, since he could teleport her head off her shoulders.

Janey put a thumb on the trigger tab. Roth hadn't seen her. His back was to her, and Janey took a silent step toward him, her stomach winding and twisting. She knew there was no way to sugar-coat this.

Janey took a deep breath and held it, flickered in front of Julian Roth, and unleashed a stream of chemical mace into his eyes and nose and mouth. Roth screamed, and Janey dropped the mace canister and grabbed his wrists and concentrated on the path she had mapped out in her head. Everything depended on Roth being too distracted and agitated by the pain to use his own power, because at any second Janey could be holding a double-handful of nothing. Janey took them sideways out of the building to one of her Eyes of the Widow symbols, straight up above the Atlanta skyline in three short jumps, and a brilliant red-orange fireball blossomed in the air as she made the final leap to the northeast.

Janey and Roth materialized in the air directly over the middle of Lake Lanier. Janey sucked in another deep breath in the second it took them to fall, and devoted every bit of strength she had to her grip on Roth's wrists as they plunged through the surface and into the lake's frigid water.

Janey had counted on two things when she came up with this idea. The first was that chemical mace, unlike pepper spray, was actually *fueled* by water, so that the tears of someone who'd been sprayed would just continue the chemical reaction that caused the immense pain. The second was that she had never seen Julian Roth teleport very *far*.

Janey could travel hundreds of miles in an instant. The resulting heat discharge went off like a bomb blast, but she could do it. Julian Roth, on the other hand—and it was pure conjecture, based off her own limited observation of him—seemed to have a much more limited range. That didn't make him any less effective, or less dangerous.

Unless that range wasn't far enough to get him out of the lake.

Janey let go of Roth. She flickered back up above the lake's surface and over to the shore, where she landed on the private dock of a huge brick house. She tried not to imagine what being dunked in water would do to the mace coating Roth's eyes and filling his nostrils and mouth, but couldn't help it. There may have been a burst of bubbles from the spot where she left him. She wasn't sure. It was too far away.

Janey stood there, staring, for a full minute, waiting for Roth to come roaring out of the lake, waiting for him to materialize behind her, waiting for something. Anything.

Nothing happened.

She didn't know Julian Roth. Unlike Trent Davis, every time she had seen Roth, he'd looked thoroughly miserable. What if Aphrodite was controlling him, the way Brenda Jorden had controlled Scott Charles? What if he had no choice?

What if I just killed an innocent man?

Tears threatened to run down her cheeks behind the helmet's face mask, but she choked them back.

Remember what Mom said. Have a breakdown later. You're not finished.

Janey glanced at the eastern horizon. No sign of sunrise yet, but no time to waste, either. She flickered thirty feet straight up, then several hundred more, and in another red-orange fireball, teleported away from the lake and back to the conference room in the office building. The hours she'd spent there, brush in hand, had been more than enough to absorb the room's essence.

Janey flickered down to the basement. Trent Davis had fallen off the work table when she'd removed the katana from his leg, and now lay slumped on the floor. Still breathing. Still not bleeding. Janey teleported back to the lobby, listening hard for Aphrodite's whispers. She heard only silence. *Aphrodite could be anywhere in here.* Janey bowed her head, concentrated, and opened up the foul, poisonous rift in her mind again that led to Aphrodite Lupo. A jolt of disgust shot through her when she realized it was much easier to do this time. She formed the words—*Come and get me*—

—and what felt like a wrecking ball slammed into Janey's back. She skidded across the polished lobby floor face-first and slammed into the far wall, and between flashes of red she saw Aphrodite Lupo stalking toward her. Aphrodite's right hand had become something club-like, thick and square, a cinder block of meat and bone, but as Janey watched, trying to get her lungs to work, that hand narrowed and lengthened and became the same kind of cluster of knives that had punched through Janey's ankle.

Concentrate! Concentrate! Get out of here!

Janey had never felt pain like this. Not when Simon Grove had broken her leg. Not when the gangbanger had shot her with the Uzi. Not when Aphrodite punched holes through her ankle. Red flashes filled up her vision, and when she tried to breathe, she felt something hot and wet spill out onto her lips and down her chin and she knew her ribs had shattered.

"I never liked the idea of talking during a fight," Aphrodite said as she leaned over Janey, her hand drawing back, "so let's keep this short and sweet."

Move move move abort abort your plan's gone to shit get out of here!

But the pain grew worse and worse, and try as hard as she could, Janey couldn't get the flickering to come, couldn't open the kind of doorway that she had hundreds of times before, and she could only lie there, every breath pumping blood up and out of her mouth, as Aphrodite rammed that cluster of knives through the Vylar and into her chest.

Aphrodite leaned close. Her jaw writhed and shifted, and her words came out horribly mangled. "I've changed my mind about letting you die fast. I'm going to keep you alive. That's why I didn't puncture anything *too* vital. I'm going to eat you starting at the feet, so you can watch as I rip off each strip of muscle."

The red flashes faded. The pain faded. Janey couldn't feel her legs anymore. Couldn't tell if she was even breathing. She couldn't lift her arms, couldn't close her fists, but she didn't need to grab hold of Aphrodite, because Aphrodite's deformed fingers were inside of Janey's chest, caging her heart.

Janey teleported both of them into the conference room. A motion detector turned on the lights, and Aphrodite Lupo screamed. The knives in Janey's chest withdrew, which hurt much worse than when they first entered her.

Whenever Janey had executed one of her nightmare paintings, it was always when she'd been frustrated, or angry, or sad, or desperate. A method of self-therapy that had always done her good—allowed her to channel whatever negative feeling had haunted her at the time into the work. A kind of catharsis. She had heard, years before, that a good way to make yourself feel better when you were upset with someone was to write a long letter to that person, explaining in detail how you felt, and then simply rip the letter up. Getting all those emotions outside yourself, outside your body, removed them from your own psyche. That was how she had always felt about the nightmare paintings.

This time was different. This time, for the first time, Janey had deliberately called up every negative emotion she could muster. Brush in hand, knowing the threat Aphrodite and her thralls posed, Janey had worked and worked until her head and her heart spun in a dark emotional frenzy, and funneled all of that anger and rage into the paint that now covered every single bare square inch of the conference room.

The memory of Aphrodite, on her knees, paralyzed in the Basement before a single painting, played in Janey's failing, fading mind. Janey coughed up more blood—she saw, out of the corner of her eyes, as it spread out around her on the floor—but she couldn't stop staring at Aphrodite.

The woman's eyes darted in every direction. When she had arrived at the building, those eyes were the same glowing yellow Janey had seen before, shot through with dancing, blood-red sparks, but now they shifted back to an unremarkable blue, and Aphrodite's hands flew to her mouth, and she turned in every direction, jerking, twitching.

Looking for a way out.

Aphrodite whispered, *"No...no...please...no..."*

Thanks to the outpouring of pain and anger and sorrow Janey had spent hours channeling out of her mind and her heart, standing in the conference room was a bit like plunging into the most grotesque Hieronymous Bosch painting ever done. The walls, the ceiling, the floor, every surface depicted images that, at first glance, seemed innocuous. A castle on a mountain. A cage set into a rock wall. A deep, dense swath of jungle. But Janey's power, Janey's gift, hadn't just seeped into these images. They were soaking in it, blasting terror and paralyzing revulsion into the eyes of the viewer. Janey had weaponized her painting, and Aphrodite Lupo sank down into a trembling heap on the floor and hid her face from it.

Janey couldn't move her legs. They seemed to have died. But her arms and shoulders worked, barely, and she hitched herself over to Aphrodite Lupo and climbed up the woman's body and grabbed her face and pulled her eyelids open.

"Look," Janey hissed. Blood dripped out the bottom of the helmet and spattered on the floor. *"Look."*

Aphrodite's screams had died away. Now she only panted. Janey held Aphrodite's eyelids open and slowly turned the woman's head, forcing her to look, to see, to bathe in the horror leaping out of the paintings. Janey knew what she was forcing Aphrodite to witness. She had felt it as the power flowed through her. She knew the unthinkable atrocities committed inside that mountain castle. She knew the depths of cruelty the demon from the cage possessed, and how glee-fully it carried them out. She knew how irresistible the creatures in the jungle were, and how they pulled in unwitting travelers, and what they did to them.

"See it all," Janey breathed into Aphrodite's ear. "Take it all in."

To Janey's horror, Aphrodite's body began shedding flesh. Janey let go of Aphrodite's head and lurched backward.

Aphrodite's skin swelled into great round nodules that split and burst, spilling gore onto the floor around her, gobbets and chunks and long shiny strings of tissue. The nodules rose all along her arms and legs and back and chest, and every time one of them burst, Aphrodite *shrank.* Her body grew smaller and smaller, but all the while her eyes never closed. Janey wasn't sure Aphrodite even had eyelids anymore. She stared, eyes huge and blue and glassy, and when her body had finished purging itself, Aphrodite was no bigger than a girl, a waif, her eyes locked open, staring far, far beyond the walls of the conference room. She made no move to attack Janey. She made no move at all, other than to rock gently back and forth. A tiny slip of saliva escaped the corner of her mouth.

Janey dragged herself across the floor. She knew she had no more than a minute before she bled out. She pulled herself through the door of the conference room and shut it behind her, and as the blessed darkness of the hallway washed over her, she reached out to Sha'dae.

Please tell me you can hear me.

Janey! Janey, thank Allah! We're here! We're here!

Information flooded through Janey's mind, and she flickered outside the building and high into the sky. A fireball lit the Atlanta skyline as Janey followed Sha'dae's beacon to Vessler's safe house.

20

Janey's mind began functioning like a corrupted video file. The world came to a halt around her. Shuddered. Moved in fits and starts. Sound abruptly halted and re-started, distorting, screeching. Somewhere along the way a thought crept into her mind.

I'm dying.

Janey had never tried to navigate based on telepathic instructions before. The concept made her want to laugh, and the thought of laughing made her want to laugh even harder. A broken, bleeding, pathetic creature tumbling sideways through the sky like a rag doll flung from a slingshot.

I'm going to hit the ground. Lose control and hit the ground and my body will rupture and splatter and scatter and there'll be nothing left of me but tiny, tiny scraps.

No, Janey! Hold on! Come to me! Follow my voice!

That cool silver channel flowed in her mind again, pure and smooth, and Janey latched onto it, dove into it, flung herself head-first into the stream and rode it. The stream did not quench the burning coals that threatened to spread out from her chest and consume her, but it made them slightly, very slightly, more bearable. Janey knew those embers were burning holes through her, burning her up, eating her while her heart struggled to pump.

I'm dying.

Flickering, flickering. Trees below her. A bird of prey swooping nearby, its cry sputtering and gap-filled as it passed.

Where am I? North...?

A plume of smoke. Frozen in place against the moon. Janey followed the stream, slipping in and out of reality, leaving fireballs in her wake. The cooling nature of the stream lost ground to the coals charring and ripping her flesh.

You're almost here, Janey! Keep going! Don't give up!

A cabin?

The rushing silver waters curved down out of the sky, and Janey followed them, followed them through a window and crashed onto a hard wooden floor in a nerveless heap and Sha'dae shouted, "She's here! She's here! Turn on the lights!"

Janey heard multiple *clicks* and a harsh glare flooded over her. Now that she was down on the earth again, out of the sky, out of the clouds, her limp, useless legs screamed at her, and she couldn't move her arms at all anymore, and the cool, soothing nature of the silver stream turned icy. The cold dug into her.

I'm dying.

Janey couldn't talk. Couldn't move her eyes. Part of her mind, the dim, distant, pitiful part that still worked, marveled that she retained any consciousness at all. She heard voices above her, all around her, and her field of vision shifted, and she realized someone had pulled her up and cradled her in a lap.

Her sense of smell still worked. It was Sha'dae. Sha'dae held her, and wept, and tears fell down onto the black mesh of the helmet's eye pieces. Janey couldn't blink, couldn't move her eyelids, but Sha'dae's soothing tears fell into her eyes.

Voices swam in and out. One said, "Get her helmet off," and another one said, "No, don't, she could have a spinal injury—you shouldn't have even lifted her," and a third said, "Oh fuck, oh Jesus, oh fuck," and Janey heard someone retching. Sha'dae—Janey recognized her voice—said, "Do you need, do you have to get the armor off, do we have to get the armor off?"

And Tim.

Tim!

He spoke from near her feet. "I don't know. I don't know. I don't think so."

I'm dying, Tim.

"Lay her down flat."

I'm sorry. I'm sorry.

Janey's head dropped again. Rested on the smooth floor. Someone said, "Is it—is it all in the chest?" She felt hands probing and prodding along her torso, and gasped. The burning coals eating through her body no longer had Sha'dae's cooling river of thought to dull the pain.

"Look! Look, there's buckles, they're, like, hidden—help me!"

Who said that?

It doesn't matter. I'm going to die.

The prodding fingers loosened the Vylar's grip on her body, but as the chest piece folded away, the pain and the cold redoubled.

Tim's voice came to her from...where? Somewhere. "Hold on, Janey. I know you can hear me. I know you're still with me. Hold on. I've got you."

Janey wasn't sure what Tim did. It felt as if a warm blanket had been spread across her, the kind of warmth that soaked in, saturated, filled the body from skin all the way to bone marrow. Janey's eyelids fluttered behind the black mesh, and she moved her head the tiniest fraction of an inch, and saw that Tim had pulled off his shirt and stretched out on top of her.

Skin to skin.

The length of his body covering hers.

The horrific burning coals receded, moving farther and farther away, until it felt as if they dropped out of her body and took the pain along with them.

Janey whispered, "Tim," and blacked out.

When she woke, Janey heard the sound of groans, and to her surprise discovered she wasn't the one groaning. Her eyes opened just fine, and didn't even feel all that gravelly, and when she convinced them to focus, she found herself staring at what appeared to be a wooden ceiling. She was cold, but not the kind of cold she remembered from her fever-dream flickering path through the night sky. Just the normal kind of cold you get from not having enough clothes or...

Janey's arms moved when she willed them to. Her hands quickly found her own bare flesh, and in a heartbeat she realized she was lying naked on a bed, covered by a sheet and a thin blanket. She surged up to a sitting position, clutching the covers to her chest, and looked down and willed her feet to move, and something between a scream and a laugh burst from her lips as they wiggled back and forth under the bedclothes.

Before Janey could do or say anything else, Sha'dae appeared from out of nowhere and wrapped her up in the tightest hug Janey had ever felt, laughing and crying. Mostly crying. "Janey, praise Allah, praise Him, you're awake, you're awake, you came back to us!"

She pulled away, and Janey saw over Sha'dae's shoulder that she sat on a bed in a small log cabin with a pot-belly stove in the middle of the floor and a stack of chopped firewood piled against one wall. A couple of rocking chairs, a square wooden table, and a corner with a few cabinets and a sink rounded out the furnishings. Nathan had just gotten up from one of the rocking chairs, and approached Janey, timid as a rabbit, his head turned so that he only looked at her with one eye.

"Are you okay? Like, did it work? Are you really okay? And are you decent?"

Janey shuddered as the fight with Aphrodite came back to her. She put one hand under the blanket and gingerly probed her chest—and felt nothing. No wounds. No blood.

Nathan went on, "'Cause you were *righteously* fucked up when you got here. I mean, your whole..." He made a circular motion around his own chest. "It looked like you'd been stuck with, I don't know, a pitchfork or something. A bunch of pitchforks. Or one pitchfork a bunch of times."

Janey heard the groan again, and leaned over to look, and saw Tim lying on the floor at the foot of the bed, and gasped.

Tim had lost at least twenty pounds. His clothes hung loose on his body, and his cheekbones stood out in sharp relief from his sunken cheeks. Janey sprang from the bed, moving past Sha'dae, barely thinking to wrap the sheet around her—Nathan threw up both hands in front of his face and said, "Whoa, whoa, hey now"—and Janey knelt beside Tim and touched his face and kissed him again and again.

He smiled weakly up at her. "Sorry if I woke you. I just ran out of food a little while ago. Mr. Vessler had some supplies here…some beef jerky and such. I kind of ate it all."

Janey stretched out next to him on the floor. She thought the sheet still covered her, but at that point didn't much care who saw what. She slipped an arm under Tim's neck and held him and laid her face on his chest and before she realized it, she was crying, the kind of crying that shakes the whole body, and Tim's thin arms came up and around and held her.

"God," Janey said, her voice hitching. "Oh Godddd…you saved me. You saved my life. Again." She craned her neck to look up at Sha'dae. "You both did. You showed me the path to come here, and you healed me. I owe you. I owe you both…everything." Janey pressed her face into Tim's chest and cried, and held onto him as if her life still depended on it, and decided that it did.

Sha'dae sat on the edge of the bed and cried along with her. Tim stayed silent, and only held her while she sobbed and listened to the beat of his heart.

Behind her, Nathan cleared his throat. "I, um. Your suit was kind of, uh…perforated? I guess? And sort of covered in blood. Especially on the inside. So, uh, I hope it didn't have any electronics in it, I mean, I didn't see any, but there's a big rainwater tank outside, and I kind of washed it out. Your boots and helmet, too. There was sort of blood all over everything."

Janey was about to answer Nathan when Tim's stomach growled

so loudly she thought for a moment that an animal had snuck into the cabin. Tim started laughing, and the laughter spread, and soon Janey's tears had transformed and she laughed along with Tim and Sha'dae and Nathan. Janey knew the laughter was at least half hysterical, but she didn't care. Eventually she sat up and clutched the sheet around her. "Where's everyone else? Mr. Vessler and Scott and…our large friend?" She glanced out the nearest window and saw only darkness. "Also, where the hell are we?"

Tim sat up. His stomach growled again. "Somewhere in Tennessee. I want to say Pigeon Forge, maybe? Mr. Vessler said to wish you the best of luck with everything, but he had to get Scott back to where he knew he'd be safe."

Janey stood and went to a window, the sheet trailing on the floor behind her. "How long was I out?"

Tim got up and came to stand beside her. "About half an hour." He put his arms around her from behind, and covered her hands with his. "I might need to put on a few extra pounds if you're going to keep getting hurt this bad."

She leaned her head back onto his shoulder.

It would have been perfect. She could have let it be perfect. Except for what lay behind the towering wall she had built so solidly.

Janey closed her eyes and steadied her breathing. *One crisis at a time.* She said, "I'll try not to make a habit of it. Hey, so, did anyone think to grab me some clothes?"

Sha'dae said, "I got a handful. I'll have to hold up the sheet for you while you change, though. The only bathroom here is outside, and it's the size of a Port-a-Potty. Unless you want to change in the woods?"

"The sheet'll do fine, thanks. I just need underwear and socks. Gotta put the suit back on."

Tim stepped away from her. "Why?"

"I need to go back to Atlanta. Find out if what I did to Aphrodite's gonna stick."

In a hushed tone, Nathan asked, "What'd you do to her?"

Sha'dae stood, wincing a little. "That might have to wait. Sorry."

Janey looked from her to Tim to Nathan. "What're you talking about?"

Tim shuffled his feet. "The reason the Plowman isn't here. We got here, and y'know, he'd been putting himself back together, from where Roth took him apart? Well, he got re-assembled to a certain point, and got a message from...whatever kind of home base it is he's using."

Janey felt a cold pit open up in the center of her stomach. "What kind of message?"

"Somebody's found his place," Nathan said. "He said, ordinarily, if it was just, like, cops or some normal humans, they'd never know it was there. But some other Augments found it."

Janey backed up until her butt touched the windowsill. "So...what does that mean?"

Tim said, "We don't know, for certain. He gave us coordinates for the place. It's in Texas. And he was kind of cryptic."

Janey clutched the sheet to her throat. "He wants us to come there?"

Sha'dae fidgeted with her hands. "He, ah, he said...if the wrong people mess with his stuff, it could send an alarm. I'm paraphrasing."

"Send an alarm?" Janey looked around the room, her eyes getting wider. "Send an alarm *where?* To the freaking *aliens?*"

Tim's face wrinkled up. "Maybe?"

Janey closed her eyes and took a deep breath. "Did Vessler leave us any kind of transportation?"

Tim said, "No. I think he was figuring on you doing your flickering thing."

"And how much time before sunrise?"

Nathan checked his phone. "Forty minutes. Give or take. But, if we're going west, that'll give us a little more time, right?"

Janey scowled. "There's no 'we.' I'll get suited up and check it out. No sense in all of us sticking our necks out if we don't have to."

Tim said, "Janey. If any one of us is going, we all need to go. You need us. You said it yourself—we saved you. You flew solo tonight, and got yourself well and truly fucked up. You might need us to save you again."

Janey's eyes shimmered. "Yeah? And what if somebody does get hurt? Using your healing takes so much out of you. What if it kills you next time?"

Tim shook his head. "I just need to grab some food to go. I'll be fine."

Janey snorted. "You'll be fine. You won't be fine if Trent Davis gets his hands on you again." That came out sounding harsher than she'd meant it to, but Tim didn't seem to take offense. He opened his mouth to say something, but Nathan cracked his knuckles and interrupted.

"That's why you bring *me* along. I'll make sure Skin-and-Bones here doesn't get hurt." Nathan broke out into a toothy grin. "*God* I've always wanted to say something like that!"

Sha'dae tilted her head to one side, and the cool, smooth river flowed into Janey's mind. *We're meant to be a "combat unit," right?*

What the Plowman had said played and replayed in Janey's mind. What if their worst suspicions were true? What if the only reason they had gotten to know each other at all was so...fake?

I guess we are, yeah.

Sha'dae nodded. *So let's act like one.*

This time Janey groaned. "Fine. *Fine.* Where in Texas, exactly? ... And where are those clothes?"

By the time Janey, Tim, Sha'dae, and Nathan arrived at a place close to the coordinates the Plowman had given them, Janey was gasping for breath and could barely stand. She sank down onto the sandy earth and pulled her knees up, resting the helmet's face plate against her kneecaps. Tim knelt beside her as, a few feet away, Nathan vomited on a low-lying cactus. "Janey? You okay?"

To their west, a small, rocky rise blocked their view, and Janey knew whatever place the Plowman wanted them to find lay just beyond it.

"Yeah. I just need a minute. That was…a long way to go with three passengers…after the night I've had." She raised her head and stared at the eastern horizon. "Just made it, too." A third of the sky had already shifted from black to gray, and pink sunlight peered through a distant tree line.

Sha'dae came over to stand on her other side. "I know you've heard this, but it's worth repeating. We should wait until nightfall before we do anything. You're crippled out here in all this…" She made a broad gesture. "All this nothing. In broad daylight."

Janey got to her feet. "If this is as dire as the Plowman said, we don't have that kind of time."

Nathan took a swig from the water bottle he'd been clutching during the whole trip, swished it and spat it out. "We could've driven. We could've gotten a car. Well—okay, *you* could've gotten a car. Do you know how to hotwire a car? I've always wanted to learn. That would be *so* cool."

Janey took a few deep breaths. "We would've wasted all day on the road if I'd taken a car." She turned to face west. "This is the best course of action. And yeah, I won't be able to do as much as I normally do, but I've still got a suit of body armor—"

Sha'dae broke in, "With holes in it. Just saying."

"—and you guys to back me up. And I've got this." Janey pulled the dark pouch around from her back, reached into it, and pulled out the hilt of the rainbow katana. "Plus the other stuff we stashed at the theater. Whatever's on the other side of that rise…we'll figure out how to handle it."

Who am I really trying to convince with this pep talk?

They had stopped along the way, as briefly as possible, so that Tim could make use of an all-night drive-through. Janey had almost laughed at the sight of him wolfing down the three triple-cheeseburgers, but… *He still looks so thin.* She knew his role in their unit, or whatever it was, was that of a healer, but she couldn't help thinking he was the one who needed healing. Tim had always been tall and lean, and hadn't had the weight to lose that it had taken to repair Janey's wounds.

"You guys just hang down here. I'm supposed to be a Scout, right? Let me go Scout something."

Tim gave her a quick hug. "I'd give you a kiss for luck, but it's kind of difficult with the helmet on."

Just for luck. Nothing more.

Don't look over the wall!

Janey murmured, "Thanks."

She dropped to her belly and climbed the slope of the tiny hill. It barely even qualified as a hill, since it was just tall enough to hide them from the sight of whoever or whatever lay beyond it. She reached the top and peered over the summit.

About five hundred yards away lay a ranch house and a barn, with a narrow strip of sun-baked road visible beyond them. The structures wouldn't have looked like much, just another small, dusty emblem of economic hardship, if there hadn't been two huge, black helicopters resting on the driveway. Janey didn't know enough about helicopters to identify them. The figures she could see—some milling about the aircraft, others standing near the house and the barn—all wore black business suits.

Feds?

Janey glanced over her shoulder at the rapidly brightening eastern sky. If she were going to take any advantage of the remaining darkness, now was the time.

Sha'dae, can you hear me?

Sha'dae's voice rang like a bell. *Loud and clear.*

Can you connect all of us? Tim and Nathan, too? But, uh...please don't do that thing where I'm seeing out of their eyes at the same time?

I make you no guarantees. The stream widened.

Tim's voice echoed through Janey's mind. *Janey, whatever you're about to do, for God's sake, be careful.*

Holy shit, can you really hear me? In your heads? Don't think about boobs, don't think about boobs, don't think about boobs—oh shit, did you hear THAT?

Pointedly ignoring Nathan, Janey addressed the group. *I think I pretty much used up whatever capacity I had for making plans last night.*

This is strictly seat-of-the-pants. I don't know what I might need you to do. I just want to be able to reach you. Y'know. When and if.

Tim again: *Don't worry. We've got your back.*

Janey scanned the space between her and the ranch house. Clumps of dry, brittle grass and a few different kinds of cactus dotted the ground, and two short, stunted trees stooped under the never-ending pressure of the Texas wind. With a burst of heat, Janey disappeared from the hillside, traveled to the shadow cast by the first tree, flickered over to the second, and paused just long enough to pick a destination in the long shadow thrown on the western side of farm house. The bark of the tree she crouched beside scorched, a tiny wisp of smoke caught up and scattered by the wind, as Janey vanished.

She emerged at the corner of the farmhouse and pressed tight to the wall. Tim's voice rippled through the stream. *Are you okay? Did anyone see you?*

I'm fine. And I don't think so. Janey peered around the edge of the house. *Okay, I've got eyes on...let's see...if I had to guess, I'd say the two helicopter pilots. Standing together near one of the choppers, smoking. They look pretty casual. Then there's some guys near the barn—oh. Great. I recognize one of them. It's Ned Fields.*

Sha'dae: *Who's he?*

Vessler used to work with him. He's one of Derek Stamford's men. Guys, if this is Stamford's outfit? Redfell? We're in the deepest kind of shit.

Nathan broke in. *Who's Derek Stamford? What's Redfell? I don't know any of this stuff!*

Tim's voice reached Janey from a distance. She could hear him clearly enough, but it sounded as if he were standing at the other end of a hallway, and she realized he was directing his mental voice at Nathan. *Stamford and Vessler used to be business partners. They run a private security business, and they've been collecting Augments. If you want to work with them, great. If not, they force you. And if they can't force you, they kill you.* His voice gained volume again. *Right, Janey?*

Right. And Ned Fields is...I guess he's a Footsoldier. Like you, Nathan. And if it's Redfell, and there's one Augment here, there's probably more.

Janey saw the barn door swing open just wide enough to let

someone out—a striking African-American woman with a mass of dark red curly hair. She didn't speak to Fields or the other two men he was standing with, and while they glanced at her, none of them spoke to her, either. Janey squinted. The red-haired woman seemed...off. She just stood there, motionless. Staring at the ground. Waiting? *Somebody else just came out of the barn. Dark-skinned woman with red hair. She's, I don't know, I think she might be drugged.*

The door of the barn stayed open, and through it Janey saw deep, inviting swaths of darkness. *I'm going inside the barn.* Before anyone could protest—and all three voices in her head immediately broke into a babble of just that—Janey vanished from the corner of the house and reappeared right inside the barn door.

Any horse stalls that might have been there at one time had vanished. Now the only feature of the large, open space was the ten-foot-wide hole in the floor. A hard-packed dirt ramp spiraled down underground. Janey was about to approach the hole when she realized someone else was in the barn with her.

A dark-haired man with pale skin stood with his back to her, facing the corner on the far side of the barn, and it took Janey a couple of seconds to recognize his posture: he was pissing against the barn wall.

Another guy in the barn—Caucasian male. And there's a giant hole in the floor.

Sha'dae: *Can you tell what's down there?*

The man in the corner zipped up his fly. In the half-second before he turned around, which would have exposed Janey and brought everyone and everything down on her head, she crossed the barn floor and, in a tiny flash of heat, flickered down into the darkness.

The ramp spiraled down, and down, and down. It put Janey in mind of the missile silo where she'd found the corpse of the Plowman's brother. *I'm under the barn now.*

Nathan: *So what's down there? What do you see?*

Nothing yet. I—

Janey completed the last curve of the spiral ramp, her boots silent on the hard-packed earth, and when the wall opened up before her and she saw what was hidden beneath the barn. Her fingers twitched. Her face felt numb.

A vast, oblong, metallic cavern spread out before her. There was no distinction between floors and walls and ceiling, as seamless metal curved from one into the other, but the lowest part—what would be considered the floor—was covered with thousands of...

Guys. I don't know how to describe what I'm seeing. Sha'dae, now might be the time to let everyone see through my eyes. If you can do it.

Um...okay...maybe if I do this... Janey felt a tremor, a shifting in the channel, and the sudden burst of voices talking at once confirmed that everyone could see what she was seeing.

It reminded her of scenes from a documentary on great oceanic reefs. Tendrils as thick as Janey's waist and easily as tall as she was rose from the floor and slowly, gracefully waved, as if moving to an unseen current. She immediately recognized the billions of pinpoints of colored light that floated and darted just beneath their surfaces as the same kind of technology the Plowman's body used. The lights shimmered and flickered in waves, undulating from one end of the cavern to the other, shifting from deepest violet to emerald green to... her stomach knotted...the luminous yellow that had glowed from Aphrodite Lupo's eyes.

Movement caught her attention, and she squinted. It was just bright enough in the chamber to interfere with her night vision, but she thought she saw...yes. There. Something the tendrils held aloft, near the center of the cavern, something like—

The shape in the center of the undulating tendrils shifted, and Janey gasped softly. It was a man, held up like someone crowd-surfing at a concert, and as he turned, Janey got a good look at his face. She had only seen it once before, through a haze of agony, right after she'd finally killed Simon Grove. But it wasn't the kind of face she'd forget.

That's Derek Stamford! He's down here! He's—

A hand hard as iron dug into Janey's shoulder and spun her around, and before she could react, a fist like a crowbar smashed across her face. She crumpled, her knees turned to liquid.

Janey

t happened are y
aney! Janey!
Talk to me! Talk to m

She never quite lost consciousness, but her arms and legs refused to obey her, and her vision slid in and out from pure darkness to out-of-focus flashes of color. She thought she was being dragged, but wasn't sure, and the only sensations she could settle on were fierce, grinding pain in her wrists and ankles, and a blinding, hot white light in her face. Those iron-hard fingers scraped around her head until they found the helmet's clasp, and she winced and turned away when someone pulled it off of her.

When the world stopped threatening to dissolve, Janey squinted her eyes and took stock of her surroundings. She sat on a rough wooden chair, her wrists bound behind her back and her ankles tied to the chair's legs, planted squarely in the doorway of the barn. The doors had been thrown open wide, and the hot Texas morning sun beamed straight into her face. People stood behind her. She couldn't tell how many. One of them said, "No one get between her and the sun. She has to stay in the light."

Janey's heart raced. Her breath locked up in her lungs.

Janey! Tim's and Sha'dae's voices blended into an odd harmony. The pounding in her head from the ferocious blow she'd been dealt made the mind-stream ripple and sway. Tim's voice took over: *Janey, what's going on? What's happening? Are you okay? All we can see is bright light!*

The people standing behind her moved around so that she could see them, though none of them blocked the sunlight washing over her. There was Ned Fields, and the two nondescript men he'd been talking with earlier; the dark-skinned, red-haired woman, her eyes still glassy; and front and center, leaning on a silver-headed cane, Derek Stamford. Stamford said, "You're sure about the light thing? That cuts off the teleportation?"

"Believe me, I'm sure," said the voice from earlier, still behind her, out of sight, and this time Janey was sure of it, and her heartbeat slammed so hard in her chest it shook the chair. The dark-haired man who'd almost seen her in the barn—the man who, she realized now, was the one who'd smashed her so savagely across the face—stepped into her field of vision.

It was Simon Grove.

In her mind, seeing what she saw, Tim shrieked.

Simon swam in Janey's sudden tears. She whispered, *"How...how—?"*

Simon winked at her. He stretched his neck, tilting his head around at various angles, so that she could see the thin line of scar tissue her father's sword had created. Derek Stamford came and stood beside him. "An honest-to-God teleport," Stamford said. He appeared to be genuinely impressed. "I have to tell you, guys—not that I'm taking anything away from you, because I'm not—but not a single one of you has the potential that this one does. I mean, can you even imagine the espionage angle? One evening spent on Embassy Row in D.C. and I'd own the Western fucking Hemisphere. I—"

Stamford cut off at the sound of whispers.

Oh no, no no no, guys, Aphrodite's here! Run! Get as far away as you can! Go!

The whispers rode the wave of Julian Roth's air-tremble as the shimmering cloud of darkness manifested in the corner of the barn. Trent Davis stepped out first. He moved with a slight limp, but that was the only evidence of his impalement and near-fatal electrocution. Davis glared at Janey with a seething hatred. Aphrodite walked out from the darkness behind him...

...or at least, Janey thought it was Aphrodite. Her body was still that of a girl, the way it had looked at the end in the painted room. She still had the same facial features, the same straight, fine blonde hair, and her eyes glowed the same violent yellow with the blood-red sparks swirling inside them. But...similar appearance or not, it was as if everything about her had changed. The way she carried herself. The set of her shoulders, her jaw. The lines of her face. Janey couldn't help but think she was looking at someone else wearing an Aphrodite costume.

She wasn't the only one who'd changed. Julian Roth, as gaunt and bony as ever, became visible inside the cloud of darkness, but where before he had always projected a deep-seated, miserable rage, now that rage had become *fear*. Aphrodite glanced over her shoulder at him, and Roth flinched. He looked past Aphrodite, and his eyes settled on Janey, and he flinched again. His body trembled. It seemed a huge expenditure of willpower for him even to stand there. "Don't go far," Aphrodite said, and Roth winked out of existence.

Janey, don't worry! I'm on my way!

Nathan.

Janey did her best not to let it show on her face as she screamed in her mind. *No! No, stay away, they'll kill you! Tim, Sha'dae, don't let him try it! You've all got to get away from here!*

Ned Fields and his two black-suited friends had immediately stepped in front of Derek Stamford, forming a protective perimeter, but Stamford didn't look scared. Not in the least. He watched Aphrodite and Davis with more bemusement than anything else. "Two teleports in one day. Knock me over with a feather. Please, miss, tell me your name."

Aphrodite turned her blistering, churning eyes on Stamford. "This body's psyche is no longer viable. For the sake of efficiency, you may still refer to me by its designation: Aphrodite Lupo."

Oh God. Janey stared in horror. *I got rid of the human part of her, and the alien part's taken over. Frying pan into the fire.*

Aphrodite continued. "I have been following that one—" She raised a hand in a horrible, mechanical way and pointed at Janey. "But now I see six more viable recruits. Yourself included." Her eyes narrowed. "These other five answer to you, correct? Command them to cooperate."

Stamford let out a low chuckle. "You've got things backward, little miss. Especially now that I've discovered what's under our feet here. For the first time, I'm about to figure out exactly what we all are. Where we came from. The machines are starting to speak to me, you see. Just a little more nudging and they'll tell me their secrets. Besides, *I* take custody of any Augments I find. They do what *I* say. Including you. Fields, Salvatore, Binkovski. Restrain our new friends here."

Ned Fields took a step toward Aphrodite, and a shockwave slammed into the crowd with such force that Janey felt as if she'd just been struck by a gigantic baseball bat. She flipped over backward in the chair and skidded across the floor of the barn, and the dark-skinned woman landed near her, grunting in pain and bleeding. Janey struggled and shifted and cranked her neck until she could see the barn doors again, where Stamford had crashed straight into the man he'd called "Salvatore." Fields, Salvatore, Binkovski, and Trent Davis all still stood. Aphrodite had fallen, but picked herself back up as Janey watched. She couldn't see Simon Grove anywhere—

—and everyone shouted and jumped as Nathan Pittman smashed straight down through the barn's roof, bounced off a beam, and punched a hole through the hayloft before thudding to the dirt floor. He groaned and rolled over onto his back, and Janey thought he might have been laughing. "What a ride," he said, his voice unsteady. "Ow. Holy shit. Ow."

Janey squinted against the shaft of bright sunlight that flooded through the hole made by Nathan's body. It surrounded her like a spotlight. *Shit.*

"*What just happened?*" Derek Stamford bellowed, blood leaking from one ear. "*What was that?*"

Ned Fields peered out of the barn, past the farmhouse. "Uh, sir? It looks like one of the helicopters blew up."

Nathan, still on his back, shot a fist in the air. "I did that!" The fist thumped limply to the floor beside him. "Whooooo!"

Aphrodite got to her feet. "Davis. Subdue these subjects." She waved a hand at Fields, Salvatore, and Binkovski. She didn't seem concerned with the dark-skinned woman, as she still lay groaning on the dirt, but Aphrodite's eyes narrowed at Stamford again. "Their leader needs convincing."

For the first time, a flash of fear danced across Stamford's face.

"Let me kill that Sinclair bitch first," Davis said, his voice low and dangerous. "Let me do that."

"You'll do as I say," Aphrodite snapped—

—and three metal canisters the size and shape of Thermos bottles came arcing into the barn through the door.

Someone shouted, "What the fuck—"

The canisters hit the ground and spewed a heavy, dense, jet-black fog into the air. Within seconds the fog had filled the entire structure, blotting out every trace of light and engulfing Janey in the most welcome darkness she had ever felt. She couldn't see anything, even her night vision was useless, but as screams and shouts and the crunching of bone sounded out all around her, she felt her way across the floor to Nathan.

"Are you okay?" Janey ran her fingers along his limbs, feeling for breaks, and didn't find any. "Can you move?"

"Janey?" His hands clutched at her. "Was that a good enough distraction?"

Janey took a firm hold on his shoulders. He was too heavy to drag, or at least to drag quickly, but in a series of short hops she teleported both of them to the hole in the floor. Janey flickered with Nathan all the way down to the bottom of the ramp.

Nathan's eyes bugged out of his head at the forest of slowly undulating, thoroughly alien tendrils. "Holy shit...it's real! Holy shit...holy shit..."

Janey left him there, and teleported back up into the fog.

Janey! She'd never heard Tim's voice filled with this much pain. *Janey, are you there? Are you hurt?*

I'm here, I'm all right, Nathan's alive, Tim what the hell just happened out there?

Hands came out of the fog. One of them clamped around her neck. The other one gripped Janey's skull, the thumb pressed against her left eye, and Trent Davis's leering, snarling face came into focus less than an inch away from hers.

Janey couldn't breathe. Davis's fingers dug into her neck, cruelly pushing in and around behind her trachea, and she knew if she didn't stop him he'd rip her throat away from her spine.

What felt like a lifetime of painful decisions compressed itself into a microsecond.

Tim I love you I'm sorry

Janey teleported herself and Trent Davis five miles straight up.

The cold shocked her most of all. Davis screamed and lost his grip on her, and she brought both feet up and kicked him in the chest as hard as she could—not to try to damage him. She knew she couldn't do that. Just to put as much distance between them as possible so that he couldn't grab her again and finish what he'd started.

Her jump had taken them above the thin layer of wispy clouds, so that pure, unobstructed sunlight bathed her as she fell. As frost accumulated on her hair and her eyelashes and her lips, she thought the golden morning sun was the most beautiful sight she'd ever witnessed.

Far, far below, so far it looked like little more than a pinpoint, she saw the fireball she had left behind. It wasn't nearly as big, she didn't think, as the one that had destroyed the basement. She hoped it wasn't, anyway. She hated the thought of Nathan lying helpless at the bottom of the ramp, consumed by fire, but based on what control she'd learned so far, she didn't think the heat discharge would reach him that far down. *Five miles isn't that much. It's the direction that counts here.*

Janey fixed her eyes on Trent Davis's falling, flailing body.

Let's see how tough you are once you've reached terminal velocity.

Davis screamed and screamed, the fear and panic in his voice ripped away by the howling winds as he and Janey plummeted, and at some point, right around the time they pierced through a wispy cloud, Davis passed out. Janey turned so she could see the ground, still far below but rushing up fast. If the cloud of black fog were still there, if she could angle toward it, if she could flicker away in the instant between when she entered it and when she smashed into the ground and died, she *might* survive this.

If. If. If.

Sha'dae's voice surged into her mind. *Janey, what have you done?*

She was about to answer—about to issue another apology, and tell Sha'dae and Tim and Nathan that she hadn't meant things to end like this—when a hand closed around her wrist and she came very close to having a heart attack. Janey torqued around to find herself looking into Julian Roth's eyes, the cloud of darkness rippling around him as he fell alongside her.

"Will you help me?" Roth screamed.

Janey tried to pull away from him, but he wouldn't let go. "What?"

"That's not Aphrodite anymore. And I'm dying. And she's going to let me die. Will you help me? If I save you, do you promise you'll help me?"

Roth didn't seem to care that they were falling out of the sky. His fear ran much, much deeper than that. "Yes! Yes, I promise!"

Roth pulled her to him and wrapped his arms around her

and the world

tore away

Janey's feet touched down, gently, on the Texas dirt behind the farmhouse. Roth stepped back from her. "I don't want to fight anymore. I just want to survive. You mean it? You promise you'll help me?"

Janey couldn't form words. She had left all the air in her lungs in the sky above them. She nodded hard.

Roth said, "All right. I'll be in touch." The cloud of darkness folded in around him and he vanished.

The ground shook under Janey's boots with a tremendous impact. From the other side of the farmhouse, someone screamed. Janey took the corner at a sprint, but skidded to a stop at the sight of what used to be Trent Davis.

Dense muscles and bones hadn't saved him. Radiating out from a two-foot-deep crater, Davis's body had turned the ground into a field of red mud and bits of what looked like uncooked sausage. Beyond that carnage, the barn still stood, but only just. It was engulfed in flames, and between the burning structure and the site of Davis's impact, Ned Fields and Salvatore and Binkovski fought...something...

Janey stared, and as she did, her guts twisted and rolled.

They were fighting Aphrodite. Or what used to be Aphrodite. Only a few strands of blonde hair gave away her identity. Her skin had turned a putrid gray-green, her red-and-yellow eyes had gone hollow and white, and thorns had erupted all over her body. Nothing but scraps remained of her clothes, shredded by the thorns—and by the long, writhing, whiplike tentacles that had replaced her arms. The tentacles ended in clusters of barbed tendrils like a pair of cat-o-nine-tails, and Janey watched in horror as Aphrodite thrust one cluster of them into Ned Fields's face.

They slid into his mouth. His nostrils. Curved around and entered his ears. Fields struggled and beat against her, but his blows had no effect on the rippling musculature of her limbs, and when she ripped the arm back, bright red blood gushed from every orifice on his head. Fields dropped to his knees, gurgling, and fell sideways into the dust.

Janey swallowed hard. A beam crashed down inside the barn, and she reached out through the mental stream again. *Nathan? Nathan, are you there?*

Yeah, I'm here. Just about got my wind back. The hell did you do?

Salvatore and Binkovski rushed Aphrodite, screaming, slamming their fists into her, but she only laughed, ready for them. Tim's voice burst into her mind.

Janey!

Tim? Where are you?

She almost choked when Tim rushed up from her right side and threw his arms around her, and the laughter that burst from her held a note of hysteria. Sha'dae was right behind him. Janey returned Tim's hug, but had to peel him off of her so she could look him in the eye. "What are you two *doing* here? I told you to get away!"

Sha'dae had started to hug Janey, too, but caught sight of Aphrodite mauling the two men in black suits in front of the burning barn. Her face went a little gray.

Tim took Janey's hand in both of his. "We're not abandoning you. We actually have an idea."

For the first time, Janey focused on Tim, really saw him, and he smiled at the realization in her face. "What happened to you? You... you look *great.*" It was true; Tim had regained all the flesh and muscle mass he had lost from healing Janey's horrendous chest wound.

"That's part of the idea," Tim said. "We ran into one of the helicopter pilots."

And he laid out the plan he and Sha'dae had come up with.

Janey never took her eyes off Aphrodite as Tim talked. It only took about thirty seconds, but that was more than enough time for Aphrodite to finish killing Salvatore and Binkovski. Both men had crumpled to the dirt, blood gushing from their heads, and Janey knew Aphrodite would look around and settle on her next target at any second.

That's a terrible plan. It'll never work.

Nathan broke in. *It could totally work! I'm almost done digging my way out! Uh...I was listening, by the way. I hope that's okay?*

Tim's thoughts managed to convey defensiveness. *Why wouldn't it work?*

Because she'd tear your head off before you could follow through with it. But we might be able to modify it. Sha'dae, I don't know if this'll pan out either, but...can you give me a boost? Mentally, I mean?

Sha'dae moved to Janey's other side and took her hand. *I can try. Guess we'll find out.*

Nathan, how close are you to getting free?

It'd be easier to tell you if the barn wasn't on fire! It's really hot down here!

Janey would have responded, but Aphrodite turned and locked eyes with her, and her face split with a grin full of fangs, and Janey knew they were out of time. She sought out that shattered, foul section in the wall of her mind, the one filled with creeping, poisonous things and gag-inducing smells and crazed gibbering—and for the first time, she directed the cool, smooth, silver stream of Sha'dae's telepathy into that noxious rift.

Aphrodite. Talk to me.

Aphrodite began stalking toward them, across the farmyard. *Aphrodite is no longer with us.*

Janey's grip tightened on Sha'dae's hand. The cool silver stream quickened, grew wider. More powerful. The walls of the poisonous rift quivered and, piece by piece...

...began to crumble.

I know she's in there. Terrified. Maybe too scared to come out. But I bet she can hear me.

Aphrodite's grotesque feet slowed their pace. The hollow-white eyes narrowed. *She is no longer viable. Your attack on her psyche proved effective. She is too weak to do what must be done. I have assumed command.*

Sha'dae groaned. Her knees started to buckle, but Janey let go of her hand and slipped a shoulder under her arm. Sha'dae clung to her. The smooth silver stream broadened, its waters rushing. A small river now.

Do you have a name, then?

Aphrodite came to a stop. The gray-green lids slid closed over hollow eyes. Her arms did not lose their thorns, but they contracted, the cat-o-nine-tails hands shrinking, and seconds later she pressed the heels of her hands against her eye sockets.

Stop. What you're doing. It won't work.

Janey gasped at the sound of Aphrodite's voice. Her real, human voice.

Aphrodite—Agnes—can you hear me? Can you talk to me?

Tim's hand left Janey's. She saw him walk away out of the corner of her eye.

A tiny, feminine voice echoed up out of the rift in Janey's mind, barely audible over the rush of the waters. *How'd you know my real name?*

Sha'dae started sobbing. "I'm sorry. I'm sorry. I won't let up. She just...she's just so alone in there..."

Janey tried to concentrate. *Agnes, can you stop this? This thing that got put inside your head, can you stop it? Or control it?*

The girl's voice distorted with despair. *No! NO! It's too strong! Don't you think I've tried? I had to do everything it said! I had to! And it'll take over again, and kill you all!*

"Maybe not," Tim said, and as he gripped Aphrodite's upper arm with one hand, he put the other hand over her heart and started vibrating. The hollow eyes flew open, and a voice that sounded not even remotely human scraped out of the throat.

"What is this? What are you doing?"

Aphrodite's arms lengthened again, turned tentacular, but wave after wave of heat poured off of Tim, and he vibrated so fast he started literally blurring, and Aphrodite *weakened*. The vibrations turned Tim's voice strange. "I figured out how to reverse the process when a helicopter pilot pulled a gun on us." Heatwaves made the air above them curl and dance. "I can heal. Turns out I can do the other thing, too." Aphrodite grunted, tried to pull away from him. She couldn't. Tim went on: "Not in the tech specs, was this? Another example of humans doing shit we weren't built to do. It's not efficient. I don't even know how long I can keep it up." He groaned, his lips skinning back from his teeth. "But you better believe it'll be long enough."

Janey made sure Sha'dae could keep her feet, and moved toward Tim and Aphrodite. She didn't dare lose focus, didn't dare divert the cool, silver river from the noxious rift into Aphrodite's mind. It was all she could do just to put one foot in front of the other, because if she did lose focus, even for a heartbeat, she had no doubt that Aphrodite would rip Tim apart. Janey crossed the horror of Trent Davis's ruined body, her boots squelching in the steaming red mud. She watched as Aphrodite diminished, muscle tissue collapsing under her skin, her flesh drawing tight against bone. Tim had begun to *glow*, radiating with an orange-red aura, and when Aphrodite finally collapsed to her knees, Tim staggered away, shining almost as brilliantly as the morning sun. Janey took a step toward him, but he waved her off.

Don't touch me! I'm too hot! Tim fell to his knees and collapsed, the orange-red energy leaching away from him into the bone-dry Texas earth. *I'm sorry, that's all I can do, but it's working! Don't let up!*

Janey didn't let up. She kept the rushing river moving, battering against the walls of the cavern where the thing in Aphrodite's head lived, and as she watched, the thorns receded and her skin went from gray-green back to alabaster. The hollow white eyes shifted back to blue.

A thin, naked, waif-like girl looked up at Janey, and lifted a weak arm to cover the tiny buds of her nipples. "It's too late." Her voice, high and breathless, combined fear with exhaustion. "You can't stop it. You'll see. You can't stop it, and once it's back, we'll kill you. All of you." The girl rose unsteadily to her feet. "All your fancy tricks won't work. Do you understand? Nothing on this planet can stop us. We'll come for you, and we'll tear all the flesh from your bones."

His clothes smoking, his skin smeared and blackened, Nathan Pittman stepped up behind the girl and drove his fist through her spine and tore her beating heart out of her chest.

The girl dropped. A sack of meat. The spark of life snuffed out. Nathan stared at the corpse for four seconds, maybe five, before realizing he still held the heart in his hands. He flung it away into the dirt, a lifeless lump of tissue.

Sha'dae stumbled to Janey's side and peered up at her. "Is that it?"

Janey looked around. At some point, the other helicopter had taken off. She didn't see Derek Stamford or the dark-skinned woman or... *Was that really Simon Grove? Was I hallucinating? Was it someone imitating him, the way Aphrodite imitated me? But why would someone like that have the scar on his neck?* Stamford and the woman and Simon Grove, if he had ever really been there, had disappeared. Either that, or they were dead inside the burning, collapsing barn.

Nathan sank down beside Aphrodite's body, his soot-smeared face creased with the kind of pain that Janey recognized. She'd felt it when her father had died. She'd felt it when Adam had gotten hurt.

Adam. Familiar shame crowded in beside the memories of pain.

Tim had stopped glowing and gotten back to his feet, and he slowly approached her. She thought for a moment that he was giving her a funny look, but realized he was actually looking past her, and she turned her head to see what had caught his attention. Her jaw fell open.

Three people walked toward them from the far side of the farm house: Zach Feygen, a middle-aged white woman she'd never seen before, and Sgt. Ashley Strandjev. Sgt. Strandjev held some sort of grenade launcher...

...the kind that might fire gas-filled canisters...

...and Nathan's words rang in Janey's ears. *"Was that enough of a distraction?"*

Tim said, "Oh yeah. I forgot to mention. Detective Feygen's here."

Janey's hands flew to her face. Her helmet was somewhere in the inferno that had once been a barn, and the bright morning sun beat straight down on her. She sighed, her eyes sliding closed. "Good morning, Detective."

Feygen glanced from Janey to Tim to Nathan to Sha'dae, and from the demolished barn to the crater left by Trent Davis's ruptured corpse to the ruined mess that had been Aphrodite Lupo. *Agnes Lorch.* "Good morning yourself." He hooked a thumb at the middle-aged woman. "This is Special Agent Grassley. She'd very much like to talk with you. And, uh, I understand you've already met Sgt. Strandjev."

Janey realized her jaw had fallen open. She closed it. "Does...does this mean the whole government knows...uh...knows—what? What does this mean?"

Feygen shook his head. "It's a long-ass story."

Reluctantly, Janey met Strandjev's eyes. "Sorry about the whole punch-to-the-face business."

To her relief, Strandjev grinned, and turned her head to show off the bruise on her jaw. She seemed to take pride in it. "It was a good shot. Right on the button."

Tim helped Nathan to his feet. Nathan sniffled and wiped his nose on his sleeve, which smeared the soot around his face even more. "I guess this couldn't get any weirder, could it?"

The air trembled.

Julian Roth's flickering cloud of darkness appeared directly over Aphrodite's corpse. He looked straight at Janey and, as Feygen and Grassley were both pulling their guns, he said, "I have no choice," and the darkness folded in on itself and disappeared. It took Aphrodite's body with it.

Janey clapped both hands to her head and pressed their heels against her temples. "Ohhhh...shit."

Tim, his skin still so warm she felt the heat through the Vylar, touched Janey's arm. "What? What is it?"

Janey looked at Feygen as she answered. "I don't think...I mean, she might not—fuck. I saw Simon Grove here. Alive and well."

Feygen said, *"What?"* at the same time that Tim said, "Shit, I *knew* that was him."

Janey went on. "Yeah. So...Roth just took Aphrodite. If that bastard Grove can come back from a fucking beheading, getting her heart torn out probably won't even slow Aphrodite down."

Nathan breathed out a long, slow sigh. "So I might not have killed her?"

Special Agent Grassley said, "Tell you what. Why don't we go back to a nice, air-conditioned office, and we can all talk about this. A lot. Sound good?"

The ground beneath their feet vibrated, then shook, and as everyone backed away, it erupted into a column of what looked like hundreds of metallic snakes spiraling up out of a hole. The snakes melded into each other, took on a humanoid shape, and resolved themselves into the Plowman, clothes and coat and weathered skin all in place. Feygen, Grassley, and Strandjev all had guns in their hands, and Janey stepped in front of the Plowman, waving them down.

"Don't shoot! Don't shoot, it's okay, he's with us!" She turned to the giant, craning her neck to look up at him. "Where have you been? What's going on?"

The Plowman's ocean-waves voice crashed out across the small crowd, overwhelming even the roaring crackle of the burning barn. "I have been assessing the damage done to my station by the human known as Derek Stamford. He has tampered with my devices." The Plowman shook his head. "I tried to get here in time to prevent the consequence, but I was too late. I am sorry, Janey Sinclair."

Janey backed up, blinking. "Wait—what're you saying? Too late to prevent what consequence?"

"Derek Stamford succeeded in translating my language, and began manipulating the technology. That interference caused an automated distress signal to be sent to my people."

Tim moved to Janey's side and took her hand. To the Plowman, he said, "And...what does *that* mean?"

The Plowman bowed his head. "It means Earth has been declared dangerous. An annexation force will be dispatched." Janey's blood flowed cold in her veins at the Plowman's next words: "I am sorry, Janey Sinclair. But it is too late for your planet."

TO BE CONTINUED IN
GRAY WIDOW'S WAR

ACKNOWLEDGEMENTS

I've never written anything (well, anything that got published, anyway) without help from other people, and this book is no exception. Enormous, heartfelt thanks go out to...

Stephen Zimmer, Frank Hall, and Linda Sullivan, for taking the chance.

John Hartness and Tuppence Van der Vaarst for being bloody invaluable.

Zach & Sarah Caylor and Clint McInnes, beta readers extraordinaire.

Andrea Judy, without whom I would have lost most of my sanity by now.

Brilliant cover artists John Nadeau (original edition) and Susan H. Roddey (Falstaff edition).

Joey-Lee Campbell, for providing some valuable guidance.

And my amazing wife, Tracy Jolley, to whom I owe...well, everything, really.

ABOUT THE AUTHOR

Dan Jolley began writing professionally at age 19. Starting out in comic books, Dan has worked for major publishers such as DC (*Firestorm*), Marvel (*Dr. Strange*), Dark Horse (*Aliens*), and Image (*G.I. Joe*). He soon branched out into licensed-property novels (*Star Trek*), film novelizations (*Iron Man*), and original novels, including the Middle Grade urban fantasy series *Five Elements* and the urban sci-fi *Gray Widow Trilogy*.

Dan began writing for video games in 2007, and has contributed storylines, characters, and dialogue to titles such as *Transformers: War for Cybertron*, *Prototype 2,* and *Dying Light*, among others.

His latest work includes the best-selling Audible Original Middle Grade urban fantasy audiobook *House of Teeth*, and a Middle Grade post-apocalyptic sci-fi novel series for German publisher Fischer Verlag called *Bad Tide Rising* (published in Germany as *Waterland*).

Dan lives with his wife Tracy and some largely inert felines in northwest Georgia. Readers can learn more about him on his website, www.danjolley.com.

ALSO BY DAN JOLLEY

ADULT FICTION

The Gray Widow Trilogy:

Gray Widow's Walk

Gray Widow's Web

Gray Widow's War

YOUNG ADULT BOOKS

The Alex Unlimited Trilogy:

The Vosarak Code

Split-Second Sight

True Chemistry

MIDDLE-GRADE BOOKS

The Five Elements Trilogy:

The Emerald Tablet

The Shadow City

The Crimson Serpent

House of Teeth (Audible Original audiobook)

FRIENDS OF FALSTAFF

Thank You to All our Falstaff Books Patrons, who get extra digital content each month! To be featured here and see what other great rewards we offer, go to www.patreon.com/falstaffbooks.

PATRONS

Dino Hicks
John Hooks
John Kilgallon
Larissa Lichty
Travis & Casey Schilling
Staci-Leigh Santore
Sheryl R. Hayes
Scott Norris
Samuel Montgomery-Blinn
Junkle